FLOATING

The Story of a Girl
Who Can Almost Fly

Jennifer Trujillo VanDyke

Capucia LLC
211 Pauline Drive #513
York, PA 17402
www.capuciapublishing.com
Send questions to: support@capuciapublishing.com

Paperback ISBN: 978-1-954920-52-1
eBook ISBN: 978-1-954920-53-8
Library of Congress Control Number: 2022922649

Cover Design: Ranilo Cabo
Layout: Ranilo Cabo
Editor and Proofreader: Heather Taylor
Book Midwife: Karen Everitt

Printed in the United States of America

Capucia LLC is proud to be a part of the Tree Neutral® program. Tree Neutral offsets the number of trees consumed in the production and printing of this book by taking proactive steps such as planting trees in direct proportion to the number of trees used to print books. To learn more about Tree Neutral, please visit treeneutral.com.

To Virginia—JTV
Everything I am or hope to be,
I owe to my angel mother—
blessings on her memory.
~Abraham Lincoln

CONTENTS

Interview 1 — The Beginning

That's when everything began? When you had the strange dream?

Yes, but it wasn't strange. I don't even think it was the first time I had it.

Why? Why is that?
I was looking down the sidewalk again. That's why I don't think it was the first time—I was looking down the sidewalk, again. There was the same long gray wall on my left, and the row of new little trees on my right. Fewer cars by the curb that time, but more clouds in the sky.

Then what happened?
I jumped.
I floated.
I flew.
Then someone screamed.
And I fell.

That Morning

Lucy Callaghan wasn't sure how she had ended up on the floor of her bedroom that morning, but through the tangle of long red curls that had fallen over her face, she could see—and hear—her seventeen-year-old sister, Maggie, standing on the other bed, screaming hysterically. Lucy rubbed her left hip, which felt like she had been kicked. Her left arm was tingling like she had hit her funny bone.

Ow.

Her father and mother, Aeden and Kelly, burst through the bedroom door a moment later, pulling on their robes. Claire, who was eleven, also popped her head, covered with golden red curls, around the door frame, rubbing her right eye. They all looked back and forth between Lucy, lying on the floor, and Maggie, still screaming her head off on her bed.

Dazed, Lucy shook her head and struggled to roll over and sit up, but her dad was already by her side settling her back down on the floor.

"Hold still, honey," he said, his deep voice soft and soothing.

At the same time, Kelly was trying to coax Maggie to come down off the bed and to stop screaming. "It's okay, Mags, it's okay. Stop yelling."

Claire, who never wanted to miss anything, plopped herself down cross-legged in the doorway and watched.

"Mom! Mom!" Maggie was on the verge of hyperventilating as she stared wildly into their mother's eyes. "Mom!"

"It's okay, Mags, we're here," reassured Kelly. She had pulled her terrified oldest daughter to her, tucking strands of Maggie's long black hair behind her ears. Kelly only glanced down at her confused middle daughter.

"Mom! Mom! She was—she was—"

"Did you have a nightmare, honey?" Kelly asked. She was smiling, but it wasn't the smile she usually gave Maggie or Claire; it was the one she reserved for Lucy. It looked a little frozen. A little forced.

"No!" Maggie panted, shaking her head violently and causing the silky strands to fall back into her eyes. "She was . . . in the *air!* Oh Dad! I think she's possessed!" She made the sign of the cross as Kelly finally pulled her all the way off the bed.

"Shhh. Honey. Of course she isn't. Let's go get some chamomile tea." Kelly shooed Claire out, hugging Maggie and leading her out of the room as well.

"Yuck," said Claire, leading the way down the hall. "Peppermint is better."

Kelly said something in reply, but it was too soft for Lucy to hear as they descended the stairs.

Meanwhile, Lucy's dad was calmly checking Lucy's eyes, her head, her pulse, her arm, and her hip. Then he patted her head and said in his deep bass voice, "Okay, Miss Lucy; I think you're okay. What happened?"

Lucy shook her still-sleepy head and shrugged. "I don't know. Maggie screamed. And I fell out of bed." She had fallen out of bed plenty of times in her life. It wasn't strange.

"Mm-hmm," he nodded. "Is that all?" he pressed, eyebrows up, head tilted to the right. He was waiting for something as they both sat there on the hardwood floor.

Lucy's brows also raised as she tried to keep her tired eyes open. "Yeah." A nod. "I think so."

"What happened before Maggie yelled?"

Lucy felt distinctly confused, unsure what he was looking for. But she always felt confused back then. For sixteen years—or as many of her sixteen years as she could remember—she always felt slightly *foggy*. That's the word she would later choose to describe her usual emotional state. Not unaware, simply uninvolved—not connected. She watched the world from the other side of a thick, foggy, glass wall.

"Honey?" her dad coaxed.

"Um . . . I was asleep?" she finally answered.

"Mm-hmm." He was nodding again, lips pressed tightly together, squinting at her with his big green eyes.

Lucy squinted back at him with her big green eyes, almost a mirror image of his expression.

A part of Lucy was always wondering something. At that moment, she wondered what they looked like, father and daughter, staring at each other with their squinting green eyes. Her long, winding red hair was all over the place. His short, wavy red hair was not gelled into the strict submission he imposed upon it every morning, but it was still tidy. She had freckles all over her pale skin, and he had blotches all over his pale skin. Lucy supposed all his freckles had merged together at some point in his life.

"Are you here, Miss Lucy?"

"What?" she asked, still looking straight at him. Her head was foggy.

"Were you, possibly, dreaming?"

Dreaming?

Then his eyebrows crept up even higher on his mottled forehead. How was that possible? How far could she raise her own eyebrows?

"Before you woke up? Before Maggie yelled?" he prodded some more.

Oh yeah.

Maggie had screamed. Her head was clearing a little now, and she knew it had been way more than a just yell. And before that?

"I was flying."

She always dreamed she was flying, and her parents knew that. She used to tell them about her dreams, but her dad always just squinted at her, and Kelly always just handed her a vitamin.

"Mm-hmm" he mumbled, tapping his lips, nodding. "You think you'll be able to get back to sleep?"

"Yeah." She nodded. "Is Maggie okay?"

"Hmm. Not sure. Maybe she had a bad dream, you think?" Lucy shrugged.

"Hmm," he mumbled, and Lucy was beginning to feel vaguely irritated by all his *hmm*-ing and *mm-hmm*-ing.

That was her very first experience with feeling irritation, though it would be some time before she could actually name the emotion. All she knew was that his mumbling told her absolutely nothing, and she wished he would stop.

That April morning was cold—not cold compared to any morning from September through March in the town of Clay, New York, which was only a thirty-six-minute drive to the icy shores of Lake Ontario, but cold enough—so Lucy pulled on her green robe over the T-shirt and pajama bottoms she had worn to bed. She found yesterday's socks in the blankets, put them on as well, and shuffled downstairs to find something to eat.

Sunday mornings always included bacon, and Lucy could already smell its tasty aroma. Could aromas be tasty? Lucy decided they could, and that this one was, and she smiled to herself.

Then she stopped on the stairway, thinking that something was weird. Something was different. She didn't know what it was, though, so she continued her descent toward the sounds of her family.

When she entered the kitchen, the combined smells of her parents' morning coffee plus the sizzling bacon made her stomach growl audibly. The rest of her family was already there, and her dad smiled up at her from the table. Kind of. It was only his kind-of smile. Her dad *kind of* smiled at her from the table where he was sitting next to Maggie.

Maggie got up and stomped barefooted out of the kitchen right past Lucy.

Kelly, who was pouring organic orange juice at the counter, glanced over her shoulder at Lucy's dad, and they exchanged a look.

Claire, curiously unbothered by the interrupted night, was jabbering away about how she had once had a nightmare—about a depressed turtle the size of a truck that came into her classroom and started eating their class hamster.

Kelly turned around with a glass of juice in one hand and a vitamin in the other. "Lucy, here's your—"

"Kelly," her dad interrupted.

When Kelly looked over at him, he gave a slight shake of his head.

She looked at him blankly for a moment then glanced down at the vitamin. She sighed. It was one of those sighs with a quick intake of air through her nose, held for a second, then huffed out her mouth. She put the juice on the counter and threw the pill down the sink. Then she started washing dishes, vigorously.

Lucy still stood in the doorway, wondering how Claire had known the turtle was depressed.

Aeden cleared his throat and said quietly, "I think it's time for a family meeting."

Kelly kept washing dishes. She could have scrubbed a hole through the cast iron skillet she was holding.

"Kel?" her dad urged gently. "Don't you?"

Kelly turned back around and looked at her husband. Then she looked first at Claire, then at Lucy, then back to her husband, giving him another significant look, head twitching sideways, eyes bulging ever so slightly without blinking. Her eyes were swollen, and the whites of her eyes looked red, which made the irises seem blue that morning. Sometimes they were gray. She finally blinked and wiped at her blue-gray eyes, then turned back to the dishes without a word.

Lucy's dad tightened his mouth. "A modified family meeting, then," he said, peering at the back of Kelly's head.

Lucy had always thought of her father as three people: sometimes he was a dad, sometimes he was a doctor, and sometimes he was a husband. Lucy wasn't sure who he was right then. He looked . . . she didn't know. She did not recognize the look in his eyes at that moment.

Claire, who was tracing the Honey Smacks maze on the back of the cereal box with her spoon, reached over with her other hand and patted his arm without taking her eyes off the task of getting Dig 'Em the Frog out of the swamp.

Kelly took a deep breath before she put the skillet down, nodded twice, and turned back around. "Okay." Then she straightened her back as if preparing for a heavy task. "I'll go tell Maggie. Then you, Miss Claire," she said, smiling her real smile. "I'll take you over to help Mrs. Decker with dusting and vacuuming, okay?"

Kelly always seemed like two different people to Lucy. She was a mom, or she was Kelly. Talking to Maggie or Claire, she was Mom. Talking to Lucy, though, she was Kelly. Lucy didn't feel bothered by it, but she did notice it, and today she vaguely wondered why she thought of her in that way.

It was Claire's turn to look like their father as she pursed her lips and squinted, though her eyes were an undecided blue-gray, like Kelly's. "Hmm," she said, completing the imitation of their dad. "Should I pretend I don't know you don't want me at the meeting, even though it's supposed to be a *family* meeting, and go dust and vacuum next door?" She thought for a moment and shrugged. "Okay," she said, probably remembering that Mrs. Decker always gave her cookies when she helped her. Sometimes they had raisins in them, but chances were decent they'd be chocolate-chip or peanut butter, which Claire loved.

Kelly shook her head slightly, ignoring Claire's comment. "Thirty minutes?" she asked Aeden.

He nodded, and Kelly turned and left.

Claire picked up her cereal bowl, dumped the leftover milk in the sink, and ran out behind her.

Aeden looked over at Lucy, who hadn't made it past the doorway yet. "Well, Miss Lucy, I'm going to go get some things," he paused and scratched his eyebrow, "things we're going to need for our meeting, so you go ahead and eat, okay?" He kissed her head, looked at her, then he, too, left.

She was alone. She looked at the whole-wheat toast, the turkey bacon, and the organic orange juice. Kelly encouraged her daughters to eat healthy, but she sometimes let Maggie and Claire eat sweet cereal if they bought it with their own money, and they shared with Lucy when Kelly said she could have some. Lucy decided she could have some that morning.

She slid her socks along the slippery tiles as she moved from cupboard to refrigerator to table, slow-motion skating around the kitchen in a drowsy dance. Then she sat herself down and enjoyed four bowls of marshmallowy sweet Lucky Charms. Afterward, she looked down at the milk at the bottom of her bowl—turned gray with artificial colors and sugar—slurped that down as well, then sat back and burped.

Then she sat there, alone, waiting for the meeting. She listened to adamant ticking of the kitchen clock, the metallic humming of the refrigerator, and the faint rumble of a neighbor's cold car engine warming up. She felt strangely antsy, so she rinsed out her bowl, glided on her socked feet into the den, and curled up at the corner of the sofa.

The neighbor's car drove away.

It was so quiet.

She began to suspect that her stomach did not like that many Lucky Charms all at once. She slid down among the cushions, pulled her feet up, and laid her head on the puffy arm of the couch. She stared at its blue-and-green plaid pattern that had little threads of white and gray. Her family had a lot of plaid in their house.

Lucy's dad came into the den then, holding a large yellow envelope held shut with a string wound around two brown circles.

"You okay?" he asked, sitting down by Lucy's feet and putting a hand on her knee.

She shrugged. "My stomach."

"Hmm . . . What did you eat?" he asked as he reached and took her hand. He was really checking her pulse and temperature but was trying to be sneaky about it. He thought he was so sly.

"Lucky Charms."

He cocked an eyebrow. "How much did you have?"

"Two or three bowls."

He raised one eyebrow.

"Four bowls."

He shook his head, then looked down at the envelope.

"I think the sugar made me sick."

"Hmm. Maybe." He started unwinding the string.

What was it with all this *hmm*-ing today? It was annoying.

He glanced up at Lucy at that moment, then at this watch, then did a quick double-take back to her face. Then his jaw dropped. He opened his mouth even wider to say something, but Maggie walked in then and huffed loudly. He turned.

"Hi Mags" he said, still looking surprised.

Maggie glared at him, not coming any closer than the green recliner by the door. "Mom said we're having a meeting."

"We are. Mom's just not back yet. Come on in." He smiled an uncertain smile. Maggie didn't budge.

Aeden kept looking at his watch. Was he wondering when Kelly would get back, or was he still checking Lucy's pulse?

Probably both. But Lucy knew Mrs. Decker liked to talk, and Kelly wouldn't want to hurt her feelings by hurrying off, so they might be waiting a while.

Kelly doesn't want to come back, Lucy thought. And she knew it. She knew it suddenly and certainly, in a moment of unfamiliar clarity. *Kelly doesn't want to come back—because of me.*

Her father cleared his throat, deciding to at least get things started, but Lucy also realized just as clearly that he was stalling. Even as he stood and looked at both daughters, he hesitated. Just a bit.

"We've had quite a morning, haven't we? Let's talk about it."

Like flipping a switch, her dad was gone, and Dr. Callaghan was there, using his very neutral, very clinical, very nonemotional doctor-to-patient voice. And though Lucy had never realized it before, her father's voice, which usually calmed her, always bugged her when he spoke in that tone. One glance at Maggie told her she was feeling the same way. And as Lucy thought about it, she realized it often bothered Kelly, too. Maybe it was the only way he could survive living in a house full of women, especially when he had to referee a confrontation between two of them. *Kind of like now?* Maybe. But Lucy honestly couldn't remember ever being in a conflict with anyone herself. Usually it was Maggie and Claire, or Maggie and Kelly, or occasionally Claire and Kelly. But not Lucy and . . . anyone.

Something was different that morning. She felt . . . something. She *felt*.

But what she felt, she didn't know, so Lucy stayed right where she was, curled up on the sofa, holding a stomach that was unhappy for some reason beyond having had too much sugar.

And Maggie stayed right where she was, still glowering from the green recliner, and looking as annoyed as Lucy's stomach felt.

Aeden looked at both un-budging daughters, then grabbed the ottoman and placed it in a neutral spot between them. He sat down, still holding the big yellow envelope.

"Margaret," he continued, using her full name, which he only used when it was a serious talk, immediately putting Maggie on full alert. "Have you calmed down enough to tell us what happened?"

Maggie let out a small puff of breath, but only gave a slight eyeroll, which meant she was not calm, but was trying to be reasonable.

"I told you," Maggie said, "and I told Mom. I woke up, and . . ." Her voice cracked, and she started shaking her head.

Lucy felt so strange. It was really distracting. Her body felt—what? Thick? No.

"And she was . . . *there*!" Maggie gestured with her hands, waving them around in the air in front of her. "Just . . . *floating* there!"

Lucy's arms felt dense. And difficult to move. What had Maggie said? Lucy looked up at her sister, but even her eyes seemed slow to do what she wanted them to.

"Were you scared?" the doctor asked, passionless and clinical.

After a big puff of breath and huge eyeroll, Maggie exploded with "Duh! Yeah!"

Lucy dragged her neck to the right to look at her dad. It took effort. And it was strange that he didn't remind Maggie not to be sassy or belligerent. He didn't scold her. He just listened and nodded and waited. And Lucy's head was beginning to ache.

Then Maggie broke down and sobbed, with her head in her hands. "Dad, is something wrong with me?"

Definitely, a lucid corner of Lucy's mind thought, but her dad looked surprised. His eyebrows scrunched, his mouth opened, his head shook, and he stood up to go to Maggie.

"Don't!" she yelled, stopping him in his tracks.

"Maggie—"

"Oh!" She was starting to ramp up. When Maggie got angry, she really got angry. A storm was about to erupt. "And just so you know? There is no way I'm sharing a room with her again." Maggie paused, casting a glance at Lucy holding her stomach. "I mean," she continued loudly, haltingly, with the threat of really becoming unhinged at any moment, "how do you even . . .? How come . . . you and Mom . . . aren't just slightly worried that one of us is . . . ARGH!" She hid her face in her hands in complete and utter word failure.

That was something Lucy had never seen, and it grabbed her attention for a moment. Maggie was smart and sassy, a talker. Not like Lucy at all. Lucy was two people now—part of her was behind her wall, sinking; part of her was noticing things around her. A strand of Maggie's black hair was clinging to her damp cheek. Maggie hardly ever cried.

Aeden reached over to put his hand on Maggie's shoulder, but she jerked away and out of the chair.

"Okay!" she shouted, standing. "Here's the deal—as if you don't know for yourself—but here it is: Either there is something really wrong with *her* or there is something really wrong with *me!* And I don't know which it is!"

His professional shell cracked a little.

"Mags—" he started.

Then, total hysteria. Screaming. "You weren't even there! You didn't even see her! But you come in after, and you see her on the floor, and I'm freaking out, and she's all acting like she doesn't know what's going on, and I tell you she looked like she was possessed! I *tell* you that! And you—just—stood—there! What were you *thinking*?!"

Is this a dream? She could never stay up. She couldn't reach . . . Maggie.

Tears were gushing from Maggie's eyes as she pleaded, "Dad? Did it really happen? I don't know because maybe it was just in my head, and you're just being nice to me because I'm crazy. Because I don't think that could happen. I don't think someone can just be in the air like that! Dad—what's wrong with me? Am I crazy?" She sat down on the sofa, and finally let her father come and put his arms around her.

"No, Maggie. I'm so sorry," he whispered. "I had no idea that's what you were thinking." She shuddered in his arms, and hiccupped, but the tears weren't stopping. "Honey," he said, pulling back, looking in her eyes and making her look back. "I promise—I promise there is nothing wrong with you. You are not crazy, and we never thought that, not for one moment."

"But, Dad," she said weakly as she cried.

"Maggie, I promise you - are - not - crazy. And as for Lucy," he began softly, as he looked over at Lucy for the first time in several moments.

"Lucy!" he yelled.
Sinking. Down and down and down.
And hot.
She couldn't move.
The last thing she heard was a splintering crack.

Interview 2 — Maggie

You mentioned playing with Maggie. What did you play?

Um. Dolls, sometimes. Or I watched her dance and sing.

Mostly I watched her play with her friends.

CHAPTER 2

Behind a Glass

At five years old, Lucy watched the world, and learned, and grew. She observed people laughing and crying and shouting, but she never laughed or cried or shouted; Lucy's responses to events, good or bad, were never extreme. She smiled softly when she was happy. She withdrew when she was sad. If emotional reactions could be measured on a scale of one to ten, Maggie used all the numbers and pushed their boundaries. Lucy's emotional range stayed evenly between four and six.

Whenever Kelly tried to comb through the snarls of orange hair, Lucy would complain, and Kelly would give up. By the time Lucy turned seven, however, Maggie had discovered the joy of arranging Lucy's fiery locks with glittery ribbons and colorful barrettes, and Lucy never made a peep when Maggie combed through it. But Lucy was still a strange-looking child who soberly watched the world around her—and the world, except for an occasional double take, paid little attention to her. Lucy heard classmates talk about her hair, freckles, and buggy eyes, but their remarks didn't bother her; she took them as factual observations, just like when they talked about Maggie. When a new student inevitably asked about the funny redhaired girl, the other students would say, "Oh that's just Lucy." She showed no reaction to their teasing; those other children were not significant to Lucy in any way.

She had Maggie, and Maggie watched out for her.

If Lucy wasn't exactly happy, she at least lived on the periphery of her family's happiness—especially Maggie's. Her joy was really just a reflection of her sister's. Maggie was like the sun, and Lucy like the moon. When Maggie was happy, she shimmered brilliantly. When Lucy was happy, she glowed quietly. When Maggie was angry, she blazed and scorched. When Lucy was angry, well, she didn't really get angry. Not like other kids. Though she did feel frustrated at times, and dissatisfied, it was more like a kind of confusion she withdrew into, becoming more distant. Again, like the moon, she could be cold and quiet, but never harmful.

Maggie was a wild beauty, running around, laughing, moody, wiggling her way into trouble, then charming her way out of trouble. Grownups always remarked how pretty she was, and that she looked like her mother. They said Lucy looked like their father.

Despite their differences, Maggie and Lucy were inseparable. Maggie took a maternal interest in Lucy's happiness, and Lucy was content to be near her. She didn't play with any of the girls in her class or in the neighborhood, but she wasn't bothered by that. It didn't even occur to her to seek their companionship. She was content.

Lucy's life followed the same routine week after week. During the week she nibbled on breakfast, took a vitamin, went to school, came home, did homework, played with Maggie or watched Maggie play with her friends, had dinner, then watched TV with her family. The weekends were only slightly different. Saturdays included chores before she would play with Maggie or watch Maggie play with her friends, and Sunday included Mass, and sometimes inviting Mrs. Decker over for dinner.

Bedtime was best. Kelly would talk and sing to Maggie and Lucy as she gave them baths; she had a pretty, clear voice. Then their dad would read them a bedtime story. Lucy usually sat on his lap while Maggie sat next to him, and she could feel her father's voice rumble against her back as he read. That's when Lucy felt the most content. After that, the family said prayers together, then Lucy went to sleep.

And then she dreamed.

She always dreamed.

Interview 3 — School

What do you remember most about your childhood?

Not much.

Not much?

No. The vitamin kept everything the same.

But you know it wasn't just a vitamin.

Yeah. But that's what Kelly called it.

Kelly?

My mom.

Why do you call her Kelly?

Sometimes she's just Kelly.

Did the vitamin keep you from remembering things?

No, I have memories. But school was just a routine. Nothing special. Everything was the same.

Did you like school?

It was okay.

How did you do?

How did I do?

In school.

CHAPTER 3

Perspective

Mrs. Agaard turned to the last page in Lucy's packet of papers. "And finally, as a class, we've been reading first-person narratives in the present tense, so the assignment was to write a story from a baby's point of view. It was a little bit of a stretch, and most children went back to using the past verb tense, as in, 'when I was a baby I crawled.' But Lucy completely got the concept right away. And she demonstrated her understanding in her writing *and* in her drawing." Mrs. Agaard handed the packet to Aeden and Kelly, who peered at what looked like a baby at the top of a ladder.

I am a baby. I like to drink milk. I love my daddy. I love my Maggie. I laff at her. I want to dans with her. I fall becaz I am sad. I am crying.

"She confused cause and effect, thinking she fell because she was sad, but that's normal. The amazing thing is her drawing," Mrs. Agaard pointed out. "She drew some stairs, which are narrower here at the top. That visual perspective at her age is so impressive. She is a very quiet student, as I've told you before, but she is observant and quick, and you should be very proud of her. I know I am. I'd love to make a copy of this work, just for my personal files, if I may? These teaching moments are what I love most about my job."

Kelly stared at the picture and Aeden chuckled. "Thank you, Mrs. Agaard. We are so pleased Lucy is in your class. You are obviously a gifted teacher."

"Oh, that's nice of you to say, but—"

"I'm so sorry," interrupted Kelly. "Aeden, what time is our appointment with Maggie's teacher?"

Aeden looked at his watch and stood up, Lucy's packet in hand. "Oh! We'd better hurry!"

"So sorry to run, Mrs. Agaard," Kelly said, grabbing her coat and heading toward the door. "It was such a pleasure talking to you."

"You too," Mrs. Agaard smiled, standing, and waving goodbye. "Have a good afternoon."

Interview 4 — Don

Tell me about Don.

He was my friend.

How old were you when you met him?

I don't remember. He lived two doors down. But his family came from Korea.

South Korea?

Well, yeah.

Seoul?

Incheon.

Uh-huh. And what did you two do together?

We watched television.

Friendship

Lucy didn't remember meeting Don; he was just there. He lived on the other side of Mrs. Decker's house, and he was in Lucy's grade at school even though he was only four months younger than Maggie. He had an older sister named Amy, whose real name was Hae-mi, but that sounded like Amy with an *h* in front of it, so that's what everyone called her. Don's real name was Tan Hyun-Shik, but the "Tan" was pronounced more like "Don," so that's what everyone called him. Tan was technically his last name, though, since Koreans say their family name first. Don's parents worked at the University, so Don came over to Lucy's house every day after school until one of his parents got home, and lots of other times too. He was practically a fourth Callaghan child. Amy never came over; she was four years older than Don, and could be alone, but not, apparently, in charge of Don.

In fifth grade, Don fell in love with Maggie. Maggie was in sixth grade and didn't pay any attention to Don, despite the fact that he was as tall as she was by then.

The next year, Maggie went to junior high school—an entirely different universe than Lucy's. Maggie was moving on. On top of that, Kelly was busy doing library research and taking Lucy's little sister, Claire, back and forth to advanced kindergarten classes and other smart-kid stuff. That would have left Lucy mostly on her own if it hadn't been for Don.

Don was a little bit pudgy, and he had black hair and black eyes. If Lucy looked closely, putting her nose almost to his, Don's eyes were actually very, very, very dark brown, but they looked black. He would definitely need braces.

Lucy and Don spent most afternoons together, riding their scooters, watching television, swinging, or playing on the monkey bars. Lucy knew that kids at school thought they were nerds, but why would she care about that? As far as she could tell, nerds were just quiet people like herself. And Don. They hardly even spoke to each other. He was her first real friend.

One of Lucy's few clear memories was a chilly fall day in fifth grade. She and Don were riding their scooters up and down the sidewalk between their houses. Don had decided they were the twin gods Apollo and Artemis, racing their chariots around the Hippodrome in Ancient Greece, and they needed to practice because that was who they were going to be for Halloween. Maggie was sitting on the front porch, doing homework, but Lucy wasn't really paying attention to her; she and Don had just finished an epic race and had collapsed on her front lawn, panting, trying to catch their breath. Lucy wasn't even aware of how much she was smiling after rushing through the autumn air, the breeze tossing her hair all around.

"Aww . . . Look at the cute little love birds!" Amy suddenly said. She was walking up the driveway with a bowl in her hand. Maggie didn't say anything and tried to hide her smile by putting her head down closer to her homework.

"Shut up!" shouted Don, throwing his sister a nasty sneer.

"Oh," Amy mocked in innocence. "Didn't you want Lucy to know that you love her?"

"I do not! Shut up!" yelled Don, red-faced as he stood, picked up his scooter, and carried it back to his house. He kicked one of the tiny rosebushes his mother had just planted for emphasis.

Amy laughed and handed Maggie the bowl she was carrying. "Here," she said. "My mom made some hotteok for you."

"Oh, are those the little pancakes with cinnamon?" Maggie asked.

"Yeah," Amy said, "but they're still hot so be careful if you eat them right away."

"Thanks!" Maggie said.

Amy left, Maggie took the bowl inside the house, and Lucy just sat there on the grass.

Frustrated.

That was the first time she actually remembered feeling heavy. Not fat. Not big. But like she couldn't get up very easily; like her body had turned into a sopping wet pile of clothes you needed to move from the washer to the dryer. She sat like that for a long time, just thinking.

CHAPTER 

Gifts

One Sunday, when Lucy was twelve, she sat with her family on the fourth pew back in the right-hand section, next to the aisle. It was where they always sat as they took communion and listened to Father Patrick's sermons. This week's sermon was on Spiritual Gifts, which made Lucy think of talents and abilities, which made her wonder about dancing and singing like Maggie, or being good at math and science and everything like Claire—were those gifts, talents, or just abilities? Was there a difference? Were drawing and painting gifts or talents? If talents came from God, then maybe ordinary, regular abilities were gifts too. And what if there were other gifts? Like the ability to run really fast or jump really high. *Really* high. And stay there. Could that be a gift? Would God let his children fly? Without airplanes or balloons or parachutes, or things like that?

Lucy felt deep within her soul—or whatever part of herself that was the most *her*; the part of herself that could never show or explain the things she didn't have the ability even to *speak* about—somewhere in that part of herself, she was convinced she *should* be able to fly. Whenever she lay down on the green grass at the park and looked up into the blue sky, Lucy felt like she could fall upward into the air and float away if she wanted to hard enough. Whenever the wind blew, pushing her hair up and twisting it around her head, she felt she should be a part of that wind, that she should be able to dance with it, to *breathe* with it. If she could just figure out how.

"Lucy?"

She shook her head and blinked, startled out of her daydream, and looked up into the gray eyes of Father Patrick, which were gazing quietly but intently back at her. The sermon must have ended because Lucy's parents had stood up and were talking to Mr. and Mrs. Cooper. Maggie and Claire had taken off somewhere, and Father Patrick had come to say hello. All this while Lucy had been thinking about flying.

"Didn't ya care for the sermon, Lucy, or the hymn? You usually like to sing."

Do I like to sing? She had never thought about it before.

Father Patrick must have seen the question in her eyes because he nodded. "Aye. I've known you since you were a wee babe, and you usually come out of your deep thoughts and sing with us, and in a clear voice that makes the angels stop and listen. You have a gift, Lucy, and you should use it."

Really?

"Aye. When you like a particular hymn, your own angel face lights up with the love of God, and I can always hear your praise of Him. I hope to hear it next week."

Finished with his gentle reminder to pay more attention in church, Father Patrick patted Lucy's arm and turned as Mrs. Cooper tapped him on the shoulder.

CHAPTER 6

Dreams

Lucy remembered being with her family, playing with Don, and going to Mass, but there were only a few things Lucy could recall about her personal past with any certainty. Those memories were usually random things like a bike, a kite, a swing set, a balloon, or a slide.

But her dreams—they were something else entirely.

Not her daydreams, though she did that a lot; her actual *Dreams*. They had always been wildly vivid—full of colors and movements and sounds and smells and feelings that stayed with her even hours or days later. They were so much brighter, so much clearer, so much more real than her awake life.

She Dreamed she could fly.

Not very high. Not very well. And not for very long. Sometimes it was no more than one long leap when she hung in the air, suspended for just a moment before landing again on the sidewalk. Sometimes she could hold herself aloft for a few heartbeats before she sank, slowly but inexorably, to the ground.

Later she wouldn't be able to recall a time when those Dreams weren't with her; they were always there. Not every night, but recurring, like holidays in a year. She used to draw pictures of her Dreams: Lucy floating above the sidewalk. Flying over a blue truck. Hovering over the flowers. Landing in a big tree.

Lucy would smile quietly—the only way she ever smiled—and give the pictures to Kelly. Then Kelly would smile quietly back—the only way she ever smiled at Lucy—and put the picture in a drawer.

Lucy hoped for these Dreams every night. She would think about them as she lay in bed with her eyes closed. Then, if she was lucky, the colors and lights behind her eyelids would slowly slide into images—a blue sky and the feel of wind, gray clouds with mists of rain, a dry golden field that smelled like dust, or a black, paved street with the hot, acrid smell of fresh tar. Then she was transported.

By the time she was in middle school, if she tried very hard, she could invite the Dreams and bring them to her. Or she could bring herself to them. Either way, she tried most nights, but it took a specific combination of sleepiness and energy that was hard to hold on to. She kept trying, though. It was part of her nightly routine: change clothes, brush teeth, say prayers, then concentrate. Concentrate gently on the lights behind her eyelids until they swirled into pictures and places. Then hover on the edge of those visions without falling completely asleep. Being completely asleep only produced the useless, *nothing* dreams, but if she could stay on that edge of kind-of-but-not-entirely-asleep, that was when she knew she was beginning to Dream. The excitement of arriving at that point, however, often woke her up. It was tricky.

But by the time she started her freshman year in high school, she was usually able to hold on to those Dreams more often than not. Then she could tell when she was Dreaming; she was awake in her sleep. And she knew she could do anything she wanted in those awake Dreams. She had no limits. So, she practiced almost every night.

Sometimes she could jump and then lightly touch down on her toes after the briefest slow-motion leap. Other times, she would jump, then plop right back down after a normal, heavy heave into the air that was no different than being awake.

But.

Every.

Once.

In.

A.

While . . .

She could stay in the air for ten or twenty weak, wobbly, wonderful seconds. She always counted.

Then one night—*that* night—she ended up inside the Dream with no effort whatsoever.

And it was different that time. She was definitely asleep—she knew that—but when she realized where she was and what she was about to do, the vagueness of Dreaming sharpened into a clear, alert, wide-awake consciousness. It felt *solid*.

She looked around and saw the city sidewalk that was a familiar scene in many of her Dreams. It felt like dusk—that quiet time after all the children had been called in for dinner but before it was dark. Then she noticed a row of little crab apple trees had been freshly planted along the sidewalk; she could smell the soft, damp dirt. She saw the cars parked along the curb were silver, red, blue, then red again, but a yellow truck that was usually there was missing. When she looked across the street, she noticed the dry cleaning store had a gate pulled down across the window and door.

And she *felt* it inside herself.

The lifting.

Please. Please let me be able to do this.

She took a full, deep breath and kicked off from the ground as hard as she could. She needed to put as much distance as possible between herself and the ground.

After two seconds she was at least ten feet in the air. And she wasn't falling.

She was above the sidewalk with the long, gray, concrete wall on her left and the little trees to her right.

She tried to push herself forward, stroking the air as if she were swimming, taking deep breaths between each movement she made with her arms. It occurred to her that swimming was the closest comparison she could make to this feeling. It was dryer, but it took the same kind of effort to stay above the ground as to stay above the water.

Desperately trying to remain afloat, she swam herself forward above the sidewalk. But she started slowly sinking by the fourth push, the sixth tree, the rusted blue Jeep. The effort became harder the farther she went. And she was getting tired. Sleepy tired.

Disappointed, having already sunk more than halfway back to the ground, she focused ahead of herself, wondering . . . sensing . . . realizing . . . that if she concentrated on something in front of her—the next little tree—she could mentally pull herself toward it. She had always tried *pushing* herself before, but pulling seemed better somehow. She was staying up longer than she ever had, and the realization gave her a tiny surge of determination.

She wafted slowly but steadily along the sidewalk, dropping and rising a few inches in a slow, predictable rhythm each time she moved her focus to the next evenly spaced tree . . . and the next . . . and the next . . .

But she was so tired.

She couldn't stay up.

She crumbled to the ground and scraped the palms of her hands on the sidewalk.

Lucy was probably a little quieter in the following days, but her family didn't notice. She was always quiet. She knew she was way more tired, but so was Maggie. The school year was wrapping up, and every teenager in the country was tired. Final exams, performances, award programs took a lot of energy.

Those normal events didn't affect Lucy much, however. Exams weren't really a big deal; she did well enough. Maggie and Claire were praised with all kinds of awards in advanced classes, but

Lucy's parents were fine with her steady B-plus average in regular classes. At Maggie's junior orchestra concert and at Claire's fifth-grade play, Lucy was fine sitting by her parents and watching.

It should be noted, however, that Lucy did, in fact, receive a white, honorable mention ribbon for a picture she had painted in art class that year. It was a watercolor of a girl with long orange hair, wearing a swirling blue and purple dress, spinning among the clouds and treetops. Her father showed no less enthusiasm for that than he did for Claire's science award for inventing a special cleanser made of toothpaste, hydrogen peroxide, and beeswax. She had made it for polishing the shell of the pet turtle she desperately wanted for her next birthday. Kelly put Claire's award on the refrigerator. She put Lucy's painting in the drawer.

It was a busy time in the Callaghan household, so no one noticed that Lucy might have been just a teeny bit even less interested in conversations at dinner, that she never paid attention to the television she was staring at, or that her gaze most often drifted down and to the left. She was remembering. And thinking.

Lucy started paying more attention to the world and comparing it to her Dreams. Her Dreams always held more color and more depth. Lately, though, it seemed like the world was becoming a little bit louder, a little bit brighter, and a little bit more colorful. On the other hand, while she still didn't talk much—she didn't have much to say—there was a growing, nagging awareness that something was missing; something was wrong with the way the world was. But what?

Her dad loved her. Her sisters loved her. Kelly must have loved her. But despite the emerging color, her waking life was really bland and tasteless compared to her Dreams. She never would have been able to explain this to anyone, though, because her thinking was muddy, and every day she felt as if she were slogging, struggling against a current of slow-moving and murky water. And comparing reality with Dreams made her more and more dissatisfied with her dreary life.

Her Dreams were full of brightness, and clarity, and freedom, and . . . and *emotion*. Flying was definitely fun, but it was the richness of her feelings that drew her back to the Dreams. Again and again. She just wanted to sleep.

She had tried to tell Kelly about her newer Dreams a couple of times at breakfast, the only time of the day Lucy talked a little more than usual. Kelly seemed only vaguely interested. She listened and handed her a vitamin, so Lucy kept it to herself when the Dreams started coming more often.

By the time she turned sixteen years old on September eighth, she was having these Dreams once or twice a week. By the time Christmas came, she always knew when she was Dreaming—when she saw that same gray wall and those little crab apple trees, or any of the half-dozen scenarios in which she could fly. And since she knew she was Dreaming, she knew anything was possible, so she tried to fly in all of her Dreams. She practiced. She got better at it. By March, she could actually *make* herself Dream about flying.

It was on a less-cold-than-usual April night in the town of Clay, New York, that Lucy was able to visit that nameless sidewalk again, and she noticed new details this time. The long wall on her left had a crumbled patch shaped like Africa. The little trees on her right were beginning to bud with tiny golden leaves. On her back, she could feel the sun shining down from between big white clouds. And her heart practically skipped at the thrill of another chance to fly.

She jumped.

She floated.

She flew.

Someone screamed.

And she fell.

CHAPTER 7

The Sofa

When Lucy awoke on the sofa, she noticed two things at the same time. First, there was a tube taped to her hand; and second, Father Patrick was dozing in the green recliner where Maggie had been sitting.

"Father?" Her voice creaked and her mouth was dry. She reached up to wipe away the gunky white stuff at the corners of her mouth and around the edges of her lips. The movement jiggled the tubing that snaked into a blue vein, causing the tape to tug on her skin.

Father Patrick started. "Oh! You're awake!" He grunted a little as he pushed himself out of the recliner.

"Uh, yeah," she said. She felt weak and trapped in a pile of blankets and a tangle of tubes. She pulled a cannula away from her nose, but the tubing snagged on her snarled hair, causing an irrational wash of fear to come over her. She would later learn that feeling was called *panic*. And she felt strange. A different kind of strange.

She felt slow.

Father Patrick was by her side by then. "Here, let me help," he said, then held the oxygen tube while Lucy freed her hair from underneath it.

"What happened? Where's my dad?" she croaked, then licked her cracked lips with a dry tongue. It didn't help. Besides feeling weak, everything seemed wrong. Different. She was at home, she knew, but it felt alien. Like she was in a place made to look like her house, but the dimensions were off a bit.

"Oh, uh, your mum and dad are just next door at Mrs. Decker's house. Uh . . ." He glanced around the room. "Will you be okay, Lucy? I only just stopped by, and they asked me to sit with you for a few minutes while they helped your good neighbor with something. I think I should run over and get them, tell them you're awake, but I hate to leave you. Can you sit tight for just a few minutes, darlin'?"

"Okay." She felt hollow, and her arms felt like overcooked fettuccine noodles, but the priest's slight accent—with *dad* sounding like *dahd* and *tight* sounding like *toyt*—brought Lucy's mind back to familiar territory.

No problem. But she also had to pee.

"Okay. Right," he said, which sounded kind of like *okay royt*. "I'll be right back in a jiffy. Don't you move."

The white-haired priest shuffled away, leaving Lucy alone and confused. Solitude and confusion, and even medical tape and tubes, were not new to her, but this was different. Where was everyone?

Her head began to clear, and she realized she *really* needed to pee but could tell her legs were too weak. It was a conundrum. Then she noticed something uncomfortable, and suspiciously weird, so she looked under the blanket.

She was wearing a diaper!

"*Ew!* What is going on?!" she asked the empty room, sitting straight up. Her brain was fully awake now. This was not okay! She would make it to the bathroom one way or another.

"Lucy!" Kelly ran to the couch and bent down as if to hug the girl on the sofa, but she stopped before the impulse was acted upon. She dropped her hands to her side and took a fractional step backward. She smiled with her mouth but not with her eyes. "I was just on my way back," she said, stepping forward again to where Lucy was perched on the edge of a cushion, "when I saw Father Patrick coming out. How do you feel?" She brushed a few frazzled locks of red hair out Lucy's face, adjusted the tubes that were dangling off the side of the couch, then straightened the blanket.

"I'm fine," Lucy said, distracted by the uncharacteristic mothering. Not that Kelly was ever neglectful; she was a good mother to all three girls. But she was not typically at ease around Lucy. At that moment, Kelly picked up a fuzzy white throw pillow as if looking for something to do, and Lucy took a mental inventory of herself.

"Well, I'm . . . kind of weak. What happened? Why do I have all these tubes, and why was Father Patrick here? And why am I wearing a *this*?" She pulled back the blanket and pointed to the padding. "Because I need to pee and there is no way this diaper thing is happening."

Kelly had bent to put the throw pillow on the recliner, but froze, still bent over, and looked at Lucy. Her blue eyes and wide mouth were also frozen, held open for a good five seconds before she blinked and straightened up. She inhaled as if to say something, but the words must have momentarily frozen, too, because no sound came out for another three full seconds.

"Well," she started, then stopped. Then started again. "Let's get you to the bathroom first, okay? Here, use this."

She pulled something out from beside the couch while still holding the throw pillow.

"A *walker*?" This was getting weirder every moment.

"Yes," Kelly said. "I'm not sure I could, well . . ." Then she stopped and searched Lucy's face. "How do you feel?"

Kelly had already asked that. But she was hanging on to the throw pillow with a deadly grip, so she was worried about something. "Honestly, mostly I just need to go to the bathroom. Genuinely."

"You don't feel . . . heavy?"

"Heavy? No—what do you mean?" But Lucy remembered the weird feeling. "Well, I felt kind of, um, slow? When I first woke up? But I think I'm awake now. What happened?"

"Well, you . . . kind of . . . passed out. Kind of." Kelly was avoiding her. As usual. She frowned a little, shook her head a fraction, then said, "Here, let's get you to the bathroom. Lean on this if you need to." She scooted the walker over, so Lucy held on to it as she got up.

She pushed it aside after a moment, though; it would just slow her in getting to the bathroom down the hall, and things were getting urgent. She practically pranced to the bathroom while Kelly followed with the thingy that held the bag of clear liquid attached to the other end of the tubes. At the bathroom door, Lucy grabbed the thingy herself. Did Kelly think she was coming in?

"I can handle this part, Mom. Thanks."

Kelly stood at the bathroom door, gaping. Lucy would have asked her what was wrong a third time, but—no—she just shut the door.

Next, she had to deal with the bunched-up padding.

"Mom?" Lucy yelled through the door. "Can you get me some real underwear and some shorts, please?" Shorts would be cold for early spring, but she knew she would be heading back to the warm blankets.

"Oh sure!"

"Thank you!"

Lucy heard her run upstairs. She was back outside the bathroom door a minute later. "Do you need help, or should I just toss them in?"

"Just toss, please!"

Kelly was still standing there when Lucy came out.

"I put that diaper thing in the garbage," she said. The very *idea* of having to use that thing made her shake her head, which made her notice she had a small headache. "It wasn't . . . used or anything."

Then Kelly laughed. Just one little huff of a breath, but it was still unusual. "That's fine, honey."

As she made her way back to the sofa, Lucy wondered why she had passed out in the first place. She didn't feel sick, but the sofa was where everyone in her family slept when they were sick for some reason—it was divinely comfortable. Then she noticed that the sofa looked wrong. The arms on each side looked right, but the middle part definitely sagged. Looking down, she saw that the bottom edge of the sofa was broken in two, touching the ground in the middle as if it had been karate-chopped. "What happened?" she asked, pointing to the injured furniture.

"Oh, it's nothing," Kelly said, scooting forward to move the blankets for Lucy. "It still works fine. Here—" she plumped the pillow and patted it, wordlessly gesturing for Lucy to sit down.

Lucy tried to comply, but the thingy with the bag and tubes required some manipulation first. "What's the deal with this stuff, anyway?" she asked as she sat back down and situated herself. She looked up at Kelly, and it was Lucy's turn to gape.

Kelly almost had a smile on her face, which was odd, and she looked like she was going to fall over.

"Mom? Are you okay?" Then she looked at the tubes again. "Am *I* okay? What happened?"

Kelly sighed. She still had that odd smile, but it was forced. It was the smile she only gave Lucy. "Here," she handed Lucy the fuzzy throw pillow for no reason whatsoever. "You're fine, honestly. But we do need to explain some things to you. Oh, and Dad can probably take those tubes out when he gets home—Mrs. Decker asked him to flip her mattress—so just try to be patient for a few minutes, okay? Try not to pull on them or anything."

"Okay, but could I have some water, or maybe juice?" Lucy could feel grime on her teeth like she hadn't brushed them in a month and a half. "And maybe a sandwich?" Or pizza. She could probably eat an entire pizza all by herself. With pepperoni and pineapple.

Kelly made some noncommittal sound, then went to the kitchen. On her way out, she said, "It's good I came back when I did. Father Patrick would have been very uncomfortable helping you to the bathroom."

Lucy laughed. "I would *die* if Father Patrick had to help me do that! But it might have been worth it to see his face."

Kelly stopped. *Again.* Mid-stride. Then continued into the kitchen.

She came back with some apple juice and a box of saltines. Not as exciting as a pepperoni and pineapple pizza would have been, but oh well.

Lucy took the juice and her eyes squinted as she drank; apple juice was never her favorite, but it tasted especially acidic this time. She made a face as she set it down and looked up to ask if it was a different brand. What she saw legitimately frightened her: Kelly's cheeks were wet.

"Mom?" Something was really wrong. Lucy could easily imagine her overprotective dad hooking her up to IV fluid if necessary; she had memories of him doing that before. But Kelly was not someone who cried often. Hardly ever. Maybe Lucy was seriously ill. Or had cancer or something equally terrifying.

"It's nothing, honey, really." Kelly brushed the dampness away, staring at Lucy, but with her head down. She almost seemed embarrassed. "It's just . . . it was nice to hear you laugh," she shrugged.

Lucy shook her head. "I—what's happening? Please, just tell me what's going on. You're freaking me out!" She put a cracker in her mouth up-side-down, as usual, and the amount of salt on it almost gagged her. But she was famished, so she grabbed another one. It was strange that she could feel so hungry while worrying that she might have the bubonic plague or something, but starvation could kill a person too.

Kelly sat down beside her on the couch and sighed again. Lucy got more sighs from her mom than anyone else in the family, and she was beginning to feel irritated.

"Lucy," Kelly began quietly, "when is the last time you remember laughing?"

Weird question. "Laughing?" she said around the dry crumbs. "I don't know. Why?"

Kelly raised an eyebrow.

"Come *on*, Mom. You and Dad have been looking at me like that all day, ever since Maggie had that nightmare. What is the *deal*?"

"Lucy? Honey, I don't want to startle you, but Maggie's—" She paused and scratched her ear. "It wasn't really a nightmare, but that's not—honey, that happened three days ago. Today is Wednesday."

Lucy stared at her.

Kelly took the glass of juice out of Lucy's hand; it was beginning to tip. "That's why you had to have an IV and oxygen, honey. You've been unconscious for three days. And that's why you had the Depends on. And that is why I am grateful beyond words that you are finally back."

Then something happened: Kelly sat down on the couch and hugged her middle daughter.

To Lucy, that was more astonishing than waking up wearing a diaper. She didn't even know what to do with that. It was almost uncomfortable. Not like with her dad—she *lived* for his hugs. Nothing was better than one of her dad's giant bear hugs, with her ear smashed against his chest, and feeling his deep voice rumble through her when he said, "Hello, Miss Lucy."

But Kelly? Her *mom*? She wasn't a hugger. Not with Lucy anyway. She hugged Maggie pretty regularly. And she hugged Claire a lot. But Lucy? She tried to think of the last time Kelly had hugged her. But she couldn't, so she just murmured into her shoulder, "But what happened? What day is it, again?"

Kelly sat back, so Lucy scraped the salt off another cracker and picked up the weird juice. "Well . . ." She was stalling, brushing some hair away from her face. "For starters, it's Wednesday. You—"

Then Lucy's dad came in and stopped dead in his tracks, looking at his wife and daughter.

"Aeden, look who woke up!" Kelly said.

Lucy's dad was across the room in less than a blink. Kelly started to stand, but he knelt down, his six-foot-three-inch frame still towering over the two small women, enveloping both of them in his long arms. He gave a big *mmm-wah* kiss on top of Lucy's head and kissed Kelly on the mouth.

Kelly smiled, then extracted herself from the tangle, and Aeden leaned back to look at Lucy. But she hung on to him anyway, again thinking her dad's hugs were the very best things in the world.

"Well good morning, Miss Lucy." His deep voice crooned. "It's good to see you today."

"She woke up a few minutes ago," Kelly said, "hungry and confused, but talking, a lot." The look she gave Aeden then—the one where she was saying something but not saying something? That was a normal look for her. But then she actually started getting choked up as she continued, which was definitely not normal. "Yeah," she nodded at his raised eyebrows. "Then she got up and went to the bathroom and—and laughed at how funny it would have been if Father Patrick had needed to help her."

"So," Aeden began, glancing around at the abandoned walker, then at Lucy, then back at Kelly.

"She's fine," Kelly said, shaking her head. Then she shrugged. "So far."

That caught Lucy's attention, as if they didn't already have it. They weren't telling her something and, fun as sitting there hooked up to tubes was, she was trying not to freak out. "Dad?"

He looked over at her.

"Am I sick?"

His lips shut tight. He looked Lucy straight in the eye, but he didn't say anything for one heartbeat.

One. Very. Long. Heartbeat.

"No," he said. But he said it with an up-sweeping tone, more like, "No?" There was definitely a "but" coming, and Lucy was irritated and, worse, scared all over again.

"Well, is someone going to tell me what's going on?" She finally exploded, hearing the volume and pitch of her own voice rise. "I feel fine—I mean I *think* I feel fine—but Mom's acting weird, she tells me it's Wednesday, so I've missed three whole days, and now you're acting weird, so now I'm not sure how I feel! Am I okay or not? Quit stalling and just tell me: what's happening?" She gestured to the tube sticking out of her arm.

Then her dad's face went through a series of various expressions, one right after the other: shock, annoyance, confusion, amusement, and something Lucy couldn't identify. Then his shoulders slumped.

"This is going to be interesting," he said, scrubbing his hands across his face.

Kelly nodded but didn't say anything.

Turning back to Lucy, finally, he said, "First of all, here—" He pulled up the ottoman to sit directly in front of her, and Kelly sat down in the green recliner, watching from a distance. Then he took Lucy's arm. "I can unhook this tube now." He glanced over at Kelly.

She nodded. "She's had some juice and crackers and has kept them down."

He detached the IV tubing, peeled off the wide medical tape that had secured the intravenous catheter, then pulled the thin, inch-long tube out of Lucy's arm. She had experienced this action multiple times in her life, but the sensation was strange this time. The feeling of the catheter actually sliding out of her vein wasn't painful at all, but it tingled in a bizarre way that made the muscles around her eyes and mouth tighten in an unfamiliar response.

With his left thumb over the small puncture the catheter had left, he picked up a roll of thinner medical tape, tore off a piece, then secured a cotton swab over the small wound.

"Thanks," she mumbled, pressing down one corner of the tape more firmly.

Aeden tied up the tubing, moved the IV contraption, then repositioned himself more comfortably on the ottoman.

"So, Lucy," he began in his professional doctor voice—the unemotional, down-to-business voice. "How do you feel?"

Seriously? she thought. *Fine, I'll play along.* But she had to stop and think about her body.

How *did* she feel?

"I feel hungry . . . and a little stiff. I want to get up and stretch. And I'd like to take a shower." Then she looked him straight in the eye. "And I want you to tell me what's wrong."

"Fair enough," he said, still all business. No emotion. "Lucy, you have had, since you were born, a physical condition which has been very perplexing. Primarily, it has to do with sudden, acute, and chronic increases and decreases in weight."

She glanced down at her sixteen-year-old body. She wasn't one of those skinny-minny girls, but she was by no means what anyone would even call chubby.

"No," he said, following her gaze. "It has nothing to do with size or proportion, or even health. As far as I've been able to observe and measure, it's only your weight."

That made no sense. She had no idea how much she weighed, but as far as she knew, weight and size had a definite correlation. She wasn't following.

"I'm going to tell you something that might be—" he stopped. He took a big breath, shook his head, and started again. "I'm going to tell you something that will definitely be very strange to hear. It might be unsettling, but you are not sick. You're so healthy, in fact, that you won't be taking a vitamin anymore. Well—not the vitamin you have been taking anyway—not the pill Mom has always given you every morning. And that's going to make things a little different." He stopped, shook his head, and started again. "Things are definitely going to be very different now. We can guess how some things will be different, but not everything. But you are growing up, and I think you're old enough to handle it now. And we believe it's time to let you laugh again."

What did that even mean?

They looked at her. She looked at them. They looked at each other, then back at Lucy.

"Well?" Aeden said.

"Uhh . . ." What were they asking? She shook her head. More must be coming. "Well, what? You didn't tell me anything." Maybe it wasn't just Maggie. Maybe her entire family was on crack. They weren't making sense.

Her dad stood up and dragged his hand over his face again. "We really didn't, did we?" He shook his head. Repeatedly. The doctor in him had left the building sometime in the last sixty seconds, and it seemed to Lucy that the dad in him had no idea what he was doing. He looked to Kelly, who was staring at the floor.

"It was me," Kelly said without lifting her head. She had a pained expression on her typically stoic face. "It was me," she said again. "It was my fault. I don't know if it was something

I had done, but I'm the one who made the choice about the Serenvidria. Your father didn't—"

"The what?" Lucy asked, at the same time her dad cut in, holding his hand up in a gesture to stop Kelly.

"No. It was both of us. We did extensive research, and we—together—made the decision. But it didn't always work, and there were breakthrough periods, like now, though not as . . . obvious. We can't keep increasing your dosage, however. Your medicine—your vitamin. It's called *Serenvidria*, and it does more than we've told you."

Discussion 1 — Neonatal Manifestations

Good morning!

How's he doing?

Uh, so far, so good.

The aggression?

Um, controlled, and his levels are back to within the normal range. It looks like he's back on the projected arc.

The girl?

She's doing very well! Yes, she's coming along remarkably well. Remarkably. But . . .

But?

W-well, we've just discovered some . . . um . . . evidence of . . .

Of what?

Well, of neo-natal manifestations.

I see.

I know, I know!

How is it possible we are just discovering this now?

Um, her, uh, father was—is—a doctor. Look here. Apparently, he administered all but the, uh, first two of her vaccinations. See? We only got into his computer this week. That was after we had found evidence of deleted hospital files. We think there may be more in a safe. In his house. We are working on that.

This isn't good.

I know, I know. But—eh-hem, *there has been no indication since, well, it would be hard to say since when, but something would have shown up if she had still been manifesting by the time she hit the public school system. It is very fortunate that she wasn't home-schooled as many of these kids are, or there would be no way of knowing. But she seems very stable now, even with early onset.*

I'm sure I don't need to explain to you that *neonatal* onset means significantly more than *early* onset. It's very dangerous.

Yes.

Keep an eye on her. On both of them.

Aeden and Kelly

Fifteen years, seven months earlier . . .

Halfway sitting up from where she had been reclined on the couch, Kelly stared at her own toes with a crinkled forehead.

"Aeden?" she asked quietly from the suede couch.

"Yeah?" Aeden replied, not looking up. The former basketball star turned theology student turned medical student when he met a cute literary major named Kellin Gunn, sat at a desk in the little family's cozy den. At the moment, he was poring over a study on myocardial ischemia, tapping his lips with his index finger as he thought.

"Something's weird, Aeden."

Aeden pulled himself out of his article and looked at his wife with an expression unique to him. His eyes were squinted, and his lips were pressed together as if he were looking at an eye exam chart and couldn't quite make out a letter. Is that a *B* or an *E*?

Then Kelly gasped for air.

"Kel?" Moving quickly but speaking calmly in his deep voice, Aeden was at his wife's side. "Is it the baby? What's happening?"

"I don't know, but—" Kelly gasped in pain, her large gray eyes flew open, and her hands grasped under her large belly. "Oh! She's . . . suddenly heavy!" She sucked in a shallow breath. "And it hurts!"

Dr. Aeden Callaghan jumped up, ran down the stairs to his office, grabbed his medical bag, and ran back to his wife's side in the den within seconds. He heard Maggie start crying in her crib upstairs, but ran back to Kelly, maintaining a practiced professional calmness so as never to distress the patient. He quickly pulled a stethoscope out of his bag and, in his soothing voice asked, "Are you having contractions?"

"No, but . . . It just—*OH!*" Kelly couldn't double over, but she spasmed as she gave a loud gasp, then curved her body around the baby and tried to roll over, using her arms to support the massive bulge. Beads of sweat covered her upper lip and forehead. "I can't breathe." She panted as tears began leaking from her right eye.

Aeden helped his wife roll over to her left side and pulled her sticky shirt up over her large belly, which was then damp with perspiration. He could see the massive bulge pulling down and stretching the skin on Kelly's left side, so he grabbed pillows from the couch and used them to support the weighty bulk. The very weighty bulk.

Finally able to breathe, Kelly continued to pant and wince as Aeden searched for the baby's heartbeat.

Kelly's eyes darted to the door; she could hear Maggie.

"It's fast, but it's strong," he said.

Then the shape of a tiny footprint pressed out and slid underneath the skin on Kelly's belly. She screamed again, louder, while a dark patch of purple blossomed and spread quickly across the stretched tissue.

"I'm taking you in," Aeden said.

Five feet one inch tall, a tiny woman even at eight months pregnant, Kelly Callaghan sobbed and gasped as her husband of three years carried her to the car while dialing Mrs. Decker's number—someone had to come take care of Maggie, their almost nineteen-month-old daughter, who was asleep in her crib. Aeden helped Kelly into the back seat so she would have more room, but she didn't sound comfortable as she cried and struggled for breath.

Mrs. Decker answered the phone.

"Mrs. Decker, it's Aeden. I'm taking Kelly to the hospital and was wonder—" A pause. "Yes. Thank you so much. Yes. Thank you. Thank you."

"Maggie?" Kelly whispered from the back seat.

"Mrs. Decker is walking over now—don't worry."

Aeden ignored the speed limit and raced to the hospital, calling the obstetrician and thinking, *Dear God, please help her. Help the baby. Help Kelly. Please help. Please . . .*

"Something's wrong," his wife whimpered.

"Almost there—hang on."

Dr. Gowers, Aeden's colleague and friend, answered.

"Ron! It's Aeden. I'm taking Kelly in. Something's wrong." A slight pause. "She's having difficulty breathing, internal bleeding, and sharp pain." Another pause. "Thanks, Ron. We're minutes away." He hung up.

When Kelly screamed again and went limp, Aeden called Father Patrick.

Aeden pulled up to the emergency room doors. He jumped out of the car and pulled his unconscious wife out of the back seat. He had a good memory for names and faces, but he couldn't recall the name of the nurse who was walking toward him with a wheelchair as he lifted Kelly's limp body from the back of the car.

"Hello, Doctor Callaghan," she said. "Dr. Gowers is prepping, and I'll be taking Kelly directly the operating room."

"I'm coming, too," he said.

"I'm sorry but, as you know, only—"

"I know the regulations, Nurse—" He wished he could remember the woman's name; it would be so much better if he could—more authoritative—but the only thing he cared about was getting his unconscious wife into the operating room. "You can call me a physician's assistant, a scrub tech, or whatever else you like, but I will be in the OR with my wife." He walked past the registration desk, ignoring the frown on the nurse's face as she struggled to keep up with his long strides.

The heart monitor beeped a blessedly steady rhythm in the operating room, but feeling Kelly's pulse was more reassuring, so Aeden didn't let go of her hand. He held his tall frame perfectly still while Ron Gowers made the first incision across Kelly's bulging belly, equipment buzzing while the entire neonatal team did their job of keeping his wife alive and delivering their baby safely.

Half his mind observed the procedure with professional coldness. He was, after all, beginning to earn a reputation as a gifted heart surgeon himself and could read the mood of an OR by the way the doctor gave orders and the way the team responded. This team was skilled, alert, doing everything by the book. No one radiated that silent tension that was always present during a procedure that threatened to end badly. They were confident.

Aeden, however, felt ill. More than once, he had to swallow back the bile that threatened to come up as he looked at his wife's splayed abdomen. But he would not leave her. He would not leave them.

At least he was used to long hours in an operating room. A simple coronary bypass normally took anywhere from three to six hours. This felt so much longer. Aeden looked at the clock when Dr. Gowers deftly lifted the tiny, lethargic, violet-colored baby from the splayed flesh of Kelly's C-sectioned belly. It had been only twenty minutes.

"It's a girl," his friend pronounced from behind his surgical mask. "I guess you already knew that, but this makes it official."

As the little baby took her first breaths and filled the room with the sounds of her angry protest, Aeden finally breathed too.

"She's hefty," Dr. Gowers commented as he handed the baby to the delivery nurse, Diane.

"Wow. You're right," she replied. Diane cut the umbilical cord and took the furious, wailing baby away while Dr. Gowers immediately began reassembling the unconscious mother.

"This way, Dad," Diane nodded, as she carried the baby toward a prepared area of the room. Aeden hesitated, however, torn between remaining by his wife and following his daughter.

"Go on," commanded Dr. Gowers, who peered at Aeden over his glasses. "Kelly is stable, and there is nothing you can do for her here. This part is going to take longer, but I see no reason to worry. Go take care of your daughter."

Our daughter. Nodding, Aeden turned away while still looking back at his unconscious wife. Then he hurried after the nurse and the crying infant.

"That's a very good cry, little one," Diane cooed. "You're getting some good color now." Handing the little bundle to Aeden, she asked, "Ready to give her first bath? We'll get her cleaned up and finish the tests while the doctor takes care of Mom."

Reverently, Aeden took his tiny red-faced baby in his huge hands, held her close to his chest and rocked her slowly, smiling weakly. "Hello little miss," he murmured soft and low. "We're so glad you're here." At the sound and vibration of his voice, the baby took a shuddering breath and stopped crying, her little chest still heaving.

"Oh, see? She knows her daddy's voice," said Diane. Then, after checking heart rate, breathing, oxygenation, muscle tone, weight, and length . . . Diane smiled and pronounced, "Five pounds, twelve ounces, fifteen inches long, ten fingers, ten toes, and a whole bunch of red hair."

"What was that weight?" called the doctor over his shoulder.

"Five twelve, fifteen inches," Diane said again, louder. "She's tiny, but she's all here and so far, so good."

"Huh," the doctor mused, half to himself. "I would have guessed heavier."

When it was time for her bath, Aeden could easily cradle the tiny infant with one arm, her head resting in the palm of his right hand with lots of room to spare. Maggie had been so much bigger—weighing such things in ounces—and she fussed and wiggled and cried the whole time. This new little one, on the other hand, opened her dark eyes a little, and seemed to enjoy the warm water. When she was dried and bundled into her first doll-sized diaper that was much too large for her, Aeden held her to his chest again, humming and rocking her. She opened her eyes again for a moment, then fell back to sleep, a perfect picture of contentment.

Diane had a syringe ready by then, so Aeden bent his tall frame down a bit so she could reach the baby.

"I'm going to need you to put her here in the bassinet for this, Doctor Callaghan," Diane smiled.

"I'm sure I'll be fine holding her, Diane."

"Doctor, it's a matter of safety. We really—"

"I'll sit here, so you can reach her." He sat down on what was, essentially, a padded circle on wheels—not even a chair. Aeden knew he was putting Diane in an awkward position. He was, after all, a surgical doctor in an operating room, used to calling the shots. Literally.

Diane looked over at another member of the neonatal team who shook her head, followed by a slight eyeroll and a micro-shrug. Aeden took that look to mean *doctors always think they can do anything they want, but whatever.* Aeden did feel a guilty twinge at that silent comment, but still refused to put the baby down. Diane sighed, pulled back the blanket, and inserted the needle into the baby's upper thigh.

When the little baby cried in angry protest again, Aeden fumbled not to drop her.

The two women looked at each other, the one shaking her head even more now.

Diane disposed of the syringe and typed something into the computer while Aeden cradled the crying baby and murmured to her once more in his deep, bass voice, "It's okay honey, it's okay. You're fine. I've got you." He looked at Diane, who was still typing. "Diane, she really does feel like she's more than five-twelve. Could we weigh her again?"

Diane nodded, finished typing, then turned to the baby. "May I?" she asked, all friendly smiles gone. Aeden nodded, and Diane took the then quiet baby and laid her gently on the scale. "Huh," she scowled. "You're right. She's eight—whoa." Diane took half a step back, raising her hands away from the scale, making a point of not letting any part of her body touch it. "It's the scale. It's definitely acting up." Aeden and Diane watched as the electronic numbers dropped quickly, then slowly, then, after a few seconds, stopping at five pounds, eight ounces. "Okay," Diane said, shaking her head, "we definitely need to get this machine replaced. She's actually four ounces lighter than we thought. Sorry. That's small, but not abnormal for coming four weeks early. Her lungs are good, though, as we've heard. She was ready to come." She picked the baby up and handed her back.

Aeden greedily took her. He rocked, murmured, and smiled at his little daughter while Diane typed into the computer and got another syringe.

"One more teeny poke, little one," she said. Talking to babies like that must be habit. "I'm sorry, but we need to know your blood type. Then you can relax."

Diane took the baby's foot and pricked her heel to draw a few drops of blood. Tears fell from Aeden's eyes at the sound of his daughter's pain. And though he held her securely, she definitely felt heavier than five pounds, eight ounces. Maybe he was just feeling the weight of fatherhood—of now having two little girls to take care of.

The private hospital room shone with gentle, indirect lighting that made the seashell paintings on the sand-colored walls shimmer and glow softly. Kelly slept beneath a bedspread of Caribbean blue that matched the drapes. She was still quite pale, but thanks to the pain medication, her breathing was soft and regular. It was music to Aeden's ears.

As Aeden held his tiny, sleeping daughter close to his heart and gazed down at her perfect little face, he gave a silent prayer of thanks to God for bringing his wife and his daughter safely through delivery. Kelly was going to be fine, and his newer little daughter was beautiful. One thing for C-section babies—they look pretty—unmarred by forceps marks or suction rings, or by having struggled through the vaginal canal. She had pale, Irish skin, lavender-colored eyelids, tiny, pouted lips like her mother's, and a mass of red curls sticking out in all directions—just like his own.

A soft knock on the door made Aeden look up.

"Am I interruptin'?" asked the Catholic priest timidly.

"Hello, Father." Aeden placed the baby in the bassinet and crossed the hospital room to greet his longtime friend and mentor.

"Hello, Aeden, my boy," whispered the gray-haired cleric as he embraced Aeden in a paternal hug, though he had to reach up to do so. He looked over at Kelly. "Is she alright now?"

Aeden sighed. "Yes. Now, at least. Thank you so much for coming, and for your prayers. When I called—" He stopped, looked at Kelly and shook his head. "I . . . I'd feared the worst. I'm relieved to say, however, that Kelly is fine now. It will be a long recovery, but she's going to be okay." Then, smiling, the proud dad put his arm around the old man and walked him to the bassinet "Would you like to meet the newest member of your flock?"

"Oh my," crooned the priest as he gazed down at the sleeping child. "What a precious angel, sent straight from Heaven. Congratulations, Aeden. I'm so glad that Kelly and this little lamb are doin' alright. Thanks be to God for your good doctor. What did he say was the problem?"

"Thanks to God, indeed," Aeden said, nodding. His eyes were squinted, his lips pursed again, as he looked at his wife. "The baby somehow broke two of Kelly's ribs, which resulted in a lacerated liver and the need for a blood transfusion. Also, the baby then struggled so hard that the placenta was torn away from the uterine wall."

Or maybe it happened the other way around. He didn't know how many of the details Father Patrick wanted to know, and Aeden didn't particularly want to talk about it. Putting his hand over his closed eyes and shaking his head, he rubbed his forehead, as if the memory of the danger caused him physical pain. "If we hadn't lived so close to the hospital, and if they hadn't been able help Kelly and get the baby out . . ."

"I'll say it again," said Father Patrick touching Aeden's arm, "thanks be to God."

"Amen, Father. Amen."

"So have yeh chosen a name?" asked the priest, looking up with twinkling eyes and a brightened tone.

"Yes." Aeden smiled. "This is Lucy Callaghan. Lucy, this is Father Patrick."

Dr. Aeden Tavish Callaghan, cardiologist, and Mrs. Kellin Gunn Callaghan, reference librarian, were elated to announce the birth of their normal, healthy, redheaded, Irish Catholic second daughter named Lucy Elisabeth Callaghan. Lucy Elisabeth Callaghan was ambivalent about the occasion, so she yawned and went back to sleep. That was perfectly normal.

But she wasn't normal.

After Lucy's traumatic birth, Kelly and Lucy spent five days in the hospital. *Had it been only five days? It felt much longer*, thought Aeden. Sleep-deprived, he drove home every night to spend time with his elder daughter, Maggie, and to get some sleep. Each morning after breakfast, he took Maggie to the next-door neighbor, Mrs. Decker.

He thanked God every day for Mr. and Mrs. Decker. Their five sons were grown and living elsewhere, so the Callaghans had adopted them. Or had they adopted the Callaghans? It was hard to tell. In any case, Mrs. Decker welcomed Maggie to her home every morning; she took Maggie to the little neighborhood park every afternoon; she brought warm, delicious meals over every evening. In fact, Aeden had begun gaining a little weight from the homemade soups, breads, and cookies that were always on hand, even after Kelly and Lucy came home.

When Aeden was finally able to bring Kelly and Lucy home, he was more than relieved to have all his girls under one roof. But he was tired. So unbelievably tired.

Kelly's recovery from broken ribs, internal ruptures, and the emergency caesarean delivery was going to take time. Mrs. Decker continued to invite Maggie to her home to play every morning, then came back to check on Kelly every afternoon. It was Aeden, therefore, who took care of tiny Lucy: holding her, feeding her, getting up with her in the middle of night, changing her, and rocking her back to sleep.

By the time Lucy was two weeks old, Kelly still couldn't sit up for very long, let alone feed or even hold the baby; it was too much for her. On top of that, she wasn't sleeping well. She cried a lot. And she had nightmares. Mrs. Decker often sat with Kelly and held her hand. Mother to five grown sons and thirteen grandchildren, she seemed best able to sooth Kelly's troubled mind, just by being there.

Aeden couldn't do that. Why couldn't he help his own wife?

He did his best to let Kelly rest while he tried to care for both of the girls: holding Lucy, dressing Maggie, feeding Lucy, brushing Maggie's hair, changing Lucy's diaper, finding Maggie's shoe, burping Lucy, putting Maggie to bed, rocking Lucy in the middle of night, then getting up and doing it all over again the next day. Kelly could sometimes sit up and read to Maggie if the rowdy toddler sat quietly next to her. Maggie, however, wasn't very good at sitting still yet. She always wanted to be stomping, dancing, running, or talking to her little sister—words no one but the two of them understood. None of that helped

Kelly much. Even walking around the house was exhausting for her.

That was why, when Lucy was four weeks and four days old, Aeden left Kelly and Maggie at home and took his newest little girl to her first checkup with Dr. Edelmann; she was a pediatrician whose office was in the same building as Aeden's cardiology practice.

He held his little daughter as she received her first immunization since the day she was born, and he almost dropped her—again. Just like on the day she was born. Her tiny body felt strangely heavy.

He really needed more sleep.

Four weeks after that, during another checkup and shot, the same thing happened.

And Aeden began formulating a theory.

The hypothesis was, logically, completely impossible. However, the unusual . . . patterns—patterns were observable, measurable, and unemotional, so that's how Dr. Aeden Tavish Callaghan chose to think of them—the patterns were clear. His wife did not want to talk about them at all, but he observed them, and measured them, and confronted them with the dispassionate professionalism he would assume with any of his regular patients.

By the time Lucy would reach fourteen months and six days old, even Kelly would have to acknowledge the reality of Lucy's condition. Aeden felt relief at his wife's managing the situation with a cool-headed, nonemotional, approach.

It would take until Lucy was twenty-four months and twenty-seven days old for Dr. Callaghan to finally find a treatment that would allow Lucy to live a happy, normal life.

But Lucy would be one hundred and ninety-nine months old before Dr. Callaghan would tell her about her strange diagnosis.

Aeden confirmed that pain triggered Lucy's heaviness by testing his theory with small pin pricks. The doctor in him knew this was necessary; the father in him felt heartbroken that he had to cause his little girl any pain at all, especially when he saw the tear-filled look of betrayal on her tiny face. Her weight gains didn't last very long, just moments, but they were sudden and acute, so even with Kelly's ribs and sutures healing well, Aeden worried about her holding Lucy at all. It wasn't much of an issue, however, since Kelly didn't seem interested in holding her. She was tired. And still in lingering pain. But he recognized the symptoms of postpartum depression, and possibly something he had just read about—postpartum post-traumatic stress disorder? That would explain the nightmares and listlessness. But he was surprised when Kelly didn't even want to talk about "the baby."

He had to tell her his theory, though. She had to know.

One morning when Maggie was at Mrs. Decker's and Lucy was asleep in her bassinet, he sat on the end of their king-sized bed and explained. He told her about almost dropping Lucy and the tests he'd conducted himself. Propped up on a pile of pillows, Kelly fiddled with the corner of the navy blue comforter as she listened, staring at her feet. She nodded every now and then and blinked slowly once in a while. On the whole, she seemed curiously not fazed by the mostly one-sided conversation. In fact, she only asked one question.

"So," she began, emotionless and barely above a whisper. Then she paused for so long Aeden wondered if she had forgotten what she was going to say. But then she spoke. "So, I shouldn't really hold the baby much. At least not right now. Right?" She finally looked up.

"Well," Aeden replied, "I think we just need to be very careful about that. I mean, only until I can figure out what's really going on. But I'm sure it will be fine when you're sitting down."

"Yeah," she nodded, looking back down at her feet. "I agree. I shouldn't hold her much."

As Lucy grew, Aeden learned that stress also triggered her alarming weight increases. She went through several bassinets, and then cribs, and Kelly had to be careful when she needed to hold the baby; one episode of Lucy's sudden and unexpected weight gains might seriously strain her back. Over the next three months, the episodes became longer, more frequent, and more intense. That is to say: she got heavier more often, and she got stronger. A lot stronger. Both Kelly and Aeden received frequent and painful bruises from Lucy kicking and wiggling when she was unhappy about something.

During all this time, Aeden and Kelly never had anyone over, not even Mrs. Decker, and they never took Lucy anywhere because they could never know what to expect. They told friends and colleagues that Kelly was still tired and needed a lot of rest. They absolutely never let Maggie hold Lucy, even if she was sitting on the couch. The poor child might be crushed! And when Grandpa Gunn came to visit from Florida, Aeden gave Lucy a small dose of diphenhydramine, otherwise known as Benadryl, to make her sleepy, so she wouldn't crash while he was there.

Aeden hoped and literally prayed Lucy would outgrow this condition. He had gone back to his practice, but when he wasn't working, he was quietly searching medical journals for any information related, even remotely, to Lucy's symptoms.

Kelly began working from home; leaving Lucy at any daycare facility, or even with Mrs. Decker, was completely out of the question. She looked for clues to the baby's condition in literary works and records. After many weeks, Aeden had found two obscure references to children with impossible and supposedly mis-reported birth weights who died, along with their mothers, within a few hours of delivery. Kelly found mythical stories and archaic legends of strong children. However, neither of them found anything that helped or explained why Lucy would get so heavy—and strong—when hurt or upset. It was becoming a real problem.

And then, out of the blue, at six months and two days, Lucy got lighter. Much lighter.

Kelly was putting away dishes, humming to distract herself from the chaos around her. The baby was sitting in her carrier on the kitchen floor—the best place for her—occasionally laughing at Maggie, who was dancing, singing, and spinning her dolly around. Kelly tried to tune out the noise as she put clean utensils and silverware in a drawer, but she had a headache, and the clattering of forks, spoons, and knives made even her own humming annoying, so she stopped. She just wanted to get breakfast cleaned up so she could have some quiet. Maybe the girls would calm down if she gave the baby a bottle and read them a story. She heard Maggie hiccup, which must have been hilarious to the baby because she started laughing. Kelly ran hot water over a glass pan and began scraping off the remains of a cheesy breakfast casserole. Maggie's hiccups continued, and the baby's laughter got louder. Then Maggie started laughing because the baby was laughing. Kelly looked over at the pair, then screamed.

The baby fell at least a foot to the floor. She immediately wailed, her face and neck turning bright red with anger and alarm.

Kelly ran to her.

The one thing that usually calmed the baby down when she was hurt, angry, or distressed was Aeden. He would hold her close, rub her back, and murmur to her until her tears dried up. But now the baby was on the floor crying, and Aeden wasn't home. And Maggie was crying; her mother's scream had scared the poor girl half to death.

Kelly got down on the floor, but the baby was too heavy to pick up and too angry to be consoled. Kelly sat on the floor next to her, crying too, not knowing what to do. She pulled Maggie onto her lap, rocking her and rubbing the baby's tummy, trying to sooth them both. "Shhh . . ." she rocked and rubbed. "It's okay. You're okay." But to no avail. The baby continued to cry, and if the baby cried, Maggie would always cry. Kelly could only rock and rub and let them cry. "It's okay. You're okay. I know. You're sad. It's okay." Rocking and rubbing.

It was more than twenty-five minutes before the baby's crying quieted to whimpers, and Maggie's crying quieted to sniffles. Then sheer exhaustion made the baby shudder, yawn, and settle. Maggie reached over and took the baby's little hand. "My baby was so sad," she said.

Kelly kissed her and put her on the floor. "Yes, she was. Thank you for helping her not be sad."

"I love my baby," Maggie sighed as she knelt down and first wiped the baby's cheeks and then her own.

"I know you do, honey. You are such a good sister."

Kelly tentatively bent over to pick the baby up. She was relieved to find that she finally could and lifted the child into her arms. When the baby laid her tired head on her mother's shoulder, Kelly rubbed her back and held her. Just for a moment.

Aeden didn't know what to make of Kelly's story. Could delirium be another symptom of the postnatal post-traumatic stress disorder? Kelly must have seen the doubt in his eyes.

"Aeden! She was floating!" Kelly yelled in a hysterical whisper, which grew in pitch and volume as she continued. "Floating! They were laughing really hard, and I looked over and—she was in the air! Floating! A good ten or twelve inches - above - the - floor! Maybe more!"

Aeden didn't realize he was shaking his head. "Kel. That's not even—"

"Oh—don't you dare tell me it's not possible," she commanded, her voice dropping in pitch but not in volume. It was her angry tone. "She - was - floating. If the other thing is possible," she pointed to the floor, "whatever you want to call it, then this is possible, too, because it happened. I saw her float. I saw her crash. I saw the dent she left in the hardwood floor! Look for yourself!" she cried, her pitch rising again to panic, on the verge of hysteria. "Aeden, I didn't know what to do. I couldn't do anything! I couldn't pick her up, or help her, or hold her, or anything."

As Kelly burst into frustrated tears for the second time in twenty minutes, Aeden stepped forward and put his arms around her and held her. She sobbed. He sighed.

The deciding event was when Lucy was twenty-five months old—the terrible twos. It was a Sunday morning, and four-year-old Maggie was dancing to the music of a cartoon on television. Lucy was moving her small feet, wiggling her chubby body in imitation, mostly going in circles, and Maggie started laughing. Lucy also started laughing so, of course, she started floating. Kelly promptly took her away from the television, so Lucy threw a tantrum, and even Aeden couldn't pick her up. She kicked another dent in the hardwood floor.

That's when they decided to put Lucy on the Serenvidria, which Aeden had procured from a facility in Panama. Yes, Panama. It took him four months to determine the correct dosage of the definitely non-FDA-approved drug, and it had to be adjusted as Lucy grew. Too much made her catatonic. Too little was ineffective for intense stimuli, like sudden, sharp pain. The optimal amount simply made her very calm. Unperturbed. Nonreactive. Pensive. Focused. And then it was perfectly safe to take her anywhere.

Strangers likely thought Lucy a little odd, but they would never have guessed she was being pharmaceutically managed. Lucy never knew it herself. All she knew was that Kelly gave Maggie and her vitamins every morning. Her parents were aware that the "vitamin" didn't work 100 percent of the time but, for the most part, it did the trick. No more heaviness. No more floating. No more anger. And for fourteen years, no more laughter.

Before/After

They were looking at her.

Lucy was sitting in the corner of the sofa. She had pulled one of the blankets around herself, holding it closed tight under her chin, though she wasn't cold at all. Well, maybe a little. No . . . she really wasn't cold. Was she? She looked at the pattern and recognized the sort-of plaid green blanket she loved to snuggle up in while watching movies. It was only *sort* of plaid because it wasn't a real *Irish* plaid and it wasn't a real *Irish* green, but it was soft and comforting.

"Well?" her dad said.

Lucy looked up at him, then at Kelly. They weren't making sense. She looked at her dad again, then dropped her eyes to stare at a piece of cracker that had fallen off the blanket while she was tripping her way to the bathroom with the IV thing.

Kelly frowned and turned to her dad. "Is it the drugs? Are they lingering and still making her numb?"

"I don't think so—I'm not sure," he said, shaking his head. "Lucy, what do you think about what we've just told you?"

Lucy chewed on her lip for a moment, then Kelly laughed. "Aeden, she looks just like you do when you're thinking about something really hard. She's just taking it in."

"Lucy?" he prodded.

This wasn't right. It just wasn't right. It was not . . . right. This wasn't right. It's not right.

"Do you understand what we've told you?"

She nodded her head. But then she shook her head.

"Those vitamins, honey. You won't take them anymore. Do you understand that?"

She nodded. Someone might step on that piece of cracker.

"And we're going to be watching you, to see how you do. Does that make sense?"

Lucy slid off the couch and stretched her right hand between the edges of the blanket, still holding it closed tight with her left hand. She bent and picked up the piece of cracker, set it on the end table next to the juice Kelly had brought her, and nestled back into the corner of the sofa.

"Aeden?" Kelly sounded stressed. That was normal. Kelly was always stressed.

Aeden shook his head. "Lucy, can you please tell me what you heard us say?"

Lucy pulled her knees up to her chest under the blanket. "You said Mom isn't going to give me the pill she gives me every morning." Then she reached over for the glass of juice and drank the last little bit of it. It was barely a swallow, and the tartness made the sour feeling in her stomach worse.

"And do you understand what that's going to do?"

She rubbed some crusty sleep out of the corner of her left eye. She wanted to take a shower. "I'm going to take a different vitamin."

"Yes. And we're going to keep you home from school for a while longer to see how you do."

She shook her head a little. "I have finals. And I have to finish some projects. School's almost out." How many weeks were left? She wasn't finished with her science notebook. She had to turn in all her notes. From labs or something.

"We can work around that, but we don't think it will be a good idea for you to go back until we see."

"See what?" She raised her head and finally looked her father in the eye.

He paused. He looked surprised. "To see if you crash, first of all."

"Crash," she repeated. That was a funny word for it.

"Yes. When you first passed out, here on the sofa on Sunday, it was several hours before we could move you. You were too heavy for us."

She nodded. "I am getting bigger." Maggie sometimes let her wear her shoes, and they fit just fine.

"No honey, it's not just that."

"Yes, it is!" She knew she would remember this moment forever: she had just shouted at her father for the first time in her life. "It *is* that. That's all it is." Her shout had died down to a weak murmur.

His lips compressed. He didn't say anything.

Kelly's face was blank, but she wasn't looking at either of them; she was sliding her silver and emerald pendant back and forth on its chain and looking at the bookshelf.

"Lucy, you need to understand that you—"

"No. You wouldn't do that to me." They wouldn't.

"Wouldn't—?"

"You wouldn't drug me my whole life."

"Drug you?"

"You wouldn't keep me drugged and separate from everything like that."

"What? Lucy, we never—"

"You wouldn't do that to me!" She pulled the blanket up over her head. "Dad! You wouldn't do that to me!" It was hard to breathe. She pulled the blanket down from her face, but it was still so hard to breathe. She felt it! Her arms—they were so heavy she dropped them, and the blanket fell from around her shoulders.

Aeden was on his feet. "Lucy?"

"She's pale," Kelly said.

"Help." It wasn't even a whisper; it made no sound. Lucy's head was so heavy. She was dizzy and there was a ringing in her ears.

"Lucy, lie down, honey! Just lie down!"

She scooted down on the couch, and blackness started closing in from the edges of her vision.

"Daddy?" There was no sound. "Help me!" She couldn't hear her own voice! She screamed as the blackness closed to a small pinpoint. Then nothing.

There was a high, ringing whistle in Lucy's left ear that wouldn't go away no matter which way she put her head against the pillow. She was so tired—the kind of tired that would take several years of sleep to cure. But it was more than being sleepy-tired. Her body felt hollow and weak but not hungry. She rolled over, trying to get comfortable. It was no use.

She opened her eyes.

The afternoon sun threw shadows to the left side of the room, and she could smell tomato soup. She was lying on the sofa again, and recollection crept back. Tears trickled from her left eye, pooled in the corner by her nose, then continued down to her mouth, tasting salty. On her right side, tears slid down into her hair. She had seen Maggie cry before—a lot in fact—and Claire a few times, but Lucy couldn't remember crying before. Ever. That realization made more tears come.

She rolled onto her back, which made tears run into her ear. She wiped those away, but more came. Her face was turning into a river! She leaned her head back and covered her face with her hands. This didn't make sense. She kept wiping her face, but the aching pressure from where the tears originated didn't ease, and tears kept coming. How many tears were inside her?

Nothing makes sense.

How could they turn off their baby like that? That's what they had done. And she knew. She knew it was true because . . . because it *was* true. She could remember now. But not the way she *used* to remember; she remembered things now that only made sense because of what they had just told her.

Kites and swings and lunchrooms and bikes and balloons. There were so many times. And they kept turning her *off*!

Lucy sobbed aloud, and Kelly rushed into the room from the kitchen. Then she stopped and just stood there, watching her daughter cry her soul out on the couch. Lucy couldn't stand it. Couldn't stand to be stared at while her world fell apart. "Go away!" Her voice was hoarse, and not nearly as loud as she had meant it to be.

After a fraction of a second, Kelly turned and left. Lucy heard her pushing buttons on her phone, then heard her dad running down the stairs with his big stupid feet. And she cried even more because she loved him. But he had—*No!* She couldn't think anymore.

And when her dad came and sat on the end of the couch, Lucy only sat up because she would drown in those horrible tears otherwise. She could hardly breathe for all the water; the neck of her T-shirt was drenched and sticky. *He did this! On purpose!* He shut her off. For fourteen years. *Why? Why did they do that to me?*

Her father sat there. Watching. There was nowhere else to wipe her hands. The back of her throat was tight and achy. Her head pounded. Her hair was damp. And her face felt raw from scraping away saltwater. And they did this. He did this.

On purpose.

She sobbed again. She wailed.

Aeden sat with her the whole time. It might have been an hour. It might have been two. It might have been a century. She didn't know. How could anyone stand this? She didn't know how to feel this way! When would it stop? How could it ever stop? There was no cure for this. No medicine. No pill . . .

She gulped some air. And then—it was the weirdest thing yet—she yawned. And the tears stopped.

No pill? Yes, there was. It was exactly the pill they had been giving her for fourteen years. The pill that turned her off and stopped her from feeling. But that didn't make sense either! She had *always* felt! She had! This - was - not - *possible.*

They had drugged her and made her—what had Kelly said? *Numb?* She wasn't sure what numb felt like, but that's what they called it. And they were okay with that! They knew that's what it did!

More tears. But they were weak and tired, barely making the effort to fall. Silent.

Lucy saw a large blurry glass of water in front of her aching eyes, and she took it.

Her nose was completely clogged, so she drank noisily, panting and gasping into the transparent glass that fogged up as she gulped. She must have cried ten gallons of water—no wonder she was thirsty. After several pauses for air, she had drunk the entire glass. The ringing in her ears had quieted to a distant scream.

She wiped her mouth with the back of her damp hand. She wiped again with the neck of her T-shirt, then gave up. She lowered the glass to her knee and looked at her dad, who hadn't said a word.

His face was also wet, his eyes were red and swollen, the front of his pale blue shirt was lined with dark streaks. She'd never seen her dad cry either. He looked older—older than before.

And that was the moment.

That was the dividing line between *before* and *after*.

Everything that happened now was all *after*. After she woke up on the couch. After she learned the truth. After they had stopped lying.

Had they stopped? How would she ever know?

They had lied before. Would they lie after?

She was sweaty, and sticky.

"I'm going to go take a shower," she said.

He nodded.

She stood up and walked past him into the kitchen, filled her glass with more water, grabbed a piece of bread out of the cupboard, then went upstairs.

Lucy sat on her bed, the tapered ends of her wet curls dripping on her shoulders and down the back of her clean, light green blouse. Her dad had put a small bandage over the puncture where the IV had been inserted on the back of her right hand, and it had come off in the shower, but a tackier adhesive remained, outlining where the wider medical tape had been. She rubbed at the sticky residue.

Her parents had *drugged* her. They had started drugging her at—what—age two? They said they had needed to. And they didn't call it "drugging," but it amounted to the same thing. All because she—

She couldn't complete that thought.

Swinging. Riding her bike. Sliding.

When she was asleep . . .

Balloons and kites.

When she dreamed . . .

Clouds and trees.

It couldn't be . . .

Laughing.

They said she . . .

Say it out loud, Lucy. Say it.

She couldn't. She couldn't even *think* it out loud, so she plopped over sideways and screamed into her green pillow to get the unthinkable thought out of her brain. All that did was hurt her throat, so she shoved the pillow away from her and wished she had more water.

But she didn't. All she could do was swallow and not think about what her parents said happened when she laughed.

Okay, then, what about the other thing—the "crashing?" That had been real. She had felt weird, and nearly sick, when Maggie was yelling at their dad that morning. No . . . that was three mornings ago. Anyway, when Maggie was yelling, Lucy had felt sick: like she might throw up, but with a thick, dense pain, like enormous boulders growing in her stomach, crushing her.

That's what her parents had called a "crash," and she had been unconscious for three *days*. Then *this* morning, after she woke up, when they said . . . when he told her . . .

She sat up and threw the pillow, wanting to hurl it across the room and smash something. But it was a fat, fluffy pillow and it only made it to the foot of her bed. Everything about today was wrong, and she couldn't even throw a pillow! She threw herself back on the bed again and covered her eyes with her freckled arm.

She sat up and looked at the clock; she had no concept of time at the moment. It was 4:36 in the afternoon. When she had woken up *that* morning, Father Patrick was there, and Kelly had come in, around 10:00, maybe? Then Dad and Kelly talked to her for maybe forty-five minutes. Had it only taken forty-five minutes to explain how she got too heavy to pick up as a baby, and then started floating, so they kept her drugged for the rest of her life? It felt like that kind of news should have taken longer. And then she had felt it—her arms felt heavy, her ears rang, the world got darker, and . . . and she couldn't hear anything, not even herself. And then the crash thing. But it wasn't the same as the first time. She hadn't felt sick that second time. No rocks in her stomach. No sickness. It felt more like she was sinking in water. And she had woken up hours later.

Was this going to keep happening?! It was terrifying! And it was painful. She had seen a big bruise on her hip when she was in the shower. That must have been from when she had hit the floor after Maggie had screamed. Did that mean the floating thing only happen when she was asleep? But could the crashing thing happen any time she was awake?

She screamed again, but only inside her mind: *I can't handle this!*

And she was hungry. But she didn't want to go downstairs. She didn't even want to leave her room. And she was so tired, still. How could she still be tired after sleeping for three and a half days?

I need help, she thought. But it wasn't a scream. It was a quiet plea, an internal whisper.

It was her first real prayer.

She sighed, feeling wrung out and hollow. And her weary mind was gently tugged to the prayer book she had kept ever since she could write. Many of her early prayers were scrawled with backward letters and slanted lines that got smaller as she tried to fit them on the pages of the little book. One prayer was actually the pledge of allegiance—it had sounded like a prayer when she was seven. But Psalm 23 was on one page, and she had read it often enough to have memorized it, so she got on her knees and bowed her head on her pillow and offered it.

The Lord is my shepherd; I shall not want.
He maketh me to lie down in green pastures: he leadeth
me beside the still waters.
He restoreth my soul: he leadeth me in the paths of
righteousness for his name's sake.
Yea, though I walk through the valley of the shadow of
death, I will fear no evil:

for thou art with me; thy rod and thy staff they comfort me.
Thou preparest a table before me in the presence of
mine enemies:
thou anointest my head with oil; my cup runneth over.
Surely goodness and mercy shall follow me all the days
of my life:
and I will dwell in the house of the Lord for ever.

She wasn't sure what it all meant, but green pastures and still waters had always seemed like a beautiful place to be—like a place in her Dreams. And she wanted God to be with her to comfort her. She *needed* God to be with her and comfort her.

Claire poked her head in the door. "Hi. I brought you a banana." She walked in, closed the door behind her, and handed the yellow fruit to Lucy.

Ah! She loved Claire! "Thank you," Lucy said, then wilted in complete gratitude. She felt her hand tremble as she set down the prayer book and accepted the proffered gift.

"And a roll," Claire said, pulling a wad out of the pouch of her pink hoodie. "And another roll, and some bacon, and a Tootsie Pop." She pulled the items out one at a time, each in its own ziplock baggie, except for the Tootsie Pop, which was in a purple wrapper. Lucy could see a white star on the wrapper. She remembered the kids at school used to say you could take a wrapper with a star on it back to the store and they'd give you a free Tootsie Pop, but she had never known anyone who had actually done that. Still, her little sister had brought her a genuine treasure.

Claire sat down on the bed and crossed her legs underneath herself.

"Thanks," Lucy said again, peeling the banana. It was a good one; the green was almost gone and there were no spots on it. When she bit into it, she decided it was probably the best banana she had ever had in her entire life.

"So can you really float in the air?" Claire never let anything get in the way of her curiosity.

Lucy slumped and looked at her sideways. "I 'on't 'ow," she mumbled around her second bite. It was banana perfection.

"Well, Maggie said she saw you," Claire took one of the buttered rolls out of its baggie and handed it to Lucy. "And Mom and Dad didn't say you didn't, or get mad at her, or say she was crazy or anything, so I think you probably did. Probably." She shrugged. But it was her turn to look sideways at Lucy.

Lucy tore off a piece of the buttered roll and put it in her mouth. "Wow. Iss iz so goo'." Buttery, salty, and soothing.

"Here," Claire said as she pulled a little bottle of Sunny Delight out of the pouch.

"Mmm," Lucy nodded as she swallowed the bread and opened the plastic bottle. "Thanks."

"So will you show me?" Claire asked.

Lucy wiped a bit of orange juice off her top lip. The juice was too tart and too sweet at the same time. It made the glands behind her jaw ache. "Show you what?"

"You knowwww," Claire said, with a tiny eyeroll that wasn't sassy, but still conveyed an unvoiced *duh*. To clarify, she waved her arms in front of her like she was fluffing up a cloudy pillow.

Lucy put the juice on the nightstand. "I don't know how, Claire. I don't know anything."

Claire looked at Lucy straight on and raised her left eyebrow.

How did she do that? Her question must have shown on her face because Claire grinned. "It's good, huh? I've been practicing! I can do it with my right eyebrow too, but not as well." For proof, she wiggled both eyebrows independently up and down.

Lucy laughed.

Claire's mouth fell open and she gasped, both eyebrows up now. "Lucy!"

"What?" She blinked and leaned back ever so slightly from Claire's outburst. Maybe it wasn't an outburst, but it had startled her, nonetheless.

"No, it's okay," Claire said as she leaned forward and put her small hand on Lucy's freckled arm. "I was just surprised. I've never heard you laugh before."

"What?"

"You laughed!"

Lucy didn't even know where that statement had come from. "Yeah?"

Claire was slowly moving her head from side to side. "You never laugh."

Lucy stared at her little sister for three seconds. "What do you mean?"

"You don't laugh," Claire explained carefully. "You smile a little, and I can see in your eyes when you think something is funny, or fun, but I've never heard you laugh before." She leaned back and opened another baggie, then handed Lucy a piece of bacon. "Here. You're still hungry."

"Thanks," Lucy said, ignoring the remark about laughing. She cautiously took the crisp bacon and bit off a piece. Her senses were immediately assaulted with savory, salty, crispy, chewy, bacony deliciousness. "Mmmm!" she groaned and closed her eyes. It was . . . wow.

"Yah," Claire said as she sat back and smiled. "I hope we go out to breakfast soon so we can order the real stuff."

"Real 'uff?" Lucy asked around another bite.

"Yah," Claire said with a perplexed expression. "That's just the boring turkey bacon Mom buys. But I brought you two pieces. Dad ate all the rest."

"Thanks," Lucy smiled when she opened her eyes and looked at her little sister.

Claire watched as Lucy took another drink of juice, shuddered, then took another bite of roll. She smiled. "You're so different."

Lucy looked up from taking the second piece of bacon out of the baggie. "What do you mean?"

Claire's smile brightened. "You . . . You're reacting. And asking questions." Lucy frowned. "No," Claire continued, "it's not like you never asked a question before," she explained in her little that's-so-obvious voice. "But you're more . . . umm . . . you're more *here*? I mean, you were sad when I walked in, then you got distracted by the food," she gestured toward the then-empty bags, "then you actually laughed. You're totally feeling things, which you don't usually. Plus, I'm not doing all the talking and filling in for you."

Lucy paused in her chewing, then swallowed. She didn't usually feel things? Yes, she did. But the talking thing . . . "I remember. You *do* do that for me." The two sisters looked at each other.

"You just said 'doo-doo.'"

Lucy laughed and dropped her head into her hands.

"Ha!" Claire shouted.

Lucy jumped and shouted back, "What?!"

"You laughed again! And you shouted!"

"Of course I shouted! You startled me!" Lucy shook her head. She didn't think laughing was a good reason for Claire to scare her half to death.

"Sorry," Claire shrugged, not looking sorry. "This is amazing," she said, trying to lower her voice.

"This is weird," was all Lucy could say.

"Yeah, but it's a good weird." Claire leaned over and hugged her. "And I'll help you."

"Thanks. I know you help me all the time."

"No problem," Claire smiled.

"Maggie helps me too," Lucy nodded.

Claire's smile dropped a fraction. "Yeah."

"Doesn't she?" Lucy frowned. Didn't she? Didn't Maggie help her? Maggie was always there. Maggie always protected her.

"She does," Claire answered slowly. "But listen, Lucy. Since you're *feeling* more now, you might, um . . . see more and hear more too. I don't know. But Maggie is still freaked out. Whatever she saw, she feels really kind of messed up about it. I mean, she's been kind of messed up for a while, but don't worry about it, okay? She loves you no matter what, okay? And I love you, and Dad loves you, and Mom, well—we all love you."

"I love you too."

Suddenly Claire launched herself at Lucy and threw her arms around her neck. "I'm so glad you're *here*! This is going to be so great!"

Lucy put her arms around Claire. She was tiny but energetic, and . . . solid. Real. *More.* She was more. This was like a Dream, but awake. As Lucy thought about it, she realized Claire had hugged her hundreds, probably thousands of times. But right then might have been the first time Lucy had truly hugged her back. Then her eyes started watering again and she gasped.

"What's wrong?" Claire asked, leaning back and looking at her.

Lucy reached up and touched her cheek. "This keeps happening, and I'm not even sad now! I don't know what's happening to me!" She could hear the despair in her own voice.

"Stop."

Lucy looked up. "What?" What had she done?

"You're freaking out." She was? Claire nodded. "Yeah. In your way, you were freaking out. Only you were doing it louder than usual."

"I—what do you mean?"

"Lucy, I didn't see you float or anything, but you are totally different than before—" Lucy noted that even Claire was calling it the *before*, "—and you're feeling things really big, and you've never done that. What happened? And pleeease don't be a grownup and brush me off. Tell me the truth."

Lucy plopped back on the other pillow, the one she hadn't failed at hurling across the room, and covered her face with her hands. Even Claire was asking her to say things out loud. What would Claire say? Lucy didn't want to tell her little sister what their parents had done to her. "I don't know if I should tell you," she finally said.

"Does it have anything to do with the pill Mom gives you every morning?"

Lucy shot back up to a sitting position and grabbed Claire by the shoulders. "How do you know about that?"

Claire made a startled face, then gently pried Lucy's hands off her upper arms. "That was scary," she said with a calm, instructional voice.

Lucy gasped and started to pull her hands back entirely, ashamed of startling the only person she trusted at the moment. "I'm so—" But Claire clutched her hands, held onto them firmly, and gave Lucy a quiet, reassuring smile.

"You didn't hurt me," she said. "You just surprised me. Like, a lot. And of course I noticed that your vitamin is a capsule in a prescription bottle, but Maggie's and mine are generic tablets from Walmart." She rolled her eyes in her typical eleven-year-old fashion, perpetually disappointed in the mental acuity of the older humans around her. "Maggie and me just figured it had to do with why you are . . . *were* the way you . . . were. Plus, when you started getting a little, um . . . bugged at things . . . last October, they switched your small pink and gray capsule to a bigger all-pink capsule. Mom and Dad never talked about it, of course, but now I can ask you—what's it for?"

Lucy had been rigid, but her body visibly relaxed at that simple question. It meant Maggie and Claire *knew*, but they didn't *know*. They weren't a part of it.

In the back of her mind, she knew her last thought sounded paranoid, like the whole drugging thing was part of some secret conspiracy to control Lucy.

Except, it *was* a plan for secretly controlling Lucy, so it couldn't be paranoia; it was fact. And Lucy was so relieved Claire hadn't known about it that she clung to Claire's hands like they were a lifeline of truth. Claire, as little as she was, was someone she could trust.

"I can tell you what they told me," Lucy whispered, glancing at the closed door, "but I'm not sure I believe them. Except that I do believe them because—" She shook her head and started again. "I believe them because what you just said about changing the pills makes sense."

Claire's mouth had been hanging open for the last half-hour. She blinked and swallowed now and then, but she didn't interrupt or ask questions. It was like she was watching a movie and couldn't take her eyes off the screen.

When Lucy finished telling her everything she knew, and a lot of the things she didn't know, and repeated her questions over and over, she felt exhausted, and plopped down on the bed. It creaked under her weight.

"Wow," was all Claire said. Then she laid down and snuggled up next to Lucy, putting her small arms around her sister. To Lucy, it was like a tiny version of their dad's hugs. More tears leaked out of her eyes, and she wiped them away. She showed her wet fingertips to Claire, who nodded. "I noticed," she said. "Feelings are hard sometimes."

"Yah. I'm learning that," Lucy replied. Then she wrapped her arms around Claire, returning the hug. God had heard Lucy's prayer and sent her own personal angel.

"But . . ." Claire began. "Will they make you take something else to keep you from . . . going . . . up?"

Lucy began shaking her head without knowing the answer. She didn't know what her parents wanted to do—or what they wanted her to do. She didn't know anything anymore. It was like she was finally waking up after being asleep for years, and nothing was how it should be or how she thought it *would* be.

She was glad to be awake, though. Awake was good, and she felt herself nod and lighten at that thought, though her body stayed where it was.

On the other hand, she was a little worried because she loved her Dreams. Asleep was also good. She didn't want to lose the one thing she lived for. She felt herself scowl and reached up to feel the bumpy ridges between her eyebrows. That was weird. She tried to relax her face.

But awake . . . awake meant having a say in things. It meant having choices. It meant getting to decide what *she* wanted to do. Herself. She could have *opinions* about things. She *did* have opinions about things.

She didn't want to take any more pills.

That thought came with unexpected certainty and, just like that, her mind was made up. With that decision, she felt like she could finally breathe after holding her breath for several minutes. She physically and metaphorically pulled the air into her lungs, into her entire body, and it filled her. It expanded her. It lifted her.

Well, no, it didn't lift her. That was an expression that carried an entire new meaning now.

She felt . . . hopeful.

"You've decided something," Claire said. She'd been watching Lucy like she had heard the entire internal dialog.

Lucy nodded. Maybe she could have both. It sounded ridiculous even in her own head, but maybe her Dreams could come true. She hugged her little sister.

"Wow!" Claire was enthusiastic in returning the hug. "You hugged first!"

"Sorry if I haven't done that before."

Claire shrugged. "It's okay."

"I love you," Lucy said.

"Really?" Claire smiled broadly, eyes wide. "I love you too!"

"Haven't I ever said that before?"

"Yeah, but—" Claire was smiling, speechless, a rare occurrence. "But this was . . . it was *more*!" The squeeze she gave Lucy then was surprisingly strong considering how small she was. "Are you going to go back to sleep? You're tired."

Lucy nodded. "Yeah. I don't know what's wrong with me." Then she erupted with a short, but almost hysterical laugh. "Other than, you know, my world turning upside-down and stuff."

"Hey," Claire sympathized, "life-changing events are exhausting, I understand." She leaned up and kissed Lucy's cheek, then left.

Lucy pushed her soggy hair over her shoulder and plopped over onto her pillow. The funny thing was, in some weird way, Claire probably did understand how she felt. After all, they were sisters.

Lucy's world seemed all about waking up in strange circumstances now, and she wondered how long she had been out *that* time. Claire was gone and light was coming through her window, but it was low, like at sunset. Or maybe sunrise—she had no idea since her room faced north. Her head ached, and her hair was a dry matted tangle of smashed curls. Aaannnd she was hungry again.

"Great," she said. Her choices were either to stay in her room for the rest of her life and starve to death or go downstairs. Her clock said 8:24, so it was definitely evening, since the light would have been brighter if it was morning. Maybe she could stay there until midnight, sneak downstairs, and cook some more bacon.

Her stomach growled a loud protest at the idea of waiting that long.

Fine.

Fine!

She would go downstairs.

But what would she say?

"Hi," Lucy said to Maggie, who whirled around from rinsing off some dishes in the kitchen sink. Her face went pale as her eyes scanned Lucy up and down, but she didn't say anything.

Lucy found some leftover pizza in the fridge and decided to make another attempt at conversation. "I thought Dad was in here," she said, and even she could tell it was a lame effort.

"He's downstairs," Maggie said, putting a plate and glass in the dishwasher. She glanced at Lucy once more before she turned and went upstairs to her bedroom. *Nice talking to you too.*

Lucy heated her pizza for exactly sixteen seconds and went to the family room. Claire was asleep on the sofa, so Lucy ate her room-temperature pizza, which was just the way she liked it, and watched the final scene of *Jason and the Argonauts* from 1963. No wonder Maggie left as soon as Claire had fallen asleep.

But now Lucy was left with only one option.

She found her dad working on his computer in the corner of the basement designated as his home office. There was a glossy, dark, old-fashioned oak desk there, with a matching credenza, bookshelf, and filing cabinet. They had belonged to his father. And there were two plush navy blue armchairs where Lucy liked to read or do homework. At least, she liked doing that before; she wasn't sure about after. Her dad's back was to her, his tall frame slightly hunched over the credenza, but he turned when he heard the creak of the bottom stair. His face showed surprise, but he didn't say anything. Kelly emerged from the laundry room, folding a fresh bath towel and looking curious.

"You kept me drugged on purpose." It wasn't a question, and the bold statement surprised even Lucy. It wasn't the first thing she thought she would say.

Kelly stepped over to the desk with an answer on her lips, but her dad spoke first.

"Medicated, yes." It was the doctor speaking, which made sense since he had been in doctor mode at his computer. "It was necessary, and it was either that or . . ." But the dad in him must not have wanted to continue the thought *keep you hidden, locked away, tied down*—all of the horrible options they must have shamefully considered when she was an infant. Medicine might have seemed like the best, kindest, most loving solution.

But Lucy wasn't sure.

"Or what?" she asked.

"Don't look at us that way," Kelly reprimanded in a light but scolding tone.

Lucy didn't know what way that was. It must have been the look someone makes when they've been told their parents have been drugging them their whole life; but why should she stop looking at them that way? After all, she *had* just been told they had been drugging her for her entire life. It didn't make sense that Kelly didn't want her to look at them *that* way. How could she not? She couldn't stop what she was thinking. And since she had asked the question, she was even more certain she wanted the answer.

"Or what?" she asked again.

"We were doing our best." Kelly's voice hadn't raised, but it had certainly intensified as she rubbed the small of her back. Was that a normal thing to do when your daughter, whom you've been drugging her whole life, looks at you the way Lucy was apparently looking at them?

"We decided to keep you on the Serenvidria until we could find a better medication, but no other medication we've tested was ever as effective at helping you maintain your emotional equilibrium."

Lucy didn't answer at first because she was distracted by something. Her mind was noticeably more . . . what? *Agile*? Was that the right word for it? Her mind had brought forward a memory and presented it for Lucy's consideration without her even searching for it. Kelly and Aeden glanced at each other, probably wondering what to expect next from their newly emotional and problematic middle daughter.

"We studied equilibrium in school, but my teacher called it *homeostasis*."

The doctor almost smiled. "Yes, they are similar."

"It's like when an animal keeps a constant temperature on the inside even if it's a cold day. Or night."

"Yes. I'm impressed." The doctor did smile then, glad that the conversation had taken an academic turn.

"But my teacher said it's not really an accurate word because *stasis* means not changing, but something inside us needs to change in order to keep our temperature the same."

He nodded. "That's also true. You have a very good memory, Lucy."

"I do. I mean, I think I do. But I couldn't really explain things before." She cringed. It was another example of before versus after. "But it feels like I can express things better now, and I can also adapt to changes now. That medicine didn't let me do that."

"Well, it did—"

"No," Lucy stated without raising her voice. Maybe she was the one scolding now, since he stopped what he was going to say. Lucy had also felt herself scowl, so she reached up to feel the ridges between her eyes. Her heart was thumping, and she felt adrenaline warming her face as her eyes began to ache and swell. She didn't want to cry again, so she mentally paused to assess her feelings—feelings, again, so numerous and intense. They blended and bubbled and merged and refused to be disentangled from each other. But she could distinguish one emotion—a new feeling she hadn't acknowledged before—and it solidified as her attention was drawn to it. Within two heartbeats, it became the dominant feeling, more certain than the others. She looked at it, held it up in her mind, and tasted it. She was keeping this one.

"No, I know I'm right." She hoped she was right. "That medicine made it so I couldn't possibly adapt. It kept me the same. I learned facts in school, and I was good at remembering them even though I didn't care about anything. But I care now. And I want to adapt to—" She tried not to choke on the words, and she almost succeeded. "—to crashing and floating."

Kelly shook her head and turned her back to Lucy, but Aeden nodded and said, "Okay. Now that you—"

"Wait," Lucy said, holding up her hand, but her dad didn't stop. He held up his own hand and kept speaking.

"Now that you are older, we can find a better solution. There's—"

"Wait. Just listen first!"

". . . nothing to be afraid of. We'll find a . . ."

"I'm not afraid! I know you—"

". . . better treatment . . ."

". . . want to help, but . . ."

". . . we can prevent the phenomenon from . . ."

"*Stop!*"

Lucy had read the phrase *the silence was deafening* before, but she had never understood it. She understood it now.

She had just shouted at her father for the second time in her life. She lowered her voice. "I don't want to prevent anything." This was the hard part. No, it wasn't. She had decided. "I want to adapt. I want to learn to control this on my own. You never even let me try."

"Lucy you were a—"

"A baby, I know, but—"

" . . . we couldn't possibly . . ."

". . . I'm not a baby now! I want . . ."

". . . explain about pain and . . ."

". . . to find out what . . ."

". . . anger and frustration . . ."

". . . I know what they are now!"

"—I'm not sure you do!"

"That's what this *IS*!" She yelled, banging her fist on the top of the gray leather blotter on top of the desk.

Her parents jumped at the loud crack and were silent. Her father looked down at the desk and tightened his jaw as he reached down to pick up the blotter that covered the surface of the desk. Kelly looked, then turned her back, stepping briskly back into the laundry room, towel in hand. Aeden's face had gone blank.

Lucy stared at a wide fracture that had splintered horizontally along the grains of the solid oak. Had she done that?

Aeden carelessly dropped the blotter back over the ruined wood. "This is what I meant by anger and frustration," he said, his jaw tight.

His father's desk—ruined.

But Lucy was still too filled with quiet but furious anger to be very sorry, so, without a word, she turned and walked up the stairs. More than the bottom step creaked on her way.

It seemed improbable that Lucy would be able to sleep anymore; she had slept so much already. But her brain was exhausted from replaying every revelation and conversation from the last—wait. It had only been one day. She had been unconscious for three days, but it hadn't even been twelve hours since she had woken up on the sofa. But her mind finally surrendered to her body's need for sleep, and she drifted off.

Her Dreams seemed clouded and muddy. The colors were dim, and the edges blurry. The leaves on the little trees were withered and brown, and the air itself seemed gray. She was by herself on the sidewalk next to the wall and aware for the first time that she was truly alone in that once-wondrous haven of sleep. It was an uncomfortable feeling.

She tried to fly, but nothing happened. She was bound to the earth, and it pulled on her body. She walked forward, but her feet were heavy. Her arms and legs felt thick, and dense, though they looked the same as always. It was as if her entire body were full of . . . something . . . something solid, like lead, and her chest ached. As she plodded forward, she lifted her weighty arm to her heart, and could feel it beating, but even her pulse seemed slow and labored.

When she reached the corner, there was an old oak desk—her father's desk—sitting dark and dusty in the middle of the sidewalk. She pushed herself forward to look at it, and the angry crack glared at her in haughty accusation. Then it split and widened. It stretched beyond the confines of the wood, spreading down to the ground and erupting into an enormous chasm beneath her feet.

Lucy screamed, flailing her arms as she fell.

Her room was dark, the glowing numbers showed 2:14, and the bed across from hers was empty.

Maggie had refused to sleep in their shared bedroom. And her father was still unhappy with her. And her mother . . .

Kelly always straddled the line between maternal love and emotional distance—not that Lucy could have explained that distinction before—but Kelly had kept even more to herself ever since the truth had been revealed. Even in her mental fog, Lucy had been aware of a difference between how Kelly interacted with her youngest and oldest daughters . . . and how she interacted with Lucy.

It was nothing new.

Maybe it all started with how Lucy had come into the world. She didn't remember much about when Claire was born, but it couldn't have been as horrible as when Lucy was born.

She could still picture one scene in her mind: Kelly sitting up in a hospital bed, smiling and holding a little bundle wrapped in a white and pink blanket.

Girls, this is Claire. Come say hi to your little sister. Had it been her mother or her father who had said that?

And now Claire was the only one in the family who hadn't really changed since Lucy had woken up on the floor that day.

CHAPTER 10

Not Being Chemically Controlled By One's Parents Is Harder Than One Would Think

It was a good thing Spring Break was the following week, because Lucy crashed a total of eleven times over the next seven days.

Once, her dad mentioned his father's desk and Lucy's temper. Lucy, who had been quite happy before that moment, became disproportionately upset, arguing that she wouldn't have gotten temperamental if he hadn't been illegally drugging her for her entire life. Then he got angry, trying to explain, then Lucy turned into the Incredible Hulk and ended up on the kitchen floor for two hours before she came around and was able to get up.

Another time, Lucy dropped a *World's Best Doctor* mug on her toe, swore, and crashed again on the kitchen floor, but only for five minutes. Her father later asked her to please try to refrain from swearing in the future, even if she dropped a ceramic mug on her foot. There were things in life no one could control, but one's choice of words was not in that category.

Once, she crashed for no reason anyone could explain, not even Lucy.

Heaviness without crashing came most often, but that wasn't a problem compared to the daily headaches, feeling nauseous, and getting suddenly hot and sweaty. She sometimes thought she was going crazy. Her life felt like a complete mess, full of questions without any answers.

She had always thought her father was so smart. A practical genius!

But no, he didn't know why she floated and crashed—there was no medical explanation. Yes, anger and pain triggered heaviness always, but didn't always make her crash. Sometimes the crashes lasted for minutes, sometimes hours, but never for days like it had the first time. Well, the first time in the *after* part of Lucy's life. But the degree of pain or anger seemed to have no bearing on how quickly she crashed or how long she was out. Also, while being sad made her feel a little heavy, it had never made her crash. So far, at least.

Furthermore, yes, her parents said she had floated when she was very small; Maggie had supposedly seen Lucy in the air as a toddler, but had never said anything about it, so Lucy didn't know if Maggie remembered it or not. And no, she couldn't show Claire the "trick" because she didn't *know* the trick.

And absolutely under no circumstances whatsoever was anyone in the family ever to divulge to anyone the nature of Lucy's condition. That's what her father called it—a *condition*. As if it were something temporary—like acne, or dandruff. Maybe he hoped it would clear up with a special cleansing astringent or tea-infused shampoo. But why they weren't supposed to tell anyone, no one knew. Maybe it had something to do with an evil government conspiracy that wanted to . . . um . . . train secret agents how to . . . nearly pass out if they were ever being interrogated by their parents. Yes. That was likely.

Plus, it did not help that Lucy's emotions were all over the place. She had made a fragile peace with her parents because all parties had tacitly agreed not to talk about "vitamins" at all. Or desks. However, even with that familial detente in place, she could go from calm, to bugged, to laughing, to snarky, to crying, to absolutely livid . . . all within the time it took Claire to watch a black-and-white episode of *The Twilight Zone*.

Her life *was* the twilight zone. Black and white. Up and down. Literally.

She couldn't handle it.

Her Dreams were still a mess—no floating. No flying, unless she counted the one night she dreamed about watching cartoons with the cute skateboarder from the Mountain Dew commercial, snuggled together in the green recliner. She woke up in that same reclined position—floating about a foot above her bed. She immediately freaked out, screamed, twisted around, and almost smothered herself when she fell face-first into her pillow, leading to the discovery that fear also triggered heaviness. She had also kinked her neck. So no, that did not count as a flying Dream; it was a waking-up nightmare.

On the eighth day of her new reality, Lucy was lying on her bed, wondering how she was ever going to go back to school next week, when Claire poked her head in the doorway.

"Hi," she said. She was wearing a fuzzy pink deely-bopper headband. It was from her Halloween costume the year before when she was an alien from the Planet Claire, which none of her friends understood since she got the idea from an ancient song from the 1980s.

"Hi," said Lucy, scooting over to make room for Claire.

Claire took off her antennae, laid down, and put her head in Lucy's lap. "Bad day?" she asked.

Lucy snorted. "You could say that." Her mom had been cleaning windows that morning, leaving a few of them open. Lucy crashed when the wind had slammed one of the bedroom doors shut, startling her. She was out for less than a minute, but she felt like one of those stupid fainting goats Claire used to watch on their dad's computer.

"You know what I do when I'm having a bad day?" Claire asked.

"What?" said Lucy.

"Get someone to brush my hair." She grinned, held up her special silver hairbrush, and rapidly batted her long eyelashes at Lucy.

Lucy half-smiled and took the brush. Claire had seen it advertised as the perfect brush for curly hair, and easily talked Kelly into ordering it for her. It was just a normal plastic brush you could get at any drug store, but Claire was devoted to it. Lucy slid the bristles through Claire's hair, which was far less curly and far less red than her own. "You're having a bad day, too?"

"No," Claire said matter-of-factly. "But since you were just sitting here, I thought you might like to be useful. Nothing makes you forget your problems better than helping someone else."

"Oh yeah? How did you ever get so wise, Miss Claire?"

"From Sister Decker."

"*Sister* Decker? Did Mrs. Decker suddenly become a nun?"

"No. I just heard someone from her church call her that. It's what people in her church call each other since we are all brothers and sisters in God's way, which I think is kind of cool, so I call her that now. Hey!" She shot up suddenly, almost hitting Lucy on the chin with her head.

"Hey, yourself! Be careful!" If Claire had come to take Lucy's mind off her problems, smacking her on the chin and making her crash again was not the way to do it.

"Sorry. But I know what you need!" Claire stood up and put her deely-boppers back on her head. "Get dressed."

Lucy looked down at her comfy pajamas. "Where are we going?"

"Sister Decker's house," Claire answered as she opened a drawer in Lucy's dresser and tossed her a pink T-shirt and green shorts. Lucy made a face. "She understands things, Lucy. She really does." She rummaged through Lucy's shoes.

"You told her?" Lucy's voice was muffled as she pulled the T-shirt over her head.

"No. You're going to tell her yourself."

"I'm *what*?" Lucy's head popped through the neck of the almost too-small shirt.

"Here," Claire pulled some red sandals out of Lucy's closet.

Lucy shook her head. "Those are too small." She grabbed some sneakers, shoved them on her feet, and obediently followed her mini guru.

CHAPTER 11

Sister Decker and Don

Lucy hung back and shoved her hands into the front pouch of her blue Buffalo Bills hoodie as Claire rang the bell at Mrs. Decker's kitchen door. The doorbell only made a one-note *ding*, but that one note somehow sounded flat. Maybe it had been rung so often during the years of raising five boys, and their friends always ringing that bell, and now Claire always ringing that bell—well, maybe it was tired.

"That's not going to work," Claire said, then she grabbed Lucy's hand and yanked her up onto the step to stand by her. She was strong for being eleven years old. Either that or she knew Lucy wasn't in the habit of putting up a fight and would come where bidden.

"What are we doing here?" Lucy whispered. She was already confused about so many things; she wasn't in the mood to be confused about something else. But how could she even know that about herself? As far as Lucy could discern, she hadn't been in any mood at all for years—maybe for Claire's entire life. Lucy had always just complied with what people told her to do; so, of course Claire would take it for granted that Lucy would do what she was told.

Lucy tried to resent that assumption, but she didn't have the energy for an emotion so complex . . . not quite anger, not quite pain, a little sadness, all mixed together. The odd thing was that she could name these feelings. Intellectually, she knew what they were. And she thought she would be able to recognize them in others. But experiencing them herself was a novel sensation . . . as if emotions were not her first language.

All this went through her mind in the few moments it took for Claire to ignore Lucy's question and for Mrs. Decker to open the wooden door to her kitchen. Through the screen door, Lucy could see she was getting ready to bottle fruit or something. She wore a pink checkered apron and was wiping her hands on a dish towel. The kitchen table was covered with mason jars, the counter had boxes and bowls of apricots all over it, and on top of the stove sat various stainless-steel pots, one on each burner.

"Why, hello, girls!" Mrs. Decker beamed. She was pretty much always happy. Lucy had seen her get upset with a couple of her sons a few times, even though they were all older than Lucy's father. She could put on a stern face and make her feelings unmistakably clear when that happened, but she loved all her boys. That was an easy feeling to detect. Lucy also remembered Mr. Decker a little bit—he had died when Claire was little, which was when Maggie and Lucy had begun coming over to help her on Saturdays. She didn't think Mr. Decker had smiled as perpetually as Mrs. Decker did, but she knew he was nice. He had helped her dad fix the toilet once. Actually, he pretty much did all the work while her dad watched, and it was really gross, so Lucy knew he was a genuinely good guy.

"Hi, Sister Decker! We came to help you," Claire announced.

"Oh, well you didn't need to do that!" Mrs. Decker laughed. Actually, it was more like a giggle. She giggled like a young girl who thought she was not supposed to be giggling, but who couldn't help it—like she was sharing a secret joke with you. Maybe the secret joke was that Claire came over to help her almost every Saturday morning, and even though Mrs. Decker never wanted to assume or impose, she would always welcome the help. Her sons came over every week to take care of the yard—which was always well-trimmed, the way Mr. Decker would have kept it—along with house repairs and big stuff. But Maggie and Lucy used to come over every Saturday to help, and now Claire came. It wasn't a job or a chore; it was just what they did. And Mrs. Decker sometimes came to their house for Sunday dinner, though she was usually at one of her sons' homes for that. Even though she said Claire and Lucy hadn't needed to come, she was already unlocking the screen door to let them in.

Mrs. Decker was the sweetest little old lady in the world who made the best chicken noodle soup in the world, along with the best bread, fudge, peanut brittle, and pumpkin cookies in the world. But it looked like the best apricot juice, jam, or jelly in the world was the project that morning.

Claire shoved Lucy inside. "Well," she explained, "Lucy needs some help, too, and I knew you'd be the perfect person for her."

Lucy made a strangled noise.

"Oh?" Mrs. Decker gave a concerned look as she walked around the counter and pulled some clean and ironed aprons out of a drawer. "Is everything okay?"

No. Lucy pulled the neck strap of a frilly blue apron over her head and tied the strings behind her back. Without a thought, she also took the fat hair ribbon Mrs. Decker handed her and tied back her typically wild curls.

"Yes, but Lucy is in a predicament," Claire said as she tied her own hair back.

This was going to be interesting.

Mrs. Decker stopped mid-stride, peered at Lucy, and asked in a conspiring tone, "Oh really? What is it?"

Lucy didn't know how other people had regarded her throughout the years, but she guessed Mrs. Decker was thinking about how Lucy hardly ever spoke. Or how she would answer questions politely, she hoped, but with little interest in conversations or events. Mrs. Decker recovered from her amazement and handed knives to both girls. "Here. While we talk, you can wash these apricots in the sink. Then cut them in half, pop out the pit, then in half again like this." She held up the quarter piece. "They are a little bruised because my son brought them to me from Utah, but it's okay because we are just making jam. Then you just put them in the pot." She picked up the pieces, dumped them in the giant pot, then wiped her hands on her apron and moved to get another box full of the golden produce. "Now, what's your predicament, Lucy?"

Lucy panicked. Maybe *panicked* was too strong a word. No, Lucy simply felt a great deal of consternation at not knowing what to say. It must have shown on her face because Claire spoke for her.

"Mmm," Claire began, "it's a little complicated. You know how Lucy has never talked much and kind of keeps to herself?"

"Yes . . ." Mrs. Decker answered cautiously and gave a significant look to Claire. She sounded as though she didn't want to admit having noticed such things. Lucy had no idea where this was going, so she looked down and tried not to drop the little apricot she was butchering.

"It's okay—Lucy doesn't mind talking about it. Aaannd . . . we've just learned that it wasn't really her fault. Some of it was a side effect of some medicine she's been on. Anyway, she doesn't need that medicine anymore, but she's feeling a little weird about talking to people and stuff now. She just kinda needs a grandma right now. Our grandmas are both dead, and our mom just doesn't understand Lucy. She doesn't understand Maggie or me, either, but we're used to that. Things are weird, and Lucy just needs some normalcy."

Claire had been nonchalantly cutting up one apricot after another—popping the pit out was strangely satisfying—and only then looked up to see both Lucy and Mrs. Decker staring at her. "I just feel that you're the most normal person I know, so Lucy and I are going to come over more often this summer so you can—" Claire paused, searching for the right words, "—get to know the new Lucy."

A football-shaped pit then slipped out of Lucy's wet fingers, landed on the floor, and skittered across the tile toward the refrigerator. "Oh no, I'm sorry!" she exclaimed. She turned two full circles trying to decide whether to put down the paring knife, wipe her dripping hands, or bend over to pick up the fumbled seed.

"Oops—don't worry." Mrs. Decker scooped up the pit, wiped up the floor with a damp cloth, and had everything back in order within three seconds. Then she straightened up and looked at the two girls and smiled a quiet smile. "I would be honored to finally meet you, Lucy."

Lucy was astonished, two hours later, when she finished summing up not only the last week and a half, but her entire life. She felt tired from talking longer than she had ever talked in her whole existence, but she also felt relieved—unburdened— somehow. Just saying it all out loud helped her synthesize all the little pieces into a comprehensive whole. Well, maybe not comprehensive—Lucy still couldn't comprehend much of it. But it was helpful pulling events and feelings out of her brain, setting them in a neat little row, and looking at them. It made them less frightening.

"That's a remarkable revelation," Sister Decker mused.

Lucy was starting to think of her as Sister Decker now too; she really was sort of like a kind nun—just a non-Catholic nun. She handed Lucy a glass of water and added, "And now that I can see the larger picture a bit better, some things I've observed make a little more sense."

"What do you mean?" Lucy asked, feeling less self-conscious than she had at first. Claire had been right. It was good to talk to Sister Decker. Her parents were too tangled up in everything, and she was still angry at them. She doubted she would ever be able to just spill her guts out like this with them.

"Well, all you girls are remarkable in your own ways," she said as she stirred the four pots of simmering apricot goo. "Claire and I have talked about this before, but even though I've thought about it a great deal, I've always had a difficult time naming what I've sensed in you, Lucy."

"You . . . you've sensed something?" Someone in the world had paid enough attention to Lucy to *sense* something? Someone had thought about her? Had considered her? That she had taken up even a crumb of space in someone else's brain was . . .weird.

And nice.

"Oh yes." Sister Decker nodded as if it were the most natural thing in the world to *sense* things—which was an unusual word to begin with—about other people. "For example, among other things, Claire has a remarkably discerning insight into people."

"We're kindred spirits that way," Claire said, nodding. She'd been unusually quiet during the entire expulsion of Lucy's clogged mind.

Sister Decker gave a modest shake of her head and said, "Oh, well, I don't know about that, but thank you. And Maggie—well, Maggie's a true musician, certainly, but so much more. Anyone who pays attention would be able to see that. She is having her own struggles, though, at the moment."

"Ya. With me." Lucy sighed.

"Well, maybe a little. But don't take it personally. Everyone has struggles only our Heavenly Father knows about."

Lucy stopped nibbling the piece of apricot she held in her hand. Even before her own world had come unraveled, she knew Maggie hadn't been her usual self for a while. How long a while, she didn't know, since it was difficult to see things through her old brain. But Maggie was *struggling*? How? All Lucy knew was that Maggie had always taken care of her, but now she wondered who had taken care of Maggie. Certainly not their mom. Not their dad, either. Lucy was realizing her parents didn't really talk about problems, or *struggles*, as Sister Decker called them. Claire? Maybe, but she and Maggie were very different from each other.

"But what have you noticed about Lucy?" Claire asked, cutting through Lucy's thoughts. Claire took a turn stirring the pots.

Sister Decker pulled the corners of her mouth down a little as she considered the question. On anyone else, that gesture would have looked like a frown, but it only made Sister Decker's dimples show up in a concerned way, as opposed to a cheerful way. "Well, Lucy," she said, "it might be a good idea for you ask Heavenly Father what gifts you have, and I am certain they are more than anyone realizes yet." She adjusted a hose on the juicer. "I understand, now, why you felt like you were separate from the world before, but I wonder if there wasn't also a gift in there somewhere." She adjusted one of the burners, then looked at Lucy. "I've always thought it lovely how you serve people."

Lucy looked down. Her entire life people had talked about her right in front of her, but it had never bothered her. Now that someone was talking directly to her, and in such a personal way, she felt something she couldn't put into words. It was uncomfortable. But she had to ask: "What . . . what do you mean?"

"You notice and think about people without passing unrighteous judgment on them. You accept people as they are. You treat everyone the same."

Everyone who? Who was there to judge? What did that even *mean*?

"I've seen that quality in you since you were small. When the Tans moved in next door, you befriended a little boy who couldn't even speak English. That didn't bother you in the least. I also noticed it with my dear, late David. Do you remember he'd had a stroke before he died?"

Lucy shook her head, tracing a swirling pattern on the countertop with her finger.

"Well, he did, and he couldn't walk or speak very well after that. And even though you were just a little girl, you weren't scared to be around him. Even some of our older grandchildren were shy around him after that, you know, because he was different from how he had been before. You weren't bothered by it, though. You came to the house several times when your mother brought us some dinner, and, one time, you noticed that David's slipper had come off his foot. You walked right over to him without a word, sat down on the floor, and put his slipper back on his foot for him. I hadn't even known it had come off until you were already putting it back on. And Lucy?"

She stopped talking suddenly, and Lucy looked up to see Claire taking Sister Decker's hand as she dabbed at her wet eyes.

"Lucy," she said, clearing her throat, "I can tell you for sure that your one little act of service meant a great deal to him." She smiled and gave Claire's hand a little shake, turned back to tend the burners, then continued. "I think it isn't a bad thing to be separate from the world. Jesus said, 'My kingdom is not of this world,' so maybe it's a gift, no matter how you came by it. And I hope you retain that gift with all your heart."

Retain that gift.

Was it a gift? Not understanding people? Not knowing what to make of them?

Lucy wasn't certain of that. She'd have to think about it.

Claire was silent as they walked home, but she held Lucy's hand.

At least Lucy had *thought* they were walking home. But instead of turning right at the end of Sister Decker's driveway, Claire pulled Lucy to the left. "Where are we going now?"

"Don's house," Claire answered in a what-else-did-you-expect tone of voice.

"Why?"

"He's going to help you too."

"Don? How can Don help me?"

Claire continued in a this-should-also-be-obvious manner, "He's the smartest person we know, Lucy."

"Smarter than Dad?" Ha.

"Mmm . . ." Claire considered. "Different kind of smart. Besides, you don't really want to talk to Dad right now, do you?"

Lucy didn't even try to answer. As usual, Claire was correct. Besides being the one who put her on the zombie drug in the first place, she couldn't begin to imagine honestly talking to him about anything. She had never needed to talk to him before. All Lucy had ever needed was to know he was there. When life got too confusing, she could just sit by him on the sofa and soak up the reassurance of his presence. In the mornings, he would hug her, and the rumble of his voice when he said, "Good morning, Miss Lucy," made her feel content. When she hugged back and pushed her head against his chest, the loud rhythm of his beating heart made her feel secure. And the woodsy scent of his cologne was home. Her dad had always been her safe place.

Now?

She didn't know.

She didn't even have an academically defined word for what she felt.

She only felt an absence of the sense of belonging he had always given her.

Then she identified the word: *resentment*. And disappointment. And sorrow. Why didn't these emotions make her heavy? At least, not *as* heavy. She felt the weight of them, but the weight stayed localized in her heart without spreading to her arms and legs.

"What are you thinking about?" Claire asked.

"Dad," Lucy answered in a thick voice.

"Could you try to think about something else for now? You are—and I mean this literally—dragging your feet, and even I'm feeling crushed by your mood."

Okay. Whatever she felt *did* affect her body—or her movement, at least. Apparently, there were subtle degrees to her weirdness. She didn't even know what to call it, so *weirdness* would have to do for now. But whatever it was, it was getting ridiculous. No—it was impossibly ridiculous from the beginning. Impossibly ridiculous weirdness.

"Okay. Help me think of something else."

"I'm hoping I get to be in Miss Butler's class next year. She is the nicest of all the sixth-grade teachers. Plus, she's pretty."

"Yes, that is an important thing to consider," Lucy replied seriously. Claire shot her a smile that showed where one of her lower fang teeth was missing. "But I thought you wanted Mr. Tuckett. He's nice." That's who Lucy had.

"He's my second choice. My last choice is Mr. Casey." That's who Don had, which made Lucy think of Don, and fifth grade, and lunchroom tables collapsing, which also wasn't something she wanted to think about. But they were at Don's house by then, passing Mrs. Tan's rose bushes that lined the approach to her front door. They only had tiny golden leaves at the moment but would have enormous yellow blooms with pink edges in the summer.

"Just tell him everything you told Sister Decker," Claire said as she rang the doorbell that played a tiny electronic version of Beethoven's "Für Elise."

"Oh right. Piece of cake. I'll just pour out my soul to Don, no problem."

"You are getting good at sarcasm, by the way. You sound just like Maggie, which isn't necessarily a good thing, in case you didn't know."

"Thanks."

"Exactly," Claire shot back while the sound of giant feet running down wooden stairs echoed from inside the house. A moment later, Don opened the door.

"Hey, guys," he said.

"We are not guys, Don," corrected Claire.

"Ohhh-kay."

"Lucy needs some help. Can we talk?" She sounded like she was calling a meeting.

"Sure," he said, not the least taken aback by Claire's grown-up nature, then turned around. Having been to Don's house innumerable times, the sisters automatically stepped inside, slipped off their shoes, and followed him up to his room.

"I knew it!" Don shouted, then spun around repeatedly on a used office chair in a bedroom that was filled with science awards, computer parts, and models of various movie spaceships. "I knew it I knew it I *knew* it!" He stopped spinning and looked at Claire and Lucy, grinning. "I knew it."

Claire had a smug expression on her pixie face, making it her turn to look like Maggie, but Lucy frowned at the boy she had known almost her entire life. The springs of the bed she was sitting on groaned as she leaned forward and demanded, "What do you mean you *knew*?!"

Don also leaned forward, putting his face right in front of hers. He nodded at the bed, indicating he had heard the tell-tale creak of her slight weight gain. "I knew." Then he leaned back, stretched, and put his hands behind his head. "I had postulated the truth when we were in fourth grade, but I've observed and collected supporting evidence ever since. I've amended my hypothesis over the years, but I knew you could fly."

Lucy recoiled. "Fly? I can't *fly*!" Don's one statement had just exposed all of Lucy's unspoken and embarrassing dreams, hopes, what-ifs, and fantasies. Speaking them aloud and putting them out into the universe was terrifying! She felt threatened and vulnerable. And, frankly, stupid. A person simply shouldn't go around saying such absurd things about another person.

Don smiled and shrugged. "Maybe not yet. But I'd bet a million dollars you could if you tried."

Even in the microsecond it took Lucy to spit out a breathy "Ugh!" and throw her hands up in exasperation, there was one part of her brain that realized she had never reacted that way to anything; that was more of a Maggie thing. And another part of her brain plugged its own tiny ears; this was too much to process. And another part of her brain perked up and paid attention; Don was a really smart guy; maybe he could help her.

"Will you help her?" Claire asked from a red beanbag chair.

"What?" Lucy blurted out at the same time Don said, "Sure!"

This was too much. This was . . . way too much! She fell back on the bed and covered her face with her hands. She wasn't sure, but she thought she might be having an anxiety attack. The bed groaned again, and Claire was by her side, pulling her hands away from her face. But Lucy kept her eyes closed tight.

"Lucy," Claire whispered, "it's okay. It will be okay." Claire tugged Lucy's hair away from her face with her right hand, still holding Lucy's with her left. She ran her fingers through a few loose strands, and breathed, "You are okay." She repeated that over and over, stroking Lucy's hair. "Breathe," Claire whispered, and Lucy realized she had been holding her breath. Claire brushed her fingers along Lucy's furrowed eyebrows. "Try to relax." Lucy tried to un-scrunch her face and made a conscious effort to relax her neck and shoulders, which were also tensed.

The bed relaxed, too, and the springs sighed a relieved screech as Lucy's body weight returned to normal.

Lucy opened her eyes when she heard scribbling and saw Don writing on a yellow graphing notepad.

"What are you doing?" She tried to hold on to the relaxed feeling she had barely managed to achieve.

"Observing and recording. Good science is good observation. This is awesome." He was nodding and smiling.

"You got that from *Avatar*," Claire accused.

"Hah. James Cameron got that from *me*."

"Ugh." Lucy squeezed Claire's hands and sat up. "I am in the hands of nerds. And I am not interested in becoming a science project." She wondered, in the back of her mind, how she knew Don was a nerd. She must have been aware, even before, that Don was also a bit removed from their peers. Not the same way she had been, but still separate somehow.

He continued to write, not even looking up. "You need to learn how to control the floating thing and the heavy thing before you can fly, so we need to keep track of all the things that make that happen." He looked at the Doctor Who clock on his wall and grabbed his backpack and his computer. "My mom is going to be home in about fifteen minutes. Can you guys come over tomorrow? That will give me time to write out my hypothesis and plan our experiments."

"Okay!" Claire chirped and jumped up, not bothering to scold Don about calling them *guys*. She and Don turned to Lucy, who was still on the bed, looking back and forth at their expectant faces.

Lucy shook her head and put her face in her hands. "This is too weird."

"Come on, Ruce! It will be fun!"

Lucy felt herself smile just a bit behind her hands. He had just called her *Ruce*. He hadn't called her that since they were little kids. Whenever Lucy went to Don's house, his mother sweetly welcomed her with, "Com een Rucy. Would you rike ah cookie?" But it wasn't a real R sound; it was more like a tongue flip that sounded like a mash-up of an R and a D. But Don knew American English didn't use that flippy sound and teased his mom behind her back by calling her *Rucy*. Or Ruce. It was probably the only mean thing she ever saw him do. But the name kind of stuck, and Lucy had become Rucy. And his mom never knew the difference.

She surrendered and dropped her hands. "Fine," she said. "Why not?" What other choice did she have? Sitting at home and hiding from the world for the rest of her life was the first option she could think of.

But maybe he can really help me, the timid but hopeful part of her brain wondered.

Shut up, said the part of her brain that didn't want to expect too much from the world.

CHAPTER 12

Scientific Method

The next day, Lucy found herself in Don's kitchen, standing on a bathroom scale. The scale showed her weight at just under 53.2 kilograms, which meant absolutely nothing to her, but Don wrote it down. Next, she stood up against the wall so he could measure her height, which was 157 centimeters. "Why can't Koreans measure in inches and pounds like everyone else?" Lucy grumbled.

"Because we're smart," Don said with a straight face. "Are you done growing?"

"I have no idea."

"We'll have to keep measuring in order to keep an accurate record of your body-mass index."

"Whatever."

"Eh-hem," Claire fake-coughed while looking through a Korean magazine.

"Sorry," Lucy said. "Thank you for helping me, Don."

But Don wasn't paying attention. He was typing into his computer. "Can you wear those same clothes all summer?"

When Lucy didn't answer, he looked up to see her staring at him with lidded eyes.

"Or just when you come over here? For weight accuracy?"

Again, no answer.

"We'll make sure she wears a T-shirt and similar shorts whenever we come over, won't we, Lucy?" Claire said, giving her big sister a pointed look.

"Sure. Thank you for helping me, Don."

He nodded, typed some more, then stood up. "First of all, go back to the scale and hold out your hand, palm up." Lucy obeyed. Don took her hand and—

"*Hey*!" Lucy yelled at the sharp pain in her finger and jumped away, taking her hand with her.

"No! Stay on the scale!" Don shouted while Lucy looked at the drop of blood forming on her fingertip. "Get back on! Hurry!"

Lucy glared at him but stepped back on the scale with her finger in her mouth.

Don looked at the scale and went back to his laptop. "Cool! You gained two-point-four kilograms," he exclaimed. Then he frowned. "But we don't know if that was from the pin prick or because you were startled. And I think we need a more accurate scale."

Lucy took her finger out of her mouth to say something snarky, but Claire cleared her throat again, so she just said, "Good idea. Thank you for helping me, Don."

Claire scowled at her.

"It's okay—this scale will work for now." He turned his computer screen around so the girls could see it. Lucy didn't know why Claire had to see it, though; her little sister wasn't the one being weighed and measured and poked with needles. "Here's the graph I made, and this is your weight today, and this is the increase when I pricked you."

"Impaled me."

"We'll need to weigh you first thing every morning, and last thing every night." Lucy wondered who he was referring to as *we*. It could be himself and Lucy, himself and Claire, or all three of them. Of course, if he believed he represented the entire scientific community, *we* could mean just himself. That wouldn't be surprising considering his cool superiority when he went into evil scientist mode. "This will give us your baseline average. We also need to weigh you before every experiment, and these are the ones I've decided to begin with today."

Lucy scanned the chart he had indicated and saw several columns of unpleasant stimuli. The first column included painful items, such as *prick finger, pinch arm, stub toe, slap face, and comb hair*. "Smart," Claire mumbled, nodding at the last one. The other columns included sprinting, jumping jacks, running up school bleachers, Zumba, bike racing, lifting weights, holding breath, and square dancing.

"Square dancing?"

"It's a good exercise that will get your heart rate up. I was going to add swimming but didn't think that would be wise. We can go to the school tomorrow to test these; I know the janitor and he'll let us in. I can design some other tests by then, too. Maybe use the rowing machines and other equipment."

"Good idea. Thanks for—hey!" Claire had kicked her!

"Hurry! Read the scale!" Claire shouted.

All three of them looked down at the scale, which read 56.2 kilograms.

"Oh, smart!" Don nodded and typed into his computer. "But again, we don't know if it's from pain or surprise. Or possibly a combination. Lucy's going to have to do most of this stuff to herself."

Lucy bit her tongue. Maybe Don should write *that* on his stupid chart.

"Claire, did you bring your jump rope?" Don asked.

"Yep." Claire patted her backpack. "And my Chinese jump rope."

"Oh, nice," Don smiled, typing.

Ugh! They weren't even asking Lucy what *she* wanted to do, or what *her* ideas were. Regardless of the fact that she didn't have any ideas, they should at least have the consideration to ask. Besides, who cares about two stupid kilograms if she's passed out on the sofa for three days?!

"Don," Claire whispered from the other side of the table, catching Lucy's attention too. "What does the scale say now?"

Lucy looked down.

"Wow!" shouted Don. The scale was at 62.8 kilograms.

"How much is that?" Lucy asked, worried by the look on Don's face. "What does that mean?"

"It means you just gained—uh . . .almost twenty pounds just while we were talking! What did you do?"

"What do you mean *what did I do*? I didn't do anything! I was just standing here minding my own business while you two were over there discussing plans for torturing me!"

"Well, you must've—"

"She was angry," Claire said with a knowing look and a nod.

"Angry?" Don asked. It was a new idea to him. "About what?"

"I'm not sure, but she was angry," Claire explained. "I could tell."

"Angry," Don said with piqued interest. "I'll need to design tests that make her—"

"Would you two stop talking about me in *front* of me!" The numbers on the scale started rising.

"Look!" Claire shouted.

The scale showed 67 kilograms then started to go up again. Don began furiously clicking away on his keyboard.

"Stop!" Lucy screamed, jumping off the scale and kicking it across the tile floor. "Stop it!"

Claire and Don stared at her.

"This is new," Don said to Claire, who nodded.

"I think she—"

Lucy yelled an inarticulate "Aaarrghhhhhh!" and stomped out of the kitchen. Her dramatic exit was ruined, however, when she bent to pick up her sneakers by the front door and ended up toppling over—with a mini "argh" that time.

"That's interesting. I don't suppose her center of gravity changed," Don mused.

"I think she just lost her balance," Claire answered. Then she caught what she had just done and spoke to Lucy. "I mean I think *you* lost *your* balance."

"What's wrong?" asked Don, coming over to help Lucy sit up.

"Lucy," Claire said, "We're sorry."

Don's expression said he didn't know what he was sorry for, but he kept quiet.

"Everyone is used to talking for you since you never used to talk much," said Claire. "We don't mean anything by it. We've always just kind of filled in the blanks for you."

"Claire is best at it," Don added. "Maggie tries, and is good at knowing what you need, but Claire reads you better sometimes."

Lucy was still on the floor, looking up at them.

"But it's not as if I never spoke." She'd almost snapped at them, but there was a question in her voice. She was newly aware that her thoughts had only vaguely floated around her mind before, without direction or order; not many even made the effort to form themselves into words, let alone struggle for the right to be spoken aloud. And again, there were multiple parts of her brain responding to this new idea, and they each saw the world differently than the other parts did. One part realized how emotionally fatiguing it was to engage in conversation; one part wanted to understand other people and *be* understood—that would be glorious beyond anything she could imagine! Another part was still singularly angry—furious at what her parents had done to her and irritated at the way her little sister and her best friend talked about her *right in front of her face*, and how they had always done that.

Yet another part must have been assigned to deciding if something was fair or not, because she could see why they—all of them—had done it. After all, she had been an emotional mute until . . . she didn't know. She didn't even know what day it was. She was reevaluating and reanalyzing and reliving every day of her life from *before* so much that the last three days had felt like a lifetime—the lifetime of a stranger. Lucy was a stranger to herself.

" . . . I should have let you say it," Claire finished.

"What?" Lucy asked, standing and putting her shoes back near the door.

"I shouldn't have told Don you were angry; I should have let you say it."

"It's okay. I didn't even know I was angry," she admitted. "Or, at least, I didn't think about it that way. Anger is new." She sighed and felt a trickle by her left eye. She wiped the tear away, then stared at it on her punctured fingertip. "It's all new."

"I wonder if being sad makes you heavier?" Don said.

Claire frowned at him, but Lucy walked back into the kitchen.

"Fifty-three-point-two kilograms," she announced.

Don went to his computer and typed. "Are you up for continuing the tests?"

The three of them stood there looking at each other, waiting to see what Lucy would say. Even Lucy was waiting to see what Lucy would say. She knew she needed help, and she knew she had just, essentially, thrown a tantrum.

"I'm sorry for the way I reacted."

"It's okay. You're—" Claire began, but Lucy held up her hand.

"I'm sorry for the way I reacted," she repeated, trying to hold on to her incomplete thought. "I'm not sure, but I think . . . I think I need to practice *knowing* what I'm feeling. And you do help me, Claire; you do. Thank you," she said, looking Claire in the eye. "But what if I can't handle it? It's already really hard, and I'm just talking about *recognizing* the feelings. I mean, everyone has strong feelings, right?" She looked at them for confirmation, and they both nodded. "Well, if handling something everyone in the whole wide world has to deal with is so hard, how am I ever going to handle the . . . the weirdness that happens when I have these gigantic . . . mood shifts?"

Don made a move to turn to his computer but stopped himself. Then Lucy rolled her eyes and nodded for him to go ahead and type, so he did. It only took a moment.

"Anyway, what I'm saying is that, yes, we can go ahead with the testing, but Don?" He looked at her. "Claire is the one who asked you to help me, and you were nice enough to say yes. But I want to be the one to ask you now." Lucy turned and looked at her friend. "Don? Will you help me? Please?"

Don smiled and nodded. "Of course."

"Thank you."

The next day was Saturday, and Lucy found herself in the empty high school gym, where Don had driven her for more tests. Lucy held her arms straight out from her sides, parallel to the ground, with dumbbells in her fists. Her arms were starting to shake.

"You're holding your breath again," said Don.

How would *he* know? He wasn't even looking at her! He was just sitting there on the weight bench with his head in his dumb notebook. But Lucy started to feel light-headed at that moment, so she sucked in some air.

"Fine! *You* try it!" She would have hurled the stupid weights at him, but her arms were weak, and she was still a little dizzy, so she dropped them on the spongy mat.

"I'm not the one who has to keep from collapsing when I get mad."

"Whatever. They're heavy."

"They're only two pounds each, Ruce."

"Don't call me that."

He looked up—*finally*! "Why not?"

"You are only allowed to call me that when I'm not mad at you."

He shrugged and looked down again, pretending to write. "Never call Lucy 'Rucy' again. Ever. There is no hope."

Lucy started jabbing him in the ribs repeatedly. "That's right! You'd better beware my wrath!"

"Hey!" Don yowled, nearly falling off the bench as he tried to push her hands away.

Lucy tried not to laugh, and her mind noticed that moment; she had never had to try not to laugh before.

Don's arms were longer, though, so when he stood up and started poking her back, she couldn't help it, and the laughter broke free like a bird released from a cage. That made Claire, who had been reading an article about space travel and zero gravity, look up and start laughing too, so both Lucy and Don turned and attacked her. Hilarity ensued, everyone chasing everyone, laughing and screaming—Don didn't scream; just the girls—until the janitor came in.

"Hey!" he shouted, clearly used to squelching any and all unsanctioned behavior with that one bark.

The bark startled both girls, who immediately slumped down and put their hands over the mouths in a move that looked synchronized.

"Sorry, Mr. Mercer," Don shouted, waving to the wiry man with white hair and very tanned skin.

"Oh, Don," the man shouted across the gym. He didn't bark that time, though he still spoke in a disgruntled voice. Maybe that voice came with the job. "I didn't see you there. What are you doing?"

"A cool science experiment involving weights."

"Hmph. Figures," he said, and Lucy detected a hint of a smile on his face as he turned around and headed back out the door, which clattered on his way out.

When he was gone, they all plopped down on the squishy mat, panting and grinning. Lucy laid down and closed her eyes, smiling so much her cheeks hurt. Her arms still felt tired, but they weren't shaky anymore.

"That's going to be hard to measure," Don said, staring at Lucy.

Claire looked over and gasped at the same moment Lucy fell about eight inches to the ground.

"Ow!"

"Lucy!" Claire screamed, scrambling over to her on the floor and practically pouncing on her in excitement! "Lucy! I saw it! You weren't even touching the ground!"

"Well, I am now," Lucy grunted as she pulled herself up into a sitting position and gave Claire a sideways hug. "Ten points to Don for insisting on the stinky mats." She rubbed her neck and looked over at her old friend.

He wasn't smiling, exactly; he had an odd, faraway expression on his face.

"Well?" Lucy asked. Even though she hadn't done it on purpose, she would have expected a big reaction from him as well. Maybe he was freaked out.

"That's my girl," he said, nodding with a slight smile. "It's good to see you again."

Back in the gym the next day, Sunday, Lucy stepped onto the scale again, took a deep breath, and tried to relax.

"Good," Don said, noting and writing down her weight. He handed her two bottles of Dr. Pepper. "Now, these are two liters each, or four-point-four pounds for you Americans, so—"

"You're an American, too, Don."

"I may be a naturalized citizen, but your imperial-based measuring system makes no sense, so I'm sticking with metric, just like Dr. Pepper does."

Lucy let her arms hang at her sides, bottles in hand. "The dumbbells were easier to hold. Why use these?"

"It's mostly psychological. How often do you walk around carrying weights in your hands? But you carry groceries and stuff all the time. Maybe I should have put them in grocery bags," he said looking down and writing in his notebook. "I've also filled my backpack to weigh precisely ten kilograms, though, so we can try that later. But, for now, holding these sort of gives you something to concentrate on. The goal is to compensate for the weight of the bottles to get back to your starting point, but let's just try lightening in general at first."

"Okay, let's." *Like he's the one doing this*, she thought, but that was on the verge of snarky, so she nodded and smiled.

"When you levitated last time—"

"Levitated? You make me sound like an alien."

"Well, you didn't just float—you ascended, so. . ."

"Okay, okay." Sometimes thinking about how much her entire world had changed boggled her mind. Now, words like *levitating* and *ascending* were being tossed around.

"Anyway, two things factored into your—relationship to the ground?"

She shrugged. It was the same thing, but whatever.

"And those were endorphins and oxygen," he said.

She nodded. "Being happy and breathing hard."

"Right. So, I'm going to play some inspiring music, and you're going to focus on breathing, okay?" She nodded again, just wanting to get on with it. The more he talked, the more unrelaxed she felt. "Slow and even breaths, okay? Think *out* - two - three - four . . . *in* - two - three - four. Like that."

She closed her eyes and tried to relax her shoulders while holding on to the bottles. It was awkward, but she would try.

With her eyes closed, she heard the buzz of the gym lights high overhead, the distant sound of the janitor power-waxing the floors, and the sound of Don pressing buttons on his phone. Then she heard the soft, static sound of an electric guitar, a drum, and some funky electronic tones. Then:

Ground control to Major Tom . . .

Lucy almost dropped the bottles when she laughed. "It's 'Space Oddity'!"

"Try to hold still," Don said calmly.

She tried, but she had to shake her head. She knew the song and remembered liking it *before*, when she didn't know why she liked it. Now, as she listened to it, it was so obvious!

"This is perfect," she said, smiling. "How did you think of it?"

"It was Claire's idea."

"Of course," she laughed. Claire, who was fanatic about old movies and retro music, would automatically search her brilliant little mind for the perfect song. When Claire first heard it, she looked it up and learned all about the singer, David Bowie, who wrote it in 1969! Claire then started listening to all his music—there was *tons* of it—and she shared every song with Lucy. That was, literally, hours and hours and *hours* of time she spent with Lucy; maybe it was because Lucy was the only one who would sit there and listen without protesting. Or maybe Claire was the only one willing to sit with Lucy for hours and hours without protesting. She wished Claire had come with them that day just so she could hug her. And thank her.

She heard Don scribbling, but kept her eyes closed. "What's happening?"

"I'm just writing down that you like this song."

She could feel herself smiling as she listened to the words . . . the countdown . . . the launch . . . the celebration! The music and lyrics told the story of an astronaut named Major Tom lifting off into space. After he stepped through the door of his spaceship, he said he was "floating in a most peculiar way," and that all the stars looked different that day.

Lucy's stars—her fate, maybe—really did look different then. A vast universe of possibilities had opened up, freeing her soul, actually lifting her.

But the whole thing was still scary. She'd never worried about her future before, and now she did. A lot. All the time.

"Lucy? Breathe."

Out - two - three - four. In - two - three - four. How weird that a person would need to be reminded to breathe.

> *Planet Earth is blue*
> *And there's nothing I can do*

She opened her eyes and set the bottles down on the ground, tired.

Don was looking at her. "What were you thinking about?" he asked.

"What am I going to do?"

He didn't say anything for a moment. "About what, exactly?"

"My life," she said. "What am I going to do?"

"That's a great question."

"That's not a great answer," Lucy half-smiled.

"I know. But it's what my dad used to say." He looked down.

"Oh, Don! Your dad! I remember! That was just—when? Last year?"

"Yeah. Last September." He clicked his pen a few times, not looking up.

"That's right! It was on my birthday!"

"I know."

"And I didn't even . . . I don't know . . . I haven't even thought about it this whole time! I'm so sorry. I didn't even help you or anything."

He looked up at her. "Yes, you did."

She frowned. "I did?"

"Yeah. You came over and sat with me while I did my homework."

"That's not very . . . helpful."

"Actually, it was. You were more yourself for a while." He paused and frowned. "I wonder if your dad changed your drugs after that because you stopped coming over around November."

Lucy thought about it, but she didn't remember any of that. "Claire said they changed my 'vitamin' from pink-and-gray to all-pink last year." Her brain slid apart again for a moment, thinking multiple things at once: What had she done that made her dad decide to give her a new dosage? How could he have emotionally tied her up like that—for her entire life? It was better now, though . . . wasn't it? Yes. She would never go back. "I didn't mean to."

He stood up and picked up a bottle. "No big deal. At least it makes sense now. Ready to try again?"

She took the bottles and got back on the scale. "Can I have a different song this time?"

Don grinned. "Yep. It's one I picked out."

"What is it?"

"You'll see." He sat down by the scale. "Okay, close your eyes, and don't forget to breath this time."

"Okay." Eyes closed. *Breathe.* She wished she'd been more help to Don. It must have been so awful for him. The thought of her own dad dying just—

"Lucy?"

She opened her eyes. "Yeah?"

"Smile. Happy thoughts."

"Right." Eyes closed. *Breathe.* Happy thoughts? Okay. Like . . .

> *Ain't it a glorious day?*
> *Right as a morning in May*
> *I feel like I could fly*

"Mary Poppins!" Lucy shouted, opening her eyes.

"I happen to know you liked watching this when we were little."

"We *both* liked it." That was a happy memory. Don's English wasn't great at first, but it didn't matter with *Mary Poppins*. And Lucy used to teach Don lots of words. "Can you still say it?"

Don shook his head, but said, "Of course."

"Say it."

"No. Close your eyes and breathe."

"Come on, Don. Say it."

He rolled his eyes. "Supercalifragilisticexpialidocious."

"Yay!" Lucy grinned and closed her eyes.

"Breathe," said Don.

Lucy nodded. *Out - two - three - four . . .*

An hour later, it wasn't so fun.

"Remember, the important thing is to breathe," he coaxed. "In - two - three - four; out - two - three - four . . . In - two - three - four; out - two - three - four . . . In - two - three - four; out - two—"

"I got it, Don!" Lucy said.

"And . . . try not to get mad - two - three - four . . . smile - two - three - four . . . Mountain Dew guy - two - three - four . . ."

An inarticulate scream erupted from Lucy's throat. "*ARRGGHH!* I'm going to kill Claire for telling you that!" Lucy stepped off the scale, nearly dropping the bottles. "It's not working, anyway," she said.

"Not completely true. You lightened by two-point-four kilograms, six-point-two kilograms, one-point-two, then point-eight."

"And no change the last time," she moped.

"Well, that's not actually true." Don hesitated, "You gained seven-point-six kilograms."

"What?!" Lucy wanted to cry as she plopped down on the mat.

Don sat down beside her. "You were just getting tired. You were really doing it at first."

"So what?" she almost shouted. "What good is lightening by . . ."

"More than thirteen pounds, at one point!" Don said enthusiastically with his goofy smile.

"Well, whoop-de-*doo*!"

Don closed his notebook and stood up, not smiling. "You're tired. We can try again tomorrow."

"I know I'm tired, Don!" She snapped. "You don't need to tell me!"

"Whatever," he said, holding out his hand to help her up. "Did you know you're tired *and* cranky?"

She grudgingly took his hand and got up. "Sorry," she said as she bent over and picked up the scale and one of the bottles of soda. Straightening, she looked at Don, who was picking up his backpack and the other bottle of soda. "Thanks for helping me."

Don looked at her. "Wow. And Claire's not even here to coach you."

Lucy huffed and spun around, marching toward the exit without waiting for him.

CHAPTER 13

Cooking Can Be Hazardous to One's Health

It was Kelly's birthday, and Lucy had chopped up the cabbage, celery, and onions, and was getting ready to move on to the water chestnuts. She was still thinking about what a jerk Don had been earlier that day, even after Lucy had tried to apologize.

Big dummy.

Maggie was overseeing the making of a celebration dinner of chicken chow mein, egg rolls, and double-double chocolate cake, plus ice cream, of course. She was almost done cooking the chicken in the electric skillet. Claire was sitting at the kitchen table, mixing up different colors of icing for decorating the cake she had baked earlier. Lucy wasn't sure what her little sister's master plan was, but she had already mixed up yellow and purple icing, and was now trying to mix red, blue, and yellow to make black. It was a rather dark lavender-gray at the moment, and completely unappetizing. But Claire was the artistic one, so the cake would certainly turn out fine, at the very least. Probably better than fine. She had just added another drop of blue when she said, "So how do you think it works?"

"I don't think you can actually make black with those colors, especially with white icing." answered Maggie. "You should have told me what you needed, and I could have gotten one of the little tubes of already-made stuff at the store."

"No, I need way more than that. But I wasn't talking about icing."

"Then how does *what* work?" Maggie had turned the skillet down to simmer and started mixing the soy sauce, water, and corn starch together in a measuring cup.

"Lucy's floating trick. I mean, I saw it at the gym, but—"

Lucy's hissed intake of breath followed by a clatter made both sisters look. She had dropped the can of water chestnuts and was holding her pinky. Bright red blood was already collecting on the tip of her finger and beginning to drip down to her wrist. She let out a tiny whimper as her knees buckled and she slid down the front edge of the kitchen counter in slow motion.

"Lucy!" both girls yelled. Claire dropped the red food coloring and started to run to Lucy, but Maggie held her back.

"Watch out Claire! Stand back!"

"But—"

"Just stay back!" Maggie ordered firmly. "Just give her a minute."

Lucy squeezed her eyes closed and completed her slow-motion collapse onto the kitchen floor with a thud that the other girls must have felt through the floor.

"But she's bleeding!"

"I'm okay," Lucy mumbled, but it came out slurred. She tried to open her eyes to prove she was okay but could only manage blinking.

"Claire, hand me a towel," Maggie said as she knelt down by Lucy. "It's okay, Luce, you're okay."

Lucy felt Maggie try to pick up her hand, but even Lucy couldn't move it. Between blinks, Lucy saw Maggie take a kitchen towel from Claire, then felt her shove the sides and corners of the towel around the edges of her hand and apply pressure and stop the bleeding.

"Is she okay? Should I call Dad?" Claire asked, almost in tears.

"It's only a little cut, Claire. She just fainted."

"No . . . I'm here," Lucy mumbled. She would not faint. She *would* not faint.

"Fine," Maggie snapped at Claire, as if she was the one who had answered. "She didn't faint. She—she did *this*." She gestured with her head at Lucy's body, flat on the kitchen floor. "It's what she *does*." The last part came out with the tiniest hint of snark.

"Did she . . ." began Claire. Then she stopped. It wasn't like Claire not to say what she was thinking.

"Did she what?" answered Maggie with a sigh. The part of Lucy's mind that always wondered things wondered if that sigh was the sound of Maggie's anger fading away on a puff of air.

Had it come naturally, or was Maggie calming herself down? Claire had helped Lucy calm down before. Did everyone just know how to do that?

"Did you always know about Lucy?" Claire said softly, like she knew she was talking to a lioness, and she didn't want to make her roar.

The lioness ignored the little cub for a moment. She tried to tuck another corner of the dish cloth under Lucy's hand, still applying pressure to the sliced finger. "I think so," she said.

Claire waited for more.

Lucy waited for more too. For the first time ever, she was glad she was too heavy to move because there was no way she was getting up off the floor when Maggie might actually reveal what she was thinking for once. She kept her eyes closed.

"When we were really little, I don't know how old I was, but I wasn't in kindergarten yet . . ." Maggie paused. "I remember I liked making Lucy laugh. And I kind of thought Lucy was my baby. It sounds dumb, I know, but Mom was—you know. And I liked making my baby laugh. I pretended I was magic and could make my baby float like a balloon." She huffed. "I really did think it was all a pretend game."

Lucy kept her eyes from popping open, but just barely. Maggie had known!

She heard Claire shift on the floor, but she didn't say anything.

"Then my baby stopped laughing one day, and the game ended."

Lucy felt tears begin piling up behind her eyelids and almost starting to seep out. She heard more movement and knew that Claire was hugging Maggie.

Then Claire scooted over and began stroking Lucy's long red hair. Only she could do that without getting her fingers tangled in the snarls. "She's crying," she said, "we should call Dad."

Lucy's eyes did pop open then. "No!" she said, struggling but still unable to get up. "I'm fine!"

"Relax, dork," said Maggie. "We aren't going to call Dad."

Lucy looked at Maggie, who was squinting at her, kind of like their dad did. But Lucy couldn't tell if Maggie was angry or amused. Feelings were so hard to name.

Lucy got up a few minutes later, a little dizzy at first, but her head cleared with a drink of cold water. Her father was a big fan of hydration, and Lucy had found over the last week that cool water really did help her recover from her . . . whatever. Claire had wanted to put a cartoon bandage on her finger, but Lucy insisted on plain old pink-brown, hoping not to draw attention to it when their parents got home. Maggie had promised not to say anything, but the shake of her head said she thought they should know. She still seemed to be avoiding Lucy, but she wasn't completely ignoring her. She was just a little more self-absorbed than . . . *before*. Lucy still hated dividing her life like that, and it drove her nuts whenever she caught herself using that term, but what else could she do? That's how her world was now. She needed to get over it.

As Lucy and Maggie finished preparing the meal, Claire put the finishing touches on her cake, and it was amazing. She'd turned a perfectly normal round cake into a bouquet of delicate purple and yellow pansies, Kelly's favorite flowers. It looked almost too beautiful to eat, but Lucy knew Claire's buttercream frosting would taste like a little bit of heaven. And in a tender mercy, their parents came home from Kelly's birthday date right as Lucy had filled everyone's glasses with—yes, water, though Kelly and Maggie would also have Diet Cokes with their meals.

Every part of the dinner was a success: her parents were happy, the chow mein was delicious, and the cake was more than divine—though much sweeter than Lucy remembered it being. Throughout the entire meal, however, Lucy mulled over the dilemma of how to get her dad to let her go to school on Monday. She didn't think Kelly would have a problem with it, but her dad was still worried about what he called her *episodes*.

The calendar kept marching forward, every day inexorably closer to the end of school, and Lucy's guidance counselor, Mr. Dibble, had called and left multiple messages on both her parents' phones asking about Lucy's mysterious sickness, and recommending that work be sent home for her to do if she was going to miss any more days. He had even asked Maggie to relay messages for him, which she was completely un-thrilled to do. Her dad had more than suggested that Lucy make up work during summer school, but Lucy was completely un-thrilled at the idea of doing homework while her sisters were having fun. After all, Lucy hadn't had a lot of experience with *fun*. She wanted to try it.

"I want to go to school tomorrow," she declared, pushing her chair back and interrupting her father's story about the time he found a belt buckle in the stomach of his medical cadaver.

Everyone had heard that story a million times, so Lucy only felt a little bad when everyone suddenly turned from looking at *him* to looking at *her*.

But no one said anything. They just looked at her. Her father didn't even blink.

"Here, let me take these," Kelly said, standing up and gathering plates.

"No, we'll do it," said Maggie, who stood up and also started picking up dishes. But Claire was drinking her water and looking between Aeden and Lucy.

"Claire?" Maggie prompted.

Claire let out a giant sigh as she stood up. "Of *course* I want to help with the dishes. I would never choose to sit and watch Dad and Lucy try to out-stubborn each other, even though it's kind of fun watching Dad finally meet his . . ." Her voice trailed off as all three retreated into the kitchen and was soon drowned out by the sound of clattering dishes and running water.

"How many days has it been since your last crash?"

She swallowed. "Three."

He squinted. "That's not very many."

She licked her lips. "I need to go back some time."

He shook his head. "But not tomorrow."

"If I wait, I'll have to—"

"You can make up the work over—"

"Dad!"

"—summer, and you'll have—"

"No, I don't want to do that!"

"—plenty of time to get things under control."

Lucy looked at her empty water glass. She felt herself getting angry. And heavy.

"It's happening right now, isn't it?" Was it her dad speaking or the doctor? Or some evil tormentor who just wanted to see her fail?

"No." She looked up. Yes, she could feel it. But she lifted her right hand to push her hair back, just to see how heavy her arm was. He studied the movement, watching as she purposefully unclenched her other hand and carefully placed both hands back in her lap.

He squinted and pursed his lips.

There was hope. She tried to relax her shoulders but couldn't manage it.

"There would be some rules," he said.

"Of course." She wasn't being sassy; their family was big on rules. They usually hadn't applied to Lucy, but she had heard him say those words to Maggie countless times just before he let her do something. She was prepared.

"You cannot tell anyone about your condition."

"Okay." Easy. Who would she tell?

"If you crash at all before Monday, you'll have to wait another week."

A blink. "Okay." She could do that. She hadn't . . . totally . . . crashed when she cut her finger. And she controlled the heaviness just now with her dad. She could do this. She *would* do this.

"You will call me if you have any problems," he said.

"Okay." There wouldn't be any problems. She would make sure.

He looked at her but didn't say anything. She didn't know who he was at that moment. He wasn't the clinical, emotionless doctor, but his face didn't have the warmth her father usually exuded, or even the sternness of when he was angry. He looked . . . she didn't know the word for what she saw in his face. He looked hollowed-out and empty. What did that mean?

"Go help your sisters," he finally said, picking up his water glass and putting it back down when he realized it was empty.

That night, Lucy opened her prayer book and read a prayer of thanks:

> *Father of Jesus,*
> *We praise you and give you glory*
> *For the wonderful things you do for us;*
> *For life and health,*
> *for friends and family,*
> *for this splendid day.*

She had copied that prayer down on a windy day in fall when golden leaves had been flying about in the wind and her hair was lifted up in billows around her head. Looking back, she realized she might have felt . . . light . . . in those minutes at the park. It had been a splendid day.

And so was today. Lucy would go back to school on Monday. All she had to do was stay calm, not talk to anyone, and above all else, not accidentally slam her finger in her locker door or anything. Piece - of - cake.

CHAPTER 14

No Wonder So Many Kids Skip School

Monday morning, Lucy took a big bite of butter-slathered toast just as her father entered the kitchen. Kelly had taken Claire to early morning safety patrol, where Claire got to wear an orange vest and tell kids not to run and stuff, and Maggie was in her bedroom, so it was just the two of them.

"Good morning," he said, omitting the *Miss Lucy* part, which made his usual morning greeting sound ominous.

Lucy swallowed. "Good morning." Her attempt to sound casual and act like this was just a typical breakfast before everyone headed off to school and work sounded weak.

"I don't think this is a good idea," Aeden reiterated as he poured himself a cup of coffee.

"I know," Lucy replied, picking up her glass of milk.

"What's your plan?"

Lucy swallowed and looked at him. "My plan?"

Aeden sat down and took a triangle of toast off Lucy's plate. "What are you going to do to keep from getting angry and frustrated at school?"

She wiped her mouth with a paper napkin. "It's just school," she defended. "I never really talk to anyone anyway, so I'll just do that. Just . . . keep to myself." It had seemed like a solid plan after Kelly's birthday dinner. And it had seemed plausible when she and Claire had talked about it earlier that morning. But she could tell her dad was not convinced.

"Hmm," was all he said as he took another crunchy bite.

"It will be fine," Lucy said. It would. She had made up her mind.

He nodded. But it was his *we'll see* nod, like he was certain he knew better and was just waiting for her to realize it too.

Lucy stood up. "I need to brush my teeth."

This was no big deal.

And for the entire two minutes of vigorously brushing her teeth, she kept thinking *no big deal, no big deal, no big deal.*

"I'm ready," Lucy said to Maggie, who was waiting for her by the front door.

But Maggie didn't move. Her mouth scrunched to the side while her eyes inspected Lucy from top to bottom then returned to her face. After a medium-sized eyeroll, she turned and headed to the door, jangling her car keys. "Let's go."

Lucy stared out the window during the twenty-five-minute car ride, amazed at how the world had exploded with color since she had woken up on the sofa a week and a half earlier. Within one block of her house, she discovered again why artists could never be satisfied with calling the sky boring old blue. No, it needed a grander description, like *cerulean*. The grasses that grew along the sides of the roads couldn't be plain green; they were *emerald*, and *myrtle*, and *chartreuse*. And the flowers? She had no name for the colors she once believed could only occur in her Dreams. But they'd been right in front of her all along, and her sleeping mind had simply shown her what her conscious mind couldn't recognize—that every shade of yellow and purple had a thousand variations. Spring had arrived and she was seeing new depths in every color and hue. The sunlight sparkled on the morning dew and made every tree, plant, and individual blade of grass stand out crisp and separate from those around it. Even the damp pebbles on the side of the road were glorious.

"They're going to notice," Maggie said out of nowhere.

"Not if I don't talk to anyone." Lucy rubbed her cold nose. Spring might be gloriously beautiful, but it was still only about forty-five degrees outside.

"Lucy, you really are different now."

Lucy sat back in her seat, only then realizing how she had been practically crawling out the window to see the world better. "Claire has said that too."

"Yeah, well, Claire's smart."

Lucy laughed. "She said that too."

Maggie looked at Lucy. Waves of irritation emanated from her body and saturated the air in the tiny hatchback before she settled her eyes back on the road exactly 1.5 seconds later. "You just laughed." It sounded like an accusation. "If you do that in school, *everyone* will notice."

Then a horn honked beside them, making Lucy gasp and jump in her seat. "What happened?!"

"Nothing!" Maggie scolded. "Don't scare me like that!"

"Don't—? What did I do?"

"You freaked out for nothing! I thought we were going to crash!"

"So did I!" Lucy shrieked.

"Look," Maggie said, clearly forcing herself to be calm, "you have *got* to relax." Then she shook her head.

Lucy didn't know what internal dialogue Maggie was having with herself. All she knew was that she had been minding her business, not talking, not initiating conversations, just like Claire had suggested, and it was Maggie who was freaking out.

"I don't see how this is going to work," Maggie murmured.

"What do you mean?" Lucy asked.

"*That*," Maggie said. "You, being different. You, looking at the sky. You, freaking out over a car horn. And you, asking 'what do you mean?' You didn't used to do any of those things. Everyone is going to know something's up."

Lucy shrugged, turning back to her window. "I'm just going to keep to myself." But out of the corner of her eye she saw Maggie nod, and it looked just like the way her dad had nodded. "It's no big deal," she added, turning further to her right so she couldn't see Maggie no matter how hard she nodded her grouchy head.

First period was U.S. History, and Lucy went to her assigned seat in the left row, four desks back. She listened, took notes, and tried to concentrate despite the fact that the boy sitting in front of her had so much cologne on she thought she might choke. The insipid fumes swirled around every time he moved, frightening away the defenseless little oxygen molecules, threatening to asphyxiate her. No one else seemed bothered, so Lucy breathed as shallowly as possible, sometimes holding her breath. After about thirty minutes, however, she had to cough. And once she let out one cough, they all had to come, and she couldn't stop. Everyone turned to look at her, and even Mrs. Hirschi asked, "Do you need to go get some water, Lucy?"

She nodded, and wheezed out a "Thanks," as she tried not to flee to the hallway for air. She coughed all the way to the water fountain, clearing her lungs. Once there, she bent to take a long, cleansing drink, but one swallow of the tepid water almost made her choke again. It tasted like metal. And dust. And it had an acrid aftertaste that she couldn't wash away with more of the foul liquid. *Yuck.* But she was done coughing, she thought, so she took a few deep breaths of air that smelled like old wood and cleaning chemicals and walked back to class.

Upon entering, every head turned to look at her. She felt her face get warm as she took her seat, and heard a few unintelligible whispers, but they quieted when the teacher resumed her lecture. The offending cologne still hung in the air, but she was able to make it through the rest of the lesson without coughing. At the end of class, a few people looked sideways at her as they all gathered their things, but no one said anything.

In her geometry class, another student coughed once in a while during the lesson, but no one looked at him. When the class was told to do some practice exercises, the other students automatically split into pairs, but Lucy was left to her own devices, so she did the problems quickly, finishing before all but two groups. She looked around at the other students, observing their interactions. Lots of whispers. Students in two separate groups were disagreeing about something, flipping back through their textbooks to settle the arguments. And one boy and girl were laughing and fighting over an eraser. She looked up at Ms. Ramos to see if she was okay with that, but Ms. Ramos was looking at Lucy. Lucy quickly looked back down at her own paper and pretended to rework a problem.

In chemistry, Mr. Bradley sent them to the lab tables, which had buckets of Legos on them. The task was to use the Legos to model the quantity of atoms and molecules during a chemical reaction called *stoichiometry*.

But on the way to the lab counters, Lucy stepped on a pen that someone had dropped, making Lucy's right foot sweep out from underneath her. She screamed, reflexively grabbing onto the counter to her right. But in the process, she nearly sent a half-dozen empty glass beakers crashing to the floor; only the quick hands of a girl walking behind her helped her stay on her feet without shattering the lab equipment and sending glass fragments everywhere.

"Thanks." Lucy righted herself and pushed her hair out of her face.

"Uh, you're welcome," the girl said. Her brown eyes were as wide as saucers and stayed that way while she helped Lucy straighten the beakers and scoot them farther back from the edge of the counter. "Are you okay?"

"Um, yah. I just—" Lucy looked down and saw the offending pen. She bent down and picked it up, showing it to the girl. "I just slipped."

"Wow. That could have been bad." But she kept looking at Lucy with her saucer-sized eyes.

"Yah. It could have," Lucy agreed. Really bad.

As usual, Lucy found Maggie at lunch and set down her tray beside hers. She opened her mouth to tell her what had almost happened in chemistry, but Maggie vigorously shook her head.

"Hi Mags!" said one of Maggie's orchestra friends who had just walked up to the table. Lucy remembered the girl played the violin. She sat down on the other side of Maggie.

"Hey, guys," said another friend with big boobs. She sat down directly across from Maggie.

Then another girl with a grumpy frown on her face sat down across from the first friend, completing a perfect little square of trays, with Lucy's on the outside.

"Is that all you're eating?" said the violinist, who looked at Grumpy's tray. It held a small side salad and a Coke.

"Yes," said Grumpy. "Just salad and Diet Coke for a month. My dad booked a family cruise to Mexico, and I refuse to wear a bikini with all this fat."

"Whatever," said the girl with the boobs. "You aren't fat."

"Ha," said Grumpy. "We can't all have your amazing body."

"You can with the right padding," said Violin Girl.

"Shut up," said Boob Girl. *Or maybe she was really just* Bra *Girl,* thought Lucy. Then she realized that even though she had sat with these same girls at lunch all year long, she didn't know any of their names. Wait—yes, she did. But it was a genuine effort to recall them. The violinist . . . she was . . . April. And the other two were . . . Sarah and Cassie. Maybe. It was weird: she could name all fifty states, their capitals, and all the elements on the periodic table, but she looked around the lunchroom and realized she couldn't have said the names of some of the kids she'd known since elementary school. She could remember the names of every teacher she'd ever had. If Mr. Bradley had said, "Lucy, please take this paper to so-and-so," could she have done it? Maybe she could have in context. Or maybe teachers never expected that of her.

"What's wrong, Maggie?" Violin Girl—April—asked.

"Nothing. I'm fine," Maggie said, shaking her head and taking a sip of Diet Coke.

"Yeah, how come you're not talking?" Sarah asked.

"I don't know," Maggi shrugged.

"Did you and Caleb have a fight?"

Caleb? Who was Caleb? Lucy turned to look at Maggie, who grabbed her tray and stood up.

"No. I have to go. Girl problems," she said, then walked away.

All three friends offered a sympathetic *oh*, *ah*, or *got it*, and continued talking about bikinis, body fat, and boys.

Lucy ate her hamburger in silence, knowing for a fact it wasn't time for Maggie to have girl problems.

When Lucy walked into the high school gymnasium, she was assaulted by sensory overload, and immediately retreated back into the safer recesses of the locker room. It took her three full minutes to brace herself, but she couldn't avoid gym class forever, so she did her best to calm herself and crept back into the chaos.

Sixty students were scattered among an array of five volleyball nets, smacking dirty white volleyballs back and forth, or running around chasing the strays that skittered across the wooden floor. The brick walls echoed brightly as many kids preferred bouncing the dingy orbs like basketballs, while the stops and starts of everyone's sneakers filled the enormous room with horrible screeches. But worst by far was the cold, drafty air that was permeated by the stench of sweat left by earlier classes that day.

How had Lucy not been overwhelmed by all this commotion before? How could *anyone* stand this? It was almost disorienting, and she had to clench her teeth to keep them from chattering in anxiety. She could feel those boulders sliding around in her stomach; they were small, but they were there. There was no way she would be able to actually play!

"Here," a man's voice said as she felt something bump her upper arm. She turned to see Coach Vazquez handing her a scoreboard about the size of a laptop computer, with red and blue numbers that flipped over. "Court number one," he said, nodding to the east wall, then walking away.

Right. I keep score, she thought, so relieved she actually smiled. Then she wiped the smile completely off her face; she'd realized early in the day that people looked at her more when she smiled. Or spoke. Or looked interested in anything at all. So she headed to court number one and sat down against the wall to put the flippy numbers in order. Having her back against the wall helped her feel less anxious for some reason. Maybe it was because the noises and movements—and even the smells—were in front of her now, instead of all around her. And she only jumped a little when Coach Vazquez blasted on his whistle, signaling for everyone to begin their games.

Everything was going pretty well until the third set. The teams traded sides, got into position, and the tall skinny kid with the red Converse sneakers served. The ball landed near Lucy, and it was out of bounds, so Lucy flipped the red "1" to record the point for the receiving team. But no one paid attention to Lucy, and both sides cheered like they'd won the point. Then a loud dispute ensued about whether it was in or out, losing the serve, gaining a point, and rally scoring.

Finally, one girl on the receiving team shouted and pointed, "Look, Lucy gave us the point, so we get the point!" That made everyone look at Lucy, which was followed by more shouting, and Lucy heard her name tossed around with *she doesn't know, yes, she does,* and . . . *just something for her to do.*

Finally, Coach Vazquez strode over, silenced the clamor, turned to Lucy, and asked. "Did you see where it landed?"

Oh crap. Opting to play it safe, she just nodded twice.

"Well? Was it in or out?" He asked in an impatient tone.

"It was definitely out."

One of the kids on the serving team swore, and two of the girls on the receiving team said, "Ha!" and "Yes!" But the rest of the kids stared at Lucy. She felt her face heat up and perspiration blossom on her upper lip just as the bell to shower and change rang.

Voices of the kids on the other teams erupted in shouts of victorious triumph or agonizing defeat, while the kids from court number one were still looking at Lucy. But they were swept away with the crowd as everyone migrated to the locker rooms.

Lucy gave herself a few seconds before pushing herself off the ground. She could feel it—her own weight pulling on her—but she managed to get up. It was okay. She would be fine. It would be fine.

She picked up the scoreboard and turned to take it to Coach Vazquez. Then, as she tripped over one of the ropes tied to the net of court number one, and as she saw the scuffs on the shiny gym floor rushing up to meet her face, all she could think was, *Oh crap.*

Lucy felt someone holding her hand. She opened her eyes, and there was Maggie, kneeling next to her on the gym floor. Standing above them were Coach Vazquez, the school nurse, and another adult Lucy didn't know. "How—?"

"You tripped and hit your head. You've only been out for a few minutes. I'm just going to sit here with you until you feel like getting up." Maggie looked up at the school nurse and Coach Vazquez, as if asking if that would be okay.

"That's fine," Coach Vazquez answered for both adults. "We sent the next class out to run laps."

Maggie nodded. "I told them that you've fainted like this at home before, when you get hurt or scared, and that it's nothing serious."

"It must be a vasovagal syncope. It's when blood pressure drops because something frightens you, or because you've been standing too long. It's pretty common; kids in choir faint from time to time, and I have to remind them not to lock their knees when standing so long. I'd say see a doctor about it, but I guess your dad sees you every day. I'll call him and let him know—"

"No, you don't have to. Like I said, she does this at home sometimes. She'll be fine in a few minutes."

"Well, legally I have to inform one of your parents."

"Call our mom then. My dad sees patients all day long."

"Of course."

"But—" Lucy interrupted and stirred, though she didn't think she could stand yet. Her mind was clearing, though, and she knew she didn't want anyone calling either of her parents. And she knew her dad was not seeing patients all day. He mostly did research.

Maggie squeezed Lucy's fingers, and gently put her other hand on Lucy's shoulder. She didn't say a word, but her look clearly said *be quiet.* So Lucy relaxed. Maggie looked up at the nurse. "Could she have some apple juice or something?"

"Of course. I'll go get some," said the nurse. She turned and jogged away.

That left Coach Vazquez looming over her with his arms folded across his massive chest, not saying a word, and the other teacher standing a few paces back with her hands in her pockets.

Lucy mentally examined herself. She felt a little heavy still, but no boulders in her stomach, no beads of perspiration on her lip, and no ringing in her ears. She looked at Maggie. "I think I'm okay to sit up." Maggie's eyebrows lifted, asking *Are you sure?* and Lucy nodded.

Maggie let go of Lucy's hand and sat back. She also scooted away just a few inches, wary of Lucy toppling over and crushing her. But Lucy felt better with every moment, so she smiled, sitting up and pushing her hair out of her face.

She looked up, and Coach Vazquez still had his arms folded, aaaannnd he was staring at her. He was the only person Lucy knew who spoke almost as little as she did. But he communicated a great deal by his looks, and his glower at that moment seemed to say he was suspicious about something.

Or Lucy was becoming paranoid. It was difficult to tell.

CHAPTER 15

After School

On the way home, Lucy struggled for something to say. She finally settled on "Thank you." There should be a better way to say, *Hey, I know things are weird, but really, thank you for helping me. And thanks for what you said to Coach Vazquez. And thanks for getting me some apple juice because, even though I hate apple juice, it was a smart way to get the nurse to leave me alone.*

And thanks for holding my hand.

It had been a long time since Maggie had held her hand.

Maggie shrugged and merged onto the highway.

"What do you think Mom said?"

"About what?" Maggie frowned.

"When the nurse called her," Lucy explained.

"Oh." Maggie's expression went blank. "They didn't call her."

"They didn't? But the nurse—"

"I listed a fake number for Mom on both our registration forms." She shrugged again.

"You—? What?" A fake number? How did a person even think of doing that?

"I signed up for a free internet phone number and recorded a message that said it was Kelly Callaghan's phone, and I get a text if anyone calls it and leaves a message."

Lucy was stunned. That was . . . not right. But it was brilliant. "When did you do that?"

"Two years ago."

Lucy was simultaneously disappointed in Maggie's deceptiveness and impressed by her . . . her cleverness. "And Dad's number?"

"No. That's his real number. Mom just can't handle some things. But you didn't want Dad to know, so I told them to call Mom's number."

"You're a genius!" It was so wrong. But so smart. "Thank you," she said again, and again, she felt like it wasn't enough.

Maggie nodded.

"Did the nurse call it? The fake number?"

"Yah. I'll call her back in a little while and thank her and tell her it's a normal thing you do."

"*You'll* call her back?"

"Apparently, I sound a lot like Mom on the phone."

"Wow."

"Yeah. But I'm keeping your secret, so you'd better keep mine."

"Absolutely." Maggie had always looked out for Lucy. Even when they were little girls, Maggie stepped in when Kelly couldn't handle things. So many memories were coming back now. Memories that were filmed in black and white were being overlaid with colors in her brain, and while the superimposed colors had a not-quite-right feeling, they helped Lucy notice things she'd never paid attention to before. But she remembered Maggie trying to make her smile. Comforting her. Soothing her. Like a mother. And she was really only nineteen months older than Lucy. "You've always helped me."

"You used to need me to," said Maggie.

"I still need you to."

Maggie snorted. "Maybe."

"Maggie?" How could she explain?

"Yeah?"

"I love you."

Maggie didn't say anything.

"It was awful. *Awful*." Lucy said, reliving the disasters at school. "Dad was right! I can't do this!" She plopped back on her bed, covering her face.

"Stop stop stop." Claire reached over and pulled Lucy's hands down. "You need to relax."

"Yes! I know I do! I don't know how!"

"Okay, first of all, school is sometimes intense. It's sometimes . . . I don't know . . . more than you think you can handle. But what happened today—those are normal school problems, not even on the top half of the trauma meter. And you've handled way worse before, you just didn't realize it, or you didn't care, or something. You can totally handle this. Maggie and I handle this kind of stuff every day, so trust me, okay?"

Lucy groaned and rolled over.

To distract herself from thinking about gym class, gifts, and the scientific method, Lucy did her homework. She did fine in all of her classes, but there was a lot to catch up on after missing a week of school, so it took her the rest of the night. Lucy got in bed and closed her eyes even though she wasn't tired. Her mind was too full of questions. It was like a television game show, and Lucy was losing.

Category: "Weird Things about Lucy's Life."

Clue: "Name a strange phenomenon that causes Lucy to float."

Music plays while the camera shows each contestant staring blankly at her podium where she's supposed to write the answer. Then the camera backs up to show that each of the contestants is a different section of Lucy's brain: One section thought about gym class, tripping next to a volleyball court and being unable to get up because she was so heavy. Another section thought about Lucy in sixth grade, sitting by herself on damp green grass at recess, watching a giant yellow oak leaf twirl to the ground from a tree near the kindergarten playground; she stood up and caught it, a little higher than she could normally reach. A third section thought about the summer before second grade, swinging at the park with Don, looking up at a bright blue sky, jumping out of her swing with a heroic pump of her skinny legs at the highest point she had ever dared, and gloriously drifting down to land on her feet while Don crashed, landing on his hands and knees in a pile of faded brown wood chips.

There was more to remember, but she fell asleep.

Lucy could feel her heart pounding with nervous excitement! *Please . . . please let me be able to do it this time,* she said to no one in particular. Maybe she was praying. Yes, she was praying in her heart.

She took a deep breath and kicked off from the ground as hard as her sixteen-year-old Dream legs could and tried to put as much distance as possible between herself and the ground. In just a moment, she was at least twelve feet in the air - and - she - was - actually staying there!

She was looking down on a row of new little crab apple trees with dark green leaves. The long, gray wall to her left had more crumbled patches. There were fewer cars parked along the sides of the curb, but the silver one was there, and she saw it had a dented fender. Across the street, the security gate of the one-story dry cleaner was pulled all the way down, and it was rusty.

The air was warm and still. Her arms were damp from humidity and sweat.

She focused ahead, forward, on the seventh tree; the eighth tree . . . But she was sinking lower and lower with each tree.

In the back of her mind, she thought of the Spider Man movies Claire loved, where he flung himself gracefully through the air, swinging up and down in gigantic arcs high above the city streets. The difference was that she was now only six feet above the sidewalk and wobbling slightly from side to side. She also had no web or anything else to hold on to, and the little trees would never have supported her weight even if she had.

Well, at least I'm not leaving disgusting sticky strings of spider webs everywhere I go.

As she neared the twelfth tree and the corner, having nothing else to mentally grasp, she knew she was done—she would sink for sure. Again.

But at four feet above the ground, she saw another focus point: a beautiful twenty-five-foot-tall chestnut tree with giant green leaves and thick, dark branches reaching out to her from a little park across the street. *That could actually hold me!*

If she could get to it, she wouldn't have to land at all.

With all the strength she had left, which, admittedly, wasn't much, she reached out with her mind and pulled—pulled as hard as she could. Willing herself forward.

She made it two-thirds of the way across the street before the toes of her shoes started scraping the ground. She either had to put her feet down, or land on her face on the cracked, gray street.

Just before she woke up, she could smell the hot asphalt. And freshly baked bread.

Transforming

Lucy did her best not to draw any attention to herself at school for the rest of the week, but it was hard. She noticed so many more things than she ever had before. From the chemical smell of the soap in the restrooms to the tangy flavor of the tartar sauce the lunchroom served with her fish sandwich, everything was *more*. She even caught herself unconsciously scraping her fingernail over the bumpy texture of her plastic chair in English class until the boy next to her looked over at her.

She was fine not answering questions or looking too interested during lectures, but she did have to stop herself from participating in Spanish class. The teacher had paired students up to quiz each other on vocabulary words about traveling. One partner would say the word in English, and the other partner was supposed to say the word in Spanish. So, when Lucy's partner said "airplane," she automatically said, "el avion."

Then two sets of eyes looked at her in astonishment.

That's when Lucy realized that the teacher always, always put Lucy into a "pair" with two other students because no one expected Lucy to say anything.

She sat there for the rest of the exercise just listening. It aggravated her because she knew the answers! Then she was shocked at herself for knowing the answers. And she was even more shocked when one student used a wrong article—*el* instead of *la*—and the other one didn't even *notice*.

This is so annoying!

Then she wiped the expression off her face—whatever it was—when her partners looked at her for no apparent reason.

By the time school ended on Friday, she was exhausted from trying not to react to anything. At all. Even mentally.

Sister Decker was a disciplined housekeeper. On Saturday morning, Lucy found the woman climbing up from a chair onto her counter to clean the plant shelf on top of her cupboards. Lucy immediately ordered her to come down—ordering anyone, let alone an adult, to do anything was another first for her—but the crazy lady insisted she could do it and that she did it all the time. Lucy mentally added that task to the list of things she and her sisters needed to do once in a while for their wonderful-but-somewhat-stubborn neighbor.

"Please," Lucy finally said, "would you be willing to let me do it? Don says I need to practice balancing and . . . being comfortable with heights." That was the best reason she could think of for getting Sister Decker to stay off the counter tops.

"Oh, well, I suppose I could let you, but be careful. I don't want you falling and hurting yourself."

"I promise," was all Lucy said in return. Then she wondered how old her parents were, and how long before they started acting crazy.

"Watch your head," Sister Decker said as Lucy climbed up.

Lucy nodded, nowhere near tall enough to hit her head on anything, even next to the wall where the kitchen ceiling sloped to its lowest point. As she took the soapy sponge and began scrubbing, she noticed there wasn't much to wipe off. That meant Sister Decker really did climb up and do this chore *all the time*. It also meant *once-in-a-while* wouldn't be often enough for the Callaghan girls to do it. Oh well. Claire would probably think it was fun to do.

Sister Decker had begun moving her kitchen chairs in order to sweep and mop under her table, and she and Lucy worked quietly for several minutes. That left Lucy time to work out how to ask the question she had come to ask.

"Sister Decker?" Lucy asked.

"Yes?" she answered as she swept around the back door.

Lucy had to think about how to ask her question. She didn't even know what her question was exactly, so she began by explaining.

"You know that Claire and Don have been helping me learn how to . . . um . . . control my . . . um . . ."

"Your gift?" Sister Decker offered, turning from the sweeping and pointing to an area above her refrigerator. "Underneath that cupboard is tricky. Be careful."

"Yeah," she replied to the woman's remark, taking the hint not to miss that tricky spot. "My *gift*. Well, Don thinks I might be able to, eventually . . . um . . ."

"Fly?" asked Sister Decker, nodding as Lucy wiped the underside of the cupboard.

"Yeah," said Lucy. Talking about this was so strange. Her parents still had a difficult time even acknowledging Lucy's Dreams, let alone the reality of her floating. And here was Sister Decker, tossing out words like *fly* as if it was just a natural part of this life that included making peanut butter cookies and cleaning her kitchen.

That spot under the cupboard actually was hard to get to. She could tell Sister Decker couldn't have reached it because it was the only actual dirty part of the entire kitchen. Lucy had to scrub.

"But, really, what's so useful about flying?" she finally said. "I mean, in my dreams I can work my way down a sidewalk or through a building without touching down, and it's an absolutely amazing thing when I feel like I'm doing it, but it's not a very useful trick. I mean, when I'm awake, I can barely lighten myself when I'm carrying a backpack, so I'm not . . ." She stopped, biting her lip and wrinkling her eyebrows as she scrubbed and thought about the right way to explain her limitations without sounding self-deprecating. "The thing is—it's not like I could rescue someone from a burning building or anything because I can't even carry myself very well."

"Oh, I don't know," Sister Decker said. "It looks like you're carrying yourself pretty well right now." She laughed.

Lucy turned and stood to look at her.

Then she froze.

In reaching for that tricky spot underneath the cupboard, Lucy had stepped off the countertop. She was now standing . . . on nothing . . . three feet above the kitchen floor.

She tried not to panic

      as she gently reached for the edge of the refrigerator

          and slid her feet back onto the counter.

"Wow," she whispered.

"Yeah!" Sister Decker laughed again. "It looks like a terrifically useful trick to me!"

CHAPTER 17

On Pins and Needles

Lucy's unsteady body bobbed in the air. She felt like a helium balloon that had lost some of its life, silently hovering just above eye level in the still air, with four or five inches of its long string coiled loosely on the floor. But there were no strings on Lucy, just long tangles of curly red hair that did not hang—they lazily swirled around her head. She had forgotten to tie her hair up before she went to sleep.

Also like the balloon, she was unable to raise or reorient herself. Only—and she knew this would sound strange—but only by *thinking* heavy would she be able to reluctantly lower herself. Even in that conscious effort, it never felt like she was actually lowering herself. It felt more like she was letting gravity claim her as she let go of the illusive, inconsistent *light* thoughts that let her body suspend itself above her bed.

She never wanted to let go. She never wanted to sink. But no matter how many times she had tried to consciously hold on to this mental effort, no matter how much she tried to figure out the cause-and-effect relationship between her thinking and her altitude—was this the tenth time she had woken up this way?—no matter how she wiggled and moved her arms and legs, she could not move herself forward or backward, left or right, or up. At all. The only option was down, so she just floated there stubbornly. Stuck.

But she had to pee.

The first few times she had woken up and found herself hanging at awkward angles in the air, she immediately crashed back onto the bed, crumpling which ever part of her body hit first. Sometimes it was her right knee or her left elbow, or even her head. She had gotten better at managing a slower descent after kinking her neck one day. Her dad could not stress how dangerous that was and wanted her to wear a neck brace to bed each night, but Lucy promised to be careful. It was still tricky.

This morning, she had woken in a reclined position, as if she had been sitting in a cushy armchair with her legs up on an ottoman—which is exactly what she had been doing in her Dream, watching an old black-and-white Disney cartoon, sitting next to the guy from the Mountain Dew commercial. She wished Claire had never told Don about that guy.

She had somehow drifted to the side of her bed, so, in that position, she had to concentrate very carefully to let herself down. Otherwise, she would crack her tail bone when she fell.

She slowly wobbled herself down to just above the hardwood floor. It happened to be her left shoulder blade that touched down first. She crumbled the last six inches with a loud thud and a pathetic groan.

Ow.

If anyone ever saw all her bumps, bruises, and even one sprained wrist, they would probably call Child Protective Services, which would be bad, so Lucy pushed herself up and made sure today's relatively gentle crash hadn't left any marks.

Nope. All good.

She stood up and looked over at the other bed in the room. It had been neatly made for two weeks now.

Not all good.

Lucy plopped down on her bed.

It had obviously been childish to assume she and Maggie would always share a room. That was before, though, when she didn't think about growing up, or leaving home, or the rest of their lives. But even if she had thought about the realities of life, it wouldn't have occurred to her that Maggie would want to move to her own room while they were both still in high school.

Lucy felt her weight becoming centered in her chest, so she took a long, deep breath to dispel it. It didn't seem fair that she wasn't allowed to be sad without other kinds of realities demanding her responsible attention. She didn't want to have to worry about how sad she was or how happy she was. She didn't want to crash *or* float. She just wanted a normal life! She just wanted her sister back.

The bed creaked.

She wasn't allowed to be angry, either.

That Sunday, Lucy followed Claire as she climbed into the back seat of their dad's silver Audi to go to Mass. Maggie got in from the other side, wearing a scowl. She was cranky because she wanted to drive herself, but Kelly had said, "No, Maggie. You'll be just fine going to Mass with the rest of us."

"Whatever."

"Maggie," their dad said, looking at her in the rear-view mirror.

What was Maggie's problem these days? Lucy could finally see that something was wrong besides being understandably freaked out at Lucy's weirdness. And she realized Claire knew it too, though she hadn't told Lucy what it was. Even Sister Decker knew Maggie was going through some struggles. Sometimes she was nice, like helping Lucy when she crashed. And sometimes she talked like nothing weird had ever happened—like when she would talk, and Lucy would not. But then Lucy would say something that reminded Maggie of all the weirdness, and then she didn't talk to Lucy for days. Those silent drives to and from school were part of what made Lucy so exhausted. Maybe Lucy could call a family meeting, or an intervention of some kind. Maggie's mood soured the ride to church for everyone. Why even bother going?

Except that Lucy liked church.

Maggie was just being dumb.

"Today, forget about weights and stuff, and just put this on." Lucy watched as Don pulled a coat out of his backpack and set the bag back on the high school gym bleachers. She couldn't believe she had agreed to come back to the school on yet another Sunday, but Don said it was the only day there wouldn't be cheerleaders practicing or the marching band tromping around rehearsing formations. She took the coat, which looked lightweight, but felt heavy. "It's not my heaviest coat—it wouldn't fit in my bag—but I put a few rocks in the pockets of this one to make up the difference.

"A few?" Lucy asked as she took the coat and slid her arms into the sleeves. The weight of the thing pulled on her shoulders, and her fingertips didn't even peak out of the cuffs. It wasn't the most comfortable thing to wear in May.

"Okay now, Lucy?" Don said, seeing her sour expression. "You've got to at least try to be in a good mood, so I brought you a surprise." He rummaged through an Asia Food Market shopping bag and pulled out—

"Choco Pies!" Lucy squealed and reached out to take the box, but Don held it out of her reach with his much longer arms.

"Wait. Get back on the scale," he said.

Lucy made a *humph* sound, but she was almost smiling when she stepped back on the scale.

"Just try to lighten yourself even though you're wearing a hot, heavy coat."

Lucy wiggled her shoulders to get an idea of how much that was. "It's got to be, like, twenty pounds!"

"Half that. But don't worry about knowing how much it weighs—that doesn't matter." He handed her one of the individually wrapped Choco Pies.

"I remember your mom used to give us these!" She took it and began pulling open the red cellophane. But when she bit into it, her smile froze—just a little. "Um," she said around the crumbs, "were they always this . . . dry?"

Don bit into the one he had just opened and laughed. "Yeah, I think so. They're shipped all the way from South Korea, so maybe they're a little stale. I guess you don't care about that when you're a kid," he said, shrugging and taking another bite.

Lucy swallowed and looked down at her childhood memory. The little Choco Pie was about three inches in diameter, and the bite she had taken left a perfect semi-circle that showed the layers: two yellow cookies that were more like cakes, white cream in between, all dipped in a layer of chocolate. She nodded and took another bite. "It's still pretty good," she said.

She almost choked on the dry crumbs as she practiced breathing *out - two - three - four . . . in - two - three - four . . .*, but she was able to compensate for the weight of the coat plus— or was it minus—43 pounds. So maybe 56 pounds all together.

She still stayed firmly on the scale, however.

After that, Lucy helped Don lug over some blue foam pads from the gymnastics area and arrange them on the wrestling mat, which was just as stinky as before, leaving a small square space in the center. Don placed the trusty bathroom scale in that space.

"Okay, get on," he said.

"Tell me what I'm doing first." She trusted him, but not completely.

He held up a shiny, silver safety pin. "It's time for you to practice not crashing."

She looked at the pin, then at the padding surrounding the scale, then at Don, but she didn't say anything.

He waved the safety pin in front of her eyes. "It will be fun," he said, as if tempting a toddler into trying a new toy.

Lucy glared at him, but took the pin, already inhaling and exhaling.

"Think happy thoughts," he said as he turned to get his notebook.

Lucy stuck her tongue out at him when he wasn't looking.

"I saw that," Don said, sitting down where he could read the scale.

"I wanted you to," she retorted.

"Okay, whenever you're ready," he said.

"Toss me another Choco Pie, please."

"*Please*, huh? You must be desperate." But he tossed it. "Don't just rely on the sugar, though. Breathe, too."

Lucy nodded, opening the pin to expose the sharp point, "I'm way ahead of you." She kept breathing as she placed the pin against the pad of her left thumb. "But just so you know, I don't think it was just the sugar that helped me with the coat. I mean, Choco Pies aren't that sweet anyway."

"What do you think it was then? Since you're stalling, you might as well tell me." His eyes were on the scale.

She glanced up at him with a slight smile at the corner of her mouth, then back at the pin. "I think it was the memory." She pushed a little bit, so that the pin dimpled the skin without actually puncturing it. "I mean, I don't remember *remembering* Choco Pies before." *In - two -three - four* . . . "But seeing the wrapping, and then smelling the chocolate . . . ?" A little more. She sucked in a breath, then controlled it. For some reason, watching as she pushed the pin into her own skin made it worse than when Don had tricked her that first time, but she breathed . . . *out - two - three - four* . . . And a little whimper escaped her mouth.

"Lucy?" Don was on his feet.

"I'm okay," she said, but there were tears coming from her eyes as she pushed the pin a little more. "I mean . . . it was such a great memory." She held the pin where it was, not pushing, but not pulling it out. "And it was really great," she said, crying for real, "having a friend."

Then she sobbed and pulled the pin out just before she dropped onto the foam pads.

CHAPTER 18

Being a Teenager Is Exhausting

Another week went by. Another week of riding to school with Maggie, of avoiding eye contact with other students, of not participating in class. Another week of doing homework, which was too easy, and of practicing with Don, which was too hard. Another week of reassuring her dad, and of not understanding Kelly—her mom. Seeing her mom—Kelly—as two different people was no big deal before; but now it was starting to bug her, and that was an entire issue all by itself.

Lucy didn't realize she had sighed, but Claire noticed.

"How come you're always so tired?" Claire asked the next Saturday morning as she buttered her blueberry waffle.

"Um . . ." That was a great question, but Lucy was never sure how much to share with Claire. She was so much easier to talk to than anyone else in the family, or in her life, for that matter, that it was easy to forget she was only eleven years old. "I think the weirdness makes me tired. If I totally, you know, crash . . . I can't seem to get enough sleep for days. And even when I just get heavy? Like when I cut my finger?" She looked at Claire, who nodded to indicate she remembered while getting butter into every square of her waffle. "I feel really tired after those times, too. Just not as bad."

"But you said you've been crashing less since Don has been helping you." Claire spoke about everything like it was perfectly normal. Lucy still felt weird every time.

"Yeah. I think it's helped a lot."

"But you're still so tired."

"Well, sometimes I don't sleep very well."

"Even though you're so tired? That doesn't make sense."

"I know. I think my dreams have something to do with it, too."

"Are you having nightmares?"

"Not really." Some were disturbing, but that wasn't the point. "They aren't bad things, just random. But it's like . . ." How could she explain something like this? She didn't even know what to call the things she saw. "Before I fall asleep, and my eyes are closed? I see things."

"Oh, me too!" Claire said.

Lucy could see the hope in her little sister's eyes and hear it in her voice. She wanted to be able to float someday, too. Who knew? Maybe she would. But Lucy was curious, so she had to ask, "What do you see when you close your eyes to fall asleep?"

Claire closed her eyes tightly and tilted her head slightly to the right, as if she were squinting into the dark to see her dream. "I always see a long room with a low ceiling, orange walls, and smelly brown shag carpet. There's a gray leather recliner and an old television set, and cartoon animals are walking around like people."

Claire had Lucy's attention—up until the cartoon animals. "Mm-hmm," she said, with her lips pursed together. In the back of her mind, she realized she probably looked like their dad at that moment. "Sorry, Claire, but I don't think it's quite the same thing."

"The same thing as what?"

"Nothing," she said. They were like . . . scenes . . . behind her eyelids. Scenes from a movie, except she was in the movie. And when it was one of her real Dreams, the movies were mostly reruns. Over and over. When she closed her eyes, but before she was asleep, the colors and lights behind her eyelids swirled and morphed into images, detailed scenes. But she didn't want to talk about it, so she rattled the new box of Froot Loops she had just pulled out of the cupboard. "There's a puzzle or something on the back. Wanna do it?"

Claire scoffed at the idea and told Lucy in no uncertain terms, "I am waaaay too old for cereal box puzzles." But she grabbed the box anyway, pulled opened the sealed bag inside, and released the unique lemony scent of the cereal, or dusting spray; they smelled very similar. Then she poured herself a bowl and sat down to find the clues to the riddle printed at the bottom.

But Lucy's mind was still on those scenes, and the way the light behind her eyes continuously danced and swirled like liquid clouds, blossoming from inside themselves for a while, then suddenly turning into clearly defined images and solid colors: mountains, houses, streets, faces, or even waffles. She would be able to feel the steam from the waffle iron; smell the hot, eggy scent; see the butter scraped across the warm, crusty surface as she pushed it around, like Claire did, so it would melt and seep into every little square. Finally, she would taste the sweet, almost-burnt flavor of the waffle, drenched in real maple syrup that squeezed out of the waffle as she closed her lips and pressed the morsel to the roof of her mouth with her tongue.

That's when she would know it was not just a dream—that it was somehow the more-real world she lived in sometimes. Those vivid smells, tastes, and uniquely tangible sensations always gave it away. Her regular dreams, the ones that might feature cartoon animals walking around and other silly things, were only sights and sounds that were fuzzy around the edges. Whereas her—what? She always just thought of them as her *true* dreams. They were more like visions, though she was not going to call them that because it sounded way too ridiculous. They were more like events. Sleep events. Her sleep events always included all her senses: sights, sounds, smells, tastes, and feelings that were so much more vivid than their waking equivalents. They gave her an awareness of the world that extended beyond what she was experiencing at any moment. They were large. And something else too. There was always a feeling of significance, often mingled with urgency, and sometimes joy, when she could fly—often frustration when she couldn't.

There were four or five of these events that repeated themselves from time to time, like television reruns, and the details stayed impressed on her mind.

The first real dream she could remember was one in which she was running after someone . . . someone who was leaving, and she chased him and wanted to stop him from leaving. She didn't want to be left behind. But her legs were heavy and hard to move, and she tripped on the edge of a rug—a big, old area rug made of multi-colored strips of fabric woven in a coil. She would always fall right on top of that rug, face down, arms and legs sprawled out, feeling the thin, ragged texture and smelling the dry dust and dirt that puffed up and made her cough as she looked up. She always looked up. And she always saw just his heel disappear as he walked out and closed the door. She didn't know who he was. Her face was always wet and sticky, and her tears salty.

She had a Dream before she was even five years old about floating around her house, and it still showed up once in a while. Her sidewalk flight with the smell of asphalt and bread reran in her head more often. Sometimes she Dreamed about floating over the rose bushes to Don's house in the dark. And her newest Dream featured large, black-and-white ceramic tiles set in a diagonal checkerboard pattern in a cold hallway that smelled like ammonia.

It didn't seem to matter what the Dream was about, however. They were all such long and vivid dreams that she often felt like she'd been awake all night.

She was always tired.

CHAPTER 19

Grades

She managed it. For the next three weeks, Lucy managed not to crash during school. She felt heavy when she walked right into another girl as she turned a corner, and they both dropped their books . . . and binders . . . and pencils . . . and purses, but the girl was nice about it, so nothing bad happened. Also, her bathroom scale showed she had gained about eighty-seven pounds for the few days she was on her period, and she felt absolutely certain everyone at school could tell it was *that time of the month*, but all she had to do was avoid Don so he couldn't weigh her. She was still not having that conversation with him. And she actually did pinch her finger in her locker one day, but it only hurt without making her feel heavy at all. Lucy decided she had earned an A in finishing her sophomore year without crashing again. That's all she'd been hoping for.

She changed that grade into an A+ when her art teacher used Lucy's charcoal drawing as a good example of chiaroscuro—using bright light and dark shadows—and the depiction of movement. It was a drawing of the swing set at the park by her house, at night, with a halo of light from the tall lamp, and some blades of grass bent in the slight breeze. Lucy hadn't thought it was a particularly interesting subject for a drawing, but it was the best she could think of to fulfill the requirement of the assignment. The teacher had pinned Lucy's artwork to the front board, and Lucy looked at it critically from where she sat at her table in the back of the room. As the teacher spoke, Lucy could see that it did show light and dark contrast. It did show movement. And it was kind of interesting, at least to her. And she could see, though it was strange to believe, that it really was good. It was . . . art.

That's when she felt herself get light. It was the lightest she'd felt at any time during school. She liked the feeling. It was more than happy. Or at least different. It was a warm and quiet feeling, but it also filled her up. It was big. She was glad she could use her drawing table to hold herself firmly to the tall stool she was sitting on, because whatever that feeling was called, it was accompanied by a strong sensation of sliding upward.

As she held herself down, she noticed the ends of her hair lifting up like little curly orange snakes.

That was new.

At least, she thought that was new. She'd never paid attention to what her hair was doing when she floated before. She'd have to think about that. But later.

For now, she simply tried to—discretely—push her hair down with her other hand. By the time she did that, however, the joyous feeling was gone. Her hair calmed down all by itself, and her butt had no problem staying put in her seat while the teacher talked about other students' drawings.

Chiaroscuro, indeed.

Light and dark.

Up and down.

Joy and despair, as she once again imagined all the possible terrible scenarios that could play out unexpectedly at any time, at any place, in her life.

Then the stupid stool she was sitting on creaked, and she had to do her stupid breathing. That made her think of Don and Claire, which made her feel glad she had them, which helped her weight shift back into the normal range.

The bell rang, ending the class, the day, and most importantly, the school year. Lucy hopped down onto the solid concrete floor. She packed up her stuff and walked out the door. She had been frustrated, but she didn't crash. For her, that was the most important lesson of all.

Academically, all three Callaghan girls had done well that year. Maggie had finished her junior year with straight As, as usual. She was grouchy, though, because her second SAT score still wasn't quite good enough to get into Yale University, where she wanted to study Law. She was already studying to take the test a third time in August.

Claire, who had skipped a grade when she was seven years old, had also gotten all As with very little effort. Plus, her science fair project had won first place at her school as well as in the county. She had only gotten second place in the regional fair because, she said, "there was another smart kid there who knew what he was doing." She'd also begun exchanging actual letters with that kid, a boy who lived about an hour and a half away in Canandaigua, since neither of their parents let them have cell phones.

Lucy had gotten an A in art class, along with the comment, "has great artistic potential."

CHAPTER 20

An Invitation

"You have to come," Lucy said in a matter-of-fact voice that verged on the edge of whining.

"The thing is," answered Don, his back to her as he typed away on his computer, "I really don't."

"But my parents said Maggie can't go unless she takes me with her, which turns *me* into a torturous kind of punishment for her being out late with her boyfriend, Caleb, which does not feel good and makes absolutely no sense."

"Makes total sense," Don said, still typing. How could he type and listen and talk at the same time?

"How? How does taking me to a party I don't want to go to make any sense?"

Don swiveled around looking her in the eyes. "Because the fact is: Maggie has always watched out for you. If you're there, then she'll watch out for you, and she won't come home late or do anything stupid with Caleb."

"Stupid with Ca—" Lucy stopped, mid-sentence. "*Eww*! You mean. . .?"

"Probably not if you're there," Don said, swiveling back around to his laptop.

"*EWW!* No way! Maggie would never do that!"

Don just shook his head a little and kept typing.

"No, Don," Lucy said in as serious and calm a voice as she could manage. "I know Maggie. She wouldn't."

Don kept typing.

"At least. . ." She thought about it for a minute and shuddered. "Anyway, I don't believe she would, but that's not the point anyway. The point is I need you there."

Don stopped typing and turned around. "Why?"

Lucy scrunched her eyes shut when she couldn't think of a good reason.

"That's what I thought," said Don, then started to turn back around.

"Well, okay, I guess I don't *need* you to come, but I want you to come. Please? Will you please go to this stupid party with me, Don?"

Don stopped mid-swivel and looked at her with what might have been a smirk. "See? All you had to do was ask nicely. Yes, Lucy I will go wi—"

He was interrupted by a flying Death Star pillow.

CHAPTER 21

The Party

Lucy assumed it was Caleb's house that Maggie was pulling up to, but they weren't even in a regular neighborhood; there was only one big house in the middle of the woods. It had three stories, was made of huge gray and brown stones with natural wood trim, and shone with about a hundred windows that glowed a soft, fuzzy gold from inside. Just the lighted windows of Caleb's house added up to more than ten times the windows in her house, which had fourteen, total, spread among four sides of two floors. And she had no idea why she was thinking about windows and math right now. The point was, she had never been to such a big house. Her world had always been just *her* world. And it was small. It never included all the other kids at school, even though she was around them every day. It never included big, fancy houses, even though her mother drove her past them all the time. And it never included feeling nervous. About anything.

That was because she had never known what there was to be afraid of. She had never had to worry about crashing in front of people. That is, not until stupid gym class showed her exactly how easy it would be to trip over a stupid volleyball rope and crash on the stupid gym floor. What would she do if she *did* crash? Here, with all these kids from school, and in this strange place? Sure, Maggie had promised to watch out for her, but Maggie hadn't even wanted Lucy to come.

Why, again, had Lucy agreed to this? For social practice? Why would Lucy need to practice going to parties at strange houses? This was a bad idea.

The car seat creaked, and Maggie shot her a look, so Lucy acted like she'd just been shifting in her seat to look around at all the cars.

She tried to relax, to breathe, but Don's spicy cologne had been wafting from the back seat to the front seat during the entire drive, leaving very little room for oxygen in the car. At least he was there. Lucy was so glad he had been willing to come. He would make sure she was okay.

She relaxed her neck and shoulders. Everything would be fine as long as no one was playing volleyball.

Maggie parked near the entrance to the large circular driveway lined with potted trees—very big trees in very big pots—and took off her glasses. She looked in her visor mirror, rubbed her nose where the glasses had rested, ran her fingers though her long, glossy black hair, checked her earrings, put fresh lip gloss on over her old lip gloss, made a little pucker, gave a nod of approval, then looked over at Lucy.

Her approval disappeared.

"Ready?" she asked. Not a hint of a smile.

Lucy looked in her own visor mirror. She didn't have nose dents from glasses, and freckles couldn't be rubbed away; she would never be able run her fingers through her frizzy hair, she wasn't wearing any jewelry, and she didn't even own any lip gloss. Claire had just said to go, watch the other kids, and do what they did. She never mentioned lip gloss. Oh well. She flipped her visor up and nodded at Maggie.

Maggie shook her head with a medium eyeroll and handed Lucy the lip gloss.

It was a glass tube with red strawberries printed on it. Lucy unscrewed the top and ran the rollerball over her lips. It smelled delicious! She licked her lips, then licked them again when she realized it was sweet.

"Don't eat it all off," Maggie said.

Lucy nodded, put some more on, and handed the tube back to Maggie. She tried not to lick the flavored oil off as she got out of the car.

Don had already climbed out of the back seat and was staring at some of the cars parked around the house. His body made a complete circle as his eyes moved from one to the next. Lucy knew Don liked *nice* cars, but she didn't really know what a *nice* car was. Maybe the blue ones? He liked blue.

Lucy felt the music coming from the back of the house as much as she heard it. It was loud, even from across the front lawn and two-thirds of the way around the drive, but the booming felt thick. Almost tangible. It filled the empty air with motion and made the darkness feel tight. She almost couldn't breathe and started to turn around to go back to the car.

Then she looked up.

Cool air rushed into her lungs as she silently gasped, immediately released from the squeezing pressure of the music. The clear night sky was filled with stars. So many stars. So much sky. And across the black expanse, a gauzy path of light stretched from the silhouetted treetops on her right to the silhouetted treetops on her left. She was transfixed. She was experiencing another emotion. Not only did she have absolutely no word for this feeling, she couldn't even have said why she felt it. She felt small. And weak. And sad? No. She wasn't sad. She was enormously happy, even though she could feel her eyes filling with tears. And the tears somehow made the gauzy path, and the stars, and the cool air in her lungs . . . clearer. She thought she might have started floating if Maggie hadn't yanked on her arm and brought her attention back to Earth.

"Come on," Maggie said, turning back toward the house.

"Maggie?" Lucy asked, as she tried to look back up at the stars and look where she was going at the same time.

"What?" Maggie grumped as she marched ahead.

"I know that's the Milky Way, but I thought you could only see it in a picture or on television or in Canada or something."

She looked up again and imagined falling upward into those beautiful points of light. But she tripped and fell instead, onto the lip of a pebbled path that led around the side of the house.

Maggie spun around when she heard the accompanying "oof" and the scattering noise of pebbles being shoved out of their carefully manicured boundary. Lucy looked up, and for brief moment, though she might have imagined it, Maggie looked like their dad did when one of his girls was hurt. Lucy wondered if that look meant she felt concerned. Maggie bent down and helped her up, brushing the gravel from Lucy's palms. Then the look was gone and, that quickly, Maggie was shaking her head again.

"Thanks," Lucy said.

Maggie didn't roll her eyes, but she didn't say anything as she turned around, wiping the gravel off of her own hands.

Don stood there with his hands in his pockets. So maybe he wasn't going to help her tonight after all.

"That's the aurora borealis," he said.

"What?" Lucy said. She pushed her hair out of her face and followed Maggie through an open gate and onto a back deck. It was lit by tall bamboo tiki torches and thousands of twinkle lights draped in strands across a space that was the size of a tennis court. Just three steps in, however, Maggie stopped, and Lucy saw her sister stiffen, just the tiniest bit.

"The aurora borealis," Don said again. "They're called the 'northern lights' because you can only see them from northern latitudes, not just from Canada because," he pointed northward, "Canada's only about a hundred sixty miles that way, in the middle of Lake Ontario."

"Huh?" said Lucy, but she was looking at Maggie, who was looking at a guy whose back was turned to them. The guy was standing next to the bar with his left arm draped casually over the shoulders of a blond girl who was looking up at him and laughing.

Maggie squinted, examining the scene. Then her shoulders relaxed, her fists uncurled, and she walked over to the couple. Don and Lucy followed.

"But you can sometimes see them from Upstate New York," Don continued, "at certain times of the year. There's not as much light pollution, which is why we can see the Milky Way so well from here."

"Hi!" Maggie practically sang, turning "hi" into a two-syllable word and smiling her smile.

"Well, not *here* here. There's too much light back *here*," Don corrected.

That smile. That big, bright smile that shone out of Maggie's big blue, mascara-clumped eyes. How did she do that? How could one person feel so much, so strongly, so suddenly? First angry, then maybe concerned, then angry, then happy. It must be exhausting. Claire said Maggie wasn't very happy these days. Maybe she used up all her happy feelings around this guy and was too tired to be happy when she was at home. Lucy felt tired just watching her.

"Hi!" The guy said, smiling like a suntan lotion commercial, but with a freshly sprouted pimple on the side of his nose. Lucy couldn't stop staring at it. He probably hadn't realized it was there or he would have gone into the house to pop it. But even with that thing on his face—*yuck*, she couldn't even look at it—he was really cute. He turned from the blond girl and wrapped both arms around Maggie and kind of rocked back and forth. He looked like a very tall child hugging a proportionately sized teddy bear. "Who's this?" the guy asked, looking at Lucy and Don.

Still smiling, but fractionally less, Maggie turned, gesturing to her followers. "This is my sister Lucy."

"Hey, Lucy." Caleb said, raising his left hand. It was resting at the end of his long arm, which was now around Maggie's shoulder, as he waved. Kind of. It was more of a flicker than a wave.

"Hi," Lucy answered back, trying to be shiny and smiley like Maggie. She'd even tried to stretch out her "hi" into two syllables.

It must not have had the same effect. Caleb raised his eyebrows and glanced at Maggie, who shrugged and rolled her eyes again.

"Uh," he said, eyebrows still raised, "this is my little sister, Naomi."

"Hey," Naomi flick-waved with her left hand, nodding her head just a little. She looked just like Caleb. Same perfect tan, same brown eyes, same puffy mouth, and same dimples. But no pimple. Lucy thought Naomi was younger than her but older than Claire, so she could have been anywhere between eleven and sixteen. She was taller than Maggie, but that wasn't saying much. She was shorter than Don and Caleb, but that also wasn't saying much because they were both tall, though not as tall as her dad. A part of Lucy's mind noticed, for the first time, that Don wasn't short anymore, which was weird.

Naomi had a kind of grown-up look, like she wasn't really paying attention to them, like they were children. Then she glanced at Don, and her face went red as she looked down, then peeked back up at him through extra-extra-long lashes that weren't all clumpy like Maggie's.

"This is Don," was all Maggie said.

Don smiled, Caleb nodded, and Naomi looked back down and turned even more red.

"C'mon," Maggie said, pulling Caleb away from them. "Let's go get a drink."

"There's only soda here, so we'll have to go inside to get something good," Caleb said.

"I meant a Coke, dummy." Maggie's voice trailed off as they walked away.

That left the other three standing there: Don smiling at Naomi, Naomi looking down and biting the nail on her left ring finger, and Lucy, staring at the two of them.

For about seventeen hours.

Or maybe seventeen seconds, but it felt like seventeen hours while they stood there. Blinking.

Don was the first to talk, which was good because it wasn't going to be Lucy, and Naomi had only moved on to the nail on her pinkie finger.

"So . . ." he said.

The two girls both looked at him.

"What grade are you in?" he asked Naomi.

She took her finger away from her mouth long enough to say, "I just finished tenth."

Lucy was wrong. She was her own age.

"Oh! So . . . what school do you go to?" Don asked politely.

Her eyes kind of darted around like she wasn't sure what the answer was before she answered, "Moore?" Or maybe she was asking. She didn't seem certain.

"Wait—what?" Don asked.

Lucy had heard her just fine. Why hadn't he?

"I go to Paul V. Moore High School. I'm in your grade," Naomi clarified.

"So how come I've never seen you?" He was kind of scowling.

Naomi shrugged then switched hands. Right ring finger now.

"Well, I'm Tan Hyun-Shik. People call me Don." Then he held out his hand.

That's right. He - held - out - his - hand.

She giggled, took her finger out of her mouth, and shook his hand. That didn't seem sanitary. "I know," she said.

Lucy might as well have been back behind her glass.

"You guys want a Coke?" she offered, pointing at the bar behind her.

"Sure, thanks!" Don laughed.

Yeah. He laughed. He laughed at being offered a Coke. And Naomi's face got even redder. And then they both turned and walked to the other end of the counter.

"You coming?" Don turned back and called.

So, Lucy followed.

Two hours later—or maybe it was three—Lucy was sitting in the middle of a wicker sofa thing. Don and Naomi were sitting across from her in wicker chairs, talking about some movie. Lucy had actually seen the movie, but that was before she paid attention to the real world, so she didn't have anything to say about it. In fact, she barely remembered anything about it except the ending, when the blond princess jumped out of a window. Her long, silvery blue dress ruffled in the wind as she slowly fell, then she was caught by a big guy with a hairy face.

Lucy's Coke was long gone, and her empty cup sat on the low wicker table that was between her and Don and Naomi. The music was louder now, though she had gotten used to it, and more kids were there, but no one was paying attention to her. Everyone was drinking and laughing. Some kids were drinking and laughing around the pool, and some were drinking and laughing *in* the pool. Some people were drinking and laughing in the house, and some people were drinking and laughing on *top* of the house. No wait. That was just a balcony. So, except for the spot next to Lucy on the seat, the entire place was crowded with drinking, laughing people.

She had no idea if Caleb's parents were home, but even though he'd said there was only soda at the bar, several kids had obviously brought alcohol. Lucy just watched; they looked so stupid. She laid her head back once in a while to look up at the sky, but she couldn't see the stars anymore—only blackness.

She sat up when she heard Maggie's voice. Maggie was over by the bar again, talking and holding Caleb's hand. He looked over then, saw Lucy, and started pulling Maggie her way. They had to weave through clumps of people to get to her, and Maggie steadied Caleb when he stumbled around a potted plant. He somehow managed not to drop his red plastic cup.

When they finally made it over, Caleb bumped the table with his leg, and Don and Naomi had to move their feet. He plopped down next to Lucy so hard that the cushion she was sitting on bounced her up a few inches and his drink splashed a little on her left leg.

"Good! Now that you're sitting down, I'm going to go get another drink," Maggie laughed.

"Um, Maggie?" Don said as she was turning. She turned back, still smiling, but it was a hard smile. A cold smile. She just raised her eyebrows at him.

"Uh," he started. "I don't have my license with me, you know?"

The smile dropped from her face completely. "Relax, Don. I'm just getting another Coke."

He nodded and turned back to Naomi, whose eyes were darting back and forth between Maggie and Don, and her brother, who was sniffing his armpits.

Lucy scooted over to the arm rest.

"Wanna go get something to eat?" Don asked Naomi. Lucy felt her eyeballs nearly pop out of her skull. He was going to leave her here? Before she could even think about whether he would ask her if she was hungry too, Naomi literally bounced up out of her chair.

"Sure!" she said, automatically flipping her hair over her shoulder and turning to go. Don was right behind her. Without even a glance back at Lucy.

Right. Some friend. She was starving *and* thirsty, but there was no way she was going all by herself to where the food and drinks were. Now what was she supposed to do?

Before she was done even thinking that thought, a guy with dark wavy hair that was trying to hide kind of big ears sat down where Don had been sitting. He was holding two red plastic cups. "Hey, Caleb!" he shouted, a little more loudly than necessary over the noise.

Lucy looked over. Caleb was zonked out.

"Caleb!" the guy shouted again. When Caleb didn't move, the guy looked at Lucy and shrugged. "I guess he's out. Want a drink?" he said in a normal voice, holding one of the cups out to Lucy.

She looked at the guy, then looked at the cup, then looked back at the guy. He was smiling.

"It's okay. It's just strawberry wine. I thought Naomi might want it, but she just left. I only brought it in the first place because Mariah likes it, but she's not here because her mom's having a baby or something." He leaned forward in a mock whisper. "They already have like five kids, but I guess it's still kind of a big deal to them." He laughed. Lucy couldn't tell if he really thought it was funny or if he was making a joke. She knew she and Maggie wouldn't be here if their mom was having a baby, but they only had three kids.

"Really," the guy gestured with the drink, "you can have it. He's not going to drink it." He nodded toward Caleb.

Lucy had only ever had wine at communion, and that was barely even a sip each time, but she was thirsty. And strawberry sounded good, so she leaned forward and took it. "Thanks," she said. She tried to smile, but it felt weird. "Who's Mariah?"

"No problem," the guy laughed. Had she smiled wrong? "Mariah is—well she's—a girl." He shook his head and sat back.

"Anyway, I'm Jonah, Caleb's not-so-handsome-or-athletic-or-smart cousin."

He laughed again. Was she supposed to laugh at him calling himself not handsome or athletic or smart? It was true he wasn't as good-looking as . . . well . . . Caleb, but he looked okay, even with his kind-of-big ears. Plus, he was nice. Lucy didn't think of Caleb as nice at all. But she didn't know what else to say, so she just said, "I'm Lucy. Thanks." Then she realized she had already said thanks, so she sniffed the light red liquid in her cup.

It smelled like really sweet strawberries, the perfectly ripe ones you could only get during the summer, so she took a drink. Then she nearly choked. It was definitely very strawberry-y. Strawberry-ish? But also, wine-tasting. And not sweet—at *all*. She wanted a drink of water. Or a piece of bread. Or maybe even a carrot—that was the first thing she could think of—anything to scrub the taste out of her mouth.

"Do you like it?" Jonah, asked, waiting for a response.

"Mm-hmm." She lied, trying to turn her reaction into a smile, holding her breath, and swallowing the lingering traces in her mouth.

Jonah laughed, "It's okay. Not everyone likes it, but Mariah hates beer. Do you want me to get you one, though?" He started to stand up.

"No—don't worry!" She had smelled beer before, and beer didn't even *smell* good! There was no way she going to put *that* in her mouth. "I like this," she said, holding up her cup. And to prove it, she took another drink. It still smelled really sweet and still really wasn't, which was super confusing to her brain, but at least she wasn't shocked this time and could give a better smile. She hoped.

Jonah looked at her but didn't say anything. He was smiling a little with one side of his mouth. She wished Claire were there to translate. She never used to notice all the expressions that constantly flash across people's faces. She knew her family. She knew their looks. And even though she couldn't have named them, she knew what to expect when her dad squinted, when her mom brought her head up in a certain way, or when Maggie huffed. But what did half of a smile mean on this guy? Was he laughing at her? Kids had laughed at her a lot in her life, and it never bothered her before—and it only confused her now. Like at this moment.

"So—Lucy, right?" he asked.

She nodded.

"So, Lucy, how old are you?"

"Sixteen."

"Really?" His eyebrows came together. "So, you're going to be a junior?"

She nodded and took another drink to avoid his eyes, but she saw him frown. He took a breath like he was going to say something, but Maggie walked up at that moment.

"Hey, Lucy," she said, stepping over Caleb's sprawled legs. "I was talking to Abbie and didn't get anything to eat. Will you hold this, and I'll bring you something when I get back?" She seemed more relaxed than she had been before. Even when she looked at Caleb and rolled her eyes, she wasn't really bugged. She even had her real smile on when she dug through the keys, mascara, perfume, hairbrush, travel-size antiperspirant, gum, money, and driver's license in her sparkly purple purse to find some lip gloss, which she took out before she handed the bag to Lucy. It was heavy. Then Maggie turned and left without another word.

"Wait—" Jonah looked back and forth between the retreating Maggie and Lucy. "You're Maggie Callaghan's sister?"

Lucy nodded, smashing Maggie's bag between her leg and the arm of the wicker seat. The bag was not little, but she didn't want to scoot any closer to Caleb, so a fair amount of actual smashing was required.

Jonah's mouth was open, and his eyes darted around a bit, as if trying to figure something out. "So, she's your sister?" he asked again.

Lucy nodded again. This was weird. She took another drink of the wine. It wasn't so bad.

"Then how come I've never seen you around?"

Oh dear. She couldn't exactly tell him this was her first time going anywhere besides school, or Mass, or Walmart. "Uh." She drank the rest of her wine, stalling. "Maggie and me . . . she's a great sister," she used to be, so that was mostly true, "but we are . . . well, we like different things."

"So, what do *you* like?"

What did she like? That was a funny question. What *did* she like? She laughed out loud. "I really have no idea!"

Jonah laughed, too. He was definitely laughing with her, not at her. "Well, you seem to like strawberry wine. Here, have mine. I really don't drink much."

"Thanks! I really do like it!" she laughed, taking the cup and another drink.

"Wow, you have a great laugh. You really aren't like Maggie at all." His kind-of-big ears really didn't matter. He had a really nice smile.

"What do you mean?" His teeth were like pieces of gum—the white gum that looked like Chiclets but tasted better even though they were sugar-free. She really did like this strawberry wine.

Jonah shook his head. "Maggie never lets herself just laugh. It's like she's there, but she's always kind of distant. Like she's behind a piece of glass."

Lucy almost spit out her wine she started laughing so hard.

"Whoa!" Jonah said.

Lucy's nose stung, as if some of the liquid had gone up into her sinuses when she nearly choked. But she couldn't stop laughing and she felt—

"Lucy!" Maggie yelled, suddenly there, kicking Caleb's feet off the wicker table and grabbing Lucy's arm at the same time Jonah said, "What the—?"

"Hey!" Lucy laughed, spilling some of her drink on the ground.

"Come on!" Maggie grabbed her bag and pulled Lucy behind her through the laughing and drinking kids. She made a detour around one of the big potted trees to grab Don on the way. "We're leaving," she ordered.

"Hey!" he shouted, as he was forcefully yanked away from Naomi and shoved toward the gate. "What's going on?"

"I just remembered," Maggie said, bulging her eyes out at Don, "Lucy is allergic to parties."

"What do you m—" he started, then took a good look at Lucy, who was smiling, still holding her red plastic cup as she followed Maggie, her left foot hardly touching the ground when she stepped. She looked like she was riding a tiny, invisible skateboard, pushing with her right foot. "Oh."

"Yeah," Maggie said, pulling Lucy to the car.

Don grabbed the cup and smelled it.

"Hey!" Lucy protested.

"I think it's wine," Don whispered, tossing the cup into the bushes.

"Great," Maggie grunted, as she yanked open the door of the car and shoved Lucy into the front seat. Lucy squeaked at the rough treatment, but Maggie slammed the door just then, so she probably didn't hear her.

Don was already in the back seat, buckling up, by the time Maggie got in and started the car. "Who gave her the wine?" he asked as she backed up and squealed away.

"Gee," she said, "I don't know. You were there with her the last time I saw her." She glared at him in the rear-view mirror.

"Hey, guys?" Lucy said.

"I didn't give it to her! Your boyfriend was with her when Naomi and I went to get some food!"

Wow. Don was shouting at Maggie. That was weird.

"Hey, guys?" Lucy said again, a little louder.

"I am in so much trouble," Maggie said, then swore.

Had Lucy done something wrong again?

In the Car

Lucy didn't think Maggie even blinked as she glared straight ahead at the road. When a misty New York rain started depositing minuscule droplets of water on the windshield, she flipped on the wipers with a jerk. Don was tapping his leg to some song in his head, trying to distract himself from the tension between the sisters. His internal music must have needed something more because he soon started making rhythmic popping bubble sounds with his lips. When the mist turned into actual raindrops a few minutes later, he started flicking his index finger against his cheek, making that weird dripping sound. Lucy could never figure out how—

"Don!" Maggie snapped.

He stopped. Immediately. She still intimidated him, after all these years. Even when she was a jerk to him.

"What?!" She snapped again. But it was at Lucy this time. Maggie kept looking at her with that look. The one Lucy saw her use with their parents when she came home too late, or when they wanted her to help Sister Decker. It was like a challenge. A dare. A defiance. Claire said she thought she just wanted them to pay attention to her. Lucy didn't think that was it.

"Lucy! What is your problem?"

Lucy shrugged.

"Well quit shaking your head."

She didn't know she had been.

"You know, you've really got to get a hold of—" She stopped abruptly. Don was there, just tapping his foot now. Maybe he had to go to the bathroom. Anyway, she must not have wanted to say anything in front of him even though she knew he knew Lucy's problem.

Maggie huffed and turned the wipers up a notch. "Please, Luce, whatever you do, don't say anything. Don't tell us how much you had to drink or what happened." She started getting louder. "Please don't explain. Please don't say a word!"

"Maggie," Don said in his quiet way.

She held up her hand, stopping whatever he was going to say next.

"Why are you . . . What did I do wrong?" Lucy asked.

Maggie's jaw dropped. "What did you do *wrong*?" she said. It wasn't a question though. It was a demand.

Lucy held up her hands, palms up. What was the problem? "I didn't crash. I know I didn't. I felt fine." Then she wondered, "Did I?" Maybe she had. Had she blacked out? She hadn't tripped or hurt herself. She didn't remember feeling sick.

"Crash?!" Maggie shouted. Lucy wished she wouldn't shout. It just confused her more. "Crashing wasn't the problem! You started—" Maggie wafted her right hand up in a swooping motion.

"I floated?!" Lucy gasped. How? When?

"You started to!" She shot back with a loud huff. Could a huff be loud? Hers was. "It was a good thing Caleb had his eyes closed—at least he did when I got there—but you were definitely starting . . . that direction! How much did you drink? I wasn't even gone that long!"

Maggie kept talking and asking questions, but Lucy didn't say anything. She didn't even know what to say. Maggie was yelling, and it made Lucy's mind even more confused than it already was. What had she done wrong? Maggie left. Don left. That kid Jonah came, and he was nice. Wasn't he? Was he nice? She remembered laughing, but at what?

There were too many questions and confusions. Her mind was always distracted by its own regular, everyday thoughts, so how could she sort through what happened at the party? What was wrong with her? And even though the glass between Lucy and the world had been shattered when her parents stopped drugging her, she still didn't know what to say to the world. She didn't even know what to say to her own sister. How does a person even begin to communicate all of their thoughts? How can you even put them in order? Lucy's thoughts were a giant tangle, like the ribbons in Claire's craft drawer. They were impossible to get straight. It was too much.

Then the world screamed as the front of the car hit something, the back end swung around, and they began to spin in circles on the wet road. Lucy's head smacked against the door window and glass sprayed everywhere. Don was yelling something, but then everything went black.

Lucy was aware of three things: cold water hitting her face, annoyance at a really loud sound, and a stomachache.

"Lucy! LUCY!"

It was Don. He was yelling, but Lucy couldn't tell where he was. She turned toward his voice.

"No! No, don't move!" he yelled. His voice was shaking. There was water. It was so cold. And her hair was in her face. She went to move it out of her eyes so she could see better.

"No! Lucy! Seriously. Do - not - move!"

Her mind cleared, but the sound didn't stop. It was the car horn.

Lucy looked over at Maggie, who was slumped against the steering wheel. Nothing made sense. Lucy was crunched up against the dashboard, right foot soaking in a puddle of water near the door. Rain was falling lightly but steadily on her right shoulder and back.

"Lucy! Listen!" Don yelled above the horn. Lucy started to look at him. Her stomach felt like there was a boulder in it.

"No! Don't move! Please," he said in a quieter voice now. His voice. "Just listen, Luce, okay?"

"Okay." She saw her breath in the cold air.

"Everything will be fine, but you need to hold still and listen."

"Okay." He was scaring her. The car tipped forward then. Just a little, but the movement made her stomach lurch, and before she could ask what was going on, she doubled over and vomited a strawberry-flavored mess of red puke all over her shoes. She closed her eyes as her stomach emptied itself. Even when it was out of wine, her stomach kept spasming, and the strawberry taste was replaced by bitter bile. She groaned as the car kept wobbling, the horn screaming the entire time, making everything worse. After what seemed like an eternity, her exhausted body relaxed, completely empty of all her internal organs, and the car stopped wobbling. She coughed and spat out the remaining taste, then wiped her mouth. Her stomach felt better, but she wanted to cry. In fact, she started to do just that.

"Lucy," Don said over the sound of the horn. "Can you relax? And take a breath?"

The gym. That's what she had been practicing in the gym. She tried to relax. It was hard with the rain, and the cold, and the horn, and Maggie . . . was she alive?

"Lucy, please." He didn't yell. It wasn't even loud. But his "please" was full of something. "Just close your eyes, Luce. Just close your eyes, take a breath, and try to relax. You need to get light, Lucy. I can't come up and help you until you do."

Then Lucy realized why the car kept moving. She looked out the window. She couldn't see anything but the lights from the road behind the car, and blackness in front. They were on the edge of some kind of cliff. So, she did what Don told her to do: she closed her eyes and breathed. She breathed in, and she breathed out. She couldn't manage a smile, she was exhausted, but she did manage to relax her shivering body.

And the car moved. It tilted up just the tiniest bit.

"Good good good," he said. She could even hear the smile in his voice. "You're doing it!"

Lucy did smile then. A little.

"Can you do it more, Lucy?"

"I don't know," she said, panting. She felt completely drained.

"Sure, you can," Don said softly. Well, softly considering he had to speak over the horn. "I know you can. You are so amazing."

Lucy started to protest, but he cut her off.

"Think of swinging. And laughing. And balloons, and kites, and dreams, and wind . . ."

No! Not swinging! But she closed her eyes again, breathed again, relaxed again, and imagined a clean breeze clearing her mind and lifting her out of this moment.

But the car only moved an inch or so, and when Don tried to come forward, it began to tilt in the wrong direction again.

"I'm sorry," she said, and the car tipped more. And rain was still coming in, adding to the sickly pink puddle she tried not to look at.

"No-no. Don't worry. It's okay! Look. You did it, Lucy. You, all by yourself, did it. And I know you're tired, but Lucy, we've got to get out of this car. And we've got to get Maggie out."

Lucy looked over at her Maggie. She didn't look hurt. She just looked like she was sleeping, her face turned toward Lucy against the steering wheel. She wasn't even wet like Lucy; her window hadn't broken. She was unconscious and beautiful. Sleeping Beauty. Sleeping Beauty hanging over the side of a muddy cliff on a rainy night. And Lucy really didn't want her to die. Things were weird. But even though her childhood was a blurry mess, Lucy knew. Lucy knew Maggie protected her. Lucy knew Maggie watched out for her. Lucy knew Maggie loved her.

But the car didn't move.

She was kind of hoping all of those loving memories would make her light.

They didn't.

"Don?"

"Yeah?"

"I have an idea."

"I'm open to ideas."

"How far back are you?"

"As back as I can get. I'm in the hatch."

"What if I crawl back there?"

"Uh. If you can do it without moving too much. Maybe."

"I'm going to try."

He didn't say anything for a second. He made that nervous popping sound, then verbally shrugged. "Okay."

She reached back and put her left hand on the back of her chair as softly as she could.

So far, so good.

But when she turned her body to reach back with her right hand, the car moved.

She froze, half turned, right arm in the air above the gear shift, where Maggie's bag was hanging.

She reached down and slid the bulk of the bag up to the seat. Nothing moved. She unwound the strap from the gear knob and slid the bag further back on the seat.

"What are you doing?" He sounded worried. Lucy knew that emotion.

"One second," she said, though she didn't know why it came out in a whisper. Whispering must have felt lighter than her regular talking. He must not have heard her.

"What are you doing, Lucy?"

So much for whispering; he hadn't heard her over the horn. She slid the bag up the back of the seat and paused when she had it sitting on the head rest. "Can you reach this without moving forward?"

"Nooo," he said. "But wait a second."

She waited. She was almost holding her breath but made herself breathe again. Breathing was better for her weight, after all.

Then, in the dark, she saw the bristled end of an ice scraper coming toward her.

"Oh. Good idea," she said, just a notch louder than a whisper this time.

She lifted the strap and wound it around the scraper as far above the bristles as she could reach. "Okay," she said, loud enough for him to hear. "Try it. But be careful because the bag is kind of heavy."

"I hope so," was all he said.

He started pulling the scraper back and paused just before the bag was about to fall off the headrest.

"Pray," he said.

She closed her eyes and began praying. She wasn't sure what the appropriate prayer was for moving a purse with a windshield scraper, so she just closed her eyes and said, *Please.*

As the bag dropped from the seat, the car began rocking.

Don yanked the bag into the back with him, yelling "crap crap crap crap crap," while Lucy kept praying "please please please please please," the car horn kept blowing, and Maggie lay gorgeously across the horn, though saliva was coming out of her mouth now, as they waited to see if they would plunge off the cliff into the blackness.

After about eighty-seven years, the car finally stopped rocking.

"Well?" Lucy asked.

"I'm okay! You okay?"

"Yeah! I'm going to try to push Maggie's head back now!"

"Oh - kay."

Lucy reached over and began to push Maggie back, but Maggie's stupid necklace was caught on the stupid windshield wiper lever thing. Lucy slid it off and pushed Maggie again. Maggie slumped back, rocking the car again, but only a little, and it stopped more quickly this time. The sudden silence from pulling her off the horn seemed really loud, and Lucy noticed a ringing in her hears for the first time. And Maggie didn't look good.

"Don? I think she's hurt."

"How bad?" It was the first time he really sounded worried. Maybe it was just because he wasn't shouting over the horn now.

"She's not bleeding, and she is breathing, but she isn't moving."

He didn't say anything but started to move forward. He sat back when the car moved again.

"Is there anything else you can toss back here?"

Lucy was finally able to sit back on her own seat, so she opened the glove box and threw back a bunch of fast-food napkins, an owner's manual, a hairbrush, a pack of gum—she was tempted to take a piece but didn't—some pens, and a box of tampons and feminine pads. Next, she opened the console between the seats and tossed back some CDs, a charging cord, a bottle of hand sanitizer, a little pocketknife, some ChapStick, and—hallelujah! —another makeup bag! Then she reached down and took off her ruined shoes and threw those back.

"Hey!"

That one might have hit him in the head. She hoped he didn't get any wine puke on him.

"Sorry."

"It's fine. Is there anything else?"

"No. Just Maggie and me."

The rain had calmed down, and they sat there. Thinking.

"Maybe someone will come along and help us."

Lucy nodded. Maybe they would. But maybe they wouldn't. And rainwater was beginning to puddle on the floor, which would also add more weight up front.

She closed her eyes. She breathed in. She breathed out. She relaxed her body, which was easier now that she was actually sitting in the seat and not crunched half on the floor. And she breathed some more. She didn't think about balloons or swings.

She thought about Maggie. Not about what Maggie did for her, or how much Maggie loved her. She just thought of Maggie.

She just.

Just.

She just loved.

She just loved her sister.

"Lucy . . .?"

"Hush."

As Lucy's body lifted, the car tipped back a little more. She kept breathing. Slow and steady. She reached back and pulled herself between the front seats, into the space above the back seat. Loving Maggie. Her big sister. Then she grabbed Don's outstretched arm as he smiled and pulled her into the hatch. Then she let go, exhausted, and crumpled down into the cramped space between his feet and the driver-side wall. The car settled almost flat.

"That was amazing," he grinned. Lucy just blinked at him. Tired and relieved.

"But we still need to get Maggie, Don, so I need your help."

"Right. I'll get out and try to—"

"No."

He frowned at her.

"The car isn't completely flat. If you get out now, Maggie is still heavier than I am, and we'll rock forward again."

"Then what do you suggest?"

"You have to slap me."

"What?!" He would have jumped back if there had been room. The look on his face was kind of funny. She'd have to ask Claire about that expression later.

"You have to slap me. Hard. Pain makes me crash."

He frowned again, "Lucy, I'm not going to slap you."

"Well, punching would be better, actually, but let's try slapping first."

"Lucy!" Oh. That was anger. Definitely.

"Don, it's the only way I know for sure how to make myself heavy. Pain does it. You slap me, I'll crash, and you go up and get Maggie out of the car. And I'll get out when I . . ." she shrugged. "Wake up."

"How long will that take?"

"I don't know."

"Well, are we talking seconds? Minutes?"

She looked at him and shrugged again.

"Hours? What?"

"I don't know, Don! It might only be a minute, like just now."

"Lucy, I've been sitting back here for thirty minutes! Afraid to move!"

The amount of water on the floor made sense then. "Oh that's good! The first time I crashed like that, I was unconscious for days, but—"

"What?!"

"—*but* it's never that long now, and we have to get Maggie! Don! We have to get Maggie!"

He looked . . . bothered? Bugged? Actually, he looked like Maggie. That I-know-you're-right-but-I-don't-want-to-admit-it look. And he looked angry. So many emotions.

"Fine. Whatever."

"Okay then."

"So, how? When? Right now?" His head was kind of jiggling, like little, tiny micro-shakes.

"Yeah," she shrugged.

Don looked at her for a few seconds. No expression. But he was thinking something. "You ready?"

"Yes."

He hesitated for a moment, then he slapped Lucy across her right cheek.

She sat there for a half a second. "Well," she said, "That didn't feel good, but it wasn't nearly hard enough. And you're not left-handed, so you're not even trying."

He looked bugged, but he didn't deny it.

"Fine! Ready?"

"Yes."

He slapped her again.

It was harder this time, and it definitely stung, but nothing happened.

"Come on, you idiot! Hit me! You stupid jerk! You—"

He clenched his jaw. "Stop it," he said flatly.

She closed her mouth as she was about to call him an asshole. She was glad she never got it out.

"I'm not going to hit you if you're trying to make me mad." Lucy could barely hear him. It was his soft voice. "I'm not going to hit you in anger, Lucy. I won't do that. I would never do that."

"I'm sorry," she said, and started fiddling with the random little things she'd tossed from the console. They were all over the floor.

"Me too," he said, then he put his arms around her and hugged her.

Not good. Lucy knew what would happen the moment he touched her. She started getting light. Like, fast!

"Oh, no," she said. Then did the first thing that came to her mind: she grabbed the little pocketknife, opened it up . . .

"Lucy!"

. . . then rammed it as hard as she could into her leg.

She heard the back tires burst just before she blacked out.

CHAPTER 23

Surviving

I'm cold.

That was the first thing Lucy thought. Second was that it was dark. Third was that she could smell a sweet spicy scent that reminded her of Don. She opened her eyes and there he was, looking right at her from a few inches away.

Whoa. She scooted her head to the left a little.

"Oh good! You're awake! Can you sit up?" he asked, black eyes searching her face, wet bangs plastered to his wrinkled forehead.

Then she realized she was lying on her back on the rain-drenched ground, her left side in a cold, shallow puddle. Don was sitting on the ground beside her. She started to sit up, then sucked in a sharp breath between her teeth as a sting in her right leg reminded her what she had done. She fell back, her head crunching onto the muddy gravel.

Ow!

"Lucy!" Don scolded as he jerked forward to try to help her somehow. But she hadn't made it very far up—probably not even three inches—before she fell back, so her head hadn't hit super hard. Bumping it didn't feel good, for sure, but the bump made her realize she had a headache. She held up her hand in a thumbs-up sign to let him know she was okay, but then she recognized the smell.

Don always wore way too much cologne, and the scent had soaked into every fiber of his down jacket, which had been draped over her, just inches from her nose. It had slid off when she jerked, and Don was pulling it back under her chin. She didn't mind the scent. She breathed it in to take her mind off of the stinging in her leg. But she had to look. She bent her leg up a little and tilted her head to see her thigh.

Interesting. The hole in her jeans had been ripped open wide, and there was a feminine pad tied to her leg over the gash with the cell phone charging cord.

Crap. They were her favorite jeans.

Lucy looked up at Don who was obviously trying not to look at her leg. Lucy wondered if it was the blood or the pad that he didn't want to look at. Probably both.

"Uh, anyway . . ." He stumbled for a moment. "Can you sit up if I help you? The police are on their way, I think."

"Maggie!" Where was she? Was she okay?!

"She's okay," Don reassured, helping Lucy sit up, but holding her so she wouldn't try to stand. "She's back there—she's fine—hold still!" He pushed her firmly down.

"Where? What happened?" Lucy asked as she scooted herself out of the puddle, pressing gravel into her hands for the second time that night and looking behind her where Don had pointed.

There was the car, still tipped over the edge of the ditch, the back tires about two feet off the ground. "Where is she?!" she cried, jerking again even though the pain in her leg spasmed. Another hissed intake of breath.

"I'm HERE!" Maggie yelled, popping her head up over the roof of the car from the driver's side and waving. But it was a weak yell. A yell that was trying not to be a yell.

"Maggie!"

"I'm FINE!" She kind-of yelled again. "Relax! I've got to hurry." The last one sounded so tired.

"But—" Lucy was squirming to see better, then hissed again as her leg protested.

"Could you please relax?" Don whisper-shouted. "We were barely able to pull you out of the car a few minutes ago, and you were really heavy. Please try to relax."

"But," she said. Her mind was fuzzy, but she distinctly remembered trying to keep the car from teetering off the cliff and into a black ravine. She looked again and saw the lights from the car shining into the blackness.

But . . . the lights were also shining on tall grass.

Don looked straight at her, then turned and pointed to the cliff.

"It only drops off about two feet right there, then there's a wide, flat, grassy area that slopes a little bit for about fifteen feet before it drops off into the ravine." He dropped his pointing hand. "We could have just stepped out of the car."

Lucy looked at him, face blank.

"Yep," he said.

"But Maggie was hurt."

"Yeah. She knocked her head on the steering wheel, she has a bump on her forehead, but she woke up as soon as I opened her door, after you—" He shrugged twice and shook his head. "Anyway, we were able to get you out after about maybe thirty minutes, so no one knows either of us was in the back. It was still raining when we got you out, though, so they might wonder why it's all wet back there, if they look. Maggie called your parents, and they called a tow truck, but just in case any police come too, Maggie is moving the stuff. If you promise to just sit here, I can go help her now. Okay?" He stood up.

"Okay."

She took a breath to ask another question, but then asked the one she should have asked sooner. "Are you okay?"

Don stalled. "Uh, yeah. I'm okay."

"Were you hurt? When we crashed?"

"Not really . . . I think I might have sprained my ankle a bit."

"How—" she began, then looked down at his feet. He wasn't putting all his weight on his left foot. "Did I . . .?" she whispered.

He smiled a little and looked down. He wiped away some water that had dripped from his bangs. "You were pretty heavy."

"Don! Oh my gosh! I'm so sorry!" *Ugh!* Maggie was right. She really did need to get control of this thing!

Then she heard Don hobble back down and felt him pulling her hands away from her face.

"Hey," he whispered, leaning closer. "You don't need to be sorry. You saved us." He shrugged and let go of her hands, scrambling back to his feet. His foot.

She made a disgusted little puffed sound; she must have learned that from Maggie. "Not really," she said.

"Okay, you're right. We weren't really in that much danger. But you didn't know that." He smiled for real then and looked Lucy in the eye. "Luce, you did it. You controlled it. You floated yourself back. On purpose."

Aaaannnnd she stabbed herself in the leg when Don tried to hug her. She didn't think he realized exactly why she had done that. At least, she hoped he didn't.

He nodded and started limping back to the car just as headlights shone around the bend, slowed down, and the tow truck pulled over a little beyond where the car had gone off the road. Next came another set of headlights that belonged to her dad's car.

Before her dad could step out of the car, red and blue police lights flashed around the bend and pulled up behind him.

This night wasn't over yet.

Lucy didn't know what she was expecting. She was so bad at reading emotions. Her dad hadn't said anything while checking them to see if they were really hurt. His doctor persona asked questions about bumps and pain and heads and ankles, but that was it. It seemed like she might be in trouble, though. She wasn't sure, but there was definitely tension. He had hugged each of them, even Don, but Lucy felt kind of, maybe, embarrassed? But she didn't know exactly why.

When they were all finally getting in the Audi, her dad in the driver's seat, Maggie in front, and Lucy and Don in back, Lucy was holding her breath. Waiting for something.

Once they were all buckled in and pulling away from the police lights and the tow truck, her dad finally spoke. "Okay gang, now that we can talk, what happened?"

All three teenagers started talking at once.

"I guess I hydroplaned . . ."
"It was raining . . ."
"We were at the party . . ."

". . . but it happened so fast . . ."
". . . and Maggie was mad . . ."
". . . to get some food . . ."

". . . I don't really remember . . ."
". . . she yelled at Don . . ."
". . . pretty early because . . ."

". . . then Don was there . . ."
". . . then we hit something . . ."
". . . Maggie said we were leaving . . ."

". . . we couldn't move her . . ."
". . . and I was on the floor . . ."
" . . . and Lucy was floating, and . . ."

"Stop!" That was maybe the first time Lucy had heard her dad shout. Maybe. Had she heard him shout or yell before? Her mom did sometimes, a little. And Maggie was loud almost daily. Claire was loud sometimes, but not when she was angry. Did Claire ever get angry?

There was silence in the car.

"Maggie." Stern—that was the word for it. He was being stern. "Did Lucy float at the party?"

Maggie shot a glance back to Lucy, who was sitting behind their dad.

"Did she?" It wasn't just stern. His voice trembled a tiny bit. He sounded a little afraid.

"Just a little. I think."

"A little? Did she, or didn't she?!"

"Well, when I came back to where she and Caleb were—"

"You left her alone?" He wasn't shouting, and his voice didn't shake. But it was worse that way, somehow.

"Only for a minute! Don was there and—"

"Lucy was not Don's responsibility—"

"I'm sorry, Sir, I —" Don tried to interject, but he was ignored.

"She was your responsibility." That was anger. Lucy knew that. Maggie was the only one who evoked that tone from their dad.

Maggie didn't say anything.

"Then what happened?" That was the doctor voice. It must be confusing being so many people at the same time.

Maggie was looking out the side window when she answered. Her voice was flat.

"She was laughing and giggling."

"She was—? She was giggling? Giggling." It was like he didn't believe her—like it was preposterous. He looked back and forth between the road and Maggie. Maggie nodded, not looking at him at all. "Well, what was she 'giggling' about?" His mouth was hanging open, and he kept looking back and forth between Maggie and the wet road.

"I don't know," was all Maggie finally said, still not looking at her dad.

"Lucy?" He looked at Lucy in the rear-view mirror. "Lucy, honey, what were you laughing about?"

Lucy took a big breath to answer, then let it out. What had been so funny? "Um—" she began but had to stop and start again. "Uh, what was that guy's name, Maggie?"

"What guy?" Maggie glanced back. "Do you mean Caleb?" She was kind of frowning.

"No, the other guy. His cousin who was there."

Maggie turned all the way around to look at Lucy. She blinked and frowned a little more. "Do you mean Jonah? Was he there?"

"Yeah, Jonah." Lucy shrugged. "He said something funny."

Her dad was squinting at Lucy in the mirror, and Maggie turned back around to the window, still frowning.

"What did he say, Lucy?" Now their dad was looking back and forth between the road and Lucy. Still squinting.

She shrugged. "I don't remember," was all she said, but it was kind of a lie. She remembered Jonah talking about Maggie—not in a mean way—but it wasn't really funny now. And she didn't know if Maggie would get mad. "We were just talking."

More squinting.

"Um, sir?" Don tentatively interrupted. Aeden glanced back over his shoulder at Don. "Maybe it was because she—"

"Don!" Maggie barked, "This has nothing to do with you!"

"Maggie." Aeden scolded with one look, then glanced back at Don briefly. "Because she what, Don?"

"Well, maybe it has something to do . . . with the, uh . . . I think she had some alcohol." Don's eye's flicked to Maggie, then back to her dad. "Lucy was holding it when we left, and it smelled like, maybe wine? I wasn't sure."

Aeden didn't say anything. Lucy looked at Don. Don looked at Maggie. Without moving a muscle, Maggie seemed to shrink down into her seat just a little.

They sat there in silence like that for about an hour and a half.

Or maybe about twelve seconds. But it felt like longer. A lot longer.

"So how much did she have?" Aeden looked at Maggie.

Maggie erupted. "Why are you asking me?! I wasn't even with her!"

"But you should have been!"

"Well, I wasn't, so I don't know!"

Lucy plugged her ears, and Don looked out his window. Lucy expected him to start doing the music bopping thing with his head and hands, but when she looked over at him, he was looking at her in the reflection of Maggie's window. He mouthed the word, "sorry," and Lucy mouthed, "it's okay."

"When I left her *and* Don," Maggie gestured toward the back seat, "she had a Coke! A COKE!"

"Don?" Aeden looked back at the boy, and it was not a happy look. Don's eyes opened wide, and he froze.

"Dad?" Lucy asked. There was a full question in that one word. It was a Dad-can-I-ask-you-something word, and Aeden heard it.

He took a deep breath. "Yes, Lucy?"

"I can tell you what happened."

"Okay," he said slowly, like he wasn't sure he wanted to hear what she had to say. Maggie rolled her eyes and Don visibly relaxed.

"Maggie was with me, but she left to get a Coke. Then Don and Naomi went to—"

"Naomi?"

"Caleb's sister. Don and Naomi went to get some food. And Caleb's friend—I mean, his cousin—Jonah—came over, but Caleb was, um . . . asleep." Aeden gave Maggie a look. "Then he asked if I wanted the drink he had brought for someone who ended up not coming to the party. My Coke was all gone, so I took it. But . . ." She stopped. She had heard her parents tell Maggie no drinking lots of times, but they had never told Lucy. They shouldn't have had to; she knew (of course she knew) they wouldn't have wanted her to drink either. But it had never come up before. She had never gone to a party before. She had never been offered wine except at Mass, and that was mostly juice.

"But what?" Her dad was being very quiet, the not-yelling quiet, which was different from normal quiet.

"But it was, um . . . wine?"

"You're not sure? Did he tell you it was wine?"

"No—I mean yes, I'm sure. He told me. He said it was strawberry wine, and . . . and I wasn't even going to take it, but . . ." Lucy shrugged weakly. "But my Coke was gone."

"Was there more Coke you could have gotten?"

"Probably. Over by the drinks."

Aeden ran his hand over his face, pulling the skin down and stretching out the mottled patches as he sighed. A very tired sigh.

"And Maggie wasn't there, and you didn't know what to do," he breathed out with an exhausted effort.

Lucy didn't know what to say. Had she known what to do? Probably.

Aeden let out another huge sigh. Actually, it was more of a whispered moan as he rubbed his forehead and turned the blinker on to take an exit. "Okay, you drank some wine and started floating. How much did you have?"

"I'm not really sure. I didn't know I was floating! Maggie came back and—" she paused. "And I'm not sure." She looked at Maggie.

Maggie turned her head back to Aeden. "She was kind of lifting up out of her chair a little. A little more than a little, but not all—" she slightly waved her hands in the air. "No one could have seen her. Caleb was zonked out—and NO, I didn't have anything besides Coke to drink—and I grabbed her and Don, and we left."

"What about this Jonah boy?"

"Urrgh! I keep forgetting about him! No! No, I don't think he noticed. Probably." Now Maggie was the one rubbing her forehead.

"Um, sir?" Don dared to speak up again. "I saw Lucy when Maggie was pulling her to the car, and Lucy was . . . she was walking, and mostly touching the ground."

"Mostly?"

"Um. Well, her right foot was stepping, but . . . not her left. It . . . was kind of floating."

Aeden rubbed his hand down his face again, but those blotches weren't moving.

"And that's why Maggie was mad, in the car," Lucy offered by way of explanation. "It was my fault."

No one said a thing.

Aeden turned onto their street. "We can talk about this more tomorrow." He pulled into Don's driveway. "I called your mom, Don, and told her Maggie had car trouble, but you should tell her what happened yourself." He paused, "I mean about the car accident. I hate to ask this of you, but I hope you won't say anything about Lucy. I know you are aware of her condition, and that's fine; I trust you. But we would really rather keep this a family matter."

"I won't say anything, Mr. Callaghan. I promise." He was already climbing out of the car.

"Thank you, Don. Good night."

"Night." Don's eyes flicked to Lucy and Maggie as he slammed the door shut.

Aeden drove two doors down and pulled into their own driveway. "And girls, let's not say anything about the floating to Mom." He turned off the car and looked at both of them. "You hydroplaned on a rainy road, Maggie. That's the truth, and I thank God you're safe. All of you. Let's just leave it at that for now. We can talk about the rest later. Tomorrow."

Lucy nodded immediately; she absolutely did not want to tell Kelly a thing, but she absolutely did want to talk to Claire to ask her about a hundred and seven questions as soon as she could.

Maggie brushed her hair away from her face and lifted her head up and down once, not seeming to care one way or the other.

Discussion 2 — Her Foot

What am I looking at?

Pictures from a party.

And?

Look there, behind the potted palm tree.

The brunette?

The redhead.

No. This is inconclusive.

Look at her foot!

Inconclusive.

CHAPTER 24

No Don, You Can't Take Communion

Don was sitting on his ergonomically designed chair, typing on his ergonomically designed keyboard, which was hooked up to his home-built two-screen computer that sat on top of an old desk painted baby yellow about nineteen years ago. Faded white ducks decorated the three drawers. Lucy sat in a red beanbag chair, playing with a Rubik's cube. She wondered if it bothered Don that he was older than all the other kids in their class at school.

"What kind of wine was it?" he asked, clacking away.

"I told you. It was strawberry wine."

"I could smell the strawberries, but what brand was it?"

"How should I know?"

"It would be printed on the bottle."

"I didn't see the bottle. He had brought the wine for someone else who didn't end up coming, and then thought Naomi might want it, but you two had left already." Which left Lucy sitting there all by herself, dying of thirst.

Sitting by herself never used to bother her before, but she realized almost for the first time that it had bothered her that night. It bothered her that Don went off with Naomi, leaving her alone next to a sprawled-out Caleb.

Don looked up. "He brought it for Naomi?"

Really? That was the part he paid attention to? "Yes."

"For Naomi?" He looked like he had just seen an error in some enormous scientific equation.

"Yes. She's his cousin."

"Oh." His face relaxed. "Right," he said, turning back and continuing with the clackety-clacking.

Lucy put the Rubik's cube down on the windowsill and picked up a glass that had five small models of H_2O molecules in it. Don had made the molecules in third grade when their class was making papier mâché projects. While everyone else had made the heads of dogs and cats and ducks out of round balloons, wheat paste, and torn-up newspaper, Don had built a model of an atom. He started with protons he painted blue and neutrons he painted red. Then he used an old wire hanger to make some green electrons orbit around the nucleus. He was finished before everyone else had glued construction-paper eyes, noses, and ears onto their animals, so he made some water molecules for the fun of it.

Mrs. Archibald liked his atom so much, he gave it to her. It hung in her classroom for the duration of their elementary school careers. Don kept the water molecules, though, for some reason. He wasn't a hoarder, necessarily, but his bedroom was cluttered with old science fair projects, awards, and small working replicas of every robot from every science fiction movie Lucy had ever heard of. And being Don's friend, she had actually heard of a lot.

"Luce?" Don was looking at her.

"Yeah?"

"How much did you have?"

"What?"

"How much strawberry wine did you have?"

"A cup. And a little bit more."

"As in an eight-ounce cup, plus more?"

"I don't know. Like most of a red plastic cup, plus part of another red plastic cup."

"You mean like one of the sixteen-ounce cups?" His eyebrows shot up. "I think that's . . . kind of a lot. Strawberry wine can have anywhere between nine and seventeen percent alcohol. The more alcohol in it, the more sugar they add, probably to make it taste good. Was the wine you had very sweet?"

She set the cup of water down and shrugged. "No. I don't know. I don't think so, but what is *very* sweet?"

"Good question."

"Gee, thanks."

Don turned to look at her. "You know, you didn't used to be so grumpy."

Grumpy? Great. Another emotion to think about. Where did *grumpy* fall on the line between *happy* and *angry* or whatever? "Sorry." She didn't know if she really was sorry, but it seemed like the thing to say since he was trying to help her.

He turned back to his computer. "It's no big deal. It's just interesting. You should probably start keeping track of your moods."

"You want to know the dates of my periods, too?" There. Choke on that.

"That's probably a good idea. Write everything down in a notebook." He didn't even skip a beat in his even typing. "Hey," he stopped to look at her. "I've heard that girls that live together sometimes have their cycles align. Is that true? I've read conflicting reports."

"I'm not going to talk about this with you." It served her right for bringing it up in the first place, but reading reports on girls' menstrual cycles was just weird. And it meant it wasn't the pad strapped to her leg that made him uncomfortable the night of the crash.

"Okay." He turned back. "Compared to grape juice then, was it sweeter than that?"

"No way. It was like—I don't know. It was strawberry, but not like Kool-Aid strawberry. More like, just strawberries. Plus the alcohol taste, but it was stronger than the alcohol taste at communion."

"Hmm. I'm not Catholic, so I've never had communion. I'll have to look up what kind of wine they use. Unless—would anyone care if I took communion?" He was still typing.

"Probably not. Maybe. I don't know." Would that be a sin if he was only trying to sample the wine, and not actually trying to commune? But he was doing a good thing, trying to help her, so maybe it wouldn't be a big sin. "Hey, Don?"

"Yeah?" He didn't even look over his shoulder at her, so she didn't say anything. He kept typing, and switching screens, and copying, pasting, and highlighting different bits of information. She bet if she were Naomi, he'd be paying more attention. She knew that wasn't reasonable because he was sitting there trying to help her on a Sunday morning. He was a good friend. He was her only friend. And he went off to get food with Naomi, leaving her all alone with creepy Caleb. So, she took the stupid wine stupid Jonah had given her.

Maybe Jonah was just being nice, but the outcome was not good. And the lecture Maggie got at breakfast didn't make her big sister suddenly all warm and friendly, either. The worst part was that Maggie used to be the one to help Lucy cope with things she didn't understand. And speaking of periods, it was Maggie who explained all those kinds of things to Lucy.

Maggie was just nineteen months older than Lucy, so she completely paved the way for Lucy in every single aspect of her life. And now? Claire was great, and Lucy was unimaginably grateful for her help, but she still wished Maggie could go back to being normal. Then just like that, another memory popped up in Lucy's wilted brain.

When she was little and asked anyone where Maggie was, she never asked *where's my sister?* or *where's Maggie?* She asked, *where's my Maggie?* And now, Lucy wanted her Maggie back.

"... is whether it was the little bit of alcohol, or the little bit of sugar, or the combination, or something else entirely, that made you float. We can experiment with sugar, but do you think your dad would let you experiment with some wine? It would be a completely controlled study, and I could write up a proposal stating our hypothesis and the control factors. We'd just need to decide which one to test for first. Sugar would be easier since he wouldn't have . . ."

Lucy wiggled her way out of the bean bag chair and stood up. A dozen tiny white Styrofoam balls puffed out of a rip in one of the seams.

"Where you going?"

"Home."

"Okay. I'll finish designing the experiments. You ask your dad how he'd feel about using alcohol. And maybe see if Maggie knows the brand of wine that guy gave you."

"Jonah."

"What?"

"That guy. His name was Jonah."

"Great. See if she could get a hold of Jonah and ask him. She could say you really liked it or something. I'll come over tomorrow."

"Okay." She lied. She never wanted to taste wine again, and maybe never strawberries, after barfing it all up in the car. When she got to the door, she turned. "Don?"

"Yeah?" He looked at her.

"Thanks. For helping me. And everything."

"You're welcome," he smiled, and turned back to his computer.

Lucy walked home, thinking about Maggie, Don, strawberry wine, and emotions. There was too much to think about. The notebook thing was probably a good idea.

CHAPTER 25

Swings

By two o'clock, Lucy was tired of thinking about feelings, so she and Claire decided to watch the movie about the girl who flies to Ireland to propose to her boyfriend but ends up falling in love with the guy who owned the Irish inn. Their dad liked the movie because it was set in Ireland, even though the actor who played the inn owner was English, not Irish. That was a big deal to him. But their dad had been to the pub where one of the scenes had been filmed, so he liked it. Irish national pride was not dead in the Callaghan household. But Claire mostly liked the movie because they used the word "poo" in it. She thought it was hilarious. Lucy mostly liked sitting next to Claire on the new sofa, which was almost as comfy as their old one, and listening to her laugh. Her laugh was real, and alive, and colorful, like Lucy's Dreams.

When the movie got to the part where the girl and the guy were chasing his beat-up little car down a hill, the doorbell rang.

"I'll get it!" Claire yelled as she jumped up and ran for the door.

The couple's car ended up in a lake.

"Lucy!" Claire bellowed from the front door. "It's for you!" Then she ran into the den to tell Lucy in person what she had just yelled from the foyer. "It's for you!" She didn't yell it that time, but her face was loud and large with emotion, eyes wide and eyebrows as high as they could go and still stay stuck to her head.

Lucy frowned. It was probably Don with more questions, but why would Claire get so excited about Don.

"Luce!" Claire whispered loudly, wanting to make absolutely certain she had her sister's full attention. "Someone. Is at the door. For *you*." She took a deep breath. "It's a guy, and he's cute even though he has really big ears, but all he would have to do is let his hair grow a teeny bit longer and then that wouldn't matter, and he smells good!"

Jonah? Did Jonah smell good? She was never close enough to him at the party to know. Claire, who was absolutely glowing with whatever enormous emotion plagued her at the moment, pranced and smiled—but it was more than a smile. It was like she couldn't wait to open a birthday present or something.

Lucy walked to the foyer.

Yep. There was Jonah, big ears and all, standing on the front step.

"Uh, hi." She gestured him and his big ears into the house. As she closed the door behind him, she noticed that he did smell good. Like cologne, but different from Don's, and not as much. She could also smell the leather of his jacket. The combination was nice.

"Hi!" He was smiling, and Lucy noticed for the first time that his eyes were blue. Not like Maggie's; her eyes reminded Lucy of electricity, really light in the center, but with a dark rim around the iris. Jonah's were a solid blue, like the sky in summer. And his teeth were super straight; he had probably had braces. But his smile was kind of frozen now. She should probably say something.

"Hi, Jonah."

"Oh good! You remember me!"

How could she forget? He was the only person she talked to at the party.

He stood there, glanced at the framed antique map of Ireland that was hanging on the wall, then put his hands in his jacket pockets. "Oh—here." He pulled something out of his left pocket and handed it to Lucy. "Maggie left this at Caleb's house."

"Thanks," she said, taking the tube of lip gloss that had red strawberries printed on it. Would strawberries plague her for the rest of her life? "Maggie isn't here, but I'll tell her you came by."

"No, that's okay. I was just wondering if," he hesitated for half a second. "Well, you left the party really fast, so I wanted to make sure you were okay, and . . . well, I didn't get a chance to get your cell number. Caleb didn't have it."

She blinked. He was looking right at her. Smiling. She had no idea what her own face was doing, but her mind had just tripped and spilled brain juice all over itself. She quickly closed her mouth because she realized it was hanging open.

"I mean," Jonah held out his hands, palms forward, like he was pushing himself away from her. "You don't have to . . . I mean, I don't know if you have a boyfriend or anything but, you know, at the party you didn't seem like . . ." He trailed off when Lucy didn't say anything. "So, do you have a boyfriend already?"

Lucy laughed, but it came out as more of a snort. Then she started to really laugh, but she choked on her own saliva and began coughing. Like, a lot.

"Are you okay?!" He looked around and saw Claire emerge from the Den.

"Hi! I'm Claire!"

Lucy was still coughing. Stupid saliva. She held up her hand and pointed to the kitchen as she walked away to get some water. She heard Jonah speak.

"Hi, I'm Jonah. Is she okay?"

"Oh yeah. She just went to get some water because she's not really good at laughing yet."

Jonah laughed. "Yeah, she definitely needs more practice!"

"She really does. Want a Diet Coke?"

"Sure," he answered.

Lucy was wiping her face with a paper towel when they walked around the corner. She had finally gotten her coughing under control, but her eyes were still watering. She watched Claire open the fridge, grab two Diet Cokes, and set them on the table. Just what did she think she was doing? Jonah was here, in her kitchen, wondering if she had a boyfriend. What was she supposed to do? She was only—wait. How old was she now? She was sixteen. She was only sixteen years old! Sure,

Maggie had had boyfriends probably since preschool, but Lucy? Absolutely not.

Another memory blossomed in her head.

The fifth graders from all three classes were herded together to gym, which was really the cafeteria, and it always smelled like bread. The walls were the multi-colored pastel tabletops and benches that were folded up vertically each day and locked into place.

The students were told to line up along those walls—girls on the left, boys on the right, tallest to shortest. Thinking they were probably going to have some kind of race, Lucy tried to find Don, so she could line up across from him. He hadn't looked over at Lucy's side at all, but she thought they would probably race each other since they were both short and were both standing in front of corresponding pale green tabletops.

"Okay kids!" said Mrs. Hoskins in her loud-but-not-quite-yelling voice that rang throughout the cold, spacious room. "Today we are going to start learning a square dance that you will perform for your parents and caregivers at the Halloween party!" Major groans erupted from the boys' side of the cafeteria; giggles came from the girls' side. Mrs. Hoskins laughed and rolled her eyes. "Come on kids; it's not a big deal—it will be a lot of fun, I promise. But first, you need to walk to the middle of the floor and line up with your partner across from you."

Pandemonium ensued immediately as boys and girls started shuffling around trying either to get away from someone in particular or line up with someone in particular. Lucy looked across at Don, and he looked across at her. Then he dropped his eyes and quietly walked about halfway down the line, far away from Lucy.

She just stood there, confused. She couldn't have really named her feelings then, but later she would recognize and name the emotions. She felt sad. And hurt. And a little angry.

She slumped back.

Against the wall.

The pale green tabletop immediately buckled beneath her weight, the lock broke, and the entire folding contraption crashed down with an enormous bang that shook the air and echoed in the large space, bumping Lucy to the side.

Kids screamed. Teachers gasped and came running over.

Since Lucy had only been bumped aside, she was ignored, but a girl named Isabel who had been standing next to Lucy had been knocked to the cold, hard floor and was wailing her head off, holding her elbow. Two teachers knelt on either side of her while Mrs. Hoskins ran out of the room yelling, "I'll get the nurse." Kitchen workers came running out to help; teachers were yelling with frantic gestures; kids were screaming; and the entire room was in general pandemonium.

Lucy stood there watching, perplexed.

When the principal came running in with the nurse, one of the teachers started ranting about faulty equipment, and the incompetent janitor who hadn't securely locked the table, and poor Isabel, and what if it had been a kindergartner!

Lucy's confusion cleared as she stood there. It wasn't the equipment or the janitor. She knew somehow that she had done it.

When the chaos was controlled and the activity resumed, it ended up that there were more girls than boys, so six girls ended up dancing together, and Lucy got to push the button to start the music. She was okay with that—since Don didn't want to dance with her.

"Lucy," Claire said, not loudly, but with a pay-attention-to-what's-going-on-here-for-heck's-sake kind of way. "Have a seat," she said to Jonah, motioning to the Diet Cokes. When he walked past the two girls, Claire, with wide eyes and a commanding expression, stepped to Lucy and shoved her toward the table. Lucy stumbled forward a step but looked back at Claire for help. What was she supposed to do?

"Well, I have to go do some homework," Claire announced to the room with a smile, then turned on her heel and practically ran out of the kitchen and up the stairs to her bedroom, which was right above the kitchen. If Claire decided to lie down on the floor next to the heating vent, she would be able to hear every word Jonah said. That might actually be helpful.

Lucy sat down in front of the other Coke, unscrewed the top and took a drink. She didn't even like Coke.

"So," Jonah started, looking at her sideways, "you never answered my question."

"Oh," Lucy stalled. "Um . . . what was the question?"

He shrugged. "I just wanted to know if you were dating anyone. Like, exclusively."

"Um." That was a little easier to answer. "No, not exclusively." Well, it was true. She had never even been on a date, unless you counted going to the gym with Don.

"Me neither," he smiled, turning to look at her fully. "So, you wanna hang out sometime?"

Hang out? What did hanging out look like? Maggie always said she was going to *hang out* with Caleb or April or some other friends, but she didn't know what they actually did while they were hanging out. Lucy always imagined them dangling from tree branches, hanging by their arms. Then she pictured her and Jonah randomly swinging from trees, which made her smile.

"I think you have a pretty smile," Jonah said, "but I'm not totally sure since I can't see it very well."

Lucy looked up from the bottle cap she had been fiddling with, still smiling a little.

"Oh yeah. You do have a pretty smile."

She reached up to touch her cheeks, which felt really hot all of a sudden. That was weird.

"Your blush is cute too."

Is that what that meant? She hadn't ever felt that before. She wondered what her freckles looked like on top of red skin. It didn't sound very cute, that was for sure.

"So, were you okay the other night? You left really fast."

"Oh, yeah," she stumbled. "We just—" Just what? Just had to leave before she started floating after having about a cup and a half of strawberry wine? "It was no big deal. We just needed to get home. Our dad . . . needed us . . . at home." That sounded lame even to Lucy. "He . . . was . . ." Was what? *Just stop talking,*

Lucy. ". . . working on something and he needed our help. At home." Why was he there? She wished he would just leave. She didn't know what to do or what to say. She took another drink. *Yuck. So gross.*

"Okay," Jonah chuckled. "Well, maybe if you're not doing anything right now, we could walk down to that little park on your street and just hang out."

With the trees! Lucy laughed out loud but managed not to choke this time.

"I really like your laugh." He was looking at her again. Or still. She wasn't sure since she kept looking down. "When you're not choking, I mean." Lucy couldn't help but smile a little at that. "That's really why I wanted to see you; to see if I could make you laugh some more. I liked talking to you at the party."

"I liked talking to you too." She smiled a little bit more. It was still a new sensation. She felt happy, she guessed. But it wasn't the same kind of happy as laughing with Claire. Lucy would ask her about it later.

"So, you wanna go? To that little park?"

"Sure." Still smiling. It was weird.

He picked up his Diet Coke, but she left hers there and they headed out the door.

"Is that your car?" Lucy asked when she saw a shiny red vehicle parked on the curb in front of her house.

"Technically, it's my parents', and they remind me of that all the time, but yeah, it's mine."

She nodded. "Maggie's car isn't really hers either, but it pretty much is."

"What do you drive?"

"*Me?*"

"Yeah you," he laughed.

"I don't drive anything. I don't know how."

He stopped walking. "But you're sixteen, right?"

"Yeah," she nodded. What was the problem?

He started walking again, slowly at first. "Oh, good. I mean, it would be okay if you weren't, but—" He shook his head. "Anyway, why haven't you learned how to drive yet?"

"I don't know." Because I've been on drugs my whole life and didn't even care about anything, including driving, until a couple of months ago? "I guess I just never thought about it." But maybe she'd liked to learn. "Is driving hard?"

"No, not really. Once you learn how the car works, all you need is practice."

"Hmm." Could she learn how to drive? Her mind was already working on so much.

"Maybe I'll teach you some time, but I'd have to borrow my mom's car since I drive a stick."

"Oh, no, that's okay! I'm not ready for that!"

"Well," he shrugged, "let me know if you change your mind. We could find an empty parking lot for you to practice in. And we wouldn't go into the city or anything like that."

"Thanks. I'll let you know." She would not let him know. No way.

They were at the park by then, and Lucy automatically walked over to the swings.

"Are we going to swing?" Jonah asked, sounding a little surprised as he tossed his Coke bottle into a city garbage can.

"Is that okay?" Was it weird to swing? Lucy loved swinging. But maybe high school kids didn't swing.

"Sure!" But he looked up at the top pole and the chains first. "I guess it will hold me." He sat in the swing carefully. It seemed to hold him fine, but he was way too big for it and his knees poked up. Lucy guessed Jonah wasn't quite as tall as her dad, but her dad was maybe six foot two? He was still way too big for a swing set built for children, though. Jonah stood up, and Lucy wondered if he had changed his mind, but he grabbed the blue plastic seat, stepped back, then tossed the whole thing up and over the top bar. He did that twice more, making the chains wrap around three times, then sat down again. His knees still poked up, but at least then he could lift his feet off the ground and actually swing. "Much better," he declared.

Lucy sat in the swing next to him. She had no problem fitting on a swing built for children. She was only five foot two. She backed up, closed her eyes, tilted her head to the sky, and flew. At least that's how swinging made her feel—like she was flying.

"You're quite the pro at that," Jonah said, bringing her back to the present.

"I love swinging." She kept her eyes closed—it made it easier to relax and enjoy the way her hair swirled around her face with each pump of her legs. She loved the breeze that her own efforts and motion created. She loved the swoop back, and the swoop forth. She loved climbing up to the clouds in the day and up to the stars at night. And she absolutely, sincerely, whole-heartedly loved that microsecond of weightlessness at the very top of each pass. She came here by herself a lot when the rest of her family was occupied just so she could feel this freedom. And now it felt even more exhilarating—more fulfilling, more real. She usually only felt this way by herself, but it made her happy in an unexpected way that Jonah had asked her to come here with him. She felt like her true self at that moment.

Another memory came flooding back as she picked up momentum and height.

Kelly had just had Claire, and Dad had sent Lucy and Maggie two doors down to make friends with the children of the new family who had just moved in. She remembered following Maggie to their house. She remembered seeing the kids sitting on their front porch, a big girl maybe in fifth grade, and a boy. Maggie had brought her Barbie and she showed it to the girl. The girl smiled and took Maggie inside her house. Lucy looked at the boy, and the boy looked at her. He had black hair and dark, tilted eyes that were almost as dark as his black hair. He was wearing blue pants and a white, ironed shirt. And he smelled like kim-chi, though Lucy hadn't known what that strange smell was at the time. She and the boy just looked at each other. Then he pointed to the little neighborhood park down the block, so they went there. She remembered they didn't even talk to each other.

And she remembered swinging.

She didn't know how it started, but she and the boy were jumping out of their swings, seeing how far they could jump. They were timid at first, only daring to jump a few inches. Then farther. Then a little farther. Soon it turned into a contest to see who could jump out of their swing the farthest. And the boy had scraped up the palms of his hands when he landed in the faded wood chips. Then Lucy's dad and the boy's mom were at the playground, along with Maggie and the girl. The boy's mom ran up to the boy and hugged him, shouting, though Lucy didn't understand what she was saying. Lucy's dad knelt down. "Hello Miss Lucy. I'm glad we found you," he said quietly. Then the boy's mom saw a hole in the left knee of the boy's pants. She scolded him as they walked home. Lucy's dad held her hand as they walked behind them.

That had really happened. She remembered. It was the first time she had ever played with a friend. They hadn't even spoken to each other, but it didn't matter. It had never mattered.

And she had floated. Just a little.

She heard some wood chips shuffle on the ground and opened her eyes. When she looked over at Jonah, she realized she was the only one swinging. He was sitting still with the chains of his swing twisted so he was facing her, just watching. She stopped pumping her legs, then dragged her sneakers on the ground to stop herself.

"Are you bored?" Lucy wasn't sure what bored felt like, but Claire had told her about it. Jonah wasn't participating, and he wasn't talking, so that might mean he was bored. But his eyes didn't look bored or uninterested. His eyes were kind of smiling.

"Nope," was all he said.

"What are you feeling?"

He smiled a little bit, a quiet smile. After a moment, he said, "You know, I don't think anyone has ever asked me that before."

What should she do now? He said he wasn't bored, but he didn't say what he *was*. She looked down at the toes of her shoes, which were buried in faded brown wood chips. She shook them off.

He finally spoke. "What are you thinking about?"

She laughed out loud, "I don't think anyone has ever asked me *that* before!"

"I'll tell you what I'm thinking," he said. "I think you really do have a great laugh."

"When I'm not choking."

Then they were both laughing out loud. Jonah reached over and took her left hand and pulled her out of the swing as he stood up. "Let's go sit down." He held her hand as he led her over to the grass beside the playground, where they both sat down. Jonah stretched out his long legs and leaned back on his hands. Lucy sat cross-legged and started fiddling with some blades of grass. She could hardly believe that he had just held her hand. It was only for about ten seconds, but she'd never held a boy's hand before at all. Unless you counted playing Red Rover in elementary school, but she didn't count that. And she never held anyone's hand in Red Rover for very long, either; the other team always knew she'd be the easiest part of the chain to break through.

"You really aren't like Maggie at all."

"Yeah. She looks like our mom, and I look like my dad." She loved her dad, but there was no denying that Maggie and her mom were really beautiful. Claire would be too, even though she had lighter hair, like a reddish-blond. Lucy and her dad both had a wild, curly mess of definitely red hair. And freckles.

"Well yeah, you look different, for sure, even though you are both really cute. I just mean that you're quiet and Maggie talks a lot." He paused for a second. "I mean, it's not like she talks a *lot* a lot, but she's definitely not afraid to say what she's thinking. I would never have guessed you two were sisters before the party. But you do kind of have the same face shape and tiny nose." He leaned over and touched her nose lightly, which was very distracting, especially when she had been trying to think of something to say. And she *had* actually thought of something, but now she had no idea what it was.

"Um, yeah. Maggie and Claire do talk more than I do, I guess." Oh brother. She needed Claire to teach her how to talk to people or she was never going to survive life, let alone talking to one boy on the grass.

"Hah! Your little sister? I didn't talk to her much, but I can tell she's gonna take over the world someday."

"Definitely. She's amazing. She's so smart and just—" How could she sum up Claire in one sentence. "She just gets people. I don't know how she does it. Everyone in my family is so different. Well—me and my dad are kind of similar I guess." That was a surprising revelation that came to her at that very moment. "But me and my mom and Maggie? We are all so different, Claire gets us all. She's really my best friend now."

"Now?"

"Um—" She shouldn't have said that part. "Maggie and I were . . . well, she's always been a really good big sister. We just—I don't know—we are just really different. Like you said, I guess."

"I get it. But that's really cool, about Claire," he added. "I'd have to say Caleb is my best friend. We were born only a few months apart, so we've just always done everything together. I might not always like him, but I love him, ya know?"

"Yeah. I know." But in her case, she guessed it was Maggie who felt like that. She was sure Maggie loved her. She still saw little glimpses of it every once in a while, but it wasn't the same anymore.

"Hey, don't be sad," Jonah said, nudging Lucy's chin up with his finger.

"Why not?"

"Cause I'm here to make you laugh, not to make you sad." That was a weird reason. But she smiled anyway. He handed her the wood chip he had been playing with. "Here. Now you can't say I never gave you anything."

"Okay . . ." she laughed.

"That's better!" He got up suddenly and held his hand out for her. She took it and let out a little squeak before she could stop it. He had pulled so quickly that she practically sprang up into the air before standing up beside him.

"Whoa! You're light!"

Crap. "Nah. Just . . . agile." Agile? Really?

"Right, you can't weigh more than—"

"Oh, I forgot to ask—" Think of a question. Quick! Think think think! "Um, since you and Caleb are the same age, does that mean you just graduated, too?"

"Yep," he nodded solemnly, "I have officially survived high school." He was still holding her right hand as they began walking back to Lucy's house. She hung onto the wood chip in her left.

"Where will you be going to college?" Act casual. How does one act casual? He was holding her hand! This was huge.

"Well, I've been offered scholarships at Dartmouth, Duke, University of Pennsylvania, and Stanford, but I decided to accept Brown even—"

"Wait. Studying what exactly?" Had he already said? He was kind of rubbing the back of her hand with his thumb. Just a little.

"Pre-med. And music. That's why I chose Brown, even though it's the only place I applied that gets even colder than it does here. I'm probably crazy, I know."

Lucy smiled again. "My dad's a doctor." It was weird that this guy who was holding her hand was making these completely mature decisions, like deciding to be a doctor.

"So is my mom."

"Really? What does your dad do?"

"He owns Edelmann Music. If you ever need any kind of instrument, from piccolos to pipe organs, he's the guy." He winked at her, and she felt her face get all warm again.

They were at her house, standing on the sidewalk by his car. He let go of her hand to get his car key out of his pocket.

"Um—" She probably should have asked this sooner, but "so that's your last name? Edelmann?"

"Yep. Jonah Edelmann, in the flesh." He reached out and tugged lightly on the end of Lucy's hair and held it for just a moment as he looked down at her. Maybe half a moment.

Then he let go. "And I'm sorry I have to go now. But I had fun hanging out with you, Lucy." So this actually had been hanging out. Okay. She could handle that. Though she couldn't imagine Maggie swinging in the park and sitting on the grass, talking.

"Me too."

"So, have you decided to give me your cell number?"

"Oh . . . yeah! Sure. Except—" Why did it feel weird to tell him she didn't have her own cell phone? It shouldn't. It never mattered to her before. But he seemed to expect that she would. "I don't have one."

Jonah took a breath as if he were going to say something, but then didn't. He opened his mouth again, then closed it. "You don't have a cell phone?"

"No."

"Did it go through the washing machine or something?"

"Uh, nope. I just don't have one."

"Oh." He shrugged it off. "Well, then—" He quirked his mouth sideways for a moment, then nodded to himself. "If I happened to maybe come by on, like, Tuesday, would you be interested in going to Scoops?"

"With *you*?"

"No, with Big Bird," he laughed. "Yes, with me."

Lucy laughed, too. She couldn't help it.

"That is such a great laugh. So, is that a yes?"

"Yes." She nodded once. "It's a yes."

"Good." He tugged the ends of her hair once more before he turned and walked around to the driver side of his car. He looked at her as he opened his door. "So, Tuesday."

"Yes."

"Around two?"

"Yes."

He smiled. Actually, he had never stopped smiling, so it was the same smile. He got in his car, started the engine, then waved and drove away.

Lucy looked down at the wood chip.

She needed a cell phone.

CHAPTER 26

Cell Phones

When Lucy walked into the kitchen, Claire was eating Oreos, expertly twisting the two chocolate cookies apart to reveal the unmarred, fully intact creamy center, with the imprint from the top cookie clearly visible.

"So?" She looked up from the successful removal of another top cookie.

"I need a cell phone."

"Yes," Claire nodded, understanding immediately. "Jonah needs to be able to text you. I'll talk to Dad about it when they get home."

"Thanks." Lucy leaned against the kitchen counter. She didn't know why or how, but Claire was the one who could talk their parents into anything. Not that she abused it; she simply knew when something was truly important, and Lucy getting a cell phone seemed to fall into Claire's category of absolutely vital to existence. "Do you think he'll care?"

"Probably not." Claire wiped her mouth and took a gulp of milk. "Maggie got her first phone when she was twelve years old, and I fully intend to have one before my next birthday, so it's perfectly reasonable for you to have one, too. You just never needed one before because you didn't really go anywhere, and you didn't have any friends. Except Don."

That was the truth. Should it have bothered Lucy? She had never felt bothered experiencing life in a semi-separated way, but now she was seeing the oddness of it. Maggie went to her friends' or boyfriends' houses a lot, plus she had a part-time job at the library, violin lessons, and sometimes after-school orchestra rehearsals and concerts. She'd also started volunteering at the assisted living center for elderly people. Claire, at only eleven years old, was also much more involved in the world than Lucy had ever been, but Claire's things were piano lessons and jujitsu. Claire had started taking jujitsu at the beginning of the school year. She had recently earned her orange belt, which was impressive even if Lucy wasn't sure how good that really was for a sixth grader.

About having friends, Lucy knew that the kids in her class spent time together outside of school. But she never felt the lack of friendship since she had her family. Even with parents working, and with sisters doing what they did, Lucy never felt lonely. There was always someone around. Always. Now that she thought about it, she wondered: had they done that on purpose? For her? There was always talk over breakfast about what was going on and who would be home and when. The discussions, like most discussions, floated around and beyond Lucy's focus. She heard it, but it simply didn't matter. Nothing mattered.

"Well, how'd it go?" asked Claire.

"What?"

"With Jonah! Where'd you go? What did you do? What did you talk about? You weren't gone very long." She looked up from an Oreo. "Please tell me you actually talked. I'm going to need to work on that with you."

"Yes, I talked!" Okay, yes, Jonah did most of the talking, but she had talked. Hadn't she?

"About what? Start at the beginning. Where did you go?"

"We went to the park."

Claire squinted at Lucy and twitched her mouth sideways. "You went to the park?"

"Yes?" Was that a problem?

"Okay . . . what did you do at the park?"

"We swang. Swung? We sat by each other on the swing set and . . . swang." Swang, swung. Neither choice sounded right. It was one of those words that sounded weirder each time you said it. Swinged? We went to hang out, and we hung out. We swung. Nope. This was going to bother her. She was turning the wood chip around in her hands.

"Lucy!"

"What?!"

"Pay attention!"

"What?" What had she missed?

"Did Jonah suggest the park, or did you?"

"Um. He did. He said we could go hang out there." We did not hang from a branch. We hung out. *Hunnnnng.*

"And did Jonah want to swing?"

"Um. I just went to the swings and sat down."

"And what did Jonah do?"

Lucy laughed out loud. "He tried to sit down, but his legs were too long, so he threw the swing around the top bar a few times so he could swing too." And they left the swing wrapped around the bar. Maybe they should have put it back the right way before they left.

"Oh, that's smart. He gets points for being nice and playing along."

"You don't think he wanted to swing?"

"Hmm. I highly doubt it. But never mind. What happened then?"

"I don't know. We just talked."

"About what?"

Lucy let out a little puff of air and set the wood chip on the counter. "I don't know."

"It's okay," Claire said, "I'm not trying to exasperate you. I'm just trying . . ."

Exasperate? Was Lucy exasperated? She turned to get a drink of water.

". . . if you're going to date him, I have to understand him."

Lucy whirled back around, choking again. "*Date* him?!" DATE him? What did that even mean? She didn't know how to go on a single date, let alone how to date a specific person!

"Yes, date him. Don't worry. I think he's okay. I just want to make sure."

Lucy's heart raced. What should she do?

"Whoa, hang on, Lucy." Claire got up and looked at Lucy but stayed where she was. "Just sit down. Where you are. Sit on the floor and breathe slowly. You're starting to panic but you don't need to. Everything is fine."

Panic? This was panic?

"Luce?"

She didn't like this feeling.

"Lucy? Sit down. Really. There by the sink. I'll sit down here by the fridge." Claire took six slow steps to the refrigerator and slowly sat down cross-legged on the floor.

Lucy held on to the counter as she sat down across from Claire. "I've never felt panic before."

"It's okay. Panic is just when you let something scare you too much. But you don't need to be scared. You just got nervous because dating is a new thing. But it's okay. That's normal. Even Maggie gets nervous when she goes out with someone for the first time."

"Nervous. This is nervous?"

"Uh, well, like I said, it's *extra* nervous, which is like fear, and you turned it into panic. But Lucy," Claire scooted closer to her sister, "you don't need to be afraid." She scooted until she was right in front of Lucy, knees touching, then leaned forward and took her hands. Lucy looked at Claire's face and grabbed her hands like they were a lifeline that could pull her drowning soul back up to the surface for air.

"Claire, I don't know what I'm doing."

"I know. Everything is new for you. But I can totally help you."

"How?"

Claire looked at Lucy for a few seconds. She squinted her eyes and pressed her lips together. "First of all, I think you need help putting the words you know to the feelings you are having. You've seen Maggie mad or worried. You've seen Mom sad or ticked off at Maggie. You've seen Dad frustrated, or—well, never mind about Dad; he keeps things pretty chill, but he gets mad and excited and happy just like everyone else, but you might not have noticed that. So, look at me! I'm totally good at being happy and excited and bugged and nervous and mad and *all* the feelings! I think that's because I'm still a kid, and I don't have to pretend not to feel things. Maggie used to be better at it, but she's getting closer and closer to being grown-up all the time, and honestly, she drives me nuts sometimes." She rolled her eyes, looking like a miniature Maggie when she did it.

Lucy laughed.

"See? I just distracted you from feeling nervous. You feel a little better now, right?"

Lucy took a deep breath and nodded. She did feel a little better. She relaxed her grip on Claire's hands.

"Thanks," Claire nodded to her hands. "Anyway, I'm pretty good at distracting people. But now you can tell me how you feel."

Lucy slumped. "I don't know how I feel. There's too much. Like, all the time! I know what the pills did, and I do feel the difference. But I can look back at before, and the thing is, I *did* have feelings! I felt things, Claire! But every feeling is bigger now. So when you say, 'nervous,' I know what that means. But honestly, I only know what it meant before. Like, I know I felt nervous every time a new school year started. But you just said

I felt nervous about—" Lucy choked a little. "—about dating. But this feeling?" She banged on her chest with her hand. "This is so much bigger than 'nervous!'"

"Yeah," Claire nodded. "Nervous is like a tiny bit of fear. But we need to keep the words separate, so maybe all you need is a plus sign."

Lucy scowled.

"Like when you get more than a B, you get a B *plus*. More. Extra. So let's say you were nervous *plus* a minute ago. To make up for the pills."

"You also said 'panic.' I don't think I ever felt panic before."

"Panic is like fear plus *PLUS*."

Lucy shook her head. "So wait. 'Nervous' is like fear *minus*, and panic is like—" She covered her face with her hands. "Never mind about that." Her voice was muffled behind her hands, but she didn't care. "Just tell me what to do! Jonah is going to come over on Tuesday and we are going to Scoops. What do I do? Should I tell him about the pills and explain why I act so . . ." Her words trailed off and she just pointed to herself. "So this."

"Um," she said. "I don't know what Dad told you, but he told me and Maggie not to say anything about it to other people."

"He didn't say anything about that to me! And he knows we already told Don!"

"I don't think Dad cares about Don knowing. He's like family anyway. But Maggie and me were told not to tell anyone anything. But it's kind of a 'duh' that you're different than you used to be."

Lucy dropped her hands. "It is?"

"Of course."

"No! Not 'of course!' It's not 'of course' to me! Nothing is 'of course' to me! What do you mean?"

"Lucy, anyone who has ever talked to you could see that you're more here now. For one thing, you never used to ask so many questions."

"Okay, never mind that." They were getting off the subject again. "So I won't say anything to Jonah about pills or anything. But then how do I explain how I'm acting?"

"Don't worry about that. For all he knows, this is just how you are." Claire stood up and got the package of Oreos off the table.

"Great."

"Very good sarcastic timing, Lucy. I give it a solid B *plus*." She sat down and offered a cookie to Lucy. Lucy shook her head. She could not deal with a sugar rush and figuring out how to go on a date at the same time.

"I think I might have been sarcastic with Don this morning, but he called it grumpy."

"Oh, that's interesting," Claire nodded, opening up another Oreo. "What happened?"

"Never mind about that. You keep getting me off the subject! Just tell me what to do—when I go to Scoops with Jonah, I mean."

"You should try the Cotton Candy, if they have it this week, with sprinkles mixed in! It's so good. Dad likes Black Cherry, but I don't think ice cream should taste like—"

"I don't mean about Scoops! I mean about Jonah!" She grabbed an Oreo and yanked it open. Some of the creamy filling was left on the top cookie, so she scraped it off with her bottom teeth before shoving it in her mouth.

"Um, are you done feeling heavy? I want some more milk, but I'd have to bring it down here to the floor."

Lucy thought for a minute. "I think I'm fine now. Thanks." When they stood up, Claire got the milk and Lucy got another glass, and they sat down at the table together.

"So do you like him?"

"I don't know—yes—I guess. I don't know."

"What do you like about him?"

Lucy chewed her second Oreo and took a gulp of milk before answering. "He's funny. I guess. He held my hand." She took another long drink of milk so she wouldn't see Claire grinning at her.

"Is he nice?"

"I guess so." She wiped her mouth. Was he nice? Now it was hard to think of it that way. He gave her a drink at the party. Sure, it was a drink she shouldn't have taken, which made her end up floating a little, and barfing, but still. It was nice of him to offer, especially since she was thirsty. And he brought Maggie's lip gloss to the house. "He said I had a pretty smile. And a great laugh."

"You laughed? Then you were pretty relaxed. That's good, Luce."

Lucy twisted another Oreo apart. "Oh." She looked up. "He said he would teach me how to drive."

"Ah." Claire nodded. "That means he wants to spend more time with you, 'cause you can't learn to drive a car in one day."

"He said he thought you were going to take over the world one day."

"Me?"

"Uh-huh."

"Well, he's smart, at least." Claire was closing up the Oreos. Lucy stood up to put the milk in the refrigerator.

"He is. He's going to study pre-med at Brown." She shut the fridge door and turned around.

"Cool." Claire took Lucy's hand to go back into the den to finish the movie. "But let Dad be the one to tell Mom you have a date."

"Duh!" They both laughed. "Oh wait!"

Lucy ran back to the kitchen counter and picked up the dusty wood chip. Sure, it wasn't much. But it was the first thing a guy had ever given her, so she was keeping it.

On Sunday, Aeden sat down on the sofa to relax before dinner, and Lucy and Claire casually walked in and sat on either side of him.

"Okay, what's going on?" he said.

How had he known something was going on?

Claire jumped right in. "Lucy is going to Scoops on Tuesday with a guy—he's Maggie's boyfriend's cousin named Jonah, and I've met him and he's nice—so she needs a cell phone."

Aeden was shaking his head before Claire even finished her sentence.

"It's time, Dad," Claire said, scooting closer to him and nodding her head in a sympathetic way. "She's almost seventeen years old."

"Her birthday is three months away," he corrected, still shaking his head.

"Exactly," Claire nodded, as if he had been agreeing with her.

Lucy noticed once again how people talked about her and made decisions for her without even looking at her, but she didn't mind this time. Claire was an eleven-year-old genius, and she probably would take over the world someday, like Jonah had said.

"She should have talked to me before agreeing to this date," he said.

Even Lucy could tell this was a weak argument.

Claire got on her knees, reached up, and gently wrapped her arms around his neck. Blinking her long eyelashes and gazing up at him, she whispered, "Maggie never once asked permission to go get ice cream with a guy."

He shook his head and looked at Claire like he'd just been betrayed by his best friend.

Claire had won.

"Hey Mom," Claire said at Sunday dinner, "will you take Lucy and me to get her a cell phone tomorrow when you get home? She's going on an ice cream date on Tuesday."

Kelly's face brightened in surprise. "Really? With whom?"

"Maggie's boyfriend's cousin, named Jonah. I've met him, and he's nice."

"Well, okay then," Kelly shrugged, then put a bite of baked broccoli with lemon zest in her mouth.

Lucy would never be surprised at anything after this.

CHAPTER 27

Scoops

Scoops Ice Cream Shoppe—with an e—in Cicero, New York, was a family-owned business that was big into community spirit. The last time Lucy had gone there with her family, it was late at night, and a local band was playing in the parking lot. She was glad it was quiet this time; before, even in her drug-induced fog, the loud music was a little unsettling, and she didn't think it would be a good idea to experience it without the fog on her first date. She still mentally tripped on the word *date*. She was on a *date*. So weird.

Jonah ordered an enormous pile of whipped cream that supposedly covered a fudge brownie with peanut butter cookie ice cream, but Lucy couldn't see anything but fluffy white goo. She ordered a small root beer float with no whipped cream.

Lucy turned to sit at one of the wooden tables around the outside patio area, but Jonah grabbed an extra spoon off the counter first and offered her one. "Wanna share?"

"No thanks," she said, trying not to make a face.

"Not a fan of whipped cream?" he asked, nodding to her un-topped float.

"I don't mind whipped cream if it's already on something, but peanut butter cookie ice cream? Yuck."

"What? How can you wrinkle your nose at peanut butter cookie ice cream?" Apparently, she had been unsuccessful at not making a face. "It's like reaching the promised land," he said, then dug deep down into the mess with his spoon. He pulled up a giant glop of brown, tan, and white, and shoved it into his happy face. It was a cute face. And his ears weren't really that big.

"I'll stick with my root beer float, thanks." Then she scraped off a root-beer-soaked layer of ice cream and put it in her mouth. "Mmm."

"Why do you turn your spoon over like that?"

"Like what?"

"You turned your spoon up-side-down before you put it in your mouth."

Lucy looked down at her next spoonful, then mentally went through the process of eating it.

"It's so I taste the ice cream first, and not the spoon."

"The spoon doesn't have a taste."

"Exactly. I want to taste ice cream and root beer, not *nothing*."

"Huh." He scooped up another heap of his whipped cream concoction. He tried to turn it up-side down, but the mess slid off the spoon and plopped on the table. "Crap. Now I've wasted an entire bite."

Lucy scraped off another spoonful of ice cream, turned it over, and put it in her mouth. "It's a skill," she said around the cold dessert.

"I'll need to practice."

"Or take smaller bites."

"No way." He held up another mountainous spoonful. "This is the perfect combination of brownie, ice cream, and toppings. It isn't possible to do that in smaller proportions."

"That's a reasonable technique for you. For me, I eat all the ice cream first, then drink the root beer that has the melted vanilla ice cream in it. That's really the best part." Another spoonful.

Lucy couldn't believe she was sitting there talking, and actually laughing, while eating ice cream on a real date with Jonah. She was actually having fun! She never even noticed his ears. There was even a point where she realized she wasn't actually floating, but she also wasn't putting any weight on wooden bench. She reached under the table and pressed herself solidly down, glancing up at the red awning they were sitting under. But then she had to wipe her hand on her pants; whoever had sat there before had left a fresh, gooey glob of what she hoped was just bubblegum ice cream.

While they ate, they talked about the perfect ways to eat other kinds of foods, about school, and about their families.

"I have an older sister named Lori who is doing medical school at Dartmouth, which is where both my parents went."

"But you said you were going to Brown, right?" She hoped that was what he'd said.

"Yeah! Good memory! Two points." He held up his right hand to high-five her, so she did. This was so strange to her. Her family didn't do that.

"And you said it was because . . ." Music? Was it music? ". . . of music?" Please be music.

"Hey, another two points!" He held up his hand again, but the high-five she gave didn't connect very well. "No, that was terrible. We need to do that again." He reached over, took her right hand in his left, lifted it up, and clapped their hands together, making a solid *smack*. "Much better," he said, still holding her hand. She pulled it back and took a drink of the remaining root beer. She wasn't sure how sticky her hand was from the goo under the table.

"Um, what instrument do you play?" she asked, eyes down.

"Saxophone and clarinet. They have a great music program and several jazz ensembles. I'll audition for those when I start in September."

"Wait—" She looked up at him then. "you're going to do music *and* pre-med? Isn't that, you know, hard to do?"

"Yeah. But I won't have to work because of my scholarships, so I think I'll be fine. My parents are worried though." He looked down and shrugged. "They're afraid my music will be a distraction. It's what I love most. But it's true; it's hard to make money as a musician."

"Um . . . but doesn't your dad own a music store?" Her mouth was getting cold, and the last word came out sounding more like "shore."

"Yeah. Music is his passion too. But when both my parents finished medical school and began practicing, it became obvious my mom was the more successful doctor, so when Lori came along, they decided not to have two doctors in the family. I think it wounds his pride a little that she earns more money than he does, even though the store is fairly successful, and he is free to do what he loves."

"Wow." Lucy didn't even know what she loved most. Her mind went blank even as she tried to think of it. She liked art. She was good at math. What else?

Flying.

She shook her head. "Wow." She had already said that.

"So, yeah, school will be a load, but I can do it. And—" he hesitated and looked down at his sundae. "It's only, like, a five-hour drive from here to Rhode Island, so I could probably come home some weekends." He looked up at her through his lashes.

She didn't know what to say to that. Did he mean he wanted to see her on the weekends? She was only sixteen years old! Why would a college guy drive five hours to see her? "Does your sister, Lori, come home a lot?"

"Not really. She's in her first year of medical school. She says it's pretty brutal." He was pushing soggy bits of brownie around with his spoon. He looked . . .

"Are you sad?"

He sort of grunted softly and shrugged. "No. Not really. Yeah, but not. I guess, kind of."

He sounded like her. Sometimes she could not think of a word to say how she felt. It was so frustrating.

"Are you frustrated?"

He looked up at her. "I really like how you ask me what I'm feeling. My family doesn't really do that. They're more about doing what needs to be done and not thinking about feelings. But yeah. I'm frustrated."

"Because you don't want to be a doctor?"

He sat back on his wooden bench and looked like Maggie did when she was being lectured. His mouth was in a kind of crooked scrunch, and he did not look happy.

"I'm sorry," she said. "I didn't—"

"No, it's not you. I'm sorry. I don't want to be all bugged on our date." So . . . he thought of it as a date too. That was good to know. "But it's funny that you get what my parents obviously can't." Then he shrugged with just one shoulder. "Or maybe they can and just don't want to. But they aren't wrong: becoming a professional musician isn't practical. I'll have to settle for playing clarinet at Jewish weddings and bar mitzvahs and stuff. I'm sure I can join a klezmer band at Brown."

"A what?"

"A klezmer band. That's what they call the bands that play at Jewish celebrations."

"Oh, I didn't know you were Jewish."

He quirked his eyebrows. "Yeah, of course. Does that matter?"

"No. I had just never heard of a—what was that called?"

"A klezmer band."

"What kind of band is that?"

He smiled and relaxed a little. He had tensed up a moment before. "Traditional Jewish celebration music. You know, like the horah, the Mezinke Tanz, 'Chosen-Kalle Mazel Tov,' 'Ot A Soi.'"

"Um, I've heard people say 'Mazel Tov,' but I don't think I've heard any of that music."

"I'll play some for you some time, if you want." The last part sounded kind of like a question.

"Okay." That would be fun.

"And actually," he thought for a moment. "I'm playing at a wedding in two weeks. Not this Thursday, but the next. You could come if you want." Another kind-of question at the end.

"Me?" She'd been to a couple of weddings before, but those were Catholic weddings.

"Well, only if you want to. It's my cousin's wedding. Oh—it's Caleb's sister. She's getting married."

"Naomi?!" She was only sixteen!

"No." Jonah laughed really hard this time. "Caleb's older sister, Talya. She's twenty-four. Her dad, my Uncle David, hired my klezmer band to play at the celebration. And we are Reform Jewish, so I think you would like it. And you'd get to hear me play. Just the clarinet, but it's kind of fun. Plus, it's probably the only time we could go out at night, since I have lessons or rehearsals most nights."

"Oh, I hadn't even thought about you taking lessons. You have a busy life." Lucy didn't have a busy life. She was barely figuring out what having a regular life was.

"I'm sorry, no." He laughed again. "I don't take lessons. Well, I do have a saxophone coach, but mostly I'm giving lessons in the evenings."

"You *teach* music?"

"Yeah. I teach beginning and intermediate clarinet and sax."

"Wow. You must be good."

"I'm okay," he shrugged, "but that's why I'll probably always come see you in the afternoon." So, he was planning on coming over often?

"I'm okay with that." She smiled. She couldn't help it! This was so cool!

"But anyway, what about you? What do you love doing?"

Crap. This was not cool.

"Ummm . . . I like hanging out with my sisters." She didn't know if watching television with Claire was considered hanging out, but it was all she could come up with. Her heart dropped a little when she realized that Maggie didn't hang out with her much anymore. Besides the whole floating weirdness, Maggie was more interested in Caleb these days. Plus, they were giving her more hours at the library, so she was sort of legitimately busy.

"I know Maggie, but Claire seems really fun for a kid. How old is she?"

"Eleven?" Was that right? Yes. Her birthday was in November. Lucy realized she needed to pay more attention to her family— birthdays and things like that. She'd never even bought any of them a present. She also didn't have any money. Maybe she should get a job. Maybe Scoops was hiring.

"She looks younger, but she seems older for some reason. I think she has an old soul."

"Yeah, she might." She thought about Claire's emotional coaching. "I'd be kind of lost without her." What could she do for Claire? Give her that blue sweater that she loved so much?

"That's really cool that you're that close. I'm not super close to Lori. But she's like, five years older than I am."

"I'm five years older than Claire. But maybe it's different 'cause we're both girls." Or maybe it was because Lucy didn't have any friends because her parents had been keeping her drugged. But that wasn't really a conversation she could have with Jonah right now. Or anyone, probably ever.

"Are you okay?"

Lucy looked up. "Yeah. Why?"

"I dunno. You looked really sad again all of a sudden. Like you did at the park."

"Oh, sorry."

"It's fine." Another shrug. "So, what else do you like to do?"

Dang it. She was hoping to slide around that question.

"Um, I like to sleep?" It was kind of a gamble: he would either think that was funny, or the lamest answer in the world.

"Ha! No kidding! I wish there could be just one day that I could sleep all day long and not have to go anywhere or do anything."

"That's pretty much what Maggie does on Saturdays." Except when she was working or volunteering, so that wasn't as true as it used to be. But Lucy hoped this would take the conversation in a different direction.

"Yeah, you two really are different." Ugh—not that direction! "I can't imagine her sitting and laughing for an hour and a half while eating ice cream." Had it been an hour and a half already? "She never sits still. She's always moving around and talking to lots of people, but not having a conversation. I've known her since third grade, I think, and she's been dating Caleb since homecoming last year, so I see her everywhere, but I don't think we've spoken more than three words to each other at a time. It's 'Hey, Jonah,' and she moves on."

"Yeah. She's always moving around." Maggie had been dating Caleb since last fall? Lucy didn't know that.

"Or brushing her hair. I've never seen any girl brush her hair as much as she does." He added. Maybe Jonah liked Maggie.

"Well at least she *can* brush it. Just try getting a brush or comb or anything through this mess." She flicked a piece of hair away from her face.

"Okay," he said, then reached over and lightly pulled on a strand of orange curls that was by her left cheek. He ran it through his fingers a couple of times then let it drop. "I like your hair. It's pretty."

Lucy felt her face get hot again.

"And your freckles," he added with a half-smile.

She immediately covered her face with her hands. "Ugh. My hair? I can handle that. But my freckles? No way. I wish there was a magic cream to make them disappear."

"Okay, stop." He grabbed her hands and pulled them down, holding them on the table. "Your freckles are cute."

She shook her head. *Nope. They are not.*

"Hey, I have freckles. Do they bother you?" He looked up and moved his face side to side so she could get a good look.

"No." That was entirely different. "My freckles are like a galaxy all over my face. Your freckles are like—" She had to think about this analogy. "—like one single constellation."

"Oh yeah? What does my 'constellation' look like?" Jonah let go of one of her hands, still holding the other, then held his chin with a serious look on his face, like a model posing in a freckle commercial.

"Mmmm . . ." If she squinted her eyes, she could imagine, "maybe a seahorse?" She laughed.

"A seahorse?" He touched his nose. "That doesn't sound very cool. Are you sure it's not something a little, I don't know, tougher? Like a dragon, or a tiger or something?"

"Sorry," she shrugged without feeling very sorry. "You asked me, I looked, and all I'm ever going to see now is a seahorse."

"Where? Show me." He pushed his empty sundae bowl aside and leaned toward her across the table. Up close, his ears didn't seem big at all. And his eyes were really pretty. Was it okay to say that a guy had pretty eyes? They weren't handsome eyes; they were *pretty*. A really pretty sky blue. "Well?" he said. And she realized they were staring at each other.

She shook her head and shifted on the bench. "Here." She reached up and barely touched her finger to the side of his nose and traced upward to under his left eye, then down in a little curl on his left cheek. She dropped her hand. "It's just a little seahorse."

Still looking at her, he quirked his mouth to the side and touched where her finger had traced. "I'll have to see this for myself when I have a mirror."

She smiled. "I could take a pen and trace it for you if you want."

He sat back, and she could breathe a little better. "Ahh, no thanks. I'll take your word for it."

He was staring at her, so Lucy looked down and took a sip of her root beer float. "This is really good. Thanks."

"I think you have a few constellations too."

She felt her face get warm. "Way more than a few, I bet."

"Hmm . . ."

She shook her head. "No, don't look at my freckles." Pretty soon he was going to realize how much nicer Maggie's face was. Or just about any girl at school. Or even any guy at school. Well, there was this one kid she'd seen in the cafeteria whose freckles were like her dad's, almost covering his entire face, but for some reason, he looked okay. It seemed that only her personal freckles were a problem.

"Now hold still and let me look."

He reached across the table with his long arms and held her face in his hands. Oh man. That was just like in the movies! She held still but could feel her face get hotter.

"You're cute when you blush."

It was Lucy's turn to make that kind of *humph* sound. She moved her eyes away when he smiled.

"I can see a little crescent moon there," he moved one hand to touch her forehead, just left of the center. "And a tiny butterfly next to where your dimple is." He touched her right cheek. "And a teeny, little heart right there." He touched her left cheek bone below the outer corner of her eye for a moment longer than the others, then let go and sat back in his seat. "See? They are cute."

Lucy frowned and shook her head.

"You do frown and shake your head a lot, though." He stopped mid-chuckle. "And now you're absolutely scowling. How come?"

"You don't have to say that."

Jonah was nice, and cute, and he was sometimes funny but, even through the glass, she always saw how beautiful Maggie was. And Claire was all kinds of adorable in her looks and her personality. But Lucy? Not at all. And she didn't like him saying stuff that wasn't true. It was mean. And she felt the heaviness coming. "I know very well what I look like," she said, then grabbed her float again. It was all melted and warm, but it was down to the best part where all that was left was creamy sweet root beer.

Jonah didn't say anything for a moment. There was clearly nothing more for him to say.

"Look Lucy, I don't want to bug you. But I think you must not know what you look like."

Lucy was looking down but could see that he was looking right at her and frowning a little. Not like an angry frown. More like a what-was-wrong-with-this-girl frown. Great.

"Look, can I just say something? Without you getting all mad?"

That was strange; she realized that she really was mad. How weird. She tried to relax and breathe. She looked up and nodded.

"I really like hanging out with you. You really aren't like the other girls, and I know that sounds dumb, but it's true. Anyway, I think maybe it's because you really don't know how . . ." he hesitated. "I don't know . . . how great you are." Lucy squinted. "I mean, I know I don't know you super well yet, but so far I've had more fun with you than any girl I've dated."

And how many would that be, she wondered.

"I mean, not that I've dated a *ton* of girls, but I've gone out a lot, and you are not just cute, you're fun. I mean, I haven't played on the swings since I was about ten, and I've never just sat on the grass and talked. You are just so . . ." Weird? "So chill. You don't have the attitude that most of the girls at our school have. And I like that you're not all into goopy makeup and stuff. You just seem so relaxed."

Lucy nearly burst out in hysterics. Relaxed? That was the very last thing she was.

"And so far," he said, "the only time you seem not relaxed is if I say anything about you being cute. But Lucy?" She realized she had looked away, staring out across the parking lot, so she looked back. His blue eyes were so intense. "You are really beautiful." He said it like it was just a no-big-deal-matter of fact. Poor guy. Maybe his amazing blue eyes needed glasses.

"You're beautiful, too." *What?!* She couldn't believe she said that! Why had she said that?!

Jonah burst out in a loud, long laugh, and Lucy could hardly believe it, but he actually blushed! He put his head down and rubbed the back of his neck, which had gone all blotchy, hiding his face, but still smiling. It was his turn to shake his head. "Well, thanks," he said, as he looked up. "I guess it is harder to take a compliment than to give one."

Where in the world had that *come* from? She wanted to die. Annnd the bench creaked. *Crap.* She slurped down the last of the flat, sweet root beer at the bottom of her plastic cup. Looking down at the foam residue left on the sides of the cup and straw, she breathed in slowly, and breathed out slowly. She relaxed her shoulders, her arms, and her chest.

"Do you want another one?"

Lucy realized she had been slurping when there was nothing left to slurp. She took the straw out of her mouth and looked up. "Oh, no. I'm fine. Thanks! It was really good." She wiped her mouth with her napkin because she couldn't think of anything else to say. Change the subject from compliments and blushing and stuff. "How was your gross brownie-peanut-butter-cookie thing?" She glanced down and saw that he had actually eaten the entire thing, even the soggy bits that he had been pushing around earlier.

"Promised land," he nodded.

"I think this was the best first date I've ever had," Jonah said as he pulled up to Lucy's house. He was radiating a buzzy energy that Lucy had only felt from Claire before. She associated it with Claire being really happy or excited, so she hoped it meant the same thing for Jonah.

"Me too." She smiled. She would not say that it was the *only* first date she had ever had.

"Uh, do you mind if I come in and get a drink of water? I forgot my water bottle, and I've got a student after this."

"Sure, come on in."

The house was quiet. The only sound they heard as they entered the kitchen was the clatter of ice dropping in the ice maker and the clock ticking on the wall. But Lucy suspected Claire was either upstairs listening through the vents or peeking around a corner somewhere. That girl always knew an awful lot about what each person in the family was up to, and she had opinions about all of it.

She filled a glass with noisy ice and cold water from the refrigerator, then handed it to Jonah. He set his keys on the counter and took it. She liked that their hands touched for a second. What a dumb thing to get excited about, but there it was. This was it. Her first crush.

"Thanks," he said, taking the glass and drinking half the water in one gulp.

She also set a cold bottle of water from the fridge on the counter. "And here," she said. "You can take this one with you."

"Oh thanks! That will help a lot." He finished the glass in one more gulp then wiped his mouth. "So, we kind of got off topic when I asked if you wanted to come to my cousin's wedding. I mean, you don't have to, but . . ."

"Sure! I'll come!" *Whoa*, that sounded way too enthusiastic. Lucy tried to turn the emotional volume down a bit, but when feelings came crashing out of nowhere like that, how was she to know when or how to turn them down?

"Really? Cool." She wasn't sure, but it sounded like Jonah just tried to turn his emotional volume down, too. But why would he have to do something like that? He's been dealing with emotions his whole life. "I'll drop off an invitation tomorrow. I'd have to meet you there since I have to be there early for band stuff. Is that okay?"

"Yeah, that's fine." That was not fine! *Arrgghh!* Too many feelings!

"Okay, good." Jonah was grinning. But then he looked at the clock when it made a click as it moved to the hour. "Oh no! I'm gonna be late." He set down the glass and grabbed the bottle. He looked confused for a moment, then leaned down and kissed Lucy on the corner of her mouth, turned, and practically ran out the door.

Lucy was staring, wondering whether he had aimed for her mouth and missed, or for her cheek and missed. These were important things to know! And—she gasped. She was rising completely off the floor! The toes of her shoes skittered along the edge of the counter as she went up. His kiss - had made - her float! At the same moment that thought crossed her mind, she heard the front door open and knew it was Jonah. She bent down and grabbed the edge of the counter to pull herself down, but that wasn't really necessary. Her fear and anxiety dropped her back to the ground like . . . like a girl who suddenly couldn't float. She kept hold of the counter, though, just to be sure.

Jonah ran back into the kitchen and grabbed his keys off the counter, not really noticing that Lucy was half bent over, arms spread wide, hanging on to the edges with both hands. "Sorry," he said, his face going red for the second time that day. Then he spun on his heel and ran out again, but he glanced back and smiled at her just before he disappeared around the door.

Lucy wasn't even a tiny bit surprised that Claire chose that moment to emerge from the den, with an empty cereal bowl, acting casual. Lucy was still holding onto the edge of the counter when she looked over, and she knew she was grinning.

Claire dropped the casual act as her jaw dropped. "What happened?"

Lucy glanced back at the door for a moment then cleared her throat. She was not sure which news was better. "I just floated again," was what popped out first, but she was thinking more about the kiss. "Like, a lot."

Claire's mouth fell even more open, though Lucy had no idea how that was even possible, as she gasped in believing disbelief. "No way! Can you do it again!"

"I don't . . . know how." Still smiling, she looked up and to the left as if trying to figure something out. The happy feelings were definitely still there, but her body was now attached to the ground like it should be. "I—I didn't even do it on purpose. It just—it just . . . happened!"

"Well, what happened? I mean *what* happened? What *happened*?" Claire demanded in a rush, shaking her head, and looking at her sister in wonder and awe.

Lucy bit both lips together hard, wanting to keep her feelings under control, but the sides of her mouth were still pulling out in opposite directions. Giving up on controlling the feeling, she settled for controlling the volume. "Jonah just kissed me," she whispered.

"I knew he liked you!" Claire screamed, doing a little jumpy dance, before Lucy could shush her.

"*Shhhhhhh*!" Lucy scowled while turning her head toward the door and waving her arms back and forth as if trying to erase Claire's words and energy from the air.

Claire's hands flew to her mouth and her eyebrows disappeared beneath her bangs as she looked at the door. When nothing happened after three solid seconds, she dropped her hands. "Why'd you shush me? Nobody's here."

"I know, I know. I don't know!" Lucy shot back, again waving her hands in the air.

Claire tilted her head and looked at Lucy with a you're-losing-your-mind expression on her face.

Shaking her head, Lucy was still trying to control something. Anything! Too many loud feelings. "I just need a minute." She covered her face with her hands and took a deep breath. "Don't worry."

"Um," Claire said in her almost-sassy voice, "I'm not the one worrying, Luce."

"Shhh!" Lucy looked up, paused, and took another deep breath, not knowing why she wanted Claire to be quiet. "It's just weird. And . . . Just shush. I have to think." Hands to her head again.

Claire rolled her eyes and walked to the cupboard. "You think too much." She pulled out her box of Lucky Charms and asked, "You want some?"

Lucy shook her head, and Claire refilled her bowl.

Lucy continued to think for the rest of the day, through the evening, and even while she slept. Her Dreams that night featured the echoing chamber that had black-and-white checkered floor tiles and gray marble pillars that she had to get past without touching down. She never knew why she needed to, but she tried every time, even though she had not yet made it. That night, her attempts had been especially frustrating. Instead of helping her float, jumbled memories of ice cream, swing sets, and freckles distracted her. She couldn't hold on to the light feelings; gravity seemed a sinister thing that mocked her and pulled her down. She slipped and fell to the cold, hard floor, over and over again.

She was tired the next morning, probably from Dreaming all night, but her mind kept thinking all through breakfast. Her family didn't comment on her silence; her quiet mood probably felt like normal to them. As she cleaned up the breakfast dishes—it was her turn—Claire gave her a hug around the waist and padded off in bare feet back to her room, leaving Lucy all alone. The silence felt strange after the momentous events of the day before.

She walked over to Don's house to practice, thinking she should have been happy about everything; she'd gone on a date, a boy had sort of kissed her, it was a beautiful day, and Mrs. Tan's roses were coming out with their pink tips emerging from the green buds. Life was good, wasn't it? But Lucy felt tired more than anything.

"And then it just happened, without me even doing anything," Lucy said, concluding her story as she played with the model of H_2O. After thinking about it all night and all morning, Lucy still couldn't believe it had happened. And she couldn't even decide if "it" referred to the kiss or the floating—both were astonishing.

That was the word Claire came up with after Lucy had told her everything. She said Lucy felt *astonished*.

"Wait. What?" Don stared.

Hadn't he been listening? Where was Don's head? "I floated," she shrugged, "right out of the blue."

"No. I got that." Don closed his eyes and shook his head. "What happened before that?"

"Jonah took me to get ice cream, and he kind of kissed me when he left my house."

"He. 'Kind of.' Wait—what?"

"Well, I'm not sure what he meant to do. The kiss sort of landed here." Lucy touched the skin next to the corner of her mouth. "So, I don't know if—"

"Your mouth. He was aiming for your mouth. You must have moved."

"But he might have been aiming for my cheek and then I—"

"No. It's simple math and probability. If he was aiming for your mouth, he was only off half an inch. If he was aiming for your cheek, it was off by two inches, and he'd be an idiot."

"That's the math, but what about probability?"

"That's the probability too."

"What do you m—"

"It doesn't matter. The problem is solved." He smiled. But it was a weird smile. "Next time you think you might crash, just think about Jonah. It's just as well, I was getting behind in my chemistry homework." He tore the pages out of the back of his chemistry notebook and threw them in the recycle box under his desk.

"What do you mean? It's summer." He was acting weird. Even more distracted than usual.

"I'm taking an online chemistry class, and it's pretty tough, so this is a relief. Thanks for letting me know." He was packing up his laptop and grabbing his earphones.

"But—"

"I'll see ya around."

Then he was gone, and Lucy was left standing by herself in Don's room, staring at the little glass of H_2O.

CHAPTER 28

Wedding

"Next, turn right on Madison Street, then go four blocks" Lucy told her dad while looking down at the app on her phone.

"To which street?"

"Um, just past University Avenue."

Lucy's dad nodded. "Good. You're doing well." He was having Lucy read the directions from her phone, even though he knew Syracuse just as well as he knew Clay and didn't really need directions. "And you're sure Jonah can take you home?"

"Yes. He only needs to play for the part before the wedding, and then the part after the wedding, but another guy in the band will play Jonah's parts for the reception."

"And that's okay? Wasn't his band hired to be the band?"

"Yeah. But I think he's doing it more as a favor for his uncle since it's his cousin who is getting married."

"That's right. And that's Caleb's brother?"

"No, his older sister, Talya. Talya's dad, *Caleb's* dad, asked Jonah to get his band to play for the wedding. But Jonah said the important thing is for him to play when the bride and groom walk in and when they leave because he promised, and then some other part."

He smiled. "Yep. Lots of parts to Jewish weddings. Just follow along with what everyone else does, like we talked about, and you'll be fine." The temple entrance was actually around the corner on University Avenue, so they drove around until Lucy's dad could find a place to let her off on Madison street. He pulled over to the curb half a block past the synagogue and looked at her. "But Lucy? No drinking. At all. Understood?"

She nodded twice with wide green eyes. "Absolutely understood." There was no way she was going to let whatever happened at Caleb's house happen tonight.

"Good." He leaned over and kissed her on the cheek. "And you look really beautiful."

"Thanks," she smiled as she looked down and rubbed her hand across the creamy soft material of her new dress. Kelly had taken Lucy shopping the day before and did her best to maneuver Lucy into an emerald-green, tea-length taffeta thing with a wide skirt. Lucy was so glad Claire had come and was able to steer their mother in another direction; Celtic pride was one thing, but Kelly's insistence on putting her in green every chance she got disagreed with Lucy even before she cared about how she looked. But now, especially when she wanted to look nice without drawing any kind of attention to herself, it was maddening.

The dress Lucy chose was a muted beige *sheath dress*, a term she hadn't even known until yesterday, with faint satiny swirls crushed into the fabric. It had a *boat neck*—another new term, which made no sense, but was probably easier than saying "the neck hole is a slit from shoulder to shoulder"—and short sleeves, and it came to just below her knees. She also wore some cute, navy-blue satin flats, small gold earrings, and a gold charm bracelet she'd had forever. Claire had been thrilled to help Lucy put on a little makeup and do her hair so her natural curls didn't turn into natural frizz. Makeup and hair maintenance may have been new elements in Lucy's world, but it was no surprise that her eleven-year-old sister had at least a theoretical understanding of all that stuff.

She tucked her phone into the little purse that matched her shoes.

"Don't lose that," her dad said.

"I won't," she answered, then stepped out of the car.

"Have fun," he said.

"Thanks," she smiled back as she slammed the heavy door shut. Did he look a little sad? "And don't slam the door!" she heard through the glass as she turned toward the synagogue. Her stomach was fluttering.

Lucy didn't know anything about architecture or Jewish history, but the front of Temple Concord reminded her of pictures of the Greek Parthenon, only smaller. Wide concrete stairs led through four two-story columns in front of three enormous doors, topped by—well, it was a flat, wide triangle shape. Above the outer doors were stone carvings of the Star of David, and above the center door was the quote

MINE HOUSE SHALL BE CALLED AN HOUSE OF
PRAYER FOR ALL PEOPLES.

When Lucy walked in, she could hear klezmer music playing but couldn't see where it came from, and it seemed like the celebration had been going on for a while. She knew there had been another *part* before the actual wedding *part*, but it seemed like she was the only one just entering the building. Before she could worry too much about that, and even before her eyes had adjusted to the change in lighting from outside, Lucy was startled when someone touched her arm and a quiet girl's voice said, "Lucy?"

She turned and saw Naomi smiling at her, and she breathed a silent prayer of gratitude. "Hi," she half-sighed.

Naomi hugged Lucy and took her hand. "Hi. I'm sorry I only have a minute, but Jonah asked me to watch for you since he's busy playing. Aunt Sharon is in the sanctuary, and I'll take you to her before I run back to help Talya." She paused and looked past Lucy. "Did Don come with you?"

"N-no. Was he supposed to?" Had Naomi invited him?

"No, I was just wondering. Here—" She hurried to turn toward a table that had a basket full of little doilies, another one full of little black hats, and a guest book. "Did Jonah tell you you'll need to wear a head covering?"

"No." Then Lucy noticed the satiny lace Naomi wore like a head band. It matched her lilac-colored dress and was wider than a ribbon but thinner than a scarf. Her shiny brown hair flowed down her back, and the long ends of the lace streamed down just past the ends. Lucy touched the top of her head. Was it disrespectful to have walked in without something on her head?

"It's okay; we have some that will actually match your dress." Naomi had already reached for one of the baskets and came back with a folded, cream-colored triangle of lace about eight inches long. She stepped around Lucy and began fastening it to the hair at the crown of her head. She had obviously done this many times before because she was done in less than four seconds. "The little combs that come with these would be useless in your gorgeous hair, so it's good they put out bobby pins." She set the clear, rejected comb back in the basket, then looked at her work and smiled a soft but satisfied smile. "You look really pretty. I like your dress."

"Thanks. So do you. I like *your* dress." Naomi had more curves than Lucy, and she didn't have even a single freckle that Lucy could see.

"Thanks. It's Talya's favorite color." She shrugged then took Lucy's hand. "I'm really so sorry, but I have to get back to Talya. Let's go find my aunt. She's saving you a seat.

Lucy followed as Naomi tugged her along, and the music got louder. She looked for Jonah when they entered what she assumed was the sanctuary and came in view of the band. He was already looking at her over his clarinet. He nodded his head and winked.

He winked!

She waved her hand a little, not knowing if that was okay to do, then lost eye contact with him as she was pulled farther into the crowd of other people shuffling to their places among the dark, wooden benches. The wink, the music, and the crowd of unfamiliar people had turned the butterflies in her stomach into bats—large, spastic bats whose echolocation was all messed up because they were crashing into each other. *Breathe*, she told herself. *Just breathe.*

Naomi stopped close to the front, next to a tall, middle-aged woman with short, dark hair and a cautious smile. Lucy had been amazed by Jonah's sky-blue eyes when they were laughing over ice cream, but now those eyes were looking at her from this woman's face, and that was weird. Of course, that meant this was his mother. The bats in her stomach did some freaky reverse-evolution thing and turned into pterodactyls.

"Hi Aunt Sharon," Naomi said as they kissed each other's cheeks. "This is Lucy, Jonah's—" then she glanced at Lucy, "—um, friend?"

Lucy wanted to die, but Mrs. Edelmann ignored the embarrassing stumble, and reached for both of Lucy's hands. She immediately kissed Lucy's cheeks, and said, "It's very nice to meet you, Lucy."

"It's very nice to meet you, too, Mrs. Edelmann."

"You may call me Sharon."

There was no way Lucy would ever do that.

"I have to go, Aunt Sharon."

"Of course. Go on," *Sharon* said, waving the already-retreating Naomi away. "Sit here, Lucy. Jonah's father will be joining us soon, but there is plenty of room." She ushered Lucy to the left, then sat down next to her, leaving an ample space by the end of the bench.

"Um," Lucy began, looking around and not sure how to ask the appropriate questions.

"Go ahead, dear. Ask me anything you like."

"Well," she nodded to the people around them. "I thought we would be, um . . ."

"Separated? Men on one side, women on the other?"

"Well, yes?" It sounded stupid because, clearly, these people were all mixed together. But her dad had told her specifically that the women and men did not sit together.

"Yes. Orthodox congregations do that still. But we are Reform. I'll admit I'm more conservative than most Reform congregations these days—" she shook her head a little at this comment, "but I agree it's simply impractical to expect everyone to be as observant as we choose to be. Not to mention guests," she gestured absently to Lucy, then waved a hand to someone behind them who had caught her attention. Waving at Jonah was probably okay, then.

Lucy nodded, since she didn't know what else to say, and looked around. A traditional marriage chuppah stood at the front of the room. It was draped with gauzy white fabric, dark green vines, lilacs in five distinct shades of purple, and tiny yellow flowers Lucy didn't know. How in the world did they get all those flowers to look so perfect in June? The one lilac bush in Lucy's yard had lost all its flowers weeks ago. She could smell the sweet fragrance from where she sat, though, so she closed her eyes and breathed it in. The scent of these lilacs was more powerful than she'd ever experienced, even from three rows back. She let her mind live in that moment, in those flowers, and consciously tried to calm her nervousness. Everything was good, Mrs. Edelmann was nice, and the pterodactyls were calming down.

"Do you know the symbolism of the chuppah?"

Lucy opened her eyes and saw Mrs. Edelmann looking at her. Clinging to the calm she had momentarily achieved, she nodded and rehearsed what she had memorized. "It represents the presence of God at the ceremony, and the house that the groom will take his bride to, and it's open on four sides to represent hospitality, which the new married couple should show to others like Abraham did, and . . ." *Crap. What was the other thing?* "And many people believe it's best if it's outside under the stars to represent having . . . um . . . many children? No—uh, a large posterity," *that* was the word, "since Abraham and Sarah only had one son, Isaac, but still had—or have, I guess—a large posterity." She looked over at Jonah's mom. She was smiling.

"I'm impressed."

Lucy shook her head. "My dad told me about it," she admitted.

Sharon's smile widened. "Is he a student of religion?"

Lucy laughed. "No. He's a doctor."

The smile that was on the woman's face dropped completely away. Two vertical wrinkles appeared between her penciled eyebrows as her gaze moved to Lucy's red curls, back to her green eyes, then scanned her entire face, all in one movement. "You're Lucy Callaghan." It wasn't a question.

But Lucy's shaky yes rose up at the end as if she wasn't completely certain herself. She had a feeling there was something suddenly wrong with who she was. Or that Mrs. Edelmann—*Sharon*—thought so, anyway.

"Of course. Forgive me," the woman verbally stumbled. "Jonah did tell me your name, of course, but I hadn't realized who you were." She was shaking her head, almost to herself, but still staring at Lucy. Actually staring; she hadn't blinked.

That didn't help Lucy's apprehension at all. What did she mean? "Who . . ." was all she got out when a large man with big ears squeezed into the space next to Sharon, who turned to look at him just as the music started. Then everyone turned to see the groom being escorted down the aisle by his father and mother.

Lucy was distracted during the entire ceremony. While the rabbi spoke, and the bride and groom circled each other, and rings were exchanged, and as family members were taking turns wishing them well or praying or something, Lucy only wished the whole thing were over so she could leave. She didn't know where she would go, but she didn't want to keep sitting there next to a woman who kept glancing sideways at her for the entire excruciating hour. How long would this last? And there were several *parts* left to go after this!

She felt it then. The heaviness. Then panic. What was she going to do? She felt the little beads of sweat form on her top lip, on the back of her neck, and in the small of her back. She closed her eyes and breathed. Slowly. Counting like she had practiced with Don. *Out - two - three - four; in - two - three - four; out - two - three - four . . .* She thought of a breeze, of swinging, of Jonah—*crap*. No! Not of Jonah, whose mother had just shifted in her seat, letting Lucy know she had looked at her again.

"Are you okay, dear?" she heard her whisper.

Lucy started, and the bench creaked. "Oh. Yes," she whispered and tried to smile.

Sharon nodded and turned back.

Out - two - three - four . . . relaxing her shoulders, her neck, her jaw, her face, arms, hands, fingers, toes . . . relaxing everything she could and still stay upright on the bench.

In - two - three - four . . . Balloons and stars and Mountain Dew.

Out - two - three - four . . . Bicycle rides and chariot races and Don.

It was working a little. She was tuning out her anxiety and focusing on feeling peace.

CRACK! "MAZEL TOV!" the whole room shouted, startling Lucy almost entirely off the bench. She should have anticipated the moment when the couple would stomp on a glass at the end of the ceremony, since her dad had told her about it, but the abrupt noise nearly undid the calm she had achieved.

It was okay, though. She would be okay. *Out - two - three - four . . .* She tried to be subtle about dabbing her top lip and it stayed relatively dry, but the nape of her neck still felt damp under all her stupid hair. Why did she let Claire talk her into wearing it down? The klezmer music started up, and the bride and groom were holding hands as they practically skipped back up the aisle and exited the room among cheers and clapping.

Sharon turned to her, smiling. "Well, what did you think?" She sounded a little more relaxed then too, with just a little tightness around her mouth.

"That was really beautiful." And she meant it. The parts she could remember, anyway. "I can't wait to tell my dad about it."

Sharon's smile froze for a moment, but she just nodded.

"Hi, Dad!"

Jonah—finally.

Lucy turned and saw father and son, a wide guy with big ears and a skinny guy with big ears, hugging.

"Wonderful job, son," his dad said when they stepped apart. "But I think Mario was a little flat."

People were still clogging the aisle. Sharon stepped into the aisle and made way for Lucy, who completed their little circle when she stepped next to Jonah. He looked really handsome in his suit. He smiled down at her, and she saw that his eyes really were like his mom's, but less worried looking? guarded? serious? Less weird, at least.

"Yeah, he was." He turned back to his dad. "But that doesn't matter right now. Did you meet Lucy?" Jonah grinned and put his hand on Lucy's back to scoot her forward half a step. Could Jonah feel how hot and sweaty her back was? She couldn't tell; his touch was momentary.

"No!" the big man enthused. "Introduce me to this pretty young lady!"

Lucy felt herself blush at that, making her feel even sweatier, and Sharon was still watching her.

"This is Lucy. Lucy, this is my dad, Abraham Edelmann."

"Hello Lucy!" His baritone voice crooned. Lucy wondered if he liked to sing as well as sell musical instruments. Anyway, he must be good if he could tell that a specific member of the band was flat. She stopped wondering about that when he took her by the hands, pronounced "It's wonderful to meet you!" and kissed her soundly on both cheeks.

"It's nice to meet you, too, Mr. Edelmann." She resisted reaching up and wiping the dampness off her cheeks. She suspected that Mr. Edelmann had been drinking at the part before the wedding.

"Please! Please call me Abe! You're family now!"

Sharon nearly choked. "Abe!"

"What? She has come to a family celebration, and everyone is family today!" He winked at his son and clapped him on the back. Jonah shook his head a little but was smiling. "Come on! Let's go celebrate!"

"I'm sure everyone can see you've already started celebrating," Sharon scolded. But she laughed and put her arm through his. "I'll need a few minutes to catch up with you," she whispered as if hatching a secret plan, and the two of them started up the aisle.

"Sorry about that," Jonah said. "He's actually a pretty quiet guy, but he does like celebrating. And showing off for cute girls," he added, looking at her.

It was Lucy's turn to almost choke.

"Oh, that's right! You're not too good at laughing!"

Then Lucy really did laugh, which was just what she needed. Plus, it was easier to relax now that his parents were off getting some wine or whatever. The bats were back, but quickly turning into happy little butterflies.

Then Jonah's eyes, which did look just like his mother's, moved to her hair and he tugged on the end of one of the coils. He glanced at the lace head covering, her dress, then back to her face. "You really do look pretty."

"Thanks. So do you." He laughed and took it as a joke, but he really did look handsome in his dark suit and vest, and his, um . . . "What's that called, again?" She pointed with her eyes.

He touched the top of his head. "A kippah. Or yarmulke. Is it weird to you?"

"No! I've seen them before. Some kids at school wear them. But I couldn't remember what they were called." She shrugged a little. "You really do look nice."

He smiled. A little pleased? A little shy? She wasn't sure. But he took her hand and led her to the reception, and Lucy decided she didn't care about his weird mom. Jonah was nice.

As they entered the reception hall, Lucy noticed there was no line forming for greeting the newlyweds. "Where are Talya and—?" *Crap*. After an hour of hearing the guy's name, she still couldn't remember it.

"Talya and Daniel will be here in a few minutes, and then everyone will dance the horah."

"Everyone?"

"Yeah, but don't worry. It's an easy ring-around-the-rosy thing in a circle, or—" he looked around and seemed to be counting. "—probably more like three circles with how many people are here. There's an easy step to do, but it's fine if you just let yourself get tugged along." He looked down at their clasped hands and gave a little squeeze. "It's okay. I'll be holding your hand, so don't worry. But" he bent down and mock-whispered in her ear, "I like holding your hand a lot, and I promise not to let go, but I will need some circulation in my fingers for playing later, so . . ."

Lucy looked down at their hands; her knuckles weren't actually white, but the skin across them was stretched pretty tight. "Sorry." She immediately relaxed her grip and counted: *Out - two - three - four; in - two - three-four . . .*

He smiled. "I'm thirsty. Let's find our seats and get some water, or a soda if you want, before they bless and pass around the challah."

"What's the challah?"

"It's a braided loaf of bread that's blessed and passed around to begin the meal. Then people can eat while the dancing and entertaining is happening."

A little stir and rumble was heard from the other end of the hall, and a few men's voices shouting: "Whoa! That's huge!" "Ha! I hope there is enough!" And a woman's voice: "Oh! It's beautiful!"

"That's the challah they're bringing in. The dads have to make a big deal over it," he chuckled with a hint of an eyeroll.

They sat down at a round, eight-place table adorned with a pale gold tablecloth and the same vines, lilacs, and yellow flowers that decorated the chuppah. Each place was set with two stemmed glasses, gold utensils, and a large, gold plate topped with a purple cloth napkin tied by a gold ribbon. As Lucy sat down, she picked up the card that had her name printed on it in gold lettering. "Wow." She'd never been to a dinner with name cards and such elaborate decorations. She'd never been anywhere so fancy. So beautiful.

She was looking up at the rectangular head table, which was decorated like theirs but with the flowers draped along the front edge, then saw a group of people approaching the table where she and Jonah sat. She immediately recognized Caleb and Naomi, but not the other four. She looked at the place card to her right, read the name *David Wise*, and hoped he wouldn't talk to her.

"What would you like to drink?"

Lucy turned to her left to see a young man in a blue, collared shirt; black pants; and a white apron.

"Oh, uh, a Diet Coke, please," Lucy replied, though she wasn't sure why. She didn't like the stuff, but it's what her family liked.

"Is Diet Pepsi okay?"

"Um, sure."

"And you, sir?"

Lucy turned to see who the server was talking to. It must have been David Wise because he was sitting down next to her while the rest of the new group read place cards and shuffled around. He was kind of short, probably around sixteen, with black hair, normal-sized ears, and a mild outbreak of acne.

"Go that direction," David Wise pointed. "She's with him."

The server nodded and turned to Jonah, who had stood up to wrangle a wild four-year-old boy who was running away from a wild, possibly five-year-old girl. "Water and a Coke," he said, barely glancing up.

"Is Pepsi okay?"

Jonah made a soft glottal sound in the back of his throat, but Lucy wasn't sure if it was about the Pepsi or about the little boy he was picking up. "Sure," he said to the server. Then to the boy, "Hey. Slow down there, Z-man." But by then the little girl was dancing around Jonah's legs. "Lily, close your eyes and count to ten." Lily complied, so Jonah set Z-man down on his feet to run away. Lily only made it to the count of four before running after him.

Jonah sat back down, shaking his head. Then he looked past Lucy and gave half a wave and a quarter of a nod. "Hey Dave."

Dave bumped his chin up a centimeter as he said, "Jonah."

"Lucy, this is Dave."

"You're the one who took my date's place," Dave said, nodding twice.

Lucy took in a breath of embarrassment, but Jonah said, "What? No way. Aunt Becky said there was plenty of room."

"Yeah, but only because my date bailed on me since her family decided to go to New Hampshire this week." Then, without turning his face, "I'll have whatever red wine you have." The server was back around to him again.

Without even a hint of a smirk, the waiter nodded and said, "The open bar is over there. Would you like me to bring you anything else for now?"

"Fine. A Coke."

"Would—"

"Yes, Pepsi is *fine*," Dave almost shouted, then turned to sulk at his name card.

"Did I really take someone else's place?" Lucy whispered to Jonah.

"No," he answered with a scowl toward Dave. Lucy was beginning to hate the name Dave. "He might have had a date, and she might have really bailed on him, but even if the girl existed and had come, Aunt Becky would have just moved some place cards around. My invitation included a *plus one*."

"Wow," Lucy mused, "I've never been a *plus one* before."

That brought the smile back to Jonah's face. "Well, I'm glad you could be *my* plus one. But I'm sorry you have to sit by Dave. He's a brat."

Lucy shrugged. At least Dave—yes, she really did not like that name at all now—probably wouldn't talk to her much.

"Welcome! Welcome everyone!" Lucy jumped. The man standing in front of the band had such a booming voice that he might not have needed the microphone he was holding. At least she wasn't the only one who jumped; his greeting had also startled a small knot of people who were standing not far from where he was. They bumped into each other as they hurried to their tables.

"Welcome!" the man said again, modifying his volume, but only a little. The clatter of people greeting each other and drinking didn't stop entirely, but it did quiet to a dull hum. "We are so blessed to be surrounded by our marvelous friends and family to celebrate the marriage of Daniel and Talya!" Cheers and whoops spontaneously erupted, making Lucy jump again.

Jonah leaned in close. "It's going to get louder after the blessing, so brace yourself," he said. His breath moved a few strands of her thick curls, and a few hairs tickled her cheek.

She nodded, bracing herself.

"We are so pleased that Talya's Zayde Joseph will offer the blessing on the challah tonight."

A few people cheered but were quieted at the sight of a bald man with a white mustache and silver-rimmed glasses walking to the table where the long, braided challah loaf had been placed. A photographer snapped some photos, and the host held up the microphone in front of the old man's mouth, but Zayde Joseph took his time as he picked up the bread with both hands. He paused, and a peculiar look came over his face. It wasn't a smile, but even from where Lucy sat a little to the side, she could see that the old man was happy. Actually—that wasn't the right word. Maybe content. But not the emotionless content Lucy used to feel. The family patriarch looked as if his life were truly all he had ever wanted it to be—like there was nothing he needed or wanted more than to be right there at that moment, holding a loaf of bread. Then he took a soft breath.

"Baruch Atah Adonai Eloheinu, Melech, Haolam, Hamotzi Lechem Min Haaretz."

Lucy had no idea what Zayde Joseph was saying, but his voice reminded Lucy of something she had heard in a sermon once. It was a story or a verse in the Bible, but she had no idea where or which book. All she really remembered was that Father Patrick had read it, and it meant that the Lord wasn't in a wind or a storm or a fire, but in a still, small voice. The exuberant speaker who had just welcomed family and friends to the celebration had a loud, thundering voice. He certainly seemed good-natured and friendly, but the weight of his greeting was unsettling to Lucy—like a storm. But Zayde Joseph? His voice was like that still, small voice Father Patrick had talked about. In it she heard a man not just praying, but truly speaking to God.

Then, in the same reverent voice, Zayde Joseph continued in English, "Blessed are you, Adonai our God, Sovereign of all, who brings forth bread from the earth. Amen"

There was one breath when the room held still, with a few whispered *amens*, then everyone erupted in applause and cheers and more whooping. And it was too bad. For those few seconds, even the butterflies had been still. She had felt more at peace than she had since she stepped out of her dad's car. And she felt light. Maybe not light enough to put her in danger of floating, but it was a beautiful feeling.

Then a man with an accordion stepped forward and began to play a slow, teasing melody. Zayde Joseph disappeared among the tables, and the host announced, "Friends! Family! I introduce to you Mr. and Mrs. Daniel and Talya Green!"

Jonah grabbed Lucy's hand. "It's time!" he said. She stood to follow but glanced back at her little blue purse dangling on the back of her chair by its thin gold cord. "It'll be fine," Jonah said. He nearly had to yell as he towed her along. The accordion was picking up volume, but the loudest commotion came from practically everyone in the hall scooting chairs out, getting to their feet, and converging around the bride and groom, who were being lifted on chairs in the center of the room.

Lucy quickly got the gist of the left-over-right then left-behind-right crisscrossing footwork of the horah. Jonah, who was much taller than Lucy, held her right hand, and an even taller man with a full black beard held her left. She couldn't help but laugh with all the guests of every age, shape, and size dancing around in three concentric circles. She even saw Lily in the ring that surrounded hers, dancing between a smiling man and woman who must have been her parents. Her little legs couldn't keep up as the pace picked up, and soon her father picked her up, and the mother held her little hand. Lucy couldn't hear her but could see the little girl giggling as she was bounced so hard, she could hardly hold her head up. Lucy knew how she felt! A violin, a clarinet, a tuba, and a trombone had all joined in the song one at a time until every cubic inch of space was saturated with sound. Lucy was in heaven.

The tempo increased and she skipped along with the other celebrants, laughing longer and louder than she ever had before. She even joined in singing the parts she could make out—all the *hava nagilas* and the *hava neranenas*. Her face began to hurt from smiling so much, but she couldn't help it. This was pure joy. And every time she looked at Jonah, he was looking at her with an enormous grin that somehow emphasized his big ears and made him all the more handsome.

At one point, the clarinetist put down his instrument and picked up a saxophone, which enriched the sound, then the tuba player traded for a trumpet, which brightened the notes, always playing a little faster than the last iteration of the song. At the front, the accordion player and the violin player urged each other on in a personal competition to see who would give out first. But neither did. These were consummate professionals who would never concede.

Inside the center circle, the bride and groom were kept aloft on their chairs the whole time. Different men held them up, and Lucy had seen Caleb in there a time or two doing his part. Lucy suspected Jonah would be in there helping if it hadn't been for her. She didn't feel one bit guilty about that. Her heart was so glad—so buoyant—she never wanted to stop.

But it eventually did stop, and on some hidden cue that Lucy couldn't see, the brass and wind instruments cut out. The accordion player continued, dramatically holding a haunting minor chord of some kind. Then the violinist ran through a complicated and dizzyingly fast upward flourish that ended on one singularly sweet high note which she held for . . . possibly hours. Then with a nod, both musicians ended in a strong and jubilant note of joyful triumph.

Everyone shouted and clapped and whooped. The band all bowed, and the accordion player and the violin player bowed separately, then kissed.

"That's my Uncle Ed and Aunt Mathy!" Jonah shouted over the cheering. "They love to show off!"

"They are amazing!" Enthusiasm was a new emotion for Lucy, and she felt it fully.

"Yeah," he said as they walked back to their table. "I'm going to miss them."

Well, that was depressing. Lucy's newfound enthusiasm poofed away as she remembered that Jonah would be going off to college in the fall. But then she saw the salad that had magically appeared on her plate and decided not to let something that was two months away bother her now. She was glad Dave was nowhere to be seen, though. She took a long drink of water, glad that the server had brought it along with her soda.

"So, what do you think about your first Jewish celebration so far?" Jonah had also taken a big drink of water and was picking up his salad fork.

"This is amazing," Lucy beamed. Yes, she could actually feel herself beaming, and resisted the temptation to look down at her plate. Instead, she looked around, noticing two little girls posing with jump ropes in the center of the floor while a teenage boy helped a woman at the microphone find a song on her phone.

"You did a great job keeping up with the dance!" Jonah stuffed a huge forkful of salad into his mouth. He must have been starving, but at least he chewed with his mouth closed.

"That was so fun," she smiled, turning back to face him. "And you're usually up there playing that fast too? I saw the guys switching instruments."

"Yeah. Joey and I can switch parts whenever we need to. It's good in case one of us can't make it. Same for Wes and Doug on the trumpet and tuba."

"What about your uncle and aunt, Ed and . . .?"

"Mathy," Jonah said, filling in the name Lucy couldn't remember. "They absolutely cannot be replaced. If one of them can't come, it's never the same. Almost everyone in our family plays something, so we could add a trombone, a cymbalom, or even a banjo any time we need to, but my aunt and uncle are the best. And besides being good, they're just a lot of fun, and everyone loves them. That's why they were up there while the rest of the family is off the hook tonight. But they don't mind. They love playing together."

"They look fun," she agreed. Then she had another question. "So, the other guys aren't family members?"

"Mario?" Jonah nearly choked on his salad. "Does Mario *look* Jewish?" He looked over where the other band members were sitting down taking a break.

Lucy guessed the two guys with light brown hair were Wes and Doug; they must have been brothers since they looked so much alike, but not at all like Jonah or his family. Joey was super blond, so probably not related. And the other guy must have been Mario. Probably in his thirties, he had a dark, tanned complexion, black eyes beneath full black eyebrows, high cheekbones, and his long jet-black hair was pulled into a loose tail at the nape of his neck. He wore a kippah, of course, but it looked odd on him. Sitting there, not talking, Mario looked like someone Lucy wouldn't want to run into in a dark alley. Then Lily skipped up and climbed up on his knee, changing everything. He broke into a gleaming white smile, transforming his features, and he suddenly looked like some unknown Latin god. Lucy felt her eyebrows shoot up at the same time her jaw dropped.

"Exactly," Jonah laughed, then noticed the server coming to their table. His eyebrows drew together a little. "I ordered the fish for both of us. I hope you're okay with that."

"Wow . . ." Lucy crooned when the server set her meal in front of her. "I love salmon."

"Good," Jonah breathed. "Or else I'd have to eat your meal, too." Then he smiled at her, his mouth already full of penne pasta with sundried tomatoes and artichoke hearts. The boy could eat.

The jump roping girls had finished their routine, and some middle school boys were now juggling beanbags and possibly softballs. They were surprisingly good, with only one or two dropped balls.

"What's that other instrument you said? A cymbal something?"

Jonah smiled. "A cymbalom. It's a string percussion instrument, and you'll see Aunt Mathy play it in a bit. It's tradition to entertain the bride and groom, so lots of family members will be doing that throughout the night. The kids all want to go first, of course."

As they ate and watched, Jonah told Lucy the names of all the performers, and there were a lot of them. The jugglers were followed by knock-knock jokes, a poem, a little girl who was going to sing a song but who got too scared and ran off crying for her mama, and various other performances of varying degrees of skill. Lucy's favorite was when two teenage boys dressed in black coats, black hats, and fake beards performed a traditional Jewish dance with bottles balanced—by strings tied around their chins—on their heads. It was hilarious because it was so bad. But then the obviously professional bottle dancers came out and showed them how it was done. It was amazing!

Then just as the dancers were finishing, Jonah and Caleb excused themselves for some mysterious reason. Naomi, who had been sitting on the other side of Jonah, slid over next to her, and Lucy could have hugged her. Dave had not returned after the horah, which was perfectly fine with Lucy, but she didn't know the other three cousins at the table, even though Jonah had introduced her to them.

"Are you having fun?" Naomi asked.

"Yeah, I love it. You have a fun family."

"Ha! Some of them are fun, but some are jerks." Naomi nodded to Cousin Dave's empty seat.

Lucy didn't know how to respond to that. She wasn't about to tell Naomi she thought her cousin was a creep, so she changed the subject. "Your aunt and uncle were really amazing during the horah."

"Yeah. They are really good. But it's always better when Jonah is playing. It's his band, after all."

"What do you mean? He said it was their band."

"Well, they play with them a lot, and they put up some money for advertising and stuff, but Jonah's the one who put the band together. They couldn't be *Jonah and the Wail* without Jonah."

"Jonah and the—?"

"Wail. Like wailing on a saxophone. Didn't he tell you?"

"No. He just said he played in a band. That's why I came—to hear him play."

"Well, you'll get to now," Naomi said and nodded to the stage. Jonah was there, adjusting the reed of a saxophone that was strapped around his neck. Caleb was there too, with another trombone, along with Mathy, Wes, Doug, Joey, and Mario. Jonah's dad sat down at the piano, and then Jonah's mom was there with just a microphone.

"Sharon sings?"

"Yeah, and she's really—oh no," Naomi said, and started getting up.

"What's wrong?"

"Aunt Mathy needs help."

Lucy looked up to see Mathy standing at a table with a flat, tray-like box with wires stretched across it. But she was struggling with the arm of the microphone stand; it wasn't staying where she needed it. She smiled and said something when Naomi stepped up. Naomi nodded and sat beside her holding the mic.

Jonah stepped to his standing microphone. "Talya and Daniel? Our band wants to congratulate you, and," he laughed, looking back at the rest of the group, who all nodded. "And knowing your love of classical music, we've prepared a special number chosen and arranged especially just for you."

The bride and groom looked at each other. Lucy didn't know them at all, but they seemed puzzled and a little suspicious.

Then Jonah's dad ran the back of his thumb down the keyboard and Jonah started playing. Then Mathy and the brass instruments joined in, producing some kind of funky, syncopated music that was an odd mix of seventies music with a klezmer twist. The bride and groom started laughing, and Sharon started singing: *Love! Love will keep us together* . . . Pretty soon everyone was laughing. But Lucy watched Jonah, and her face started aching again from smiling so much. She hadn't really seen him playing for the wedding ceremony. Now he was in line with the other horns, turning side to side and stepping to some corny but impressive choreography. She turned to take her phone out of her purse.

"They're good, aren't they?"

Ugh! People here really needed to quit startling her! It was creepy Dave, showing up out of nowhere.

"Yeah. They're incredible." She laughed when Mathy and Naomi started singing background *doot-doots* to Sharon's words. She opened the camera app on her phone and sat up as high as she could to get a better shot.

"Want me to take your picture? With the band behind you?"

"Oh." That was actually a good idea. "Okay. Thanks." She felt kind of weird standing up at first, but the bride and groom and other people were heading to the dance floor, so it was okay.

"Hurry, so we get a clear shot without the crazy dancing people." He rolled his eyes, but not in a mean way.

"Here?" She tried to smile, then decided to just go for a happy expression. Smiling still wasn't something she could do on demand.

"Yeah. Perfect." He took about three pictures, moving to get the band over her shoulder, then looked down at her phone. "Want me to send these to Jonah?"

"Okay. Thanks." Maybe he wasn't a complete jerk. Maybe he had just been grumpy because his date couldn't come. That might have been a grump-worthy scenario; she'd have to ask Claire.

His thumbs slid all over the screen. "I need to log you on to the Wi-Fi here first." A few clicks later he handed her phone back. "I think I got some good shots."

She took the phone and sat down, looking at the pictures. He had taken six, and Jonah was in the background of all of them. Naomi, too. Counting the pictures she had taken of Claire and her dad, she now had a grand total of eight pictures on her phone. Then she felt herself smile for real. She was becoming a real person. She was going places and meeting people. She even, maybe, sort of had a boyfriend. She was having fun, and she had controlled the heavy feelings before, with his mom. She was actually living a life. Jonah smiled at her when their special number was done and everyone was laughing and cheering, and Lucy smiled back. It was easy.

CHAPTER 29

Front Porch

They left the reception at 10:30, but the celebration was still going strong with a few smaller children zonked out on their dads' shoulders or sprawled on a blanket underneath a table. The band was still cranking out the music, and Jonah would go back and help pack up band equipment after taking Lucy home. He didn't seem to mind, though; he was holding her hand as he drove. Lucy did her best to act casual about that—like, *No big deal; lots of guys have held my hand while driving me home from a date at a wedding reception where he was in the band. This is just a typical Thursday night.*

Except a typical Thursday night would have entailed watching an old movie with Claire.

"What are you smiling about?" Jonah asked.

Lucy didn't know she had been smiling. The sensation was becoming less foreign. She hoped it didn't look weird. "I was just thinking about Claire. She's probably eating cake batter popcorn and watching a black-and-white sci-fi movie right now—she's been into those lately." Lucy was beginning to suspect she wasn't the only odd one in the family; that's probably what had made her smile.

"What's cake popcorn?"

"Cake *batter* popcorn. You melt white chocolate and stir in yellow cake mix and sprinkles, then coat the popcorn with it. It's really good, and Claire loves it like you love your weird peanut butter ice cream thing."

"Excuse me—it's peanut butter *cookie* ice cream. Big difference." He rolled his eyes in solemn indignation. "And I can't believe you'd ever try to compare it to white chocolate anything." He made a face.

"I'm sure Claire could come up with a way to make peanut butter cookie popcorn—she's kind of a popcorn prodigy—and you could have it all to yourself."

"Is that an invitation?" He raised his eyebrows and plastered on a broad smile. "Because I would never say no to peanut butter cookie popcorn."

"Sure," she laughed. She hoped Claire would be okay with it because Lucy could make stuff she already knew, but she couldn't snap her fingers and create a brand-new recipe like Claire could. "Want to come over on Sunday?"

"Mmm. That's rehearsal day, and then we have a birthday party that night. But I think I have a night off on Tuesday. Let me check with the guys; we are all trying to make as much cash as we can before Caleb and I head off to college."

"Okay!" Poo. She forgot about him heading off to college.

When they got to her house, Lucy wondered if Jonah would kiss her again. Really, though, she'd been wondering that all night. She wanted him to, but it could be problematic. And possibly terrifying if they were outside and she floated away into outer space and was never seen or heard from again. If he was going to kiss her, it would be by the front door. She and Claire had watched Maggie kissing her dates there plenty of times, so that must be the place. With that in mind, she made a straight line for the door so she could hold on to the door handle in some sneaky way, just in case. And there was an eave overhead if things went completely wrong.

"Uh," Jonah said, looking confused. "Are you in a hurry? Are you going to get in trouble?" He looked at his watch.

"No!" Crap. She must have walked too fast. "I just . . ." Just what? You just *what*, Lucy? "I just thought you had to get back to help the band." Good save. She shrugged and casually put her hands behind her back, then put one hand on the door handle.

Jonah relaxed. "Well, I will, but they'll still be playing now." He laughed. "Actually, the reception could go on all night, but the band is only contracted until midnight."

"Huh. I never thought about needing contr—"

He kissed her. In one motion, he'd carefully but firmly held her by her upper arms as if to keep her in place, and he kissed her. It wasn't a long kiss, maybe like two and a half seconds, but he had definitely been aiming for her lips that time. No question.

And it was nice. Her first official kiss, not counting the half-kiss from the other day, was almost perfect. It probably would have been better if she'd actually kissed him back, but she'd been too surprised.

Lucy almost let go of the door handle, then grabbed it all the tighter. She did feel light, but she could also feel her feet on the rough welcome mat, so she relaxed her grip again. She tested her gravity for a moment, then let go.

"Thanks," she said. *Ugh!* That was wrong! You don't say *thanks* for a kiss! But what else do you say? It made sense. But it was still probably a weird thing to say.

"Sorry," he chuckled. "It's just—I kind of wrecked it by hurrying last time, so I wanted to do it right."

He was sorry? *She* wasn't sorry. She liked it. She felt her face go all warm and looked off to the side because she couldn't look him in the face! She didn't know what to do. Girls in movies jiggled their keys and said something like, *I had a really nice time tonight, Albert,* and *then* he would kiss her. And then the girl would go inside. But this was all out of order. "I didn't think you wrecked it."

"Then, would you let me kiss you again, since I really should get back?"

"Okay."

He took her hands, which had been fiddling with the flap of her purse, bent down, and kissed her—twice. He was smiling when he straightened up, and so was Lucy. She'd actually kissed him back.

She had approximately two heartbeats to enjoy the moment before she felt herself rising. "Good night!" she yelled as she flung herself around, grabbed the handle, and threw herself inside.

"Dad!" Lucy screamed, clinging to the inner door handle as her feet continued to drift upward, pulling her into an angle as if she were sliding head-first down a little hill. "Mom!"

Aeden raced out of the family room, Claire and Don right behind him with their eyes bugging out of their heads. Lucy tried to reach with one hand to make sure her dress wasn't sliding up her legs, but her dad reached her before that was necessary and pulled her into his arms. Kelly ran down the stairs and halted to a stop on the last step. All four of them were talking at once.

"Are you okay?"

"Cool!"

"Huh."

"What happened?"

And Lucy was laughing.

"Thanks!" She said, wrapping her arms around her dad's neck. Her little purse dangled from the strap caught in the crook of her right elbow.

Her dad carried her into the family room. "Did anyone see you?"

She shook her head, still laughing, nearly breathless. "No, I don't think so, but it was close!"

"What happened?" Kelly asked for the second time.

Lucy's laughter cut off, but she was still smiling.

"He kissed you!" Claire squeaked then started jumping up and down. "He kissed her good night!"

Lucy looked at her dad, who was looking back at her through squinted eyes, mouth scrunched tight. He didn't say anything, but Lucy knew a question when she saw one.

"Yes," she said, measuring his response to know if her dad would be okay with that. He didn't respond. That meant he was being the doctor at the moment. She squirmed to be put down. "I think I'm okay now."

The doctor hefted her for a moment and must have decided she really was okay because he set her on her feet. Then she looked at Kelly, who didn't look like she had a problem with Lucy being kissed; there was a slight smile on her face, which was actually kind of weird. Nice, for sure. But weird.

"I told you! I told you he likes you! *Likes* you likes you." Claire continued her smug little victory dance.

Don hadn't said anything besides his *huh* when she first came in. The scientific wheels in his brain must have been spinning like crazy. He probably had a ton of questions.

"Are you sure he didn't see you levitate?" That was the doctor.

"Levitate? No, he didn't see me float. We were right by the door, and . . ." She didn't really want to go into all the details right here, right now; she wanted to just enjoy the experience. But there was no use avoiding it. "And he kissed me—just quick—" No need to mention that there were three—THREE—kisses in all. "—and a second later I could tell what was happening, so I said goodnight and I ran inside."

"That was kind of rude," Claire said, scowling from the new sofa.

"Claire, please," Kelly said.

Claire didn't sulk; she was not a sulky person. She just lifted her hands in the air as if to say, *Well, it was*, then picked up the bowl of the predicted cake mix popcorn and started munching.

"That was smart," the doctor continued. "Were there any problems the rest of the evening?"

"Nope." She sat down by Claire and took some popcorn. "The wedding was nice, though the men and women sat together," she said to her dad. "And then the reception, which was the fanciest thing I've ever been to, had music—Jonah's band—and dancing. Oh! I danced the *horah*! And I heard Jonah play the clarinet *and* the saxophone, and he's really good. It really is *his* band; it's called 'Jonah and the Wail.' Isn't that funny? It was so fun! So yeah, no problems!" She grabbed another handful of popcorn. "Oh," she turned to Claire, "I told Jonah you'd make him some peanut butter cookie popcorn."

"I can do that," Claire nodded.

"Uh, I'd better get home," Don said.

"Bye, Don!" said Claire.

"I'll bring over your mom's eye drops tomorrow evening," said her dad.

"Good night, Don," said Kelly, who walked him to the door. "Thanks for watching that ridiculous movie with Claire, whatever it was."

"*Zombies of the Stratosphere*!" Claire shouted toward the entry.

Lucy knew her dad was back in the building when he kissed the two girls on the tops of their heads. "I love you," his voice rumbled. "Don't stay up too late." They nodded. He started to leave, then stopped and turned around by the green recliner. "Lucy, we are going to have to come up with a way for you to manage your episodes." Episodes? That sounded ominous. "Let's think of some ideas and talk about it tomorrow."

"Okay . . ." She couldn't tell who was talking at that moment, but she didn't like the sound of it.

He smiled and left.

Lucy frowned.

"So . . .?" Claire goaded, poking Lucy in the ribs.

Then Lucy proceeded to tell Claire everything, including the three kisses.

Discussion 3 — We Found Something

We found something!

The Cosson Girl?

No. *Even better.*

Alright, you have my attention.

CHAPTER 30

Going Viral

That night, Lucy Dreamed she was at a party in the school gym, and everyone she knew was there. In real life, it would have been a pretty small party since she still didn't know a ton of people, but her family was there, along with Father Patrick, Don, the girl in her chemistry class who helped her when she had almost fallen, and other random faces from school. Coach Vazquez was there, too, flirting with Sister Decker, who was teaching canning techniques by the weight machines. After a while, things started getting weird: Father Patrick led the school choir in singing "YMCA," Sister Decker was swatting Coach Vazquez away with her dish towel, Jonah and Dave were holding hands in the choir, and Lucy and Don were ignoring everyone and laughing their heads off making up their own new choreography to the song. She was laughing so hard she needed to pee, which was what woke her up.

In the air, arms over her head in a sloppy Y shape.

Oooh! She couldn't move herself around like she could in her Dreams sometimes, but she had floated close enough to the wall that she could push off it and maneuver herself down the hall to Claire's room. It was tricky, though. She might be light as a balloon, but she felt fragile as a bubble. Too much jostling would surely make her pop and crumble to the floor.

She made it down to Claire's room, and the door was open, but Claire was already downstairs for breakfast. *Crap*. Lucy tried making a three-point turn in the hallway, but it ended up being at least a seven-point turn, bumping a plant stand and nearly knocking it over in the process.

"Let me sleep!" Maggie yelled from behind the closed door across from Claire's room.

Ignoring her, Lucy eventually turned herself around and made it to the stairs.

This could hurt. But, like Don said, she'd never get anywhere if she didn't try.

But she didn't know how. She'd always concentrated on thinking happy things to compensate for crashing. Could she think of . . . what? Sad things? Painful things? to make her less floaty? She grabbed onto the railing, as a precaution, then tried to think of something sad. But Lucy's life was pretty good at this moment, which was probably why she could hold her altitude, and she didn't want to think of sad things, anyway. So she pulled herself down the stairs hand-over-hand, using the banister, toward the smell of waffles and bacon—which was pretty smart, if she did say so herself. And it was still tricky.

It turned out worrying about falling on the stairs was enough to make her sink a little, so she gritted her teeth and pushed away from the railing. She thought happy thoughts about floating, which seemed like a weird meta-referential thing, but it worked. She glided down the stairs, caught herself on the edge of the kitchen doorway, and swung her feet around so she was looking into the kitchen.

"Hi family!"

So many things happened at once. Kelly screamed, Aeden jumped to his feet, knocking over his chair, and Claire yelled a very long and high-pitched "Woooooh!" The combinations of those reactions popped Lucy's fragile bubble, making her bang her face into the door frame halfway to the floor, sliding her lip up over her nose the rest of the way down. Kelly covered her eyes, Aeden swore, and Claire gasped.

Lucy woke up where she had fallen, top half in the kitchen, bottom half in the hallway, an icepack on her face. When she groaned, her father's face appeared over the edge of the icepack. Claire was behind him, drinking a glass of chocolate milk.

"Hi," he said.

"Hi," she said.

"How do you feel?"

"I have to pee."

Everyone else had finished breakfast, so Lucy ate the rest of the waffles and turkey bacon by herself. "Hey, could we get some regular bacon next time? I want to try some." She licked her lips, feeling the strange sensation of her upper lip being fat and swollen, with a tinge of the taste of blood up near her gums. She reasoned that Claire's chocolate milk would help with that, so she stood to get some. Even with her swollen face, there was yummy food, she had floated, and Jonah had kissed her. Life was pretty good.

Her dad sat down, took a piece of her bacon, and bit it in half. "Sure," he said after he swallowed. "It tastes a lot better than this. But it's not very good for you, so we usually settle."

Kelly sat down across from him and clasped her hands on top of the table.

Lucy turned around, forgetting about the chocolate milk. "What's going on?" Was this what her dad had felt when *he* knew something was going on?

"Lucy," Kelly began, "we are certain you don't want what happened last night or this morning to happen again, so it's important that we regulate your moods. Dad can adjust the dosage of the Serenvidria so that—"

"Kelly, Serenvidria is bipolar medication. She is not bipolar."

"I realize that, dear," Kelly continued, her mouth drawn tight. "But it is what works best, so—"

"No. It is not what works best. This is what I've tried to explain to you for years. Yes, we need to find a way to help her, but we cannot continue to regulate her moods to the point where she is catatonic. That medication, when we first discovered it, was preferable only because of her age, but we need to address the real problem, which is—"

"Which is that she can't stop these episodes!"

"—which *is* that we have been treating the wrong disease!"

"You have always insisted that she does not, in fact, have a disease, but now—"

"No, of course. You're right; it is not a disease. It is a disorder. But she does not have unusual mood shifts; she has normal, everyday, middle-of-the-curve mood changes. She also has no problem carrying out tasks. She also has no problem concentrating on schoolwork. And her prior low activity and energy levels are a negative side effect of the Serenvidria, not a symptom of her condition. And under no circumstances would any psychiatrist diagnose Lucy's condition as *bipolar*. We simply cannot continue—"

"And just how would we know that, Aeden? How would we know no psychiatrist would diagnose her condition as bipolar since she has never *been* to a psychiatrist?"

"And you know very well why that is, Kelly."

"Aeden, psychiatric medicine is not like it was in the fifties. It's not even like it was ten years ago! Or five! So much has—"

"Yes, a lot has changed. But much has *not* changed. I'm a medical doctor, and I have no problem prescribing medication if it's the correct medication, but Serenvidria is not the correct medication. And you've read the same reports I've read, Kelly. There is an incalculably high probability that the psychiatric tests and treatments would be far, far worse for Lucy than what she's already gone through!"

"You mean worse than what you've *put* her through."

"Here we go." He threw up his hands and turned his back on her. "Make up your mind, Kelly. Am I the bad guy for taking her off the medicine, or am I the bad guy because I put her on the medication in the first place? I keep forgetting." He stood up, and Lucy had to move as he went to the refrigerator and began rummaging.

"Lucy," Kelly turned to face her daughter, which didn't usually happen when people were talking about her. "You know we love you, and we would never want you to go through anything dangerous or scary. And yes, we would be concerned about taking you to another doctor. But I can't imagine how frightened you must have been when you started . . ." She trailed off.

"Floating?" Lucy completed the thought for her. "I wasn't scared." That wasn't quite accurate, though. She definitely hadn't wanted to fall and get a fat lip this morning, but she wasn't seriously hurt. And she had successfully lowered herself down the stairs, kind of, and had maintained it, more or less! She also didn't want to float off into the sky last night because that would have been bad, but she handled it, and everything had turned out fine. Better than fine. Jonah had kissed her. Three times! These were definite wins.

"Of course you weren't," Aeden said, then turned back to Kelly. "That smile is a one hundred percent normal reaction. She had a fun night, and a boy she likes kissed her. Her physiological response is atypical, and we don't know why or how the floating happens, and we *do* need to think about her safety, but there is absolutely nothing wrong with her mental processing. She will not be going back on the Serenvidria."

"That's for sure," Lucy said, sitting back down at the table with her chocolate milk.

Both parents looked at her. They seemed to have forgotten she was there again, listening as they discussed her mental and emotional and psychiatric *whatever* health. She didn't care. She was not going back on that stuff, whatever it was or whatever it did. She took a drink, letting the milk lap over her upper lip, giving her a mustache, but oh well.

"Well, what do you intend to do if you start to, you know," Kelly gestured upward with her hands, on the edge of coming unglued, "and there is no door to hang on to?"

That was a valid point. Lucy wiped her mouth but didn't say anything.

Her dad sat back down and took Kelly's hand, but he was looking at Lucy. "We do need to think about your safety. That's the primary concern at the moment. And I am not saying medication is not something to consider, but—"

"Dad! I'm not—"

"But" he overrode her protest, "not Serenvidria. And not now. But Lucy, if there is a medicine that can help you, we will consider it."

"Who is *we*?"

"What do you mean?"

"Who will consider it? You and Mom? Or you and Mom and me?"

"Certainly, we will consider our options as a family. Of course."

"I don't see the *of course* in that." She wiped her mouth again—then winced at the napkin's rough and abrupt contact with her sore mouth—while they unanimously frowned at her. "You've never let me have a say in anything before." She put the half-melted ice bag back on her mouth.

"Honey," Kelly soothed, "that's only because you were so little. You wouldn't have understood."

She lowered the bag. "Was I little last month?" They looked at each other. She stood up and pushed her chair back. "Because I knew last month, I knew last year, and I knew when I was nine that I was always behind a glass. Now I finally know what that glass was, and I know you both put me there, and I am not going back behind it."

Lucy stood and took her plate to the sink, ran water over it, then walked out. The floor shook and the table rattled as she did so, but she didn't crash. *Out - two - three - four. In - two - three - four.* The steps creaked as she climbed the stairs, but she didn't crash. *Out - two - three - four. In - two - three - four.* The box springs protested when she lay down on her bed, but she didn't crash. She did fall asleep, however. That's all it was. Just a deep sleep.

Lucy didn't wake up until 1:23 that afternoon. Her mind quickly cleared, and she evaluated her situation. She was determined to fight for her right to *feel*. She would refuse—she *did* refuse—to ever take that terrible drug again, that little pill that separated her from the world, from emotions, and from caring about anything.

True, she obviously needed a way to manage her literal up-and-down relationship with gravity, but she was working on it! She refused to give up the vivid sensations she used to feel only in her Dreams. She realized those amazing greens and blues and reds and yellows . . . they were only a shadow of what she had been missing her entire life. No! She would not retreat. She would figure it out. After all, she had successfully banished the weighty anxiety she had experienced sitting next to Jonah's mother at the wedding; and she didn't crash when her parents were yelling at each other about *her* in the kitchen earlier. She had wanted to scream at them! Maybe she should have.

Maybe that would have made it worse.

Don would help her.

First lunch, then Don.

" . . . you can't tell who posted it first. That's why it's called going viral, *Doctor* Callaghan." Lucy could hear that Maggie was in full sass mode before she even got to the bottom of the stairs. "It's been shared so many times no one knows who started it! Look! Just this one picture has been shared more than three *thousand* times, and that's just since last night! It's going all over the place. And my friends have shared about a dozen different memes that are floating around now."

"What are you looking at?" Lucy asked as she opened the refrigerator and gathered food.

"And there she is," Maggie snarked in her typical tone. Maggie was becoming fluent in Snarkese. She could teach a class.

"I fell asleep." It was probably just a normal nap. Probably. "What's going on?" Lucy closed the refrigerator door with her arms full of lunch meat, pickle chips, Miracle Whip, and a tomato. But she froze when she saw her entire family looking at her. Maggie's eyes were squinted to a slit, Kelly's lips were pressed tight together, Claire's mouth was hanging open, and her dad—his mottled face was crimson. Lucy almost dropped the Miracle Whip, but Claire closed her mouth and took the food out of her arms. "What's wrong?" *Breathe*, she thought, but she didn't even know why she needed to. *Out - two - three - four.* Slowly. *In - two - three - four.*

Her dad held out a chair. "Sit down." Lucy complied. Always two people, the doctor had probably noticed her breathing, but the dad was not happy. She'd only seen him like this with Maggie and once, a little, with Claire, but Lucy had never been on the receiving end of this level of anger. And he was truly livid! *Why?*

Maggie, who was nearest to her, took the phone out of their father's hands and shoved it at Lucy, who looked at the image on the screen. It was a picture of her taken from behind, and her first thought was *Why is my hair like that?* The wild curls looked as nice as Claire had been able to make them last night, but they were swirling up and around, like she was swimming in water. But the photo was taken while she was hopping around in a circle with Jonah, so that explained the hair. She could see

Talya and Daniel laughing on hoisted chairs in the center, and the circles of people skipping and dancing around them. Jonah was holding her right hand and she could see the tall man who was holding her left, but half of him was cut off by the edge of the frame. She looked up at her family. "We were dancing the horah. It was fun."

But her remark fell flat. The serious faces staring back at her were not interested in whether it was fun. Claire's face looked worried, but her father's, Maggie's, and Kelly's faces looked respectively irate, indignant, and cold.

"Your feet," Claire whispered.

Lucy looked down again. Whoever took the photo had caught Lucy in mid-leap as she tried to keep up with the longer strides of Jonah and the man on her left. That explained her hair too. She still couldn't see a problem, so she looked up.

"Keep swiping," Maggie said.

Lucy slid her finger on the screen, going to another picture of her and Jonah and the tall man, but from a different angle, or as the dancers had progressed farther around the circle. This photograph showed the dancers feet crossing over or behind at the same time; Jonah, Lucy, and the tall man were stepping across all at the same time, but Jonah and the tall man's feet were solidly on the ground. Lucy's crossed feet were not. "Well—" Lucy started.

"Keep swiping," someone said. It was probably Maggie, but Lucy wasn't really listening now. She was swiping. One after another, pictures from different angles, different lighting, and different degrees of focus showed Lucy, her feet not touching the ground - in - any - of - them. There were also some that had been cropped and turned into memes. *Challenges of an Anorexic*; *If you can be anything, be a balloon*; *I don't dance often, but when I do, I Riverdance*; and *They're after me Lucky Charms*.

The last photo was a closeup of Lucy, looking happy, with Jonah and the Wail behind her.

She knew who had taken that one, at least. "Dave," she said.

"What? Who's Dave? I thought you were out with a kid named Jonah."

"Dave's his cousin. He took this last photo." She felt herself getting heavy before her anger even registered. That . . . that . . . she let out an inarticulate "*Urrrghhh!* That creep! He took pictures of me in front of Jonah's band—with *my phone*! Then he sent them to Jonah! That's what he *said* he did, anyway!" She really felt it. Her entire body felt like lead, but it didn't pull her down; she didn't even feel hot. Or sick. No ringing in her ears, just anger. The floor creaked, causing everyone to back up except for Claire, so Aeden pulled her back himself.

"Where's your phone? You can see who he sent it to," Claire said.

The floor and staircase pounded as she ran up to her room. She grabbed the tiny purse off the desk and yanked the phone out of it, then spun around and ran back downstairs. The entire house felt her anger.

"Here." She tried not to shout as she pushed her phone toward Claire. "How can you tell?"

Claire danced her thumbs around the screen even more adroitly than stupid *Dave* had. She started shaking her head.

"He didn't text or email it, or he was good about deleting them and emptying the trash before he gave your phone back. How long did he have it?"

"For about as long as you've had it," Lucy answered, not sure how long that was.

"Well, he could have been fast about it. Or he could have airdropped it. Were you connected to Wi-Fi?" Claire asked.

Lucy nodded, furious. "*Dave* logged me in."

"That means he could have airdropped it to himself, too. Or to anyone who was nearby."

Ooh Lucy hated that guy! Her fists were balled up and she felt herself scowling. The floor creaked again.

"Okay, we all need to calm down," her dad said, meaning Lucy needed to calm down. "What's done is done. But I think we can all agree that you aren't going out with that boy again."

"*What?!*" Lucy spun to face her dad so fast she almost fell over. Aeden automatically held out his hand to catch her, then, on second thought, held out his long arm to scoot the others away from her. But she didn't fall. She was solidly on her feet. "What do you mean? *He* didn't do anything wrong!"

"That we know of. It could have been that Dave guy or Jonah. Apparently, the Fischer family can't be trusted."

"*What?*" Maggie asked.

"*Fischer?*" Lucy asked.

"Wrong," Claire said, shaking her head.

It was Aeden's turn to look confused, looking back and forth between all three daughters. "Fischer. They're both Caleb's cousin, right?"

All three girls were talking at once:

"... different names ..."
"... mother's side ..."
"...oh, Dad ..."

" ... not Fischer ..."
" ... Edelmann ..."
"... paying attention ..."

Suddenly Aeden held up his hands. "Stop!"

The talking didn't suddenly stop, but it died down and fizzled.

Aeden sat down at the table and put his head down, covering his face with his left hand. "Lucy," he said quietly, pointing right at her without looking at her. "What is Jonah's last name?"

"Edelmann," she answered.

"What is his mother's name?" he asked, still pointing at her without looking.

"Um, Sharon." Her anger was gone, replaced by confusion at her father's sudden change of demeanor.

Then her father breathed in, held his breath for a moment, then let out a quiet but exasperated sigh. He looked up at Kelly, who had been sitting quietly at the opposite end of the table, and his eyes were so tired.

Lucy followed his gaze and saw that Kelly was wide-eyed and pale, dry lips parted. Maggie went to the sink and got her some water. Claire sat down next to her and took her hand. "What's wrong, Mom?"

CHAPTER 31

Checkups

A eden rocked baby Lucy in his arms as he read a journal article on childhood diseases that was posted on the blue, green, and yellow-painted wall of the pediatric exam room. When Dr. Sharon Edelmann entered, she was looking down at the clipboard in her hand. "Hello, Aeden," she greeted warmly but professionally. "Where's Kelly and cute little Maggie?"

"A car ride is still a bit much for Kelly right now, and Maggie is with our good neighbor, who is probably giving her too many cookies at the moment." He tried to greet his colleague with a smile, but he doubted his blood-shot eyes were cooperating. Dr. Edelmann was still looking at the clipboard.

"Yes," she nodded. "I was just reading about the traumatic birth." She kept scanning. Nodding. Murmuring an occasional *hmm*, and then shaking her head. "Left ninth and tenth ribs broken, damage to the costal cartilage, *and* placental abruption? That's incredible." She'd said it like it was merely a fascinating case study in some textbook, not an event that had threatened the life of his wife and child.

"Like I said, car rides are a bit much."

"Indeed," she agreed, still scanning.

"But this is Lucy," Aeden interrupted, turning his sleeping daughter toward her new doctor.

Dr. Edelmann was a highly respected and sought-after pediatrician who took Maggie as a patient eighteen months ago only as a professional courtesy, so Aeden tried to hide his irritation that she hadn't even looked at him or the baby. He hoped he never treated his own patients that way.

She set the clipboard down, washed her hands, then finally looked up. "Well, I'm sorry not to see your wild child, but I'm glad to meet this little one." She pulled back the blanket a bit and put her finger into Lucy's tiny fist, which grasped reflexively. The doctor nodded. "That's a good grip."

Aeden watched as the pediatrician examined Lucy head to toe. At one point, the doctor glared up at him, and he realized he was literally towering over her and needed to take a step back. He felt anxious, and more protective of Lucy than he remembered being with Maggie. Was that because of Lucy's difficult entrance into the world? But then, Kelly had recovered so quickly from Maggie's birth, hardly skipping a beat and taking to motherhood with such positive glee, Aeden hadn't felt especially needed back then. Now, with Kelly still recovering, unable to even feed the baby, Aeden was Lucy's only lifeline. She did need him.

He stepped back and watched, lips pressed tight together, wary of any reaction or expression on Dr. Edelmann's face that would indicate problems. But she gave nothing away—poker face the whole time. Throughout the procedure she doled out her pronouncements stingily.

Normal heartbeat.

Normal weight gain.

Normal reflexes.

Normal oxygen levels.

Normal, normal, normal.

Aeden released the tension in his shoulders he hadn't known was there.

Dr. Edelmann asked Aeden to hold the baby while she gave Lucy a shot.

Lucy wailed, which was normal, her face turned red, which was normal, and then Aeden almost dropped her.

Perhaps that was normal when an angry baby was writhing in your arms. But what wasn't normal was how shockingly heavy Lucy had suddenly become. Aeden recovered his balance within one of Lucy's gasps, but he was sure Dr. Edelmann had noticed. She didn't say anything, of course, but she must have been wondering how Maggie had survived his clumsiness.

He just held Lucy more snugly, rocking her awkwardly, and talking to her until her cries stopped, and she calmed down with one final, shuddering whimper. The heavy feeling only lasted a few moments and must have been due to his fatigue; all the nighttime feedings must have made him more tired than he had realized.

However.

When the same phenomenon occurred at Lucy's two-month checkup, Aeden wasn't taken by surprise. He didn't admit to himself that he had been waiting for it. He didn't say a word. To anyone. But he deliberately turned his professional attention to the study of pediatric medicine and decided that he would be Lucy's doctor as well as her father. It would not be ideal, but it would be necessary.

He procured a baby scale, weighing and measuring Lucy every day. He researched. He took meticulous notes and kept them in password-protected files on his own completely un-networked computer. He kept hard copies in a home safe.

When Lucy was four months old, Dr. Aeden Callaghan was the only person Lucy's father trusted to administer her next vaccination. He took Lucy into his home office and carefully placed her on the baby scale. It read 12 pounds, 1 ounce. That was on the tiny end of the spectrum, but not abnormal, and completely in line with Lucy's projected growth. When it came time for the actual shot, he hesitated, squinting at his daughter. She stared at him with large green eyes. He stood with one protective hand on her torso, thinking. She babbled and reached toward the blue and yellow birds hanging from the mobile above the scale. He tapped his pursed lips with his index finger. She yawned.

Finally, he decided. He took the syringe in one hand, held her little leg with the other, and carefully pushed the needle into her delicate baby skin.

Before her cry had reached his ears, the scale collapsed with a crunch and a clang.

The next day, Aeden went to the medical clinic early. He went to the records department. He took all of Lucy's physical files and completely erased her computer records.

CHAPTER 32

Long-Lost Pediatrician

Lucy was sitting at the kitchen table, frowning. The heaviness had left her; she didn't even feel like crashing. She was too astonished.

"So . . ." she said, without knowing what to say. "Mrs. Edelmann, Jonah's mother, was my doctor? And she knows about me? About my . . . problem?"

"I'm not sure what she knows, but she read about your delivery, and Kelly's trauma, and . . . doctors talk. That clinic was full of gossip, which is why I started my own practice later that year. That also made it possible for me to be around the house more. The main concern, however, was I couldn't erase or take Kelly's records; she was an established patient, still recovering, and in need of treatment." He looked at Kelly then, who was looking down at her glass of water. Claire was still holding her hand.

"But that was forever ago! How could she possibly remember one baby she only saw one time? She didn't even remember anything until I mentioned *you!*"

"You told her who I was?!"

Oh crap. "Kind of."

"What did you say? What happened?" His eyes no longer looked tired. They were practically stabbing her with their intensity.

"Nothing." Why did she feel like she was in trouble? Or rather, why did she feel like she was in *more* trouble when she hadn't done anything wrong? "She asked if I knew about the . . . the chuppah thing, and I said you'd told me about it. Then she asked if you were a religious person, and I said you were a doctor. Then. . ." Lucy paused. She knew this was the worst part. "Then she looked at me weird and said, 'You're Lucy Callaghan.'"

"What did you say?"

"I said *yes!* What else should I have said?" She was getting angry again, but she didn't care. She took a deep breath but only so she could tell them exactly how ticked off she was.

"Lucy—" her father started. He was going to tell her to calm down or something, but she wasn't going to let him.

"How was I to know that, besides not telling anyone about my freaky problems, I shouldn't tell anyone who my dad is, or my last name, and I should ask everyone if their mother might possibly be a pediatrician I never knew I'd had for about a minute and a half when I was barely born, just in case I run into her at a Jewish wedding! How was I supposed to know that?!" Her chair creaked and she stood up.

"Lucy! Calm down! You're going to hurt your—"

"And you are out of your mind if you think I'm not going to see Jonah anymore!" She took a breath and quieted her voice. "He is a nice guy who makes me actually laugh. He's not the one who's been lying to me my whole life, who gets mad about someone else taking pictures of me, who keeps telling me things I should have been told a long time ago, and who keeps getting mad at me for something *I* didn't *do*!" The quietness didn't last long.

"I'm not mad, Lucy. But—"

"Well, you sure sound mad! I've heard you get angry at Maggie enough times to know what that sounds like, but I didn't do anything wrong. But you have. And I get to be the mad one today because you have to stop keeping things from me!"

"We weren't keeping anything from you! We also couldn't have predicted that you'd run into Sharon Edelmann!" He threw his hands up in the air and sat back, shaking his head. Then he scrubbed his hands over his face, still shaking his head. Lucy's brain had split into multiple sections again because, as furious as she was, she could also see that her dad was just about to explode with exasperation, and he looked completely wiped out. Kelly was crying. Claire was patting her hand. And Maggie was standing by the sink, grinning.

Lucy didn't know what to do. She was feeling heavy again and needed to breathe. She wanted to sit down but didn't want to lose the high ground. She shifted her feet and folded her arms to hide her *in - two - three - four.* "Well, so what if she knows? How bad could that be?"

"Worst case?" Aeden lowered his hands and looked off into the distance. "The worst-case scenario would be: she gets curious, digs up old files, asks questions, looks at pictures on the internet, makes some phone calls, sends some emails, calls in favors, writes a paper, reports on Patient L, draws all sorts of attention to you, scientists come and ask questions, I lose my license and go to jail, and you, Lucy, will never have a private moment to yourself for the rest of your life. That's the worst-case scenario."

Lucy's brain noticed her dad's insane resignation, her mother's swollen eyes, Claire's gaping mouth, and Maggie's perfect stillness.

"Okay, yes, that would be bad," Lucy said as she leaned back against the refrigerator. It jiggled a little, and every eye turned to her, wondering if she was crashing. Miraculously, she wasn't. She was just tired. And she needed to think, so she straightened up and walked out.

"Where are you going?" Aeden asked, his chair screeching as he stood up.

"For a walk," she shouted, not looking behind her as she tried not to slam the front door behind her.

CHAPTER 33

Prayers

"Why, Lucy!" Sister Decker opened the screen door and invited Lucy inside. She was dressed in a skirt and blouse without her customary apron. "I'm so glad you're here. I'm hoping you can do me a favor."

"Sure," Lucy said, though she hoped the favor didn't involve mangling fruit again. She wasn't even sure why her feet had brought her there.

"Can you pluck my eyebrows for me?" Okay—that was definitely the last thing Lucy expected her neighbor to ask. "I'd need my glasses on in order to see that closely, but I can't really pluck my eyebrows with my glasses on."

"Um, yes. I'd be happy to. But Claire or Maggie would be so much better at it."

"Oh, you'll be fine," she answered and handed Lucy some stainless-steel tweezers without the slightest doubt that Lucy could do it. "There are three or four I can feel with my fingertip, and they are driving me crazy. One of my daughters-in-law usually helps me, but I have a meeting this afternoon. I'd be so grateful."

"Okay," Lucy agreed, hoping she didn't hurt the woman—or wreck her eyebrows.

"Thank you," Sister Decker said, sitting down at the table, back straight, chin up, eyes closed, with her face toward the light.

"Are you sure you want me to do this?" Lucy wanted to give her every opportunity to change her mind.

Sister Decker opened her eyes and looked sad. "Well, if you really don't want to—"

"Oh, no—I don't mind at all," she said, ashamed of making her feel bad after all she'd done for Lucy. "I just . . . have never done this before."

Sister Decker smiled and closed her eyes, resuming her pose. "You'll be fine. I trust you."

"Okay . . ." Lucy placed herself in front of the dear lady and used her left hand to tighten the delicate, creped skin above her left eye. With her right, she gently but firmly plucked the first offending hair, which the aged woman's skin let go of easily. *Ha! Success!* Funny how a little thing like that could give her such satisfaction. Lucy imagined her father feeling a little like that after performing some tricky medical procedure. She moved more confidently to the next tiny hair. "Sister Decker, can I ask you something?"

"Of course," she answered, eyes closed, brows raised.

"Well, I just want to ask if you would mind not telling anyone what I told you? About, you know, my problem?" It was somehow easier to ask since Sister Decker's eyes were closed.

"Oh, of course," she said again. "What is spoken in my kitchen *stays* in my kitchen." Her simple declaration carried with it the promise and certainty of tradition. Maybe her sons had talked to her about personal problems in this very room, at this very table. What would it be like to be truly able to talk to one's mother? But Lucy was still trying to grasp the idea of truly talking to anybody at all.

"Thanks," said Lucy, not knowing what else to say.

"But," Sister Decker added, "I do talk to Heavenly Father about you. And those prayers go from this room, or from my bedside, straight to His ears. But He already knows what you're going through, so I'm not really telling Him anything new."

Lucy sat back and paused in her plucking. "You pray for me?"

"Oh, yes. Every night. I pray for everyone I care about."

"I don't know what to say." She *prayed* for her?

"Well, there's nothing you need to say. Like I said, it's not like I'm telling Him anything He doesn't know."

"You really think he knows about me? About these problems, I mean."

"Of course he knows about you. You are His child, and He loves you. Like he said to Jeremiah, 'Before I formed thee in the belly I knew thee.' I mean, He might not have ordained you to be a prophet, or a prophetess," she giggled at that, "but he ordained you for something."

She said it all like it was no big deal. She'd even said *of course* as if everyone knew and believed it. But Lucy had never really thought about what God meant for her to do—other than the basics, like honoring her father and mother, and she might have to talk to Father Patrick about that one now. But she had no intention of killing, committing adultery, stealing, or bearing false witness against Sister Decker.

Lucy continued plucking. "Thank you," she said.

"Mm-hmm," was the reply. No big deal.

"You really pray for everyone you care about?"

"Mm-hmm," again, was the reply.

"You must say really long prayers."

A guilty giggle quietly burst from her mouth. "Well, my knees aren't so good," she whispered, "so I sometimes say them from my bed. I just hope He forgives me for falling asleep in the middle of those long prayers once in a while!"

Having successfully tweezed Sister Decker's eyebrows and gotten a little perspective, Lucy turned left at the sidewalk and marched over to Don's house, not even acknowledging the newly opened roses. Their fragrance, however, triggered a whole new set of memories that Lucy ignored. She was not going to be distracted from her goal. Also, since she knew his mom was teaching at the University, she didn't ring the bell that played Beethoven; she banged her fists on the door. Repeatedly.

She'd come over three times that week, but he'd never answered the door even though Lucy *knew* he was home each time. He was not going to ignore her today, so she kept pounding.

After about five minutes, she finally heard his dumb loping feet clomp down the wooden stairs, one - step - at - a - time.

He even took his time unlocking the bolt and opening the door, and he didn't say a single word when he saw her standing there.

Lucy swallowed. "Will you please drive me to Cicero?"

He turned and walked away, leaving the door open, so Lucy waited.

He came back forty-five seconds later with his keys and shoved his feet into his sneakers on his way out the door. Lucy followed him to his blue Honda Civic.

Ten minutes later, Lucy and Don were walking up the concrete stairs to the Sacred Heart Church. If she just counted Sundays and ignored holidays and other events, Lucy had walked up these stairs more than eight hundred times in her life. No—she had probably been carried for the first two years of her life, but still . . . she was very familiar with the building.

A woman in a purple dress came out one of the glass doors just as Lucy and Don approached the entrance. "Hi Lucy," the woman casually said as she briefly held the door for them and continued on her way.

"Oh, hi," Lucy said, waving back to the retreating woman.

"Who was that?" Don whispered, entering the edifice.

"I don't know," Lucy whispered back. "Her name might be Gina. Or Jenny. Or maybe Joy. I think she works in the office, but I'm not sure." Just like school, Lucy had gone to Mass and interacted with all the people there without knowing their names or much about them. And this was the first time she had ever come here on her own.

"What are we doing here?" Don asked, walking softly behind Lucy.

"Just wait there." Lucy said. Don didn't ask any more questions as he sat in a pew at the back of the nave.

Lucy walked forward, straight down the center aisle that was covered with low, purplish-gray carpet. She took in the high, slanted walls made of warm, wooden planks. She saw the altar in front of her, with a Bible propped open on it. Behind the altar was the tabernacle—a small white box that held the sacramental host. Above and behind everything, suspended in air by wires, was a tall carving of Jesus nailed to a cross. This is what she had come for.

She stepped forward to the altar stairs and knelt down. She knew the prayer she wanted to say; it was one she had written in her prayer book two years ago. But her prayer book was at home, so she hoped it would be okay if she didn't get every word exactly right.

She took a calming breath, then clasped her hands together, bowed her head, and whispered:

Heavenly Father, in my need, help me believe
You are aware of me and will do what is best for me.
Give me the strength to trust you
and put everything in your hands.
Grant this through Christ, our Lord.
Amen.

Back in Don's car, Lucy sat back and closed her eyes, feeling good about what she had done. After all, if Sister Decker was praying for her and her whole family, Lucy should be praying for them too. And that big a prayer seemed like it needed some extra effort.

"Was this all about the pictures?" Don asked, pulling out of the church's parking lot.

Lucy wasn't even a teeny bit surprised that Don had seen the photos, or that he'd guessed why she'd shown up at his door, so she just nodded.

"And that they could be a problem for not just you, but for your dad too?" he continued.

Lucy nodded again.

"Even though you know people will just think they were photoshopped?" There was no impatience in his voice. He was just walking his way through Lucy's brain, following the path as far as he could. "What am I missing?" Yep. He was so smart he knew there was more to the story.

"As it turns out, Jonah's mom was my pediatrician for my first shots."

Don nodded, seeing the problem immediately. Then he smiled. "Ha! I guess that means 'bye-bye Jonah.'"

"That is not what it means!" Lucy said, sitting up and glaring at her friend. She was surprised by her own vehemence. She hadn't even really thought about Jonah since her dad had suggested the same thing—it was more than a suggestion—but she was not going to stop hanging out with him.

Unless, of course, he didn't want to hang out with her anymore. She slumped back in the seat, oblivious to the fact that Don had entirely stopped talking to her. He just drove in silence while Lucy thought about what a wreck her life was.

Don pulled into Lucy's driveway. "Thanks," she said as she got out, but he just nodded with his mouth shut tight. "Fine!" she shouted. "Don't talk to me!" She slammed the door shut and stomped into the house.

All her good feelings about praying were completely gone.

Lucy's Dreams were a confusing jumble that night. She started out on the sidewalk, swinging between the trees, never able to move herself in a straight line—only dips and climbs between the little trees whose leaves had begun turning red and brown. But when she got to the end of the sidewalk, she was in front of Don's house, trying desperately to float over it. Or toward it. But she couldn't even make it over the rose bushes. Every leap was heavier and heavier, until she could hardly lift her feet. Then she was in front of the fancy house where the party had been, and Jonah was there, laughing. He leaned down toward her, and Lucy noticed again the little seahorse constellation his freckles made—right before he kissed her. He kissed her mouth, very softly, and she relaxed. Then she started floating upward, toward the Milky Way. Then the wind blew. It wasn't hard, but there was nothing to hold on to as she was carried higher and higher into the sky. Then she was caught in a dizzy current of air that began whipping her one way and then another.

That time, it was Lucy who screamed, waking herself at the moment she crashed. Hard. Half on the bed and half off, smacking the floor with her knee while her upper body hit her mattress then slid off to join her legs on the floor. She landed in a heap on her left side, facing the bed.

Maggie reached her door first, followed by Claire. Maggie flipped the lights on and stared. Claire started to go toward Lucy but Aeden, who was only a moment behind her, yanked her back.

"Hey!" Claire protested at the uncharacteristically brusque treatment but seemed to realize at the same moment why he'd moved her out of the way.

"Lucy?" It was the doctor who touched her shoulder, but it was her dad's hand that froze when he felt her immovably dead weight.

"I'm okay," she whispered, but she felt tears sliding toward her left ear. Her right knee hurt, and her shoulder and head, but the tears weren't from the pain; she didn't even know why she was crying. But she started breathing *out - two - three - four . . .*

"Can you move?" Aeden asked, touching her forehead and cheek, glancing at his hand when he felt the dampness.

"Not yet." . . . *two - three* . . . "Give me a minute." *In - two - three - four.*

"Are you hurt?" The doctor seemed a little more emotional than usual.

"Not bad," Lucy said, but her voice cracked, and more tears gushed out. Crying, she discovered, made it impossible to breathe calmly. "Please, just give me a minute." It came out as a plea. As she breathed, she saw Kelly grab a pillow and hand it to Aeden, who placed it on the floor near the back of Lucy's head. She managed to roll onto her back on an *out - two - three - four.* Her head was mostly on the pillow then, and she was eventually able to steady her tears and release the heaviness completely. *In - two - three - four.* A few more tears slipped out, making rivulets down her cheeks, but they were quiet about it.

"That's really good," Aeden said. "The breathing, I mean." He moved his hand to her knee.

Lucy nodded and kept breathing, letting go of the fear, letting go of the frustration. Letting go of the anger, though she hadn't realized she was angry before that breath.

Claire knelt beside her, holding a glass of water.

"Thanks," Lucy said, but she didn't move. Claire reached out and held her hand, and Lucy gave it a little squeeze.

Their dad watched it all—the tears, the breathing, the sisters . . . Lucy felt him apply a little pressure to her leg and saw his face relax when he was able to move it.

She took one last deep breath and held it a moment before she said, "Okay. I can get up now."

"Are you sure?" Kelly said.

"Yep," she answered, with a little impatience and a little embarrassment. But for what? "Yes, I'm fine," she answered more gently as she pushed Aeden's hands away and sat up on her own, her back against her bed.

"What happened?" Aeden asked, sitting back on his heels.

"Just a bad dream," Lucy dismissed, as if nothing more needed to be said.

"Were you . . . flying?" Aeden asked cautiously.

Lucy looked him straight in the face. "Yes, Dad," she said, though being pulled up into the sky wasn't the same thing as flying. "I was. Why can't you just say it? I dreamed I was flying. It's no big deal." But she knew it was.

Aeden's lips tightened, and he stood up. "Can you get up?"

Lucy wished she hadn't displayed so much bravado the moment before. She wasn't heavy anymore, but she was weak. She wasn't going to let him see that, though. She put her hand on the mattress and used that—just a little—to stand up. But she winced at the pain in her right knee.

"Will you let me look at that?" Aeden said, looking down at her leg.

She nodded, sat down, and pulled back the edge of the over-large T-shirt she had worn to bed. Her mind noticed, however, that it was the first time he had ever asked her permission to check on a bump or a bruise. He had always just said, "I'm going to," or "Here, let me . . ." It was kind of sad. She had successfully asserted her independence, and he had respected it, but it seemed like another *before/after* moment—a necessary but sad one. She wasn't a helpless child anymore, but . . . she wasn't his helpless little girl anymore, either. Why should that minor distinction feel sad? She blinked before another tear could escape. Fortunately, he wiggled her kneecap at that moment, and she winced.

"Nothing is broken, but I'm guessing it will bruise up pretty nicely and be sore. Ibuprofen and—"

"Hydrate," Claire finished for him, handing Lucy the glass of water. "And take it easy for a few days."

Everyone laughed, including Kelly and Maggie, and Aeden shook his head and pulled Claire into a side hug.

As Lucy drank the water, she guessed he was glad to still have one little girl to look after. Did that mean Lucy was now more like Maggie? She looked over at her big sister, but she was gone, and Kelly was turning to go too.

"Claire, will you go get Lucy the Ibuprofen?" Aeden said. Claire nodded and darted away. "And Lucy, I think you should let me wrap that and put some ice on it to keep the swelling down, okay?"

"Okay, thanks," she said. She liked that he had asked again.

He only kind-of smiled just as Kelly came back in with the Ibuprofen. She handed it to Lucy, bent down, and kissed her forehead. Then she handed Aeden an ace bandage and an ice pack, then left. Lucy had never noticed before how in-sync her parents were with each other.

Claire popped back in. "Mom beat me to the other stuff, but here." She handed Lucy a pink and yellow stuffed hippopotamus she'd won at a carnival the year before.

"Thanks," Lucy said.

Claire nodded and watched their dad wrap Lucy's knee. "Will she have a contusion?" she asked.

Aeden did smile that time. "Probably," he said.

Then the smile disappeared.

Lucy suspected Claire had wanted to help him relax. But, besides bruising, Dr. Callaghan wasn't exactly sure what Lucy's strange body would do, and it seemed the dad in him wasn't happy about that.

CHAPTER 34

No Driving Lesson

The next afternoon, the doorbell rang, and Lucy ran downstairs as quickly as she could without putting weight on her tender knee, hoping it was Don. It wasn't.

"Jonah!" she said in genuine surprise, mixed with excitement, mixed with disappointment.

"Hi! I know I'm way early, but are you busy?" He was practically bouncing with excitement.

"Uh, not really." She was absolutely not busy because she should have been practicing not-crashing with Don, but he hadn't answered the door any of the three times she had hobbled over that morning. He was being so . . . she didn't know the word. But it was immature of him not to even answer the door. Immature! *Yes!* That's what he was being.

"Cool! I had two students cancel at the last minute. And I don't even care that their mom said they were sick—when I'm pretty sure they're going on a vacation she forgot to tell me about, and she just doesn't want to pay for the cancelation. And do you know why I don't care?" He grinned, and his ears sort of flared out a bit.

It was surprisingly hard to muster curiosity, so she went for humor. "Because they're really terrible clarinetists and listening to them practice hurts your ears?"

He stopped bouncing and shook his head at her sad attempt. "Actually, they're both pretty good . . . on the saxophone. But the point is: I have two and a half free hours to teach you how to drive before we go to Scoops!"

He held up his car keys and Lucy's mouth fell open, but no sound came out.

"If . . . you want," he added, finally sensing Lucy's mood. But she recovered quickly.

"That would be . . . amazing, but . . ." then she glanced down at her bandaged right knee, so she wouldn't have to lie. She probably could have managed driving—physically—since her knee didn't hurt that much. But mentally? Even if she was certain it would be *legal* for Jonah to teach her to drive, which she wasn't, it would not be a good day for her to concentrate on operating a car—or any heavy machinery—or even a hair dryer.

"Oh man! What happened?"

Lucy had already worked this part out. She hated to lie, but telling him the truth was not a possibility. "Nothing really," she said as she invited him inside. "I'm basically a klutz, and I hit my knee when I yanked the car door open really hard."

"Seriously?" He sounded dubious. "You must have hit it pretty hard."

"Yeah, well, I think I'm okay. It's just a little sore. But I'm sure you know what it's like when one of—or both, for you—your parents is a doctor."

"Ha! I totally get that." Good. "My parents made me wear a sling for like a month when I twisted my wrist once. I always took it off at school or when I went to Caleb's house. By the way," he looked down and his face went a little blotchy. "I'm really sorry about what Dave did at the wedding reception."

"Dave?" Was Jonah talking about what Lucy thought he was talking about?

"Yeah. He used to do that kind of crap to me and Caleb all the time—ever since we beat him up for picking on Naomi when they were in fifth grade."

"That kind of crap . . .?" Lucy wasn't certain.

"Yeah. Editing pictures of us and posting them online. I mean, he's pretty good at it, but it doesn't take a ton of creativity to give me Dumbo ears, or to give Caleb donkey ears. But anyway, I'm sorry about that. Everyone knows what a d— what a jerk he is, and I already told him what we'd do if he ever pulled that . . . crap . . . again."

"You . . . you what?"

"Yeah. He loves all his tech, and I let him know what we'd do with it if he ever bothered you again. So," he shrugged, "I think the problem is solved."

"Wow," was all Lucy could say. Jonah's chivalrous yet slightly thug-like defense of her was kind of flattering, and she was glad

Dave had a reputation for posting edited pictures. But no editing would have been needed in Lucy's case. Unless she hadn't really floated, and Dave just coincidentally chose to make Lucy *look* like she had been. "What did he say?"

"Oh, he denied it. But everyone knows it was him. He likes pis— he likes ticking people off."

Lucy smiled. It wasn't like kids at school didn't use foul language around her every single day. But she had already noticed that Jonah didn't, and she liked that he was trying not to say exactly what he thought of stupid Dave. "Well, just forget about him," she said. "Will you still take me to Scoops?" She felt like celebrating.

"I like your bracelet." Jonah nodded at it as he loaded his spoon with another bite of brownie, ice cream, and topping. "You wore it to the wedding."

Lucy looked down at her left hand, which was holding the cup of her root beer float. She didn't remember having put the bracelet on that morning. "Thanks. I've had it forever."

He reached over and lifted up her hand to look more closely, and Lucy's heart gave a little leap. His fingers were warm and hers were icy.

"Is this your birthstone?" he asked, turning the first charm over with his other hand.

"Uh-huh. It's a sapphire."

"When's your birthday?"

"The eighth of September."

"That sounds like a song," he said. Then to Lucy's surprise, he started singing, but only loud enough for the two of them to hear: "*Try to remember the kind of September, when life was slow and oh so mellow.*"

"Mellow?" Lucy said in a strangled laugh. He had a really nice voice, but singing to her outside of an ice cream shoppe was a little too weird even if she did like that he was holding her hand. Using the word *mellow* just put the whole thing over the top.

Jonah chuckled, still in a quiet way. "What can I say? I grew up around music of all kinds, playing in orchestras for every high school and middle school production in the county. I've probably heard that song a thousand times and could play it in my sleep. And now I'll think of you every time I hear it for the rest of my life."

"Uh. That's pretty heavy for a guy who has ice cream on his nose."

"What? Really? No, I don't!" But he still reached up to rub at his nose, dispelling the intensity of the moment before. Lucy really did laugh then, and Jonah just shook his head. "You're hilarious," he said.

Lucy just smiled. He was still holding her hand.

"So, what's this one?" he asked, holding up the next charm. "A daisy?"

"It's an aster, my birth flower."

"Ah, I see a theme emerging. And this one? Is it a teardrop?"

Lucy couldn't see the charm, but she knew which one was next. "It's a light bulb because the name Lucy means *light*."

"And this one is a girl on a swing, because I know you like to swing."

"Yep. I always have."

"And this one? A . . . stagecoach?"

"It's a chariot."

"Um. But it's a stagecoach. Like in an old Western movie."

"No, look." Lucy twisted her bracelet around and looked at the charm painted with red enamel. It had doors on both sides, windows all around, tiny wheels that moved, and a place for the driver to sit . . . in front. It was, indeed, a stagecoach. "But—" she was confused. "It's supposed to be a chariot."

"I hate to break it to you, but you've been cheated."

Lucy frowned. "But—" Oh no! Another memory!

Don had given her this bracelet! For her birthday when she was just . . . ten maybe? He had said the store didn't have a chariot, so she should just pretend. And she did. All she had ever seen was a chariot.

"Are you okay?" Jonah asked, looking at her with his eyebrows scrunched together. He wasn't frowning, but he was definitely wondering what was wrong with her.

Lucy shook her head. She wanted to get off the subject. "I must have forgotten. Like I said, I've had it forever." And Don's mom had taken him to buy her a new charm every year for five years. The last one was when she had turned fourteen—that was the sapphire. What happened the last two years? She didn't know. She shook her head a second time. "Anyway, when's your birthday?"

"December thirtieth. I was three weeks late, and my dad said my mom was as big as a whale. So when I came, they decided to call me Jonah."

Lucy laughed out loud. "No way! He did not say that! That would be horrible!"

Jonah was laughing too. "He really did! My mom confirms the story and shows pictures as proof! She was huge!"

"Oh, man!" Lucy had to wipe a tear from her eye. She'd never laughed so hard that her eyes actually leaked.

"Wow," Jonah smiled quietly. "I really like it when you laugh like that."

"Ugh!" Lucy covered her mouth with her hand, which made her charm bracelet rattle a little.

"What about you?" he asked.

"What about me?"

"Do you have a birth story?"

Lucy choked, inhaling some of her own saliva, and started coughing.

"Lucy," Jonah said, shaking his head and pushing a cup of water toward her, "you have got to practice laughing more. You're going to asphyxiate yourself one day if you don't get better at it."

"I know," she wheezed, as she grabbed the water. She coughed a little longer than absolutely necessary, just to give her a second to think and change the subject. Then she took a nice long drink of water.

"Are you going to be alright?"

She nodded. "Can we leave? I bet everyone here suspects I have the plague or something." She coughed once more for emphasis.

"Yeah," he smiled as they scooted out of the booth.

When they stepped outside, Lucy took a deep breath. "Okay. All better I think."

Crisis averted.

CHAPTER 35

The Park at Night

When Lucy got home, she limped up the stairs. Her knee was sorer and stiffer than it had been that morning for some reason. She probably needed some acetaminophen or something, but that was back downstairs, and she didn't want to bother. Besides, walking straight wasn't bad; it only hurt bending her knee and putting weight on it to climb steps, so she only stepped up with her left leg, pulling her right leg up behind her. She remembered climbing stairs that way when she was little. Maggie used to hold her hand as they went up the four stairs in front of the cathedral Lucy had prayed at the day before.

When she needed to go back downstairs for a late dinner that night, her knee didn't feel any better, so she did the motion in reverse, stepping down with her right foot, then bending and lowering herself with her left knee on each step. See? She could totally handle things. Life was good.

But dinner totally burst her happy bubble. Most of the topic revolved around curfews, Maggie complaining and being grounded, their dad lecturing about Caleb and coming home late without calling, and Kelly trying to intervene, which ended up causing more friction among all of them. Claire, normally the family peacemaker, sat there and let the argument roil around her without saying a word. Lucy tried to discretely ask her what was wrong, and Claire looked and sounded alarmingly like Maggie when she raised her chin and answered, out loud, "Dad said I can't have a cell phone until I'm twelve, which is a ridiculously arbitrary day on the calendar, and it's halfway through the school year."

"November is not halfway through the school year, young lady," answered their dad, taking his focus off of Maggie for the moment. "And there's no need for an eleven-year-old to have a cell phone."

"Except for the fact that you know I'm not a typical eleven-year-old, that I'm a year ahead in school, and that I'm more emotionally capable than either Maggie or Lucy!"

"What?!" shouted Maggie.

Lucy just looked at her little sister.

Their parents sat in stunned silence for a moment, as if there was no argument for any part of Claire's statement.

As if a red haze were clearing from her brain, Claire blinked, and her mouth fell open as she turned to look at Lucy. "Lucy, I'm sorry. I—"

"Oh!" jumped Maggie. "You're just sorry to—"

"Girls!" Aeden interjected, cutting off all discussion. "Enough! It's late. It's been a long day. We are all tired and have said things in frustration and anger. Let's just finish our dinner, clean up, and then we will all take some time to think before we say anything further."

Maggie made a disgusted noise as she shoved a piece of chicken into her mouth.

"Maggie," Aeden warned. He was making it clear he wanted silence and would tolerate nothing else.

Kelly took a sip of water.

Claire glanced at Lucy before wiping a tear away from her right eye. She hardly ever cried.

Lucy retreated. She wasn't behind a glass, unaware and emotionless like she used to be, but she sat as still as possible, breathing as quietly and as deeply as she could.

An hour later, she walked out. She needed to think. If it hadn't been so late, she'd have gone over to Sister Decker's. All the lights were off at her house, though, so she walked to the park. When she reached the swings, she carefully lowered herself into one of the seats, but bending and straightening her knees enough to really get going hurt too much. She tried using only her left leg to push off and pump, but that only made the chains twist and jounce.

"Great!" She huffed. "Even the swing set has turned against me!"

She was tempted to swear as she lowered both feet and brought the jangling contraption to a halt, but she didn't. Instead, she sat there with her hands squeezing the chains by her ears for possibly an hour. She didn't cry, though her eyes watered up more than once during the time she sat, thinking. She didn't even let herself feel angry. She breathed. And she paid attention to what was happening inside herself. It was as if she could feel chemicalized emotions swirling around in her brain, then down millions of nerve fibers through her torso and into her arms and legs, her fingers, and toes. A slight breeze moved the leaves and grass, so she knew she wasn't the cause of her hair moving and tickling her cheek.

After a while, she bowed her head and closed her eyes.

"God?" she whispered, "please help me."

Was that a good enough prayer? It didn't feel like the one at church had helped, but maybe it wasn't the right one. She didn't know any prayer, however, that mentioned upset friends, or parents possibly going to jail, or angry sisters, or—oh yeah—her fear of floating up into the sky. Or her desire for it. How could she want something and fear it at the same time? What if God wasn't even there?

That didn't feel right. She knew God was there. But what if he was too busy with people who were praying for help with droughts, or famines, or wars, or locusts? What if, in the grand scheme of things, it didn't really matter if someone's sister hurt her feelings. Or if boys were confusing. Lucy knew those were trivial things! And maybe even the floating thing was just . . . She didn't know. Maybe she was being selfish by thinking so much about her own problems. But not wanting her dad to go to jail because he had tried to help her, even though she wished he had told her the truth a long time ago? That wasn't trivial. That seemed like a good reason to pray.

"Is it, God? Is it a good enough reason to ask for help? I don't want to be selfish."

Down the street, a dog barked.

"Was that a yes or a no?" she said. Then she chided herself for being disrespectful. "Sorry," she added, as part of her prayer.

Then four things happened at almost the same time: another dog started barking, closer that time; some sprinklers sputtered on at the house next to the park; a man's voice swore; and a dark shape stumbled out from behind the hedge that separated that house from the park. Lucy jumped to her feet, startled, then almost fell as her sore knee protested. She caught herself with the swing chains and hobbled back from the shape that was approaching her.

"Hey, Lucy," the man's voice mumbled.

She stepped back, keeping her right knee straight that time. "Who's there?" she shouted, looking around to see if anyone was around to help. Her neighborhood was not downtown Manhattan or anything, and she was only half a block from her house, but being alone and approached by a strange man at night was not a good thing anywhere.

"It's me," the voice said as he stumbled nearer. "Caleb."

"Caleb?" she whispered to herself. What was Caleb doing there? Then he came within the ring of the playground light, and she knew that it was, indeed, Caleb. And he was all wet.

"Hey," he said, lifting his chin up in the same way Jonah and Dave had when they greeted each other at the reception.

"What are you doing here?"

He wiped his hand over his damp face and said, "I was coming to see Maggie."

"Where's your car?" This didn't make any sense.

"Oh," he chuckled, gesturing over his shoulder, "it's back there somewhere. I had some car trouble."

He had walked across the faded wood chips and stopped right in front of her. She took half a step back, on her good leg, and he took a full step forward. She felt something she'd never felt before: a mixture of nervousness, and fear, and she didn't know what else. She just knew she didn't like that he was there. She turned as casually as she could and took a step toward her house. "Why are you all wet?"

He walked with her. "Oh, I got caught in some sprinklers back there." He gestured again as they walked.

"But why were you there, behind the hedge?" She wanted to walk a little faster but didn't want him to think she was freaking out—which she was. This was weird.

"Well, like I said, I was coming to see Maggie, and you kind of look like Maggie in the dark. Did you know that? I noticed that at the reception." He bumped his shoulder into hers in a joking-around way, but it made Lucy stumble. "Hey are you okay?" He asked as he grabbed her arm to keep her from falling.

Lucy twisted her arm out of his grip. "I'm fine, thanks," she said, and kept walking. But she could smell the alcohol now, so she put a little more space between them as they walked. He closed the gap.

"Whoa, Lucy. Why are you in such a hurry?"

"Don't you want to see Maggie?"

"Well, yeah, but like I said—" Then he paused and laughed. "I keep saying 'like I said.' That's funny!"

Lucy didn't think it was funny. They were four houses away from home now.

"Anyway, like I said, you kind of look like Maggie, so it's kind of like I'm seeing her now. Except your hair. That's different. I noticed it when I saw you dancing." He reached over to touch her hair, but she stepped away, and felt the heaviness coming.

Not now, she thought. *Please, not now.* But it was too late. She started breathing . . . *out - two - three - four*, but her heart was pounding. *In - two - three—*

"Hey," he said, "it's okay. I'm not going to hurt you." He grabbed her upper arm again.

"Don't!" she said, shaking his hand off and running away—trying at least. *Swings, and ice cream, and out-two-*

"Lucy!" She heard him stumble, and she was glad he was drunk.

Three houses away. Don's house was next. "Don!" she yelled as loud as she could. "Don!"

She jumped.

But this wasn't a Dream. It was real life, and she could feel the weight coming. Then Caleb was behind her.

"Be quiet!" he yelled, grabbing a handful of her hair, yanking her back, and spinning her around—her weight on her bent right knee.

Lucy screamed, swinging her left arm around with her momentum and catching Caleb across his right eye.

He didn't even make a sound as he collapsed on the sidewalk.

Lucy turned and stumbled a few more steps toward the fragrance of Mrs. Tan's pale yellow and pink roses, now in full bloom.

She crashed right on top of them.

Lucy!

Lucy!

She thought she could hear someone calling her, from miles away it seemed. The sound was distorted and difficult to focus on. She started to turn her head toward the voice, but something stung her cheek by her right eye. She drew in a sharp breath at the pain and noticed a familiar fragrance. Don's mom had once told her they were called peace roses. That was a strange thing to remember as she lay face down across two of the bushes she had crushed . . . when she crashed. How long had she been there?

"Lucy? Lucy!" It was her mother's voice, and her fingers were lightly brushing the left side of Lucy's face. She was crying. Kelly never cried, but maybe her mother did. She wasn't sure. Kelly and her mother always seemed like two different people. She hardly knew her mother.

"*Eommaga, jeongwon gawi gajyeowa!*" That was Don. "*Bbali! Bbali! Gajyeowa!*" Lucy knew the word *eommaga*. It was *mother*. Don was yelling at his mother. Maybe Mrs. Tan was upset about her beautiful roses.

She tried to move again, but thorns stabbed and scraped her body everywhere: her face, neck, torso, arms, and legs . . .

She hissed and sank a little heavier onto the already flattened bushes as she was pulled into unconsciousness again. She heard Don yelling again, "*Eommaga! Bbali! Bbali . . .*" The sound was traveling away, though, leaving her in the dark.

When Lucy opened her eyes again, the world was a noisy, chaotic mix of movement, color, and darkness. There were lights flashing red and blue, people talking, and a static ringing buzz coming from somewhere deep inside her head. She was lying on her back under a blanket, and someone was holding her left hand.

"Hi," a small voice whispered.

"Claire," Lucy softly croaked as she moved her eyes to the right to see her little sister sitting cross-legged on the grass.

"Hold still. They can't know you're awake yet. I need to tell you what Don and Dad told the police."

"The police!" Her alarmed words came out as another croak, only slightly louder than the first one, but Claire still hushed her.

"Shhh," she whispered, holding still, glancing up quickly. "Listen. Dad told me to watch you, but one of the police officers— the lady—keeps coming back, so I have to hurry. Squeeze my hand if you understand."

Lucy squeezed, but she could tell it was weak.

"First of all, if they come back, say you found Don's baseball bat in his front yard and hit him—the guy, Maggie's boyfriend—in the head. Okay? Do you understand?"

Lucy squeezed again. The memory of the park, Caleb, his weird behavior, his grabbing her . . . it all came back. And—had she hit him? Had she hurt him?

Claire continued, "Okay, when Don heard you scream and ran outside, he found you in the bushes and the guy, Caleb— did you know that's who it was?—he was unconscious on the sidewalk. Don couldn't move you, so he ran and got Dad—all of us. Dad checked you first and saw you were probably okay, but the guy, Caleb, you must have hit him pretty hard. Dad had to call 911. He and Mom argued about it, but he said he had to. He said . . ." Claire paused for the first time and took a deep breath. She lowered her voice to the point where Lucy could barely hear her. "He said his injuries were life-threatening."

Life-threatening? She nearly choked as she asked, "Is—did I . . ."

"Hush," Claire commanded, sounding like Kelly. "He's alive, but I don't know how he is; they took him to the hospital. But listen. While the ambulance was driving here, Don got his baseball bat, and he and Dad pressed your left hand around it, so tell them you used the bat to hit the guy. Your left arm is bruised, but just say that's from him grabbing you, okay? Do you understand?"

Lucy squeezed again. Had she hurt him? She had just wanted to get home! She just wanted to get away! Tears started leaking from her eyes, and she started shaking.

"Stop!" Claire commanded, squeezing Lucy's hand hard. "Dad said you might go into shock, but you can't, Lucy. Breathe. Do your breathing."

"Okay," Lucy whispered, voice shaking. But she nodded slightly and began counting in her mind. *Out - two - three - four.*

"Good," Claire said. "That's good. You just can't get heavy again. Dad refused medical attention for you, but the police—" she looked up. "She's coming now."

Lucy was still crying, but she squeezed Claire's hand and kept breathing.

"I love you," Claire said.

Lucy squeezed, still breathing. Still counting. *Out - two - three - four. In . . .*

A woman police officer crouched down next to Claire. She looked young, with smooth brown skin, dark eyes, and black braids pulled into a bundle at the nape of her neck. Claire started to get up, but the officer put her hand on Claire's shoulder. "You're fine," she said. Claire sat back down, scooting over a bit for the officer.

Thank you, God, Lucy thought when Claire was allowed to stay.

"Hello Lucy, I'm Officer Penelope Thomas. How are you feeling?"

"Cold." It was the first thing that popped into her head. Then she realized she was clenching her teeth together to keep them from chattering, and she was shaking.

Officer Thomas nodded as Claire tucked the blanket more closely around Lucy. "It's a cool night, but you may be experiencing some shock after a traumatic ordeal."

Lucy nodded. She understood what shock was, but she hadn't been hurt—not really. "I'm okay," she said. Officer Thomas gave a sympathetic half-smile and nodded. She must not realize what Lucy had done, or she wouldn't be smiling at her. "How's Caleb?" Lucy asked.

"Do you know him? The boy?" The woman didn't answer Lucy's question, and her own question didn't seem real. It seemed like the police officer already knew the answer but wanted to know what Lucy would say.

"He's my sister's boyfriend."

Officer Thomas nodded again. "Do you mind if I ask you some questions?"

Lucy shook her head. Her jaw was really starting to chatter, and Claire squeezed her hand. *Out - two - three - four . . .*

The officer took out a notepad and looked down at it, as if she had to remember what the first questions should be. "Can you tell me what happened tonight?"

Lucy swallowed. "I was down at the park, on the swings, and he came out from behind the bushes. I didn't know who it was at first. He said he had car trouble. And he was coming to see Maggie. And we started walking to the house, and—" Lucy stopped. And what? He'd teased her? He'd only touched her hair—Jonah had done that lots of times, so what? He kept her from falling. She could hear her teeth clicking together. She couldn't stop them.

"You were at that park," the officer pointed, "just down the block?" Lucy nodded. "What time was it?"

"I don't know. Maybe about 10:30?"

"Was anyone else with you?"

Lucy took a deep breath and let it *out - two - three - four*. "No."

"And you started walking to your house?"

Lucy nodded.

Officer Thomas watched her breathe in and out slowly several more times. "Can you tell me what happened next?"

Lucy sniffed and coughed. She could feel her sinuses draining down the back of her throat.

"Do you need some water?" the officer asked.

Lucy nodded. "Thanks," she said as she raised her left hand to wipe away tears that were stinging her face, then winced as her fingers brushed the cuts that left pink traces of blood on her fingertips. She also felt a bandage on her check below her eye. The officer stood up and walked away, and Lucy looked at her arm. It was covered with scratches too. Some were so fine they were already scabbing over, but three bandages covered what must have been deeper cuts. There was also a long, dark bruise on the side of her wrist beginning at her thumb and extending halfway to her elbow along the edge of the radius.

"Remember what to say," Claire whispered.

Lucy squeezed her hand and whispered, "I'm glad you're here."

Officer Thomas came back and handed Lucy a bottle of water. "Do you think you can sit up?"

Lucy thought for one second then nodded, "Yeah," she said, giving Claire's hand one more squeeze when she saw the concern on her face.

Claire took the blanket as Lucy sat up and wrapped it around Lucy's shoulders so she could hold it with her hands. "Thanks," Lucy said, then stared at the scratches the thorns had left all up and down her legs. They probably weren't any worse than those on her arms—she looked at both arms for comparison—but there was so much more surface area on her bare legs that they looked much, much worse. There were at least twenty bandages covering what felt like deep slices and gouges in her skin. Her T-shirt and shorts also had snags of various sizes, and she could feel where the thorns had stabbed her on her chest and stomach. She reached up and felt the scratches on her neck, along with two bandages.

"It's Claire, isn't it?" Officer Thomas said, turning to Lucy's lifeline.

"Yes, ma'am."

Officer Thomas smiled, obviously thinking she was addressing an ordinary eleven-year-old. "Do you see that officer over there talking to your parents?"

Claire nodded, not inclined to disillusion the officer by speaking more than was strictly necessary.

"That's Officer Dunn. Would you go ask him to bring me one of the cards we talked about when he's done, and ask your mother to come over here, please?" Claire nodded and ran off.

Officer Thomas twisted the lid off another water bottle as Lucy twisted the cap back on the first one, which was empty. "Here," the woman said.

"Thank you," Lucy said, taking the bottle. She hadn't realized she was so thirsty.

"Would you like another blanket?"

"No. I'm okay." Her teeth had stopped chattering, and her shivers had calmed to an internal tremble. She kept breathing. Breathing was important for so many reasons.

Kelly came over and knelt down on the grass, immediately taking Lucy's right hand. Lucy looked down at their hands, then up at Kelly. Kelly was looking down at the grass, but she gave a slight squeeze. Claire must have told her to do that.

"You said you and the boy started walking to your house. I know this is difficult, but can you tell me what happened while you were walking?"

"He said . . ." What had he said? "He said I looked like Maggie—that he'd noticed that at the reception, when I was dancing."

Lucy felt Kelly stiffen

"The reception?"

"Um." Why was it so hard to think? "His sister's wedding. I was there with Jonah. They're cousins—Caleb and Jonah."

"Okay. He said he noticed you at the reception. Then what?"

"He touched my hair." Tears started coming again. Why? He'd only touched her hair. Lucy's mom squeezed her hand and held it tight.

The officer nodded. "And?"

"And I started walking faster, and he grabbed my arm." More tears.

The officer nodded and said, "Take your time."

"Then I pulled away and told him to let go." Had she really said that? She couldn't remember. She had wanted to yell at him.

"I think he told me to be quiet, but I tried to run away." All she had wanted to do was get away! "And he grabbed my hair and pulled me back. And . . . and I hit him." Kelly squeezed her hand really hard.

"With what?" asked the officer.

"With . . ." Lucy squeezed her eyes shut. "With a baseball bat."

"You had a baseball bat with you?"

Lucy shook her head. "No. It was Don's. It was in the yard. I grabbed it, and when he pulled me back . . ." More tears. "I . . . I hit him as hard as I could." All she had wanted to do was go home! "I'm sorry," she yelled with her entire heart, feeling thick and heavy, but not crashing. Her mom put her arm around her, and Lucy leaned against the small woman's shoulder. Kelly tensed but leaned into her daughter's weight. "I'm so sorry," Lucy kept saying.

Officer Thomas gently rested her hand on Lucy's knee. "Lucy, you're okay now. You're safe." Then Officer Dunn was there, handing the woman a card. "Thanks," she said, taking the card and looking up. "Jeff, look around for a baseball bat. It's evidence."

Officer Dunn nodded. "I saw it by the kid," he said, then left.

"Lucy," the woman said softly when she turned back around, "How did you end up in the bushes?"

"I . . ." How had she ended up in the bushes? "I turned to get away, but I crashed . . . into the roses."

Kelly nodded, "When the neighbor heard Lucy yell," she said, "he came out and found Lucy passed out in the bushes. That's when he ran over and got us, and we called 911."

Officer Thomas nodded, writing in her book for several seconds before she closed it and looked up. "Lucy," she said, "you are a very brave girl. You're understandably upset because you had a very frightening experience tonight, and you didn't want to have to hurt anyone. But you never, ever have to be sorry about protecting yourself." She looked like she was waiting for Lucy to say something but went on when she didn't. "It's a lot to process, and you are going to feel all kinds of emotions about it in the coming days, or weeks, or even years."

Lucy sniffed. She wanted to sink, to be swallowed up by the earth, in fact, but she was afraid of getting too heavy for her mom to hug. She just wanted to be normal. She should never have walked out of the house angry and upset. Her parents were only trying to help her.

"I'm going to give this card to your mom," the officer continued. "It's a free twenty-four-hour helpline if you ever want to talk about what happened, or how you're feeling. And I strongly recommend counseling," she looked at Kelly then, "so she can work through this. Too many women think they are weak if they need help, but counseling is vital in recovering from assault. If you don't have insurance or the means, this helpline can also tell you where you can go for free group discussions."

Assault? He'd only touched her hair! He'd only grabbed her arm!

"Thank you," Kelly said, accepting the card. "We will make sure she gets some help."

Lucy began crying again. So many tears. She'd just wanted to go home. She sobbed some more.

"Good. See that you do." She turned back to Lucy. She sat there and watched as Kelly—as Lucy's mom—rocked her middle daughter. Then she spoke again. "Lucy, your dad denied medical help for you, on account of him being a doctor. It's very lucky for you that he is, but your injuries aren't just to your body; your mind needs to heal too, and you might need to get a different kind of help for that. I know that for a fact. Do you understand?"

Lucy nodded. She just wanted to go home.

Officer Thomas then handed Lucy a card. "This is my card," she said. "If you remember anything else about tonight, or if you have any questions, call that number."

"Thank you for your help, Officer," Kelly said. "We truly appreciate your kindness."

"You're welcome, ma'am." The officer watched as Lucy stood up, helped by her mother, then walked away.

Discussion 4 — Nothing to Observe

What do you mean there is nothing to observe?

> *She hasn't gone anywhere. Except for two trips to the store with her mother, she hasn't left the house since the park."*

She hasn't. . .? What about the boy?

> *Which one?*

The musician.

> *He has gone to the house several times, but—*

Specifics, please.

> *He has gone to the house five times in the last three weeks. He stayed seventeen minutes the first time, two hours and thirty-six minutes the second time, forty-seven minutes, twenty-two minutes, then eleven minutes. But the girl never left the house.*

Get Tech on this to get us eyes and ears in the girl's house.

> *Right.*

Thank you. That's all.

CHAPTER 36

Processing

Lucy didn't open her eyes. She had woken up naturally, finally having gotten a full night's sleep, and was 100 percent comfortable snuggled into the blankets of Claire's double bed. She didn't want to wreck that feeling by opening her eyes and facing the world, so she kept her eyes closed and enjoyed the moment.

Kelly had protested when Lucy first started sleeping in Claire's room. What if Lucy crashed and hurt her little sister? But Lucy's nightmares had become problematic, making her tired, irrational, and more prone to crashing during the day, so Kelly relented on the condition that the girls keep a pillow between them so Lucy couldn't roll over on top of Claire. But it hadn't been a problem; Lucy hadn't had a single nightmare in the two weeks since she'd moved into Claire's room. She hadn't had any glorious flying

Dreams either—since the rose bushes—but she didn't care. As far as she was concerned, no floating and no crashing was the goal. Just stay normal. Just maintain equilibrium. Just be normal.

Just don't feel anything.

She must have been sleeping in the same position all night because her muscles suddenly wanted to move. She took in a deep breath and stretched, tensing every muscle, and held it for a good six seconds before relaxing and letting her breath out in a loud, satisfying woosh.

"Good morning," Claire said.

Lucy opened her eyes to see Claire peering at her from over the pillow.

"Hi," Lucy said, in a croaky voice. "What time is it?"

"Seven thirty-two."

"Wow. That's early for a Sunday morning."

"Not really," Claire said. "I've been awake since six forty-seven, but I didn't want to wake you up, so I've been writing in my diary." She held up a little, pink, hard-bound book with an unlocked gold clasp on the edge.

"What did you write about?" Lucy asked as she scratched sleepy crumbs from the corners of her eyes.

Claire shrugged. "Just stuff. I stopped when I heard you wake up."

"You heard me wake up?"

"Yeah."

"How do you hear someone wake up?"

"I don't know." Claire shrugged again. "Wanna ride our bikes to the movie theater after Mass?"

"No," Lucy groaned, then got up out of bed.

"You know, you really should get your driver's license, so we wouldn't have to ride bikes everywhere."

"Not today, I shouldn't." She headed for the door. She didn't want to talk about going to movies, or getting her driver's license, or anything.

"Then let's invite Don," Claire offered, sitting up. "He can drive us."

"I don't want to go to a movie, Claire." With that, she walked out.

In the bathroom, she flicked on the light, locked the door behind her, and stared at her reflection in the mirror. She pulled antiseptic ointment out of the drawer and dabbed it on the cut below the outer corner of her eye. It was mostly healed, but still visible. It could have been hidden by makeup on most girls. When Lucy tried that, however, she also covered the skin around the scar, making the freckles in that spot lighter. The result looked weirder than just leaving the little scar alone, free to stare back at her.

She also dabbed ointment on the cut at the right edge of her upper lip. That one hurt when she smiled, but that wasn't much of a problem these days.

Jonah had left for Brown University the week before. It was earlier than he'd planned, but he'd joined a band up there, so that was that. Anyway, things hadn't been the same since she'd given his cousin a concussion, along with short-term memory problems. Caleb supposedly didn't remember anything about that night and had no idea why his car was found rammed into some juniper bushes three and a half blocks from Lucy's house. His blood-alcohol level at the time had explained it, but Maggie still blamed Lucy for ruining her boyfriend who, apparently, kept forgetting to call her when he said he would.

Lucy also still had a few cuts on her arms and legs. The one on the side of her right knee, where a thorn had made a long gash, was the worst. She peeled off that bandage. It still looked angry, but it wasn't infected. She dug a new bandage out of the same drawer to stick over it. It would heal like all the others had. All of them would eventually fade. Probably.

Until they did, those little cuts were a good excuse not to go anywhere. Her dad wished she would at least go to church, but her mom was her unlikely ally on that topic, saying Lucy had "been through a lot," and of course she felt "self-conscious," and to give her "time to let her cuts heal."

The truth was, Lucy didn't care what she looked like. She'd never really cared before, so it was easy not to care now. She just didn't want to go anywhere. Ever again.

Someone banged on the door. "I need the bathroom," Maggie shouted.

"Hold on! I'm peeing!" Lucy shouted back.

"Well hurry!"

"Fine!"

She heard Maggie stomp away, so Lucy threw the ointment in the drawer and the bandage in the garbage, peed, washed her hands, stuck her tongue out at herself in the mirror, and went downstairs. On the way, she rubbed the outer corner of her eye to make the cut seem worse than it was. She wasn't sure how much more mileage she could get out of the remaining scratches, but she was determined not to go to Mass.

The kitchen scene was typical. Claire was already there, opening a cereal box to get a little plastic toy that was supposed to perch on the edge of her bowl. Kelly—her *mom*—was eating whole-wheat toast, and her dad was getting the cream for his morning coffee, which was percolating. He looked over at Lucy when he shut the refrigerator door.

"Good morning, Miss Lucy," he smiled.

She acknowledged him with a fake half-smile and a "Hi."

"I hope you'll come to Mass with us today," he said as he stood waiting for the coffee to finish dripping.

"Dad . . ." Lucy protested. She thought she had slept well, but she suddenly felt tired.

"I think it's time, honey."

"Next week, okay?" She wouldn't want to go next week either.

He poured his coffee and kissed Lucy on top of her head on the way to the table. "It will do you good to get out."

"Next week. I promise." Great. Now she'd have to go.

He gave her a look as he sat down. That one look communicated just as much as actually saying, *I'm not going to argue with you on this, young lady, but I'm getting mighty tired of you moping around the house like this. And you should at least take a shower.*

Maybe his look didn't say that last part. Maybe Lucy just knew she needed to take a shower. It had been . . . a while. She sniffed her shirt.

"It's fine, Lucy," Kelly said, interrupting Lucy's olfactory assessment. "Maybe we should all go out for ice cream after Mass. How does that sound?"

No! Ice cream meant Scoops. And Scoops meant thinking of Jonah. And thinking of Jonah meant thinking of his—

"No," answered Claire, and Lucy wanted to hug her! "We should all go to the movies." Then Lucy wanted to kick her.

"The movies?" Kelly mused.

"Yeah," Claire continued. "We haven't gone in for*ever*, and I'd be perfectly content with any one of the three PG movies that are playing at the mall right now."

Lucy sat down and glared at Claire, who was already smiling triumphantly. She was using her crazy voodoo powers on her parents again, and Lucy knew what their answer would be.

"That's a good idea," Aeden nodded in approval. "We'll all go to the movies this afternoon." Lucy didn't even get her mouth open before he added, "As a family." That meant no excuses. They were all going.

Lucy sighed.

Lucy lay on her bed and listened to the sounds of her family leaving the house, getting into the car, and driving away. With all the visiting her parents would do before and after the service, Lucy knew she'd be able to sit there alone without anyone bothering her for almost two whole hours. She felt the tension leave her body at the thought. She almost smiled.

Almost.

Then her phone rang.

"Hi," she said.

"I saw you weren't in the car. My mom made mandu."

Lucy might have salivated like Pavlov's dog at that moment. She knew *Don* knew that the little pork dumplings his mom made were just about Lucy's favorite thing in the world to eat. If his mom's mandu wasn't on the menu in Heaven, Lucy wasn't sure she wanted to go. Was that sacrilegious? She didn't think so; she would bet even God would like to have some of those little pockets of fried perfection dipped in soy sauce. Besides, the Bible said Jesus ate fish after he was resurrected, so why not mandu? Except for the pork, maybe? But the veggie kind was almost as good, so maybe that would be the compromise. If Heaven only had veggie mandu, Lucy decided she would still want to go.

"Lucy?" Don prompted.

"Fine," Lucy sighed. "But only because I don't want to offend your mom."

They both hung up.

She wondered why they never said bye to each other like most people.

Lucy stopped at the walk up to Don's door and stared at the new little bushes that had been planted there, replacing every single one of Mrs. Tan's rose bushes. They were each about fifteen inches high with smooth, light-green leaves. A few of them had two or three grape-sized clusters of tiny, yellow-white flowers. She bent down and picked one off, holding it up to her nose to smell it. The scent was light and clean, not at all like the strong, almost cloying fragrance of the peace roses that had grown there. She stood up, tossing the cluster on the ground, and saw Don standing by the front door.

"They're called privet bushes," he said. "No thorns."

Lucy glanced down at the foliage again, nodded once, then proceeded to the house.

Inside, Lucy slipped her shoes off and was glad to have the aroma of sesame oil, pork, garlic, ginger, and other delicious ingredients fill her nose, banishing thoughts of roses and thorns and crashes and scars. Her mouth actually did water as she stepped into the kitchen.

"Hello, Lucy!" Mrs. Tan said.

"Annyeonghaseyo," Lucy replied in her typical salutation to her best friend's mom. She almost stopped herself in the middle of the greeting, however, realizing that the last time she heard Korean being spoken was that night. Lucy decided she might not like speaking Korean anymore . . . ever again. Not that she could speak it. She only knew how to say *hello, goodbye, yes, no,* and *mother*. Plus, she could count to ten. The numbers six through ten kind of sounded like 'Yuck! Chill pal! Cool ship!' The bad thing was those words only worked for counting certain things, but Lucy never knew what things, so that's as far as she ever got.

"Mandu, Lucy?" Mrs. Tan asked, offering Lucy a plate. She still said Lucy's name with an accent, but she'd gotten better at it over the years. Lucy, on the other hand, hadn't gotten any better at saying the word for the other Korean dish she loved: bulgogi. *Bulgogi* didn't actually have an *L* sound, and Lucy couldn't make that in-between sound it was supposed to have, and Mrs. Tan smiled every time Lucy tried to say it. That one sound, plus the two ways to count things, made Lucy realize that even though she would never be fluent in Korean, she would always be fluent at eating mandu and bulgogi; she was practically a pro with chopsticks.

She took the plate with an attempt at a smile. Mrs. Tan smiled back . . . a real smile.

As they sat there eating and talking, Don and Mrs. Tan speaking mostly English for Lucy's sake, Lucy wondered for the first time ever how Mrs. Tan had handled everything. Lucy imagined it would have been hard to move to the United States without being able to speak or understand English, even though her husband could. Lucy knew Mrs. Tan had Korean friends, but she hadn't been able to speak to her neighbors at first. Lucy didn't know how or when Mrs. Tan started teaching at the University, but that had to have been hard too. And then her husband, Don's dad, died just last year. Lucy didn't remember much about how he'd died, but it must have been so awful for both of them.

If something happened to Lucy's dad—her stomach dropped, and Lucy had to stop that thought immediately before the rest of her body decided to follow. But there was Mrs. Tan, laughing at something Don had said, while Lucy sat there and watched. It was like she was behind the glass again, but this time she was the one who had put herself there.

"Mom? Can I borrow your phone this afternoon?" Don asked, which caught Lucy's attention.

"My phone?"

"Yeah. I want to teach Lucy and Claire that game we used to play with Dad."

"Ani," she began, shaking her head and frowning a little. Lucy knew that meant *no*, and Mrs. Tan went on with more Korean.

"Eomma," or *Mom*, he said, cutting her off. Then he whispered the rest, as if not wanting Lucy to suddenly understand Korean and hear what he was saying.

Mrs. Tan's eyes softened, and she looked over at Lucy with a sad smile. "Ne," she finally said, giving Don a small nod.

"Eomma, gomawo, Jeongmal gomawo."

Lucy sat cross-legged on the floor of Claire's bedroom, waiting while Don loaded the app on her phone. Claire sat there, too, holding Mrs. Tan's phone.

"I think it might be time for me to get one," Claire mused to herself, as if getting a cell phone was only a matter of her deciding it should be so.

"Okay, here you go," Don said, handing Lucy her phone. "Lucy, you're Ruce, and Claire, you're Mrs. Tan. Sorry."

Claire nodded, and Lucy waited for further instruction.

"Now," Don said, "turn the *play* dial all the way to the right, and that will take us to the waiting room."

The girls complied.

"Claire, you're the purple guy," Don explained, pointing to her screen. "Lucy, you're the one with the big hoop earring."

"Aww . . . I wanted a big hoop earring," Claire teased.

"Maybe next time." Don winked. "Now, remember we aren't playing against each other. We have to work together to keep our ship from blowing up or falling apart or being sucked into a wormhole. Read your prompts at the top out loud to tell the rest of us what to do, and listen to what the rest of us are saying, so you can do those things on your screen below. You'll get it once we start."

"Okay. . ." Lucy wasn't sure about this.

"Ready? Okay. Engage meditripod!" Don shouted.

"What?" Lucy shouted back, startled.

"Connect exercising people!" Claire shouted.

"Tell us the commands you see, Lucy!" Don shouted again. This was, apparently, a very loud game to play.

"Activate cubic valve! Activate cubic valve!" Claire yelled.

"You don't have to yell," Don yelled. "Appreciate art!"

"Disengage meditripod!" Claire shouted. "Lucy! Say the commands!"

"Set metered . . .," she began. "Set metered . . . what's that word?" she asked, while the other two kept shouting bizarre commands that didn't make any sense.

"Just do your best!" Don laughed.

"Enable F spout!"

"Set star prism to two!"

"Activate roto grid!"

"Roto grid? I don't—! Oh, here it is."

"Kick moon pocket!"

"Metajib—oh, that's me!" Claire laughed.

"Engage meditripod?" Lucy shouted. What the hell was a meditripod? *Oh no!* Lucy just *swore* in her head! She thought about it and decided, yes, that was the first time she had . . .

"Everybody shake your screens!"

. . . ever sworn at all, even though it wasn't out loud. The question was whether or not she wanted to be a person who—

"Lucy! You can't zone out now! You have to listen! Shake your screen!"

"These aren't even real words!"

"Time alert!"

"Activate cubic valve! Activate cubic valve!"

"Activate solar fans!"

"Time alert! Somebody hit 'time alert'!"

"Sorry, that's me," Lucy said.

"Solar fans!"

"Surv . . .Survobucket? Survobucket!" Lucy shouted.

"Flip! Flip flip flip!"

"What?"

"Flip your phone over! We have to do it all at once to avoid the wormholes!"

Lucy flipped her phone.

Then their respective phones all made a repeated twitching sound.

"Uh . . . we're dead," said Lucy, feeling responsible for the demise of the little digital spaceship.

"Wow, we stink at this," said Claire, who seemed genuinely disappointed even though she was smiling.

"No—everyone stinks at first. You'll do better this time." He was smiling, too.

That was just like Don . . . not mentioning the fact that it was Lucy who pretty much let them be sucked into a wormhole—or whatever.

Three games later, as Don desperately tried to help both girls—mostly Lucy—find the right switches on their respective screens, Lucy was smiling, too, and she knew what Don was trying to do.

"Activate quasifold!"

"Uh . . . D-driver. Turn on D-driver."

"Engage globu . . . globular fork. Engage globular fork!"

"Activate quasi fold!"

"Ah!"

"There's slime on my screen! What do I do?"

"Wipe it off! Wipe it off!"

"Shake! Shake your screens!"

"Set dark fork to one? What's a dark fork?"

"Ugh! There's more slime on my screen!"

Their screens dissolved in a checkerboard pattern, and Don yelled, "Good! Okay, next level!"

"So, this is a simulation of what it's like to be an astronaut, right?" Claire laughed.

"Yeah, they have to worry about globular forks all the time."

"Okay—next level!"

Eight games later, as she felt herself getting lighter, she decided she didn't care.

"Z-yoke? Set Z-yoke to two!"

"That's you!"

"Turn on kilo hive!"

"Bind . . . um subfield."

"Fire clip buckle."

"Uh, no no no . . . W-jacket. Unbind W-jacket"

"Unbinded! Activate spin thumb!"

"Um . . . subfield. Bind your subfield.

"Turn off kilo hive! Didn't we just turn on the kilo hive?"

"Engage Z-yoke!"

"Crank volatile V-yoke!"

"Engage your Z-yoke! Oh—you got it."

"Uh . . . spin knot to zero. Oh—that's me."

"Set keplar fluid to seven!"

Lucy let her crisscrossed legs unfold beneath her as her laughter began lifting her up. Claire saw what was happening, gasped, and started to say something, but Don just bumped her with his elbow, and yelled, "Deactivate your spin thumb!"

"Oh—right." Claire said, keeping one eye on her screen and one eye on Lucy, who was laughing at the game and at how good it felt to laugh . . . and to float.

"Deactivate it! Deactivate it!"

"I did! I did!" Claire protested.

"No, you didn't!"

"Keplar fluid to three! Yeah! I flipped it!"

"Set . . . uh bind your subfield . . . again," Lucy said.

"What?!" Don yelled.

"Bind your subfield again!" Lucy yelled with genuine glee.

"Ahhh! Everything's falling apart!" Don yelled! And Lucy knew he really did not want the ship to get destroyed because this was his master plan. She was floating!

"Jiggle hemivector!" Lucy yelled.

"Engage tesla hook!"

"Kick ultra tape!"

"My panel is falling apart!" Claire yelled.

"Jiggle the hemivector again!"

"Set luminous hook to full power!"

Lucy was completely off the ground, hovering in Claire's little room like an astronaut in the vast expanses of time and space as she tried to manipulate the tiny control panel on her phone while laughing at the sheer joy of the moment.

"Asteroid! Everybody shake! SHAKE!" Don yelled, and Lucy could hear the smile on his face, which made her lift up even higher.

Plus, shaking her phone in mid-air was a strange sensation without gravity. The movement caused her body to wobble, tipping her a little forward and to the left. It was hilarious! And she was laughing harder than she ever had—in her life!

"Set aeropuffer to one!" She yelled.

"Set octowhisk to zero!"

"Octowhisk!"

"Coddle binoculars!"

"Enable infinity!"

"Engage R2D2!"

"Deactivate parking meter!"

"Wormhole! Flip your phones!" Lucy flipped her phone, which made her rotate a little in the opposite direction, so she was more or less . . . straight again? Not tipped to the left, at least, but still forward, her feet more behind her than under her in a mostly relaxed position. She tried to consciously relax the tension in her body except for what she needed in her neck and arms in order to play the game.

"Set gyro nanojack to two!"

"Match your socks!"

"Plunge spin engines!"

"CLEAN UP VOMIT!"

And with that, Lucy gave up and simply laughed, not caring about asteroids, wormholes, or the demise of their digital ship as she hung in the air. Laughing was so much fun! And that thought lifted her even higher. She looked down at Don and Claire, who were looking back at her—Claire with a huge smile on her face, and Don with a pleased smugness on his. Lucy felt tears at the outer corners of her eyes and reached up, phone still in hand, to wipe them away.

"Look," she said, smiling and holding up her damp fingers. "Actual happy tears. I never knew how that was possible."

"Do you feel stable? Up there?" Don asked, ever the scientist.

Lucy nodded, then touched Claire's bookshelf to steady herself when the movement tipped her body a little to the right. "It's weird, for sure, but," she whispered, "it's amazing."

"Is there a feeling of adrenaline?" Don asked. "Like swinging?"

Lucy thought. "Maybe. Maybe a little. But . . ." it was hard to explain. She patted her chest. "I just feel . . . good."

She felt good.

What a simple thing to say. It didn't seem like a deep enough word, so she looked at Claire.

Claire nodded. "Good is good," she said.

Don nodded, too. It seemed he knew when to turn off his brain—or at least when to make it be quiet—and let Lucy enjoy the moment.

"Now what?" Lucy asked.

"Luce?" Claire said, standing up.

"Yeah?"

"Can . . ." She hesitated, which was unusual for Claire. "Could I touch you?"

"Sure!" Lucy said, holding out her hand.

Claire almost tiptoed the three steps across her purple area rug and reached up for Lucy's hand. Lucy, who was about five feet off the ground, reached down and took it.

"Uh. Maybe just don't get underneath her," Don suggested, quietly but with a slight warning in his voice.

Lucy looked down at her little sister, who was beaming the smile that took up her entire face. She was pure joy at that moment. And then her face got a little bigger as an idea popped into her head.

"Let's go show Dad!" It was a whisper, but it was a loud whisper.

Lucy slowly nodded her head. "Yeah," she said. "I think I can totally do that."

Claire ran and Don walked quickly downstairs to be in the family room when Lucy made her appearance.

Lucy drifted, basking in the pure joy of wafting herself down the hallway, using the door frame and walls to direct her toward the stairs.

Movement out of the corner of her eye caught Lucy's attention, so she turned her head to the left . . . which made her start to tip over in air until she compensated by making a kind of sideways jackknife motion with her hips and legs. It seemed that moving one part of her body in mid-air would require her to move another part of her body to balance things out. Spinning herself around just to see if her mom was dropping off clean laundry was turning into a complicated maneuver. She thought about how funny she must look, which made her lift high enough that she could use the ceiling to help reorient herself. Lucy realized that ceilings got dirty; she could feel the dust on her fingertips.

A few inches closer to her room, Lucy saw through the crack between the door hinges, but what she saw didn't even register as she wiped the fingertips of her right hand on her pants leg and had to move her left arm forward to compensate. Then she looked again.

Someone was standing on her chair with their back to the door, reaching up with something in their hand. It was a man, but it wasn't her dad. Had her parents called someone to repair something she didn't know was broken—or maybe to clean the ceilings? No. He was putting a small electronic something on the very top of her bookcase, near the ceiling. It looked like a little camera, and she would never have seen it if she hadn't already been up in the air so high.

The man turned to get down, and fear made Lucy sink—a slight automatic drop that didn't surprise her—but she was not expecting the retreat; her body floated backward without her even thinking about it. Under other circumstances, she would have wanted to analyze, once more, the cause-and-effect relationship between her emotions and her propulsion, but this was not the time; she had to stretch to catch herself on the door frame to keep her feet from bumping into the opposite wall and knocking down a picture of some old Irish castle. Then she had to focus hard to twist her body in the air and redirect herself.

She wanted to get away, to tell her dad or mom or anyone, but moving quickly was impossible as she struggled to keep her balance without bumping into things! Even in a straight line without obstacles, the fastest she had ever been able to . . . fly, she guessed . . . was only equal to the pace of a very slow stroll.

On her feet, she would have been down the stairs, through the kitchen, and into the family room in less than five seconds, but not without making a lot of noise. Floating was silent, assuming she didn't knock anything over, but not speedy.

Trying not to panic, and trying to stay afloat, she looked back over her shoulder, jackknifing, as she drifted away from her room. No one had come out of the room after her. Yet.

Down the stairs she floated, head down, feet up in the air, trying to let go of the light feelings just enough to let gravity help her. But not *too* much.

Help. Help. Help.

When she got to the family room, Lucy managed to get her feet underneath her in time to make a quiet landing—she hoped. Kelly, sitting on the edge of the recliner turned a puzzled face to her, while Claire and Don looked at her from the sofa in disappointment. "Mom!" she whispered frantically, "there's a man in my room!"

"What—" her mother seemed confused, turning toward the other side of the room.

Then Lucy saw her dad looking out the window with his phone to his ear. He was listening intently to whoever was on the other end but turned when he heard Kelly's voice. Lucy turned back to her mother and realized the expression on her face had not been puzzlement, but anxiety. Claire and Don hadn't been disappointed; they were relieved to see her. Don stood up and took her hand, pulling her to the sofa.

"What's going on?" Lucy demanded, keeping her voice quiet but wanting to shriek.

"It's that police officer from . . . from that night," Kelly said.

"The lady? Officer Thomas?" Claire asked.

"No, the other one," Kelly began . . .

Lucy stood up and said at the same time. "Tell her there is a man in my room!" she said.

". . . the man," Kelly finished.

"What? Hold on," her dad said into the phone. "What, Lucy?"

"Dad! Tell him there's a man in my room!"

"A man? What do you mean?"

"There's a strange man in my room right now! He didn't see me, but I just saw him."

"What?" Kelly said, looking at the door while Claire and Don began whispering to each other.

Aeden turned and spoke into his phone. "Lucy says there's a strange man in her room right now." He listened for a moment, then held up his hand for everyone to be quiet. Claire stopped whispering to Don, and all five of them sat there, Kelly looking back and forth between the door and her husband. "Yes, just a minute ago." He raised his eyebrows at Lucy, wanting confirmation.

Lucy nodded vigorously while Aeden listened some more.

"Where's Maggie?" He suddenly asked, looking at Kelly.

Kelly shook her head. "At the mall, I think."

"She's not at home?"

Kelly shook her head again.

"We are all in the downstairs family room . . . straight back, behind the kitchen," he said into the phone. "Five of us—my wife, two of my daughters, and a neighbor. Our other daughter is not home."

Lucy started her breathing. She wasn't feeling heavy, but she sat back down next to Don and counted silently to herself, trying to get ahead of it.

Don nodded and took her hand again.

"Yes," Aeden whispered into the phone, then put his finger to his lips, gesturing for everyone to be silent as he walked away from the window.

"Second floor, first one on the right," he answered as he stepped next to Kelly. Then, "Yes," he said, and nothing else.

Then they sat there.

In silence.

And waited.

"Yes," Aeden whispered into the phone, a long while later.

Lucy tensed when she heard the front door open softly; it hadn't been locked.

After a few seconds, a police officer wearing a helmet and protective padding crept down the three steps into the family room, gun drawn and pointed downward, with his hand held out in a gesture that seemed to say, "Stay silent; stay calm; we are handling this."

"Yes, they are here," Aeden whispered into the phone. He nodded and hung up.

Over the next few minutes—which seemed like hours—Lucy heard tromping around and doors and closets being opened throughout the house—upstairs, in the front room and kitchen, and in the basement.

Finally, another police officer walked casually down into the family room, visor up, gun holstered. "All clear," he said. We didn't find anyone."

Lucy's entire family, Don included, let out a collective breath and the thick tension seemed to evaporate.

It was strange, then, that Lucy's body chose that moment to grow suddenly heavy. It washed over her like a wave that would have knocked her off her feet if she had been standing. She began breathing, and the hand which had been calmly resting in Don's hand now clutched at it in panic.

OUT - TWO - THREE - FOUR - IN - TWO - THREE - FOUR - OUT . . . much too rapidly to do the good it was supposed to do. She was getting dizzy!

"Lucy," Don said, not loudly, or harshly, but not quietly either. To anyone else, it would have sounded as normal as if he were about to ask her to hand him a pencil, or something equally noninteresting. All he did was say her name, and gently press his left arm against her right arm and breathe . . . with her.

Out . . .

In . . .

Out . . .

No need to count.

She would be okay.

He was there.

It would be okay.

"Lucy, tell us what you saw," Aeden said, bringing her attention back to what was happening. By sheer force of will, she calmed herself. She still felt heavy, and hoped this sofa was stronger than the last one, but she refused to crash.

"There was a man in my room," she began. "I saw him when I was coming downstairs. The door was mostly closed, but I could see he was standing on my chair and putting something on top of my bookcase."

The second officer took off up the stairs.

"Did you see what he looked like?" the first officer asked, writing in a notebook.

"Not really. His back was to the door. He was wearing dark clothes. Long sleeves, I think, but that's all I could tell." She didn't even know what color his hair was.

"Can you describe his size? His shape? His height?" he asked.

Lucy shook her head and shrugged. "He was just normal, I guess. Not fat, but not really skinny."

"How tall would you guess?"

"He was standing on my chair. I don't know."

"Could you—"

The second officer clomped down the stairs. "We didn't find anything," he said. "Can you come up and describe where you allegedly saw him?"

Allegedly? Didn't he believe her?

Lucy nodded, taking a mental inventory of her status. She didn't think she'd make the floors creak or anything, so she stood and followed the officer, the rest of the party trailing behind.

"Right there," Lucy pointed. "He was standing on that chair, reaching up and putting something on the bookcase. On the corner." She was trying not to whine or shout like a frustrated child.

"Did you see what it was?" Officer number two asked. She was about to start calling them Thing One and Thing Two.

"It looked like a little camera," she answered. "Like a little video camera or security camera or something. But it was really small."

"How small?" Thing One asked.

"Like . . ." Like what? She looked around her room for a comparison, but nothing seemed to fit. "Like . . . a little toy car, maybe?"

"How many inches?"

"I don't know." She looked down at her fingers and tried to imagine holding it. "Like maybe two inches by one inch by one inch?"

"Like a Matchbox car?" Claire offered.

"Claire, hush," Kelly said, but Lucy nodded.

"Yeah, like that," she said. "And it was dark colored, but I could see a little lens on the end," she offered by way of description.

"Okay, well, we will file a report," Thing Two said. "That's about all we can do without more information. Let us know if you think of anything else."

With that, Thing One and Thing Two started down the stairs.

"What happens now?" Lucy's dad asked, following them downstairs with the rest of his clan.

"We will let you know if we find any other cases or recent incidents in the area that match your report," said Thing One, turning around at the door.

"In the meantime," added Thing Two, "we suggest you install a security system in your house; an alarm at the least, but an alarm with security cameras would be best."

"Good idea," Aeden said. He sounded distinctly unsatisfied, but added, "Thank you, officers. We appreciate your help."

"You're welcome," both Things One and Two said in unison. Then they turned and left.

When Aeden closed the front door behind them, he looked down at their cards. "I'm glad Officers Jack and Ass came to help, but I can't say much for their investigative proficiency," he said.

Lucy began wondering if she had heard her Dad use words like that before, but Claire's eyes almost fell off her face. "Daddy!" she said.

"Sorry, Sweetie," Aeden said, touching her shoulder. "Your dad's not handling things very well today."

"No," she said, "I'm impressed!"

Kelly snorted and began herding Claire into the kitchen when there was a soft knock at the door.

Lucy tensed and held her breath as Aeden looked out the peek hole, then relaxed when he opened the door. "Officer Dunn. Thank you for coming over," he said, inviting the middle-aged man in.

"Doctor Callaghan," he nodded, removing his hat and displaying a shaved head that had gray stubble around the edges.

"You just missed the officers who were here," Aeden said. He gestured with his arm to invite the man into the kitchen.

"No, I talked to them," the man said, then paused when he saw Lucy standing on the bottom stair with her hand on the banister. "How are you doing?" he asked her with a stern and discerning look.

"Fine, thank you," she answered automatically. She was still trying to hold herself together.

The rest of the family halted in their retreat to the kitchen and turned to watch the exchange, but Officer Dunn didn't reply. He just stood looking straight into her green eyes.

Lucy wondered what he was waiting for. It felt like he was seeing her, and she realized that was an odd thought as soon as she had it. She opened her mouth, not sure what she was going to say. "I don't think they believed me," is what came out.

"What makes you say that?" he asked.

Before she could decide how to respond, she heard Don, on the stairs behind her, let out a quiet, "Uh-oh."

Then she crashed.

CHAPTER 37

Recruiters

"Thank you for agreeing to meet with us, Doctor and Mrs. Callaghan, and Lucy, of course."

Lucy didn't know anything about men's clothing, but the man looked like a salesman. He had on a snug gray suit with a faint pattern of wide squares, matching vest, black shirt, and a gray tie. When he sat down, Lucy saw that his socks were green. Not like Irish green, though. Like Christmas green. And his shoes were super shiny black. Maybe this was just a part-time job, and he was a shoe salesman the rest of the time. He was really tan with short black hair, and he sat on a sofa of the Callaghan's seldom-used front room, next to the lady who came with him.

The lady looked like she could be an anchor on the ten o'clock news. Her suit jacket was a solid royal blue with a tight matching skirt that went to just above her knees—a little higher when she sat down, but she could still probably get away with wearing it to church. Her shoes were a shade darker than her pale skin, but the heels were impossibly high. How did her feet bend down from her ankles enough to walk in them?

"You're welcome," Lucy's dad said, "though I was more than surprised when Officer Dunn suggested I meet with you. I understand you know his niece, Emma?"

"Yes," the woman smiled and nodded. "We do not usually share the names of our students, for their own privacy and protection, but we can tell you that Emma recently finished her last year with us at Newton University. We've helped her focus her unique talents, and now she has accepted a scholarship to an Ivy League school for her graduate studies."

"Her, uh . . ." Aeden cleared his throat. "Her unique talents?"

"Yes," was the only answer the woman gave.

"Lucy," the man said, taking over as if on cue and looking at Lucy. "First and foremost, we want to reassure you that there is nothing wrong with you; you're not ill; you're not a mutant."

Okay, well that thought hadn't occurred to Lucy until this very second.

"—you haven't been bitten by a radio-active bug . . ."

Was he trying to be funny? Because it wasn't funny.

"—you're not at all abnormal . . ."

How could she not be abnormal? The opposite of abnormal was normal, which this wasn't. Even this conversation wasn't normal. But at least her parents were listening, not ignoring the issue.

"—and, believe it or not, you're not alone."

There was a silence, maybe five seconds of silence, as they all stared at each other around the rectangular coffee table. The man and woman were on one small sofa, and her parents were across from them on a small loveseat, and Lucy sat in one of two stuffed chairs at the small end of the configuration.

Lucy waited for more.

Kelly shifted in her seat next to her husband.

"I'm sorry," Aeden said. "We aren't even that comfortable talking about this . . . situation, even among ourselves."

You're not, thought Lucy, *but I want to hear what these people have to say.* She admitted to herself, in the very back of her mind, that her feelings seemed rebellious. Not really against her parents, and not against anything she could name. She just wanted answers.

"That's completely understandable," said the woman. "Every culture has enduring myths about people with particular gifts. And every culture has either deified these people, sainted them, mythologized them, or burned them at the stake because the reality of their lives didn't fit into the carefully constructed societal mold that most people cling to. Our job is to help you, Lucy, and your parents, not only to face the reality of your challenges—which, let's be honest, can be wildly inconvenient in the early stages— but to embrace the possibilities of your gift . . . a gift that can be turned into something terrifically useful and fulfilling."

Aeden shifted and said, "Okay. We're listening."

I think she was talking to me, thought Lucy, not sure if her dad meant to include her in that comment.

"Our agency," said the man turning again to Lucy, "was founded with the sole purpose of finding and training young people, like yourself, who have discovered they have extraordinary talents. And the help we provide is not just for the students; we also provide ongoing support for your family through your own personal counselor. We are on call every day of the week to address all questions or concerns your parents might have at any time. You will have a team of caring experts to help you throughout your experience at Newton University."

University . . . going to college . . . that seemed too long to wait. Lucy was going to be a high school junior in the fall. How could she handle another two years? She needed help now.

"The Newton University campus—here's a brochure," said the woman, handing one copy to Lucy and one to her parents, along with a single-page report of some kind, "is in Newton, Massachusetts—the other paper is information on safety ratings, median income, and other demographics of the town. It is a privately run university of little distinction in general, but we keep it that way for the privacy of our students."

"The mission of our school is twofold," said the man. He had pulled a laptop out of his briefcase and turned it around to show the presentation. This was practically choreographed. "First of all, we provide our students the opportunity to study in any of a wide variety of academic disciplines from art and music to medicine and law, and everything in between: education, engineering, business, history, sociology, psychology . . . you name it. We have the most outstanding professors and advisers that money can buy, but our classes are small, typically from ten to twenty students, so students receive individual one-on-one instruction. But you see, helping our students in their educational goals is only one of our endeavors.

"The main focus is to give individual students the specific training they need in order to help them control and develop the unique skills that each possesses. We are impressed with the degree of control Lucy has exhibited in these early stages of her skill development, but we know it is a challenge for her to remain constantly on guard so that her skills do not manifest themselves without her conscious control. As you are painfully aware, Lucy cannot allow herself to get drowsy or too relaxed, or even too excited, anywhere but at home when only her family is around. She must avoid being noticed and, Dr. Callaghan, while we commend your robust efforts and success at keeping anything that would be problematic off her official medical or school records, unless you want Lucy to remain trapped here, in this house, for the rest of her life, she must be trained to consciously control these abilities and to be able to access these skills only when she chooses to."

The man seemed to pause for dramatic effect as a slide show played on his computer screen. It showed students smiling in classes, playing Frisbee on a campus lawn, and laughing while eating lunch together. Lucy glanced down at the brochure, which had many of the same photos on its front cover.

"Even though Lucy has just completed her sophomore year of high school," said the woman, "we think you should consider allowing Lucy to enroll at Newton University this Fall."

Lucy sat up!

"In light of the fact," continued the woman, "that she began public school a year later than her age group . . ."

Wait. What? She would be seventeen in September . . . and . . . what?

". . . and would normally be starting her senior year of high school, we believe Lucy would not be too young to easily transition to college life, especially with the tutoring our staff will be able to provide."

Lucy was trying to listen while figuring out how old she was when she started kindergarten.

Lucy's dad then shifted in his seat, glanced at Lucy, and almost imperceivably began to shake his head.

"While most of our students are between eighteen and twenty-five," the man said, nodding to acknowledge Aeden's reaction, "we do have a few whose talents have emerged earlier—whose gifts are a little more conspicuous. Obviously, Lucy's gift is more challenging to hide than, say, not needing to breathe while under water . . ."

Seriously?

". . . and, of course, Lucy will be able to complete her high school studies, then go on to college courses while learning to master her abilities." The man lifted his hands, palms upward in half a shrug, as if it was a natural, foregone conclusion that they would agree.

Lucy agreed! She absolutely agreed! It would be scary, leaving home, going away to *college*, but yes! It would be perfect! They would help her!

She could see, however, that her parents were not totally convinced.

Her mom didn't look even a little bit convinced; she had her face in her hands.

Aeden's mouth was hanging open . . . just a fraction of an inch, but it shouted volumes about the mental shock his mind was under. "When you say, um . . . 'not needing to breathe,' you're being facetious, correct?"

"Not at all," answered the woman. Aeden's mouth was still open as she continued. "Our students fall loosely into two categories; those who want to learn to control their abilities so that they can live their lives, well, 'normally,' for lack of a better word. For them, the goal is to go on to establish careers and lifestyles that have nothing to do with their unique abilities. Then there are those who wish to apply their skills to help them succeed in a number of fascinating and fulfilling careers. More than just providing career counselors, we at Newton see ourselves as talent agents of a sort.

"I mentioned that our institution is privately funded; well, we receive several endowments from private contributors and government organizations who are keenly interested in the research conducted by faculty and students at Newton. Furthermore, many of our contributors eagerly scout out students and recruit them for careers in their organizations. They sometimes give us a wish list of sorts, stating the skills that they are looking for and the salaries and benefits they would offer individuals who have varying degrees of proficiency in those specific skills. During their training, students are presented with the opportunity to learn about the interesting career possibilities that are open to them."

"You see," said the man, "we do not advertise or market our school to attract new students and, for those who do happen to inquire on their own, tuition is disproportionately high due to the school's markedly undistinguished academic ranking. Therefore, those who potentially could afford tuition probably would not be interested in it. As a side note, though," the man continued, lowering his voice, "you should know that our students do achieve remarkably high academic scores; we simply do not report them as such. It would be quite . . . unethical, if you will, to compare students who have exceptionally high mental acuity to the rest of the national student population."

Aeden looked at Kelly with what Lucy took as skepticism verging on suspicion. She could practically see him thinking, *this has to be a scam.* But Kelly still had her face in her hands and was beginning to rock forward and back in her seat. Lucy had never noticed before how often her mom was on the verge of a breakdown.

But Lucy was more hopeful than she had felt since this whole mess began. Yeah, this whole presentation was weird, but what else would they expect from a school who helped kids who were like Lucy?

Aeden sat back and folded his arms across his chest. "Forgive me. This is a very impressive—and well-rehearsed—sales pitch. But let's skip ahead to cost. 'Disproportionately high' tuition sounds like a barrier to entry, indeed. How much are we talking?"

"Yearly tuition at Newton University typically runs a little higher than those at Columbia, Northwestern, and Brown

Universities." Brown? That was where Jonah was going! Not that it mattered, but Lucy had gotten the impression—

"Columbia and—" Lucy's dad interrupted her thought, almost sputtering. "We can't possibly—"

"Not to worry, though," the man continued, seeing the look on their faces. "We are here to officially offer Lucy a full-ride scholarship to Newton University."

The woman then handed Lucy a large, thick, official-looking envelope, with her name printed in embossed lettering. "Lucy, if you choose to enroll in our program, your tuition, books, lab fees, housing, and meals will be provided. This scholarship would cover these costs for the full term of your time at Newton, up to six years."

Lucy felt herself lifting up, and her father's arm reflexively shot out, as if he could reach over and keep her from doing so. "Wait!" he exclaimed frantically, as Lucy let her body rise up out of the chair and straight for the dusty ceiling.

Kelly sobbed.

The man and woman looked at Lucy with twin smiles.

Don froze with his chopsticks halfway to his mouth. He had gone to Han's Asian Supermarket in Syracuse for kimbop. Lucy always thought kimbop looked just like sushi, but Don had told her, explicitly, that it was absolutely not the same. He had naturally offered to share, and Lucy was excited to try it with her newly awakened sense of taste.

It was absolutely divine, and she mentally added it to the list of things she hoped were in Heaven when she got there. After her good news that day, she was re-committed to going to church. Maybe Don would take her to Cicero so she could offer an extra-sincere prayer of thanks.

"Lucy," Don said.

She opened her eyes, still chewing and coming back from her reverie of enjoying the yummy rice, egg, ham, sesame oil, carrots, cucumber, and other stuff, she definitely wanted to thank God for. It was sooooo good!

"Lucy!" he shouted, startling Lucy into opening her eyes a second time, without realizing she had closed them again.

"Sorry," she said, swallowing. "This is just amazing!"

"Hold on," he said, blocking her chopsticks from picking up another round circle of deliciousness.

"What do you mean you're 'going to college' in the fall? You're only going to be a junior, like me." He had a weirdly intense look in his eyes.

"I know! It's so weird! But one of the police officers from that night has a niece who is—well not like me exactly, but she has some kind of thing going on with knowing things ahead of time. Anyway, she went to this school in Massachusetts that helped her, and he—Officer Dunn—thought maybe I needed some help too. Apparently, our trick with the bat wasn't convincing, but he said it was okay because whatever I did was still obviously self-defense. So, he called his niece, and she called Newton—

that's the name of the school—and they found me! And they found the pictures online, and they knew something was up! Ha! 'Up!' That's funny since I'm lifting up right now!" Lucy laughed then but held on to the table so she could have some more kimbop. "Anyway, they offered me a scholarship, and now I can get some real help with this." She gestured to her body with her chopsticks, then pointed to the kimbop to tacitly ask if she could have another piece.

He nodded, lowering his own chopsticks without taking a bite.

"What's wrong?" she said, now sitting firmly on the chair with no fear of floating away.

"Nothing," he shrugged. "That's really great."

They both sat there.

She stared at him, wondering what was happening, kimbop forgotten.

He wiped his mouth with a paper napkin then scratched his eyebrow.

"You don't seem happy for me," she said, then wiped her own mouth.

"Sorry," he said. "I'm just surprised. But it will be good. I'm actually going to be taking full-time classes in Syracuse in September too."

"Full—wait. What do you mean?"

"I finished all my high school credit requirements six months ago. And I tested out of most of my college freshman courses last January, so I'm almost a college sophomore now."

"What? You never told me that! That's so cool!" Lucy sat back in her chair, beaming at her friend.

"It's not that big of a deal," he replied, standing up. He pointed to the plastic container of food. "Do you want any more of that? If not, I'm gonna put it away."

"No, that's okay," she said, though she really wanted some more.

"Go ahead," he said, with a hint of a smile.

"Just one, thanks," she said, grinning and using her chopsticks to help herself.

Don cleaned up the table while she chewed and savored.

"But how come you never told me?" She asked as she took her plate to the sink. "I mean, I've seen all your college books around, but I thought it was just science classes. I didn't know you were going to college this fall."

"I wasn't going to. But I can now, so it's all good."

"You can *now*? What does that mean?"

He rolled his eyes and started wiping off the table. That was literally the rudest thing she'd ever seen him do!

"What's that for?" she asked with an indignant tone. He'd actually just shaken his head and rolled his eyes—at *her*!

"You know," he said, standing up straight and looking right at her, "during all the years I've known you, almost our entire lives, yes, you were quiet, hardly speaking. But I knew you saw things. I knew you felt things. I just never realized you were so dense."

The world.

Suddenly.

Stopped.

Then the shock—the hurt—the indignation—flooded Lucy's brain all at once. Her cheeks were instantly hot. She almost felt fevered. Ironically, it was as if her entire body were suddenly exactly what he had just said: dense. Dense with too many feelings that had nowhere to go, all crammed together inside in a way that surely must have been visible. She looked down at her body. It looked the same.

But the floor creaked.

She looked up at Don. How was it possible that he looked both cold and troubled at the same time? What was he feeling?

"Lucy, I—"

"Don't," she said, holding up her hand in quiet command. She didn't really want to know what he was feeling.

Dense.

Yep. It was true. He was brilliant. She was not. She couldn't even name her own emotions at the moment.

Embarrassment?

She reached up and touched her hot cheeks.

Definitely. The floor creaked again as she walked toward the front door.

"Lucy, don't go. I'm sorry," Don said, not moving from where he was. He clearly didn't want to get crushed if she crashed.

No wonder she was embarrassed. Her smart neighbor, who she thought was her friend, had practically been babysitting her all summer. She hadn't even wondered why. Sure, she was certain he cared about her, but it wasn't like . . .

She slipped on her shoes.

. . . it wasn't like hanging out with such a dense, un-smart, girl could have been tons of fun for him.

She walked out the door, past the new privet bushes.

So why had he been so nice?

She walked to her house.

He took all those notes.

She opened her front door.

He planned all those experiments.

She heaved her body up the stairs.

He always loved science experiments.

She sank into her bed.

She had been his own personal science experiment.

Now, more than ever, she wanted to leave. Leave the parents who lied to her, the sister who hated her, the ice cream shop, the swing set, the high school, the . . . the everything that was home.

Discussion 5 — I Will Inform the Board

Well?

> *She's coming.*

And her parents?

> *They aren't happy about it, but they signed. I did end up offering the full-package scholarship.*

Fine. So, with her and the other boy you met with, that brings new enrollment to. . .?

> *One hundred and seven.*

That's a bit less than previous years.

> *Yes. But we already have at least that many in view for the following year.*

Fine. I will inform the board. Thank you.

CHAPTER 38

Take Your Protein Pills and Put Your Helmet On

Newton University looked like it did in the pamphlet, except the sky wasn't as blue, the grass wasn't as green, and the bricks weren't as red. And the random students walking from building to building looked less confident than their counterparts in the student life photos of the school brochure.

When Aeden found a parking space close-ish to the dorms, Lucy jumped out before he turned off the car. She was nervous, but she wasn't about to let her dad see that.

The dorms were proud, three-story colonial buildings with blue slate shingles, white trim, and dormer windows on the top floor. The only thing that distinguished one building from the next was the large, blue wooden numbers affixed to the corners of each structure. Lucy's was number eight. To hide her jitters, she took a deep breath and filled her body with the first scents of autumn that hung on the late August air; it was perfectly still, unbothered by the chaotic bustle of students. Mythical Titans disguised as maple trees were beginning to turn yellow, orange, and red; they regally presided over the campus, silently observing and judging the new freshmen. They looked like they were waiting for something to happen.

Lucy and her dad spent an hour and a half being greeted by incredibly enthusiastic students from the photogenic welcoming committee, checking in, going on a brief tour, and finally carrying her two suitcases of clothes, three boxes of personal belongings, a backpack, and a black trash bag of bedding and towels to the third floor.

Lucy's dorm unit had a mini-kitchen by the entrance, then a long narrow living area. Lucy paused when she saw fuzzy pink and orange throw pillows neatly arranged on a brown plaid sectional sofa. They reminded her of Maggie. On the coffee table there was a bottle of lavender-scented oil with little sticks poking out of it, and several magazines arranged precisely in a semicircle. A faded wooden bookshelf held a baby fern, and Lucy wondered if her sister had magically flown in ahead of them, decorated her dorm with bright colors, then whisked herself away before Lucy and their dad got there. But only the old Maggie would have wanted to do that. The new Maggie wouldn't even have thought of it.

"This looks nice," Aeden said.

Lucy looked up at him, and he nodded to the wall between two windows at the far end of the room. A plasma-screen television that still had the protective plastic on its surface was mounted to the wall.

Then she noticed the two bedrooms, one on either side of the living area.

The bedroom door on the right was closed and decorated with a homemade sign that said, "Tea and Anandi's room." She turned and walked through the open door on the left. The bare room had two twin beds, two small desks, two small closets, and one impossibly tiny bathroom. Another girl Lucy didn't know had been assigned to be her roommate, but no one else had been there yet. It was empty, musty, and cold.

"Do you want me to help you put your stuff away?" Aeden offered, stalling, as he looked in the bathroom, opened and shut a drawer, switched the lights on and off, and checked the closets.

"No, it's fine, Dad. I'll do it later."

He nodded, standing there, looking down at his daughter. "Well, I guess," he began, and then cleared his throat. "I, uh, guess this is it, kiddo." Then he looked up and around, avoiding her eyes, clearing his throat, trying not to let her see that his eyes were watering.

She studied his features and his fidgety stance, and Lucy knew this was more difficult for him than it was for her. Then she felt a twinge of—what? Shame?

No.

Guilt? Maybe. But guilt about what? She hadn't done anything wrong. What is that feeling when someone you love is sad or hurt, but you, yourself, don't feel sad or hurt about the same thing? Regret maybe. Not for her choice to leave home, but for the consequence—the pain it was causing her dad.

"Yeah. I guess so," she shrugged, hands at her side, looking straight at him.

He nodded. "You have your schedule, and your map?"

"Yep." She held up the paper one of the less enthusiastic but more official-looking staff members had given her.

Moving from home for the first time and going away to school, leaving your family, was supposed to be a difficult thing to do. Especially since her seventeenth birthday was still a week and a half away. Lucy was anxious for her father to leave. Looking up at his morose expression, she did feel a guilty tug on her heart because she knew *he* knew she didn't feel the same pain of separation. And he knew it wasn't drugs now that numbed her emotions. She couldn't help it. It wasn't that she was angry at him anymore. Or at her mom. She shrugged to herself as she realized she was ready to get on with things. She wanted to see who she was, away from them.

He opened his arms and she stepped into his enormous hug, putting her arms around his waist, and letting herself be enveloped one last time before he left.

"I love you," he said.

With her ear against his chest, she felt the deep, familiar rumble of his voice and listened to his heartbeat. She felt herself relax, releasing the tension she hadn't been aware of until that moment. She really did love him—that had never changed. "I love you too," she said, squeezing him hard to show she really meant it.

"Thanks," he whispered, and let go. His emotions were put away now and he tugged on her chin, commanding, "Call us." Then he ducked through the door and left, clearing his throat again on the way out.

Alone.

Taking a big, slow, deep breath, still smelling a trace of her dad's aftershave, she puffed the air out as she looked at the empty doorway. Relieved, and feeling light, a smile crept onto her face, and she almost started to laugh—a sensation she still found fascinating.

Her phone vibrated. It was Kelly's phone.

> Hi! It's me, Claire
> Good luck today!
> And Mom says hi

> > Thanks. Hi back to Mom
> > I left my blue sweater for you
> > It's in my closet

> Really?

> > Yep

> Thanks!
> BTW I got Mr Casey for 6th grade ☹
> And Hayden is in my class! ☺
> Mom says to call us. Love u!

> > You're welcome.
> > Yay for Hayden. Boo for Mr Casey
> > I promise to call. Love U 2

Lucy's mom had stayed home because it was Claire's first day of sixth grade, but Lucy knew she probably wouldn't have come anyway. They had made peace with each other, but Kelly still avoided her. More than ever, lately.

Lucy got it; she knew her mother loved her absolutely, but she had also seen how fragile her mother's nerves were, especially around Lucy. Claire, on the other hand, was a balm to their mother's worries. Not dramatic and hormonal like Maggie, nor problematic like Lucy, Claire was just an easy child. Always exuberant. Always happy. Feeling everything *so* much and *showing* her feelings so much. Lucy admired her. While she was becoming familiar with her own emotions, recognizing them, naming them, and communicating them, she doubted she would ever be as open with the thoughts in her own head as Claire always was with hers. She would miss her little sister—who had become an emotional mentor over the last few months. She hoped her parents would buy Claire her own cell phone soon so she could text her directly.

She didn't expect to hear from Maggie.

Looking around the dorm room, she thought it was like her soul right now. Empty. Cold and echo-like in its bareness. But she would fill it with her new experiences, her new memories, her new self. She would claim this space, and she would claim her heart and give it permission to feel—to react—to finally be *alive*.

Choosing the bed by the window, Lucy pulled out the new comforter her mom had bought for her. It was green, of course. Kelly had always chosen to dress Lucy in green when she was little because it brought out the green in her eyes. Lucy thought green just made her hair look more alarmingly red, but she also knew Kelly thought of it as a soothing color, and an undeniable *Irish* color, so she appreciated the thought.

Now that her dad was actually gone, she recognized that she was a little . . . *What do I call this?* She was still nervous for sure, but this feeling was more like eagerness. She felt eager to begin this new life. Eager to go to her first class, which started in—"Oh crap!"

She grabbed her schedule, her binder, her bag, her key, her map—and ran.

The Beginning

THANKS

My heart is full of gratitude and love. First, to our Heavenly Father, who loves us all so much that he sent his Son, Jesus Christ, to die for all of us so we can live again.

Second, to my husband, Wesley VanDyke, who always believed in me. Plus, I'm now working on the second book, and he never grumbles when I sneak into the other room in the middle of the night to write a scene I've just thought of.

Next, to Kasey with all the love a mother could possibly feel.

Also, to friends and colleagues who helped me throughout this journey with every possible kind of help, including enthusiasm, inspiration, coaching, and feedback; medical, scientific, religious, linguistic, and cultural consultation; or just listening when I needed to talk: Sheila Sconiers, Beckie Baily, Natalie Knight, Sharon Fuller Adams, Aneisa Dickerson Phelps, Jennifer Briggs Durham, Joanna Briggs Liddell, Hyeon Ju Han, Jae-Ran Grandy, Joe Grandy, Laurel Richmond Shiner, Carole Decker Draper, Dr. Adrian S. "Buzz" Palmer, Dr. MaryAnn Christison, Dr. Brian

Alder, Robert M. (aka Tony) Bradley, Amy Delis, Amy Reimann Hudson, Debra Ellis Smith, Alycia Calvert, Mathy Wasserman, Mara Haslam, Marnie Pehrson Kuhns, Libby Vargas, Yvonne Leavitt, Michelle Baumann, Laura Hess, Thomas Perkins, and everyone at Capucia Publishing: Christine Kloser, Carrie Jareed, Heather Taylor, Jean Merrill, Penny Legg, and all the rest.

Finally, to my mother. I miss her every day.

You may have tangible wealth untold;
Caskets of jewels and coffers of gold.
Richer than I you can never be—
I had a mother who read to me.
~Strickland Gillian

ABOUT THE AUTHOR

Jennifer Trujillo VanDyke's love of reading was first ignited when she was twelve years old, and her mother gave her the boxed set of C. S. Lewis's *The Chronicles of Narnia*. Although she excelled in writing classes throughout her school years, Jennifer never imagined writing a book of her own one day.

When she married her best friend, Wes VanDyke, she became a mother and also sprouted the idea for *Floating*. She wrote and re-wrote amid many other endeavors: earning a master's degree in applied linguistics, teaching English as a Second Language, singing in the Tabernacle Choir at Temple Square, and taking drawing, painting,  and pottery classes. Then, with the onset of the pandemic in 2020, she was finally able to dedicate time to completing this first book in the trilogy of Lucy Callaghan's fantastic story.

Jennifer and Wes split their time between family and friends living in Northern Utah and Southern Nevada. In her spare time, Jennifer enjoys playing with her grandson and solving crossword puzzles.